An
AFFAIR
of
SPIES

ALSO BY RONALD H. BALSON

An
AFFAIR
of
SPIES

A Novel

RONALD H. BALSON

ST. MARTIN'S GRIFFIN
NEW YORK

Published in the United States by St. Martin's Griffin, an imprint of St. Martin's Publishing Group

AN AFFAIR OF SPIES. Copyright © 2022 by Ronald H. Balson. All rights reserved. Printed in the United States of America. For information, address St. Martin's Publishing Group, 120 Broadway, New York, NY 10271.

www.stmartins.com

Designed by Gabriel Guma

The Library of Congress has cataloged the hardcover edition as follows:

Names: Balson, Ronald H., author.
Title: An affair of spies / Ronald H. Balson.
Description: First Edition. | New York : St. Martin's Press, 2022.
Identifiers: LCCN 2022019290 | ISBN 9781250282460 (hardcover) |
    ISBN 9781250287427 (international, sold outside the U.S., subject to
    rights availability) | ISBN 9781250282477 (ebook)
Subjects: LCGFT: Historical fiction. | Novels.
Classification: LCC PS3602.A628 A33 2022 | DDC 813/.6—dc23
LC record available at https://lccn.loc.gov/2022019290

ISBN 978-1-250-90601-4 (trade paperback)

Our books may be purchased in bulk for promotional, educational, or business use. Please contact your local bookseller or the Macmillan Corporate and Premium Sales Department at 1-800-221-7945, extension 5442, or by email at MacmillanSpecialMarkets@macmillan.com.

First St. Martin's Griffin Edition: 2023

10 9 8 7 6 5 4 3 2 1

This book is dedicated to my ancestors who lived in Odessa and emigrated to the U.S. from Ukraine a hundred years ago. It is also dedicated to the gallant people of Ukraine, who at the time of this writing are bravely fighting a cruel Russian despot. Unfortunately, history does repeat itself.

PROLOGUE

The Letter

On August 2, 1939, Albert Einstein of Old Grove Road, Peconic, Long Island, delivered a typewritten letter to "F.D. Roosevelt, President of the United States, White House, Washington, D.C." It was two pages in length and, in a dispassionate yet urgent tone, alerted the president to the most lethal danger of the twentieth century. The letter began: "Sir: Some recent work by E. Fermi and L. Szilard, which has been communicated to me in manuscript, leads me to expect that the element uranium may be turned into a new and important source of energy in the immediate future. Certain aspects of the situation which has arisen seem to call for watchfulness and, if necessary, quick action on the part of the Administration."

"L. Szilard" was Dr. Leo Szilard, Einstein's protégé, who was strikingly similar to his famous mentor in several respects: he was a genius, he was Jewish, he fled Germany to escape the Nazi persecution in the early thirties, and he was one of the founding fathers of the atomic bomb. It was Szilard, in 1934, in London, who patented the concept of a nuclear chain reaction. It was Szilard who was the first to use the term "critical mass" to describe the minimum amount of uranium required to sustain a nuclear chain reaction and its potential to cause a violent explosion.

Four years later, in 1938, Lise Meitner and Otto Hahn at the Kaiser Wilhelm Institute for Chemistry in Berlin discovered that bombarding uranium with neutrons left a residue of barium created by the breaking apart, or fission, of the uranium nucleus. They were the first to split the atom. Nuclear fission became a reality, and so did artificially created radioactivity. Meitner, also a Jew, fled to Sweden. Hahn stayed in Berlin to become a leading figure in Germany's nuclear program.

As clearly as any two people in the world, Einstein and Szilard foresaw the destructive power of a nuclear bomb. The letter to Roosevelt went on to say, "This new phenomenon would also lead to the construction of bombs, and it is conceivable—though much less certain—that extremely powerful bombs of this type may thus be constructed. A single bomb of this type, carried by boat and exploded in a port, might very well destroy the whole port together with some of the surrounding territory."

By the time Einstein's letter was delivered in August 1939, Hitler had already marched into Austria and Czechoslovakia with the world's largest and most powerful military force. Thirty days hence, on September 1, 1939, he would send over a million German troops in a blitz-krieg over peaceful Poland and ignite the Second World War. The thought of Hitler with a nuclear bomb was Einstein's and Szilard's worst nightmare.

Einstein knew that it would only be a matter of time until the technical applications of his theoretical work would be achieved by one regime or another. He proposed the immediate appointment of a director to head up a committee with sufficient funding "to speed up the experimental work, which is at present being carried on within the limits of the budgets of University laboratories."

Over the next year and a half, one advisory committee followed another, while the scientists continued their research in university laboratories scattered across the country. In 1941, Dr. Arthur Compton was appointed to consolidate the research. In 1942, Roosevelt placed the entire program under administrative control of the U.S. Army Corps of Engineers with the goal of creating an atomic weapon. Foreign intelligence sources confirmed that Nazi Germany was on the same track, but no one was sure how close Hitler was to achieving that goal.

CAMP RITCHIE
NOVEMBER 1943

A black Lincoln with U.S. military plates pulls to the side of the road in Frederick, Maryland. After consulting his map, the driver heads north beside the pristine lakes and forests of the Catoctin Mountain range. The treetops display a palette of autumn colors on the hills of northern Maryland. There is a chill in the breeze, and the driver rolls up his window. A family of white-tailed deer lifts their heads and calmly watches the car glide by. All in all, picking up a passenger seventy-five miles from Washington, D.C., on this fall day has turned into a pleasant duty assignment for Corporal William Johnson.

He comes to a stop at a crossroads, checks his map again, nods, and turns off the two-lane highway onto Cascade Road, a bumpy wooded stretch that meanders past a crystal blue lake and abruptly comes to a halt at a military checkpoint. The corporal hands a large white envelope to the sentry, and after examining the contents, the sentry waves him on. "Camp administration office is straight up on your right," he says.

As the corporal approaches the compound, he has to blink. There are German Wehrmacht soldiers in full battle gear marching in formation beneath an iron sign that reads CAMP RITCHIE. He sees another group of young men in GI fatigues gathered in a circle, appearing to study map coordinates. On the other side of an expansive meadow, he is stunned to see what he's damn sure is a Nazi Panzer tank and a German half-track, both with a *Balkankrauz* insignia, the white and black cross that is the German national symbol. "What in the hell is this place?" he says out loud.

The camp has dozens of stone buildings that undoubtedly serve as barracks. A few are larger and rectangular, and the corporal surmises they must be mess halls and assembly halls. The design of the administration building is no less out of place, with Gothic-like turrets, but to the corporal's relief, an American flag flutters on a twenty-foot post. It is indeed an American camp, albeit nothing like Corporal Johnson has ever seen.

After a few minutes in the reception area, the corporal is shown into an office where a uniformed officer sits behind his desk. The corporal snaps to a salute. The officer is a full bird colonel. The bronze name plate on his desk reads COL. CHARLES Y. BANFILL. His short-sleeve shirt has several rows of bars and ribbons. A lit cigar sits on the lip of his ashtray.

The corporal clears his throat. "Excuse me, sir, I have orders to pick up a Nathan Silverman."

Colonel Banfill smiles, picks up his cigar, sits back and says, "Do you have a name, soldier?"

"Oh, yes, sir, I do. I mean, it's William, sir. William Johnson. Corporal William Johnson. Sir."

"A pleasure to meet you Corporal William Johnson. For what purpose are you here to pick up Staff Sergeant Silverman?" The colonel has close-cropped gray hair, a ruddy complexion, and a square jaw. "Shall I assume that the envelope in your hand contains your orders? Is that right, Corporal?"

Johnson immediately places the envelope on the desk. "Yes, sir. This is for you, sir."

Banfill takes his time reading the order. He hasn't been given the usual heads-up and he is curious, if not peeved. "What does the Army want with my Sergeant Silverman? He is a nice young man and one of my best. He's a squad leader."

"I can't say, sir. I was just told to come pick him up."

"Well, what if I don't want him *picked up*? I have plans for him. The Army has plans for him. He's fluent in German, you know? He could be driving one of those Nazi tanks out there and you wouldn't know the difference."

"That's a scary thought, sir."

"I hope so. Where is he going next? And why?"

Johnson hesitates. He knows his response won't go over well. "I'm sorry sir, I believe that's in the orders. The reasons are classified."

"Classified? You mean I don't have the clearance? I'm a colonel and his commanding officer."

Johnson doesn't say a word. He swallows hard.

"That's all I'm going to get out of you isn't it, Corporal Johnson?"

"Yes, sir, that's all I know."

Banfill rises, walks to the door, and tells his adjutant to fetch Sergeant Silverman. "Tell him to bring his gear, he's being reassigned."

———————

Fifteen minutes later a stocky dark-haired man walks briskly to the colonel's office with his duffel. He snaps to attention. "Sergeant Silverman reporting, sir."

"At ease, Nate." Tapping the envelope on his desk, Banfill says, "Corporal Johnson here has come to pick you up for a new assignment. Sorry to see you leave us, Nate, I wish you the very best."

Silverman is confused. "Sir, I didn't put in for a transfer. I'm a Ritchie boy, through and through. Ritchie boy to the end. I've been trained to do intelligence work. I intend to go over with my unit when it leaves for Europe. Rumor is we're pulling out in a few months. That's the reason I joined. The only reason. I'm going back to Europe and fight those Nazi bastards for what they did to my community and my family. That's what I've been training to do."

The colonel sadly shakes his head. "Welcome to this man's army, Nate. The orders say you are to go with Corporal Johnson. It comes from Army headquarters. He's been sent up here to get you. In a limo."

Silverman stands his ground. "Colonel Banfill, sir, I don't want to go to Army headquarters. I don't want to be reassigned. You know my story, what happened to my people back in Germany. I enlisted to go back to Europe and fight. You gotta help me, Colonel. Can't you get these orders rescinded?"

Banfill raises his eyebrows. He holds the paper for Silverman to see. "These orders come down from the office of General Leslie Groves. I don't have veto authority here, Nate. Chin up, it might be a good move for you. If General Groves wants you, it must be pretty damn important." The colonel holds out his hand for a farewell shake. The discussion is over.

Silverman sighs, picks up his bag, and walks toward the door. "Drive safely, Corporal," the colonel says, "he's a damn good soldier and smart as a whip."

Johnson nods. "Yes, sir, I will."

2

REASSIGNED

Nathan cranes his neck to watch Camp Ritchie, his home for the last ten months, fade out of sight. He turns to the driver. "Do you know what this is all about?"

"No, sir, I don't. I'm nothing more than a delivery boy. Get my orders same as you."

Nathan nods and settles into the soft leather seat. Other than training maneuvers in and about the surrounding hills, he hasn't been out of the camp since he arrived from Fort Bragg. And that was on an Army bus with eight other men. His reassignment to Camp Ritchie was the first of the Army surprises. He hadn't put in for that transfer either.

He recalls the day he received his orders. He was preparing for parachute training that afternoon when he was called into Captain Lawson's office. "I'm recommending you for intelligence training, Silverman," the captain said. "The Army's put out a call for recruits familiar with Germany and fluent in the language. That would be you, right, Nate?"

"Yes, sir, but I'm quite happy where I am. I'm doing my third jump this afternoon. I'm an infantry soldier, that's what I joined up to do. I was studying at Columbia when I saw the poster that said foreign nationals who had received residency cards were eligible for the draft and could sign up. I went straight to the Army Recruiting Station, passed my interviews, passed my physical, and four weeks later I was sent down here. I want to be with my unit whenever we land in Europe. More than most, I got a score to settle. You don't know what they did to my family and others like me. Look, Captain, respectfully, sir, I don't want to be in intelligence, I don't want to sit at a desk and analyze data. I don't want to be a spy. I want to fight. I got a right. It said so right on the poster: 'Uncle Sam Needs You to Fight For Your Country!' That's why I joined up."

The captain smiled. "Hold on, Silverman. No one's telling you to sit at a desk. You're a German emigrant and you have skills that the Army can use. You should be proud. From what I understand, you're going to be transferred to an elite camp and trained with other boys that came over here from Germany to assist our ground troops once we start our invasion, whenever the hell that'll be. You know the language, you know the territory, the customs. You can be very valuable. That's something we didn't have in the last war."

"But sir, my unit . . ."

Captain Lawson closed his file folder. Negotiations were done. "I'm sending you to Camp Ritchie for intelligence training. It's top secret stuff. You'll thank me. Get your gear."

So, Nathan was off to Camp Ritchie, where he'd spent the next ten months learning how to interrogate German prisoners of war, how to navigate the terrain in France and Germany, and how to distinguish the difference between the German uniforms, insignias, and patches so that his commander would know the rank and function of any captured German soldier. From map coordinates and aerial photos, he had learned to recognize the churches, village squares, and principal structures of rural France and western Germany.

Now, after all those months of study, and after he has become comfortable with his new role, the Army in its infinite wisdom decides to pull him out of Camp Ritchie and send him somewhere else. And to make matters worse, rumors have it that all of his buddies in his Ritchie unit are scheduled to ship out for England in the next few months.

Nathan gazes out of the backseat window with glassy eyes. The car moves silently on. Suddenly his vision sharpens. "Excuse me, William," he says, "it doesn't take a map expert to know that Washington is southeast, and you are headed north."

"Yes, sir, that's true. We're not going to Washington. And it's Bill, sir. Just Bill."

"Well, where the hell *are* we going, Bill?"

"New York, sir. Manhattan. My orders say to drop you off at 270 Broadway. You are to report to the offices of the Army Corps of Engineers on the eighteenth floor."

Nathan feels his blood boil. "I'm not an engineer. I don't know anything about engineering. There must be some mistake. They got me confused with some other Nathan Silverman."

Corporal Johnson chuckles. "Wouldn't be the first time this army SNAFU'd. But these are the orders and I'm sure they'll explain it all to you when you get there. My advice is to just sit back and enjoy the ride."

"New York," Nathan says wistfully. "That's where I was living when I joined the Army."

Corporal Johnson tips his head toward the back. "If you don't mind my saying so, you sure don't sound like any New Yorker I ever knew." That brought out a laugh from the two of them.

"I was born in Germany."

"I figured you for a German," Johnson says, "that accent and all. When did you come to America?"

"Nineteen thirty-eight. Seems like a long time ago." Nathan leans back and closes his eyes. "Like a hundred years ago." There he was, looking down from the rail of the steamship, seeing his mother's aunt Gertrude wildly waving her arms back and forth. That silly straw hat of hers. She had agreed to sponsor him and guarantee his welfare with a financial affidavit, or he wouldn't have been able to come to America at all. The U.S. immigration office wouldn't have issued him a visa without Aunt Gertrude's affidavit.

"I guess you were lucky they let you out before the war started," Johnson says.

Nathan nods. "Yeah, fortunate for me, but not so lucky for the ones that I cared about and left behind."

"They wouldn't let them leave?"

"Back then, in 1938, the Nazis didn't give a damn how many Jews left Germany. They'd just as soon the whole lot of us, all five hundred thousand Jews, would have left. Hitler even said he would put all the Jews on ships tomorrow if he could. Hell, he said he'd supply the ships. But he knew that no country would take us in."

"Is that right? No country? Not even the U.S.?"

"Did you ever hear about the steamship *St. Louis?*"

"No, sir."

"In May 1939, four months before the war started, the MS *St. Louis* left Hamburg with nine hundred German-Jewish refugees, all holding Cuban visas. They were trying to escape the persecution in Germany. Two weeks later they docked in Havana, but the Cuban government changed its mind and wouldn't let them off the ship. Cuba had passed a new law revoking the visas and they turned them away flat. The *St. Louis* circled around Florida trying to find a place to dock, but the U.S. Coast Guard kept them away."

"Why would they do that?"

"Ask Cordell Hull."

"The secretary of state?"

"That's right, the U.S. secretary of state. The U.S. wouldn't take in the refugees or let the *St. Louis* even dock. The ship's captain then tried to take them all into Nova Scotia, but Canada wouldn't let him dock either."

"So, what happened to the refugees?"

"They had to take them all back to Europe."

"And?"

"Got caught up in the war, I suppose. Anyway, after that, it was too late for people to leave."

"But America let *you* in."

"That was 1938, a year before the war. Still, it wasn't easy for me. An immigrant had to prove he had the means to support himself before the U.S. would issue him a visa. No matter how wealthy you were, no matter how much money or property you had in Germany, you couldn't count it toward a visa, because Germany wouldn't let you take it with you. Germany passed a law they called the 'Flight Tax.' In order to leave Germany, you had to obtain a tax clearance certificate. In 1938, the tax was ninety percent of the total amount of your assets. And they would search you at the border. So, my parents couldn't give me money, the Nazis would have taken it away. I couldn't show the U.S. I had the ability to support myself unless I got a U.S. citizen to swear in an affidavit that she had the financial wherewithal and would promise to support me. That was my aunt Gertrude."

"You're lucky your aunt had money."

Nathan sadly shakes his head. "She had very little. She borrowed from friends to show a bank balance sufficient to justify an affidavit, just big enough to support one refugee. Otherwise, my mother and my sister could have come with me. I had to leave them in Germany."

"Geez, that's tough. I'm sorry."

"Yeah." The car falls silent as it motors through the Pennsylvania hills toward New York City. Nathan reflects over those last days, and sad memories wash over him. His mother had called him into the bedroom. "I've heard from Gertrude. She's put together enough for one visa. You're going to go to New York." Nathan was shocked. He shook his head. "No, Mom, you go. Or send Rachel. I'll be fine here."

There were tears in his mother's eyes as she gently placed her hands on his shoulders. "No one is fine here, Nathan. I don't know how long they'll keep your father working at the Institute, but I have to stay with him. Rachel is too young to make it on her own in New York. You go, finish school, become a big deal in America. You have the talent. The Jewish Aid Society has a ship leaving in two weeks. Go, and God willing, we'll all be together soon."

The day came for him to leave. His mother had packed a brown leather suitcase. She looked into his eyes and said, "Listen to me, Nathan, they won't let you leave with more than a few Reichsmarks. You can't rely on Gertrude for support when you get to America. She has nothing."

"I'll get a job."

She shook her head. "From what I hear, it's not so easy. I'm giving you my wedding ring; it's worth a lot of money. You take it and sell it in New York," she said. "I have sewn it into the shoulder padding of your jacket. They will search you, but they won't find the ring. Just be careful when you go through immigration control."

Nathan had protested, but his mother was firm. "Take the ring, sell it and start a new life." He hugged his mother tightly, not wanting to let go, until she finally pushed him away. "Go now. Write to me. Be a *macher* in America."

While he never knew her precise age, he knew that Gertrude was his mother's aunt, so she had to be at least in her early seventies. She had a small two-bedroom apartment she shared with another woman in New York's Lower East Side. She was a sweetheart, and never would have raised a fuss, but she really didn't have room for Nathan. She made him his meals and he slept on a small settee in her living room, but after a couple of weeks, he decided to sell his mother's ring. He had delayed the decision as long as he could, hoping to get a job, but his mother was right. They were hard to find in 1938. Thus far his efforts had failed. Language was a problem for him. He spoke Yiddish, so he could get by in the neighborhood, but applying for a job was a different matter.

Aunt Gertrude recommended a jewelry shop on Forty-Seventh Street to sell the ring. "While I would never say you should give your trust to any jeweler in this city," she said, "Feingold's is *heimishe*. Ask for Moishe. Tell him Gertrude sent you and he better do right if he knows what's good for him."

With some of the money from the ring, Nathan rented a room on Ridge Street, a block off Delancey. Finally, a neighbor told him that Mazer's in the Meatpacking District was hiring and Nathan, a strong and stocky boy, found work. He worked long hours, made a few friends, and saved his money with the hopes of sponsoring his family. He wrote often, but the letters from Germany stopped coming in 1940. There was no way to find out what had happened to his family.

Nathan was a voracious reader, and he studied tirelessly to learn English. In the spring of 1941, he felt comfortable enough to enroll in an evening course in literature at Columbia. That was followed by a course in American history. He had decided to take two more courses in 1942, when he saw the Army recruitment poster in the main hall of the university: UNCLE SAM NEEDS YOU. He learned that the Second War Powers Act of 1942 lifted the restrictions on foreign-born men serving in the military. They could enlist, they could fight for their new country, and it provided a fast track to citizenship.

Here was a chance to turn the tables, help defeat the Nazis and maybe find out what happened to his father, his mother, and his sister. Six weeks later he took the military oath and was on his way to Fort Bragg. Then, four months later, he was pulled out of Fort Bragg and sent to Camp Ritchie. Now he was sitting in the back seat of an Army limousine headed full circle back to New York City, to an Army engineering office, no less. It was hard to think that any of this made any sense at all.

3

MANHATTAN ENGINEER DISTRICT

The Continental comes to a stop in front of a twenty-eight-story white brick building across the street from New York's City Hall. "Here you go, sir. Two-seventy Broadway," Johnson announces.

Nathan takes another look at his orders. "Manhattan Engineer District. Eighteenth floor." He grabs his bag and holds out his hand. "Thanks for the ride, Bill. And for the company."

"Good luck to you, sir," Johnson replies. "I hope everything works out for you and for your family."

Nathan enters the lobby and is immediately stopped and questioned. He shows his orders to the uniformed security guard and is directed to the elevators. When doors slide open on the eighteenth floor, Nathan is surprised to see what looks like an ordinary office hallway. At one end, a uniformed officer is stationed outside a glazed door that reads ARMY CORPS OF ENGINEERS, MANHATTAN ENGINEER DISTRICT. He reviews Nathan's orders, nods, and opens the door.

Nathan enters the office on tentative steps, unsure of what surprises will happen next. There is a young lady sitting at the reception desk and she smiles at him sweetly. Her light brown hair is permed. She has a white poplin blouse and a dark skirt, tight at the waist. Nathan returns the smile and says, "My name is Sergeant Nathan Silverman. I'm not exactly certain who I am supposed to see here. Or truthfully, why I'm even here at all." She giggles. He places his orders on her desk.

"The orders are signed by a General Groves," Nathan says, "but . . . I think this all might be some kind of mistake."

The receptionist feigns surprise. "Oh, my goodness. A mistake? Hmm. That would be something. General Groves doesn't usually make mistakes." She gestures for Nathan to be seated and she carries his orders into an inner office. Moments later she returns and says, "Please come this way, Lieutenant Silverman."

"It's sergeant, ma'am," Nathan replies as he follows her into the office. Behind a large oak desk sits a man in his midforties. His uniform reveals that he is a three-star general. He has thick dark hair with wisps of gray above his forehead. To his right sits a man in a suit and tie. He is thin, with short curly black hair, an oval face, and what Nathan thinks is an unusually long neck.

Silverman snaps to attention. The general nods casually. "At ease, Sergeant, have a seat. You're probably wondering why you're here."

"Yes, sir."

"My name is Leslie Groves, and this is Dr. Robert Oppenheimer." Nathan settles into a chair, still not at all certain why he is sitting in this room. The general continues. "Your father, Josef Silverman, he's a physicist back in Germany, is that right?"

"Yes, sir."

"We understand that he works at the Kaiser Wilhelm Institute in Berlin, is that correct?"

Nathan shrugs. "Well, he was working there when I last saw him, but that was in 1938. Is he all right? Do you know something about him?"

"No, I'm afraid not, son. We do get some information about the Institute from our sources every now and then, but I haven't heard anything about your father in some time. I'm sorry to say, that's not a good sign."

"I understand."

"Did your father ever take you with him to work? Have you ever been inside the laboratories at the Institute?"

"Yes, sir, several times, but I was a teenager."

"As you probably know, these days, the Institute's current operations, all of its research, is a tightly guarded secret."

"I'm sorry, sir, but I don't know anything about its current operations."

"Are you familiar with Dr. Günther Snyder?"

Nathan nods. "He is also a physicist at KWI. He has worked with my father. My father got him the job. I've met him a few times. He likes my mother's cooking; I can tell you that."

Groves chuckles. "That may come in handy someday."

"My mother's cooking?"

"Do you think you could recognize Dr. Snyder if you saw him?"

"No doubt. He's a portly guy with curly hair. About five-eight I'd say."

Groves glances at Oppenheimer, who nods.

The general continues, "Just as important, Nathan, would Dr. Snyder recognize you?"

"I'm sure he would."

Dr. Oppenheimer interrupts. "Sergeant, at your mother's dinner table, did you ever hear your father and Dr. Snyder discuss the work they were doing?"

"Sometimes they'd make reference to it, but not in any detail. It's not exactly dinner talk, you know. They were theoretical physicists. Pretty boring stuff. They studied chemicals and their atomic structure. Atoms and protons and electrons, that kind of stuff. Way over my head."

"Understood."

"My father is a genius, the smartest man I ever knew, but Dr. Snyder got promoted over him." Nathan raises his eyebrows. "I believe it was because Snyder wasn't Jewish. Opportunities stopped for my father in the mid-1930s. But getting back to your question, I can't really tell you any details about Snyder's work."

General Groves taps his fingers on the desk. "We have information that Günther Snyder wants out of Germany. He's sent signals that he wants to defect to America. Does that sound like him?"

"Could be. I never knew him to be an enthusiastic Nazi. He used to complain about the way the Nazis fouled things up. He didn't like the way they ran the Institute, I know that. I think it's very possible he would like to defect."

"If he does, we want to help him."

Oppenheimer adds, "We're also very interested in the work that Dr. Snyder and his colleagues are doing. Did he and your father ever discuss fission or fusion in your presence?"

"No, not really. I remember they discussed theories about atoms and elements, but I was young, and it wasn't something that interested me."

"Did you ever hear either one of them talk about making weapons?"

"Weapons? Like artillery? Oh no, sir, never. They were peaceful men. Scientists. Theoretical physicists. Eggheads. Those guys didn't work for Germany's war department."

"Well, in fact they did. The war department owns the KWI."

Nathan leans back in his seat. The statement is shocking.

The general stands and looks at his watch. "We'll talk about it. Why don't we order up a late lunch and we'll discuss our assignment for you, Nathan?" He presses a button on his desk. "Molly, send Rickert over to Katz's and bring us back some chow. There's three of us. You know what I want."

Nathan sits up. "Excuse me, sir, but if you are ordering from Katz's Deli . . ."

"You don't like pastrami?"

"Oh no, sir, I love pastrami. But I've been traveling since early this morning and I'm kind of hungry. I wonder if you might add a side of potato latkes. That's all. They make the best."

4

NEW ORDERS

"Nathan, do you know why you've been assigned to the Manhattan Engineer District?"

Lunch is over. The plates are sitting on the conference room table. Two of them still have half of a sandwich. Nathan's is empty. "No, sir, I sure don't," he replies. "I'm not an engineer. That's why I thought it might be a mistake. But then, this doesn't seem like what I'd expect an engineering office to look like. Are you really an engineer, sir?"

"Indeed, I am. I helped design and build the Pentagon. But the title of Manhattan Engineer District is a bit misleading. On purpose. I'll explain it all to you in a moment, but what we're about to discuss here is highly classified. As classified as it gets. Top secret. Not a word of this goes anywhere. Do you understand me, Nathan?"

"Yes, sir, General, I understand. I won't divulge a single word without your permission."

"That's right. Now Robert, let's give Nathan a little background."

Oppenheimer leans forward. "We'll start simple. Do you know the parts of an atom?"

Nathan nods. "I'd better, my father is a physicist. The parts are proton, electron, and neutron. The proton has a positive charge, the electron has a negative charge, and the neutron is neutral, no charge, I think."

"That's right. You're up to date. The presence of neutrons is a very recent discovery, but certainly one which your father would have known. Simply put, physicists theorize that if you bombard an atom of uranium-235 with a neutron, you can cause a nuclear fission; that is, the atom will break apart, split. That splitting will release other neutrons which will bombard other uranium atoms causing other fissions, releasing quite a bit of heat and energy. We call that a chain reaction. If the amount of uranium is large enough, what we call a critical mass, and if the chain reaction is allowed to continue, it can cause quite an explosion."

Nathan's eyes widen. "So that's what you meant when you asked if my father and Snyder were working on weapons. Are we talking about making a bomb out of uranium?"

Oppenheimer nods. "The most powerful bomb in the history of mankind, capable of killing millions of people. Conceivably."

"Do we have such a bomb?"

Oppenheimer hesitates and looks to Groves for permission. Groves approves, and Oppenheimer says, "Not yet. Dr. Compton at the University of Chicago is in charge of coordinating all of the scientific research necessary to make this chain reaction a reality. I have been appointed to head a committee to design and develop a working nuclear bomb. That's what the Manhattan Project is all about. We're working on it right now and we're getting closer, but at the present time, we're not there."

"Does Germany have this bomb?"

"We don't think so, at least not yet, but we don't know for sure. They certainly have the scientific know-how, but it's one thing to create fission in a laboratory, and quite another to engineer an atomic bomb. It would take a large facility and a lot of money. Otto Hahn, Fritz Strassmann, Abraham Esau, Kurt Diebner, Günther Snyder, and presumably others have the theoretical knowledge and they are hard at work in Berlin. Maybe your father as well, though I haven't heard. Germany had a significant head start over us: some of the best scientists, a strong industrial base, sufficient materials, and the interest of its military community. But we don't know how far along they are."

General Groves leans forward. "Unless and until we receive positive knowledge to the contrary, we have to assume that German scientists and engineers are working on an atomic program with the full support of the Reich Ministry of Armaments and with the full capacity of the German industrial complex at their disposal. Any other assumption would be unsound, dangerous, and frankly, foolhardy. Right?"

Nathan nods, not sure where this is going.

"Nate, last September, I received a referral from General George C. Marshall. You know who he is, don't you?"

"Yes, sir, he is the chief of staff of the United States Army."

Groves smiles. "Well, when George makes a referral, it carries some weight. He says that Adolf Hitler has been making noise that we believe is directly related to developing a nuclear weapon. He brags that Germany is developing a 'secret weapon.' When we add his speeches to the reports we are receiving about Germany's nuclear activity at the Kaiser Wilhelm Institute, we have to take that possibility seriously. General Marshall thinks we should develop a military unit to go to Germany and determine the extent to which Germany has achieved nuclear weapons or chemical weapons. That mission has been given the code name ALSOS.

"Because of the work we are doing here at Manhattan Engineer District, ALSOS was referred to me for oversight. As you know, in September we landed in Italy. I intend to send part of the ALSOS unit to Italy to proceed north with our troops. Whenever we land on the west coast of Europe, a second unit of ALSOS will travel with our expeditionary force. As you can imagine, reaching Germany with either of these alternatives is many months, if not years, away. It will take quite awhile before we get any information from ALSOS.

"I want to know sooner. Günther Snyder's defection provides that opportunity. So here is where you come in, Nathan Silverman. I want to sneak someone right into the heart of Berlin, someone who knows the city, someone who knows the inner workings of the Kaiser Wilhelm Institute, and someone who has connections with one or more of the physicists, like Günther Snyder."

Groves smiles and points his finger. "And someone who has been trained by Camp Ritchie to go back into Europe on intelligence missions. Sound like anyone you know?"

At that point Molly enters the room with coffee service. She places the cups around the table, saying, "One for you General, one for you Dr. Oppenheimer, and one for you Lieutenant Silverman."

Nathan smiles. "It's sergeant." She smiles back.

General Groves dumps three spoonsful of sugar into his cup and takes a sip. "So now you know why you are here. That's your new assignment, Nate. I want you to go back to Germany, to Berlin. Meet Günther Snyder and find out what we need to know about Germany's nuclear program. He'll tell you what he knows. And what he doesn't know, he can find out. How far along are they? Have they constructed a workable nuclear reactor? How and where are they doing their isotope separation? Where are they enriching uranium? Have they calculated and achieved critical mass?"

Nathan is sitting with glassy eyes, like a deer in the headlights. All of these concepts are beyond his education or experience.

Groves adds, "And maybe you will learn if your father is still alive. If he is, we can help to get him out."

Nathan swallows hard and clears his throat. "General, sir, I'm not trying to beg off this assignment, I'd love to get back to Berlin. I'd love to help Professor Snyder defect. Most of all I'd love to find out what happened to my family. But I don't have any scientific background. I just wonder whether I am the right guy to lead a mission to assess the progress of Germany's nuclear program. I don't even have the basic knowledge to understand what I would be looking at. Not to mention, how do I get into Berlin and get the information back to you?"

The general nods. "We're aware that you don't have a scientific background. What you have is high-level military training, intelligence training, and a connection to Dr. Snyder. We have no indication that Dr. Snyder intends to change his mind, and we presume that he will bring the information to us."

"But sir, what if something happens to Dr. Snyder, or what if—"

"We have considered that possibility and the possibility that he may not possess all the information we need. For that reason, we have assigned Dr. Fisher to go with you. Dr. Fisher is a brilliant physicist and has been working with Enrico Fermi and Leo Szilard in Chicago for the past year. Dr. Fisher is capable of understanding and analyzing any information you uncover from Dr. Snyder or from the KWI, and will help us to determine exactly how close the Nazis are. Additionally, Dr. Fisher's presence will give you more credibility with Dr. Snyder."

Nathan is doing his best to process everything he is hearing. "I'd like to help," he says, "I really would. For many reasons. Tell me if I've got this right: you want me to travel to Europe, which is presently occupied and fortified by the German army, make my way to Berlin with some old scientist in tow, assess the progress of Germany's nuclear weapon program, find my father if he is alive, sneak him, Dr. Snyder, and Dr. Fisher back out of Europe, and then report it all back to you."

The general smiles broadly and smacks the table with his palm. "Exactly!" He turns to Oppenheimer. "You see, I told you he was perfect."

Nathan's jaw drops. "But, General . . ."

General Groves wags his finger up and down. "Isn't that what you Ritchie boys have been trained to do? To go back into Germany? We'll put you in a Wehrmacht uniform; you can easily pass for a German officer. You know your way around Berlin, you've been to the Institute, you know Günther Snyder and he knows you. He'll see you and Dr. Fisher and be more comfortable when he defects. You've got all the map skills to get you across France and Germany, you know the terrain. You've been working on it for months. You're perfect!"

Nathan sighs. "Okay."

"Good. First, we're going to send you to meet up with Dr. Fisher in Chicago and hopefully you'll get a better sense of what we're looking for."

"When are you expecting me to leave?"

General Groves looks at his watch. "The train to Chicago leaves in two hours. You'll meet up with Dr. Compton at the University of Chicago's Metallurgical Laboratory. They call it the MetLab. As Robert just told you, Dr. Compton is the head of research for the

Manhattan Project. He will introduce you to Dr. Fisher, Dr. Fermi, and Dr. Szilard. They will tell you exactly what information they will need to know in order to make an assessment of Germany's progress. Then you and Dr. Fisher will return here to New York where we will brief you on the remaining details of the mission. We'll provide you with your European contacts and give you the tools you'll need before proceeding to the Continent."

The general stands and holds out his hand. "Godspeed, *Lieutenant* Silverman. You can pick up your tickets, your new orders, and your lieutenant's insignia from Molly. Congratulations."

5

THE TWENTIETH CENTURY LIMITED

Nathan stretches his legs and laces his fingers behind his head. "Pretty posh," he says aloud. Nathan is sitting in a private sleeper called a "roomette" on his way to Chicago's LaSalle Street Station aboard the jewel of the New York Central line, the Twentieth Century Limited. He is dressed in his uniform, now stitched with a gold rectangle signifying his rank as second lieutenant. There is a white carnation in his buttonhole, given to him by a porter when he boarded the train in New York's Grand Central Station.

Wouldn't the folks back home be surprised? he thinks, gazing out of the window at the cityscape. Actually, his thoughts are never far from the family he left behind. From time to time, the American newspapers have printed dreadful stories about Jewish persecution in central Europe, and they disturb him deeply. Reports of mass arrests. Reports of prison camps. But Nazi persecution is nothing new to Nathan; he witnessed it, though the extent of the cruelty now being reported sickens him. He worries about his family. Is his father still alive? Is he still working at the Institute? Are they forcing him to work on a bomb? Nathan hopes his father would refuse such an assignment on moral grounds, but then what would become of him? Would he be fired? Or punished? Or killed?

What about his mother and his little sister? Rachel would be nineteen now, not so little anymore. When he left her she was fourteen; always full of life, full of energy. Nathan hasn't heard from any of them since 1940, when he received his mother's last letter. Still, they are never out of his thoughts.

He makes his way to the dining car and is shown to a table by a porter who keeps calling him "Colonel." Inside the car, white tablecloths are set with fine china, silverware, and crystal stemware. Outside the car, the countryside, now dimly lit by a half-moon, glides by at sixty miles an hour. The train whistle sounds every now and then as the Century passes through a town center.

The porter approaches to take his order. Nathan ponders the menu and says, "I think I'll have one of those filets, medium rare, a baked potato with sour cream and chives, and in honor of this trip, I'll have a Manhattan." The porter smiles and leaves to place the order.

Nathan is enjoying his dinner when the porter seats a couple across the aisle. He has to take a second look. He could swear that it's Lena. Same long blond hair. Same figure. Nathan stares. She has the same mannerisms, same expressive way of talking with her hands. Lena radiated confidence. And Lena broke his heart.

He started dating her when they were sixteen. Her father was an industrialist and seemed to have weathered the Depression just fine. Lena's family had money and connections. But that was unimportant to Nathan. He was intoxicated by her vivacity. Everything she touched sparkled. He was Jewish, she was not, but it never seemed to matter to them. They had a large circle of friends and Lena loved to socialize. At any gathering, she was inevitably the epicenter.

They were eighteen in 1933, swearing their everlasting love and planning for a future together, when President Hindenburg appointed Adolf Hitler as chancellor. His anti-Semitic rants frightened the couple, but Lena's father brushed them aside. "He's good for business," Mr. Hartz said. "Good for Germany. All that other stuff is just talk."

Less than three months into Hitler's rule, the Nazis staged a national boycott of all Jewish businesses. It was presented to the public as a reprisal against a so-called international Jewish conspiracy that was accused of trying to damage Germany's reputation. Nathan's uncle had to close his hardware store that day, but it was vandalized. Lena was fond of Nathan's uncle and she was angry at the government for promoting such a horrible program. She even helped to clean up the damage caused by the hate-filled vandals.

Three weeks later, the government passed an act entitled "A Law Against Overcrowding in Schools and Universities." There was no overcrowding; that was a lie. To relieve the so-called overcrowding, the law limited the number of Jewish students in any public school or university to 5 percent. Nathan was allowed to remain in school, but Rachel, who was in the sixth grade, was forced to leave. Once again, Lena was furious and did not hide her disgust. She loved Rachel. Some of the Jewish members of their social group were forced to leave the public high school and many enrolled in a private school, which had the effect of separating them from their friends in and out of school. Social gatherings became less inclusive. Parties tended to be either Jewish or non-Jewish.

As the months progressed and Hitler's anti-Semitic campaign intensified, Lena's discomfort in Jewish circles became perceptible. There were times when she might beg out of an invitation to a predominantly Jewish party. From time to time, she'd make excuses and not come to dinner at Nathan's home. Nathan started feeling a chill when visiting the Hartzes. When he would raise his concerns with Lena, she would brush them off. "You're being overly sensitive," she'd say. "Everything is fine."

One night, Lena let it slip that her father was urging her to broaden her social circle. By that, he meant for her to date other boys. "The way Germany is headed, it would be wise for you to form relationships with other people in addition to Nathan Silverman, people who will have a secure future in this country," he said to her. When she mentioned the conversation to Nathan, he asked her point-blank, "Is that what you want to do?"

"Of course not," she said, but then she added, "You must admit that it's pretty hard for a girl like me to be totally comfortably in all-Jewish groups these days." Nathan felt bad for her because she was getting pulled in opposite directions, but he was confident that their love was strong enough to survive the challenges. It wasn't.

In 1935, their time together grew less frequent. In July, Lena said she wanted to have a serious talk. They sat on Lena's front porch. The excuses she offered, the explanations she gave, were entirely unnecessary because Nathan had known for some time that the relationship was unsustainable. That night she gave him back the necklace he had given to her on her birthday. She said she didn't feel right keeping it.

Nathan was twenty years old and devastated. He had never considered a break-up with Lena. His mother tried her best to console him. She said he was young; he had a whole life ahead of him. He had so many wonderful talents. He would find another girl, but Nathan shook his head. He would do his best to put Lena out of his mind forever; he never even wanted to hear her name again. He vowed never to be so vulnerable, never to let another woman inside his defenses again. He would construct impenetrable walls. And at least to this date in November 1943, he has remained true to his vows.

In retrospect, holding on to Lena in Nazi Germany was like trying to hold a handful of water. Whatever they once shared had slipped away. Had it not dissolved that night on the Hartzes' porch, it would have collapsed soon afterward. That September, Germany passed the Nuremburg Race Laws depriving Jews of their Reich citizenship and making it a crime for a Jew to marry or even have sexual relations with a person of "German Blood."

Now, looking across the dining car at the girl with the blond hair, Nathan feels a tug. He remembers the warm nights, not the cold shoulders. Long ago, Lena had a place in his heart. No doubt she left a scar.

Nathan stands, leaves a tip for the porter, smiles at the couple across the aisle, and walks off to his compartment. Tomorrow is sure to be an interesting day.

6

PLAYER WITH RAILROADS

Nathan is enjoying breakfast in the Club Car as the Century slowly rolls past the steel mills in Gary, Indiana. Orange smoke rises from the chimneys. Glimpses of Lake Michigan appear in between the factory buildings. Less than an hour remains of the journey.

His instructions are to proceed to the Palmer House Hotel, check in, and take a taxi to the University of Chicago where he is to meet with Dr. Compton in his office at the MetLab. General Groves wasn't sure if Dr. Fermi would be there. Fermi had made a quick trip to another Manhattan Project location in Oak Ridge, Tennessee.

Dr. Compton was to introduce Nathan to Dr. Fisher and Dr. Szilard. They were to take as much time as necessary to educate Nathan on what they presumed would be key indicators of Berlin's progress in nuclear development. Then Nathan and Dr. Fisher were to return to New York for a final meeting with General Groves before heading to Europe.

Pulling slowly into the LaSalle Street Station, the Century passes acres of rail yards, evidencing Chicago's status as rail hub of the country. From his literature class at Columbia, Nathan recalls Carl Sandburg's poem, *Chicago*. A melody of phrases rings out: "City with the Big Shoulders," "Hog Butcher for the World," "Player with Railroads," and the "Nation's Freight Handler." From what Nathan can see, it appears to be that kind of town.

The station is on the south end of Chicago's Loop and seven blocks from the hotel. Nathan grabs his bag and heads out onto the streets of the Second City, so named because of its rebirth after the Great Chicago Fire of 1871. An elevated train rumbles loudly overhead as Nathan passes Van Buren Street. There is a strong breeze off the lake and many pedestrians have pulled their coat collars up as they walk briskly to their destination. Chicago is a busy town, gritty and brusque. No meandering permitted here; it has no time for dawdlers.

By contrast, the Palmer House is elegant and stately. The immense reception hall has brilliant chandeliers, and sconces and columns that line the walls, directing the eyes to a short staircase at the south end that rises to a curtained doorway, almost like a throne. To Nathan's mind, the scene resembles an ancient Egyptian palace. High above the hall, the ceiling is painted in an exquisite French fresco. Nathan stands with his bag at his feet gawking at the glorious expanse when the desk clerk says, "May I help you, Lieutenant?"

She hands him a key to a room on the fifth floor. Nathan opens the door to a larger and more luxurious bedroom than he has ever slept in. After a quick shower, he flags a taxi, motors south along Lake Shore Drive, and arrives at the Hyde Park Campus of the University of Chicago. He is scheduled to meet Dr. Compton in his office in Eckhart Hall at noon.

The campus befits one of America's most revered universities. Stately limestone buildings dot the landscape, many styled in Gothic architecture. Nathan stops a student to inquire where he might find Eckhart Hall. The young man points across the quadrangle to a large building. Its facade is also Gothic, with three ornate pointed arches rising to a steep maroon roof. Nathan is confused. Eckhart Hall looks like any other college building. Is this the Metallurgical Laboratory? The MetLab? Is this the place they are researching an atomic bomb?

A uniformed guard ushers Nathan down the hall and into the office of Dr. Arthur Holly Compton. Behind a desk of papers sits a thin man in a light gray suit. He has a short brush of a black moustache beneath his nose, not unlike that of Adolf Hitler. His hairline is receding and comes to a widow's peak. All in all, Nathan thinks he looks very much like one would expect a Nobel Prize winner in physics to look. Compton gestures for Nathan to take a seat.

"Quite a dangerous assignment you've volunteered to undertake, Lieutenant," he says.

Nathan smiles. "Volunteer is a generous term, Dr. Compton. I was reassigned to this project from a military base. I received a brief introduction into the kind of scientific work that's being done here and in Germany, and then I was directed to come to Chicago to meet with you and Dr. Fisher."

Compton looks at his watch and shakes his head with a touch of annoyance. "Obviously, we're waiting for Dr. Fisher, who is swimming, I presume. When weather permits, Dr. Fisher takes a daily swim at the Fifty-Seventh Street beach. Or, if the weather doesn't permit, in a swimming pool. Quite an athletic person, as you will soon see. The youngest member of Dr. Fermi's team."

That brings a smile to Nathan's lips. "I told General Groves that I was worried about making my way across Europe dragging an old professor in tow. I imagined myself and some old geezer trying to run through enemy lines."

"Hmm. Well then, you may be in for a surprise. How much do you know about the work we're doing here?"

"Very little, I'm afraid. General Groves and Dr. Oppenheimer met with me in New York. They briefly explained that you are heading a research team developing nuclear energy and the possibility of creating a very destructive bomb. They also indicated that Germany is doing the same thing. They want me to go to Berlin, help one of the physicists defect, and bring back enough information about Germany's nuclear program for you to assess the threat."

"That's my understanding, as well."

"I personally know the man who is supposed to defect. He was my father's colleague and a friend of the family. But to answer your question more directly, I have no conception about the work you or the German physicists are doing."

"Isn't your father a physicist in Berlin?"

"He was. Maybe he still is. I haven't heard from him in three years. I told General Groves that I personally have no background in physics and that I am not really qualified to report on nuclear research, so he sent me here to meet with you and Dr. Fisher, who is supposed to accompany me. I think the general hopes that I will learn something basic before we go to Germany, especially in case something happens to Dr. Fisher."

Compton raises his eyebrows and wiggles his moustache back and forth. "Basic, huh? Our nuclear program in a nutshell, is that it?"

"Sort of, sir."

"Well, to start, in 1939, President Roosevelt was alerted to Germany's efforts to create a bomb out of fissile uranium. He consulted with several members of the academic and military communities to assess the risk. One committee followed another with nothing much being done, and then, in 1941, he directed the head of the Office of Scientific Research and Development, Vannevar Bush, to create a committee that would study the use of uranium-235 and plutonium-239 for use in weapons and then report back to him. Vannevar appointed me as head of the committee. At the time, research in nuclear fission was being conducted in several universities spread out across America: here at Chicago, at Cal-Berkeley, Columbia, Princeton. My first move was to consolidate the research. We moved it all here.

"I brought Enrico Fermi over here because he was already working on calculating the critical mass of uranium-235. Leo Szilard, the holder of the patent on a nuclear fission reactor, was working with Fermi at Columbia, and he came as well. About six months later, the Army Corps of Engineers assumed control of the project, now named the Manhattan Project, under the management of General Groves. I remained in charge of the scientific research, but Groves needed to put someone in charge of designing, building, and testing a bomb capable of being dropped from an airplane. That testing could not be done in the middle of a big city on a college campus. It needed a large footprint in the middle of nowhere. I recommended my good friend Robert Oppenheimer to head that part of the program, which we called Project Y. He selected a remote location in Los Alamos, New Mexico."

Suddenly, the door to the office swings open and a tall young woman enters. Her dark hair is wet. She's a little out of breath. "Sorry I'm late, Arthur."

"Lieutenant Silverman, allow me to introduce you to an old geezer. This is Dr. Fisher."

"Old geezer?" she says, as she extends a strong right arm.

"It's an inside joke," Compton replies.

"I'm so embarrassed," Nathan says. "No one told me I would be working with a woman physicist. Dr. Fisher, I had assumed . . ."

Fisher smiles. "Well, I'm the only woman on Enrico's staff, so that's a fair assumption. But old geezers prefer to be called by their first names. I'm Allison." Nathan shakes her hand and stares at her hair. "Were you just swimming in Lake Michigan?" he says.

"In November?" she says. "It's freezing outside. What is Arthur telling you?"

"He said you took a daily swim at the Fifty-Seventh Street beach. And your hair is wet, and . . ."

She laughs. "U of C has an indoor pool."

7

CHICAGO PILE-1

Allison and Nathan leave Eckhart Hall and head across campus. "In order to fully appreciate the work we are doing here," she says, "you need to see the nuclear reactor. Enrico named it the Chicago Pile. You said you wanted to know more about the science, and that is the ideal place to start." They cross the Midway and arrive at a football field.

"This is Amos Alonzo Stagg Field, where the University of Chicago plays football and other field sports. Right now, it's not in use. It hasn't been used since 1939." They take a seat on the wooden grandstands. "About a year ago, after Enrico and Leo were brought here by Dr. Compton, they decided they needed to build a secure nuclear reactor—a large container, for lack of a better word—where a controlled nuclear chain reaction could take place and be observed. Do you understand what a chain reaction is?"

Nathan hesitates. "Dr. Oppenheimer said that when you bombard an atom with a neutron, it could . . . I'm not real sure."

"Fair enough. Let's start at the beginning. In 1932, a British professor at Cambridge, James Chadwick, discovered the presence of 'neutrons' in the nucleus of atomic elements. Before that, we believed that atoms had only protons and electrons. Protons are positively charged, and electrons are negatively charged. Chadwick discovered the presence of neutrons, which have no electric charge but add to the atomic mass.

"In 1934, Enrico Fermi conducted an experiment to determine whether he could induce artificial radioactivity by forcing a neutron into the nucleus of a heavy atom; he chose uranium. The result of his experiment was to cause a change in the element itself, in addition to creating radioactivity."

Nathan nods. So far, so good.

"Did your father know Dr. Leo Szilard?"

"I think so."

"He was one of several Jewish scientists who worked at the Kaiser Wilhelm Institute in Berlin before fleeing Germany when Hitler came to power. Dr. Szilard settled in England. In 1934, he patented the idea of a nuclear chain reaction by using neutrons. He theorized that if he bombarded the nucleus of a certain element with a neutron, that nucleus would absorb the neutron, and also free other neutrons. The freed neutrons could then be absorbed into other nuclei and do the same thing over again, causing a series of reactions. But it was just a theory at the time. Are you with me, so far?"

Nathan shrugs and then nods.

"All right then, try to follow the old geezer. In December 1938, Otto Hahn, also at KWI in Berlin, found that bombarding uranium-235 with neutrons caused the uranium to undergo a change. A month later, Lise Meitner, along with her nephew Otto Frisch, also Jewish physicists in Berlin, explained that Hahn's experiment really amounted to splitting the atom. They repeated the experiment in January 1939 and gave it the name 'fission,' because they split the uranium atom into parts.

"Today we know that certain heavy elements with an odd atomic mass, like uranium-235 or plutonium-239, when bombarded with a neutron, will absorb that neutron and split. If we bombard uranium-235, it will absorb the neutron, change the element into barium, and release 2.4 other neutrons, creating heat and energy in the process. If those 2.4 neutrons are then absorbed into other uranium atoms, those atoms will also split and repeat the process. Ergo, a chain reaction. It's a violent process that results in a lot of heat and a lot of energy. Boom! Are you still with me, Lieutenant?"

"With you."

"Last year, Enrico and Leo decided to build a reactor to carry out this chain reaction and study how the process could be controlled. They decided to build the reactor at the Argonne Laboratories a little south of Chicago, but they ran into all sorts of construction problems and the project was stalled. Enter Miss Allison Fisher to save the day." She takes a slight bow. "I knew that beneath this grandstand, the one you're sitting on, there are squash courts. This area is basically abandoned, there is no one using this football field and there are squash courts underground that are made out of concrete and they are unheated."

"You knew that?"

"I play squash."

"Of course you do."

"I suggested to Enrico that he might use the court for a reactor. And he did. The work began last November, and Enrico achieved the first sustained chain reaction in history, just this last January." She stands up. "Want to see the Pile, the world's first nuclear reactor?"

They walk down the stairs, past a guard, and arrive at a group of squash courts. Nathan looks into a doubles squash court and shakes his head. "I don't get it," he says. "It looks like a twenty-foot box has been built inside the squash court and then stuffed with thousands of bricks."

Fisher nods. "Forty-six thousand graphite blocks. The graphite acts as a moderator. When the atom is split and a neutron is released, it goes very fast. Too fast to be absorbed by another atom. The graphite moderates the speed—slows it down. Like swimming through molasses. We find that graphite makes a great moderator. So does heavy water, but heavy water is expensive to produce and ship. The result of the moderation is a slower neutron that can more easily be absorbed by the uranium atom, which will then split and free up other neutrons. The graphite is a way of controlling the chain reaction."

They stand there for a moment and then turn to leave. "Any questions?" she says with a smile.

"No. I think that is all this little brain can absorb without splitting."

"Ha! Where are you staying, Nathan?" she asks on their way up the stairs.

"The Palmer House Hotel."

"Ooh. Fancy that."

"No kidding. The Army is doing it all first class. They bought me a ticket on the Twentieth Century Limited in a sleeper compartment. They picked up the tab for everything I ate and drank. They reserved a fabulous room for me at the Palmer House. All on the Army's dime."

"Did you eat dinner in the Empire Room? I always wanted to eat there. I hear it's the best in Chicago."

Nathan shakes his head. "I just got here this morning."

Fisher smiles. "What about tonight? Do you want to take an old geezer to dinner on the Army's dime?"

"Sure."

"Great. But first, let's go meet Leo Szilard."

———————

D r. Szilard's office is also in Eckhart Hall. He has a pleasant round face and rich dark hair with occasional strands of gray. He is forty-four years old and speaks with an accent, though it is not German. Nathan learns that he was born in Hungary.

"So, you are Josef Silverman's boy?"

Nathan nods and smiles.

"I was only briefly at the Institute, but I knew your father. He is a brilliant scientist."

"Thank you."

"I'm sorry that he did not leave when the rest of us did. I know he was talking about it in 1934, but he was so dedicated to his work, he wanted to stay. I don't think he believed the country would deteriorate so quickly and so badly."

"I know. He was working with Otto Hahn and Günther Snyder, and he thought they were close to proving their theories."

"And they were. That is what is so troubling now. Not that Josef would ever permit the results of his work to be used as a weapon, but he had visions of the peaceful development of nuclear energy. 'Mark my words,' he would say, 'someday there will be nuclear power plants all over the world.'"

A tear comes to Nathan's eye. "I agree. He had great vision, my father. I miss him dearly."

"Well, let's hope he is alive and survives this terrible epoch. Meanwhile, I told Arthur that we should make sure you are alert to the possibility of an enrichment facility in or near Berlin. To the extent it exists, that will tell us how worried we should be."

Nathan is confused. "Enrichment?"

Before Szilard can explain the concept, Allison interrupts. "Leo, let me tell him about it at dinner. He's absorbed a lot today and I don't want his brain to split. By the way, we are going to the Empire Room for dinner."

"Lucky you."

8

THE EMPIRE ROOM

Nathan sits alone at a polished oak bar, nursing a martini in the quiet of the Empire Room. It is seven fifteen and Dr. Fisher is not due to arrive until seven thirty. He swirls his glass. So, Dr. Fisher is an attractive young woman, certainly not what he had anticipated. "What are the odds?" he says aloud.

"Pardon me, sir," the bartender says. "Did you need something?"

Nathan smiles. "Oh, a little sanity in this world would be appreciated. Can you help me out there?"

"Wish I could, sir. But I could get you another martini."

"Sounds like a decent alternative."

Ten minutes later, Nathan sees Allison enter the bar. She is definitely dressed for a night out. A navy V-neck dress with padded shoulders, tight at the waist and hemmed just slightly below the knees, all of which gracefully complements her figure. Nathan stands to greet her and at once realizes that in her heels she is taller than he is.

"I still have a full martini," he says to her. "What can the U.S. Army order for you?"

She smiles. "I'll have the same."

———

Knowing that their conversation would cover delicate subjects, Nathan asks the hostess to seat the two of them in a booth off in the corner. "For a little privacy," he says. The hostess smiles and leads them to a quiet corner of the room, lays two menus on the table in the booth, nods, and departs.

"I received my doctorate from the University of California at Berkeley," Allison says quietly over appetizers. "I was working for Dr. Ernest Lawrence in the Radiation Laboratory, what we called the Rad Lab. He had invented and constructed a cyclotron they named the Atom Smasher, for which he was awarded the Nobel Prize in 1939. Last year he built a bigger model that he named the Calutron. It spun around at great speeds. Unfortunately, it wasn't as efficient as he wanted, and he told General Groves to use other means. That was about the time that Dr. Compton transferred me to Chicago."

"Was he using the cyclotron to split the atoms for a chain reaction like in the Chicago Pile?"

She smiles. "You learn fast, Lieutenant. But no, it was to separate the uranium isotopes."

Nathan furrows his forehead signifying yet another concept he does not comprehend.

"Do you remember this afternoon, when Dr. Szilard mentioned enrichment, and you didn't know what that was?" He nods. "So, now I'll tell you. Uranium is a gray metal; it is extracted from the ore uraninite, also called pitchblende, which is mined like any other ore, like silver or copper. There are only a few places on Earth where uraninite is found in abundant enough quantities to be mined: Canada, Russia, and the Congo are major sources. And also Czechoslovakia, which is now, of course, under Nazi occupation. Like many other elements, uranium can have different varieties, what we call isotopes. Uranium in its oxidized state is ninety-nine percent of the isotope uranium-238, or U-238. It is not fissile, which means it does not start a chain reaction by bombarding it with a neutron. It is also only minimally radioactive.

"The other one percent is the isotope U-235. It is fissile, which means it can be split. Nuclear fission will occur when you bombard U-235 with a neutron. And it's very radioactive. The challenge is to separate the U-235 from the U-238, so that you can achieve a critical mass of U-235. That critical mass, when detonated, can blow you to kingdom come. Separating out the U-235 is called enriching the uranium. We need enriched uranium to make a bomb."

"And that takes a large facility?"

"Correct. It takes quite a bit of uranium and other materials to separate out a sufficient amount of U-235." She leans over and whispers, "In addition to knowing how close Germany is to building a bomb, Dr. Szilard thinks Dr. Snyder would know where the raw materials are being stored. Or where they are coming from. Or where the German scientists are doing their enrichment. There is a lot that Dr. Snyder can tell us, whether or not he ultimately defects, and hopefully, he will be willing to tell us."

Nathan begins to understand his assignment better. He thinks Snyder will give him the information, willingly or not.

Allison raises her eyebrows and shrugs. "So that's the plan." She flashes a coquettish smile over her cocktail glass, takes another sip of her second martini, leans back, and says, "So, what's your story, Nathan the Soldier?"

"Ah, nothing really."

"Don't play coy with me, I'm putting my life in your hands. This mission may seem like nothing to some sharpshooting army guy, but I'm heading to Nazi Berlin in the middle of a war to sneak out information and frankly, it scares the hell out of me."

"So . . ."

"So I get to know who I'm going to die with. Are you married?"

He chuckles. "We're not going over there to die. The plan is to come back with information, and maybe a defector. And no, I'm not married."

"Girlfriend?"

"Definitely not," he says firmly.

"Uh-oh, do I sense a bad break-up?"

"Yes, you do, but it was a long time ago. I don't want to talk about it."

She places a finger on her chin. "Hmm. Well, as for me, I'm not married, and I've never been in a relationship serious enough to have had a bad break-up."

"Good plan."

"Don't get the wrong idea. I'm not a misandrist; I'm open to the idea. Someday, with the right guy. You know, husband, little children, white picket fence. So far, it's just too early in my career to be side-tracked by some guy with marital intentions. I got my PhD two years ago when I was just twenty-six. That's a lot of hard work in a short period of time, which doesn't permit the distraction of romantic entanglements."

"I applaud your focus. So, did you always want to be a nuclear physicist? Did that come from your parents? Are they professors?"

That question brings a smile to her face, and she shakes her head. "Far from it. They are Iowa farmers. My dad has two hundred and fifty acres east of Ames and he grows corn. It was the depths of the Depression, times were tough, and they wanted something better for their only child. After high school, I enrolled at Iowa State just down the road. I was seventeen, and it was 1934. I studied chemistry, because I thought I might learn something to help increase my dad's efficiency and yield."

"It's a long way from studying chemistry at a farm school to working with Fermi and Szilard at the nuclear reactor at the University of Chicago," Nathan says. "How did you make that jump?"

"Well, first of all, ISU is not a *farm school*. They've had a strong physics program since the 1800s. And for your information, Iowa State is very involved in the Manhattan Project. Much of the pure uranium in Chicago Pile-1 came from the pilot project at ISU. Anyway, I took a couple of physics classes, became interested, wrote a couple of research papers that were well received, and I got a call to come work for Dr. Lawrence at Cal-Berkeley, where I got my doctorate.

"Last year, Dr. Compton took me away from the California sun, where I was comfortable and happy, and brought me here to frigid Chicago to work with Enrico and Leo who are studying chain reactions. And now that I am comfortably settled here, you come along to take me away to Berlin on some impossible scheme to steal information from Germany's nuclear laboratory and help a German scientist escape."

Nathan nods. "I guess that's right. Similar thing happened to me. So, what do you say to all that?"

She tips her head. "I say I must be crazy, and I'd like another drink.

Then I want you to tell me how in the world we are going to get this done. How do we get into Berlin? How do we get inside the KWI lab? How do we get back again? With Dr. Günther Snyder? Tell me that, Nathan the Soldier."

"I have not a clue. General Groves has those answers—I hope— and we are going to meet with him when we get back to New York. The train departs LaSalle Street Station tomorrow at three o'clock. We get into New York at eight in the morning and we meet with Groves immediately thereafter. He will brief us on the details of the mission and, no doubt, he will have answers to some of your questions. I suspect, however, that we will have to improvise along the way."

"That doesn't make me comfortable."

"Sorry. You speak German, don't you?"

"No. Why would you think that?"

"Only because it would make sense, but then again, nothing in the past week has made much sense to me. Isn't a lot of the nuclear research written in German?"

"It is, but we get it translated. I speak English and college French."

"Well, maybe that will come in handy." He pulls a folder out of his pocket, lays it on the table, and slides it over to Allison.

"What's this?" she says.

"Tomorrow's ticket on the Century. Car number seven. Cascade Glory. Compartment fourteen."

She opens the folder and studies the ticket. "Guess I better get home and pack. I suppose we could be gone for quite a while." She narrows her eyebrows. "This is a sleeper car, right? With beds?"

"That's all they have on the Century. It's a sixteen-hour ride from here to New York. We get there in the morning."

"What car are you in?"

He shrugs. "Car number seven. Cascade Glory. Compartment fourteen. It's a double roomette, I think. Two beds."

"You're sleeping in *my* roomette? Excuse me, what about respecting my privacy?"

"I suppose you could complain to the general; he bought the tickets. But maybe you should have considered your privacy before agreeing to accompany me all over Europe. Did you think we're going to have separate room arrangements everywhere we go? Do you want a separate bedroom in the field? I'm sorry, but you can rest assured that I have no interest in invading your privacy. Believe me, I am only interested in getting the job done and coming back home in one piece. I'm sorry if the arrangements offend you, Dr. Fisher."

"It's Allison, Nathan. Just Allison. And I've never been in the field. Nor have I ever been sneaking behind enemy lines. Or rescuing defectors. Or dodging bullets. I work in a laboratory. I'm a scientist. That's how I get the job done."

"I know. Splitting uranium to make bombs."

Allison's eyes narrow; her lips tighten. "Hold on. That's not fair. All these dedicated men and women . . ." She counts them off on her fingers. "Einstein, Fermi, Szilard, Compton, Lise Meitner, Otto Frisch, your father, brilliant scientists all, didn't study the atom in order to make bombs. They studied it to understand the universe, and they realized that it could be a valuable source of energy, for *the good of mankind.* And it's a damn shame that generals and majors and military minds have decided to bastardize the science and use this energy source for malevolent purposes. Who will win the race? Who will be the first to use atomic science as a weapon of war and kill people? Isn't that what you're all about, Lieutenant?"

"Damn right. And we need to win that race. Because Hitler doesn't care who he kills. Or how many. I lived in Germany; I saw the hate, the rage. He'll use whatever murderous weapon he can acquire. He'll wipe out an entire city without a second thought. *Deutschland über alles!* You think he wouldn't have used it on Poland, if he could have? Or Moscow? So, we have to do whatever we can to stop him from getting this bomb. That means getting the bomb before he does, and maybe that's the only thing that will stop him. And *that* is what I'm all about."

"Right. Win the race and build the bomb. And then what, Nathan? Would you use it? Would you drop the bomb on Berlin, if it was your decision? Would you kill four million people? Because the atom bomb doesn't know the difference between a Nazi and a child. It doesn't discriminate, it doesn't have a conscience. A neutron enters a uranium or plutonium atom and starts a chain reaction without a single moral thought."

"So why are you doing it then? You and Fermi and Szilard and Compton and all the others? Why are you making this bomb? How do you justify what you do?"

Allison's jaw is quivering. "First of all, Fermi and Szilard and *all the others* aren't making bombs. They're being made in Los Alamos by Oppenheimer and Teller and their group, all under the auspices of the U.S. Army." She pauses, exhales and shakes her head. "I know that was not an adequate answer or a justification for what I do, because we are giving them the science to make it work. We're just as guilty. But you must understand that it all started out as scientific research for the good of man. Understanding the atom and how it works, that's what it was all about. Science finds ways of making good use of its discoveries, like finding a dependable source of energy."

With her hands folded on the table, she says quietly, "People with evil agendas, they corrupt scientific discoveries. Professor Einstein warned President Roosevelt about the destructive application of uranium because he knew Germany had the science and would have the bomb sooner or later. And like you, Einstein was a German who saw the evil of the Third Reich. Our research didn't make weapons. We alerted the president to the possibility of weapons."

"No." Nathan shakes his head in a dismissive manner. "No, no, no. You and Fermi and Szilard and the rest of your nuclear physicists— even Einstein—you can't wash your hands. You can't blame the military for using the result of your research. You opened the gates of hell. You started splitting atoms, and by doing so, you set in motion a deadly chain reaction. And now it's in the wrong hands, and you come to the military, the ones you so readily condemn, and beg us to make sure that the wrong hands don't use it. You want us to put the genie back in the bottle. You want the U.S. Army to stop your chain reaction."

Allison lowers her eyes. She knows there is no simple retort.

They finish their dinner in relative silence. Nathan signs the check. They stand to leave. "I'll see you in compartment fourteen tomorrow afternoon."

9

A FATEFUL PROMISE

Hearing a knock on the door, Allison calls out, "Come in," and Nathan enters with his duffel. She is sitting on a padded couch which also serves as the roomette's lower bunk. A book is in her hand. She tips her head toward the upper pull-down. "You're on top. No secondary meaning intended."

On the opposite side of the roomette, there is a small closet, a sink, a mirror, and a single seat. Nathan calculates the dimensions of the upper bunk and shakes his head. When pulled down beneath the sloping ceiling, there is very little room for a stocky man, or a tall woman for that matter. Allison sports a guilty smile. "Squatter's rights, I guess. Sorry."

Nathan flips his duffel onto the luggage rack, points to the single chair and says, "I think I'll just bunk here. I sleep pretty well anywhere, even in a chair."

They sit quietly staring out of the window while the Century moves slowly south, out of the station and through the railyards. Across the tracks and east of the park, Lake Michigan's whitecaps crash against the shore. "Did you swim today?" he asks.

She nods. "Indoors. Those waves are easily six-footers down at Fifty-Seventh Street, and freezing cold. Besides, no matter what the weather, I don't swim when the waves are high. What about you? Do you work out? You look fit."

He shrugs. "I'm in the Army; we do a lot of physical exercise. I was in parachute training at Fort Bragg. All the jumpers are fit. And they worked us hard at Camp Ritchie. We did calisthenics every day. Ritchie has a bitch of an obstacle course. The Army keeps us moving, keeps our muscles strong and builds our endurance. But I'm not a swimmer or a runner. When did you start swimming?"

"High school. I swam competitively my junior and senior years. I didn't pick it up as a fitness regimen until I lived in California. I was also on the volleyball team in high school and at ISU. I was one of the taller girls, so I had an advantage. I was active as a kid, especially growing up on a farm. What about you? When you were growing up in Berlin, did you play sports? Were you athletic? I bet you were."

Nathan responds with a short shrug and a nod. "Sports were always front and center to the youth in Germany, myself included. And doubly so after the Nazis came to power with their emphasis on German physical superiority. For years there were numerous clubs and leagues all throughout the country. There were school teams, church teams, and what you might call semiprofessional teams competing in various leagues. That changed in 1933 when Hitler became dictator."

"So, you were excluded from playing competitive sports?"

Nathan shakes his head. "No. They permitted Jews to play on Jewish teams, but not in the official DRL leagues. Jewish sports clubs began to flourish, especially the Maccabi Clubs, both for men and women. Soon there were thousands of members of these Jewish sports organizations. I played on a youth football team, what you would call soccer. We had a league of ten teams in Berlin, and for tournaments we'd travel to other cities. It was always so exciting, especially when we went to Munich or Cologne." Nathan pauses to let a memory soak in. He has a faraway look in his eyes and Allison picks up on it.

"Did she go? Did your girlfriend go to the games?"

Nathan hesitates. There is regret in his voice and he answers slowly. "Yeah, she did. Lena was her name. I would look to the sideline, rain or shine, and there she'd be, screaming and yelling and jumping up and down. No matter where we were."

"I'm sorry," Allison says. "I shouldn't have asked."

"It's okay. It's over. Years ago. Did you have someone cheering you on?"

"My dad. I didn't have a relationship like you did. You were lucky to have what you had."

"Maybe. We parted friends."

"You had those years, no one can take them away. I'm surprised that the DRL didn't try to shut down the Jewish leagues."

"In the midthirties, there was little interference with Jewish athletes playing in Jewish leagues, especially as the 1936 Olympics was approaching. You remember, seven years ago, Germany hosted both the winter and summer Olympic games. There was a lot of international talk about boycotting the games because of Germany's racial laws, especially in the U.S. Hitler knew the world was watching and he knew that there was pressure to boycott or hold alternative games."

"I read about it. But the games went on."

"Hitler temporarily cleaned it up, at least superficially. He took down the anti-Jewish signs. They paused the daily racial crap that ran on the front page of the newspapers. He let our Jewish leagues exist just so he could boast about it. He even promised that the German Olympic team would be open to Jewish men and women. Of course, that was basically a lie. Our league had several athletes good enough to be on the German football team, but we were not permitted to try out. Gretel Bergmann was the best woman high-jumper in the world, and she was not allowed on the team."

They sit in silence for a moment. "I'm hungry," Allison says. "Let's go to dinner."

———————

They are greeted at the dining car by a porter in a white jacket. "Welcome back, sir," the porter says. "That was a surely quick turnaround for you, wasn't it?"

"It was indeed, Charles. Do you have a table for two?"

"Not right this minute, sir. It'll be a half hour or so. But the bar is open. You can get your Manhattan there. I'll come get you when I have a table."

"You have a good memory, Charles."

"Yes, sir."

In the club car, with their drinks in their hands, Nathan proposes a toast. "To the first leg of a successful mission."

"Hear, hear," Allison echoes. "And to each leg thereafter. How many legs do you suppose that will be?"

"Let's make a deal," he says. "Let's have a pleasant dinner, good food and drinks and light conversation. No arguments about science, no talk about the assignment, no talk about the Nazis or their racial laws, no talk about uranium bombs, no questions about what we did in high school, and definitely no questions about Lena. Okay?"

"No arguments? I don't know. That might be out of character for each of us."

"You see? You're starting already. What kind of music do you like?"

Allison takes a sip of her Manhattan and says, "All right. I'll tell you, but you're going to say I'm a type."

"Really, a type?" Nathan grins. "Do you like farm music? Square dances? 'Turkey in the Straw'? That type?"

"Oh, you're asking for it. I suppose I should ask you if you like military marches. 'Battle Hymn of the Republic,' maybe?"

"Well, I kinda do."

"I prefer classical music. And opera, though I doubt either appeals to you."

"And that's your type because you're a serious scientist? An egghead? Serious music for a theoretical physicist."

"Not so theoretical anymore. And you, Army boy, what is your musical choice?"

"I cut a mean rug."

A burst of laughter explodes from Allison's mouth, spitting a mouthful of Manhattan onto Nathan. "Oh, I'm so sorry," she laughs, "but that was your fault."

"I would say no it wasn't," he says, wiping his jacket with a napkin, "but then that would be arguing, and I would be breaking my rules." He gestures to the bartender for two more drinks. "So, what did you think was so funny? I happen to be a good dancer."

"You'll have to prove it. There will come a time and I'll put you to the test."

Charles appears, takes their drinks on a tray, and bids them to follow him back to the dining car.

———————

Toward the end of their meal, only a couple of tables remain occupied, and the dining car is quiet. The train speeds smoothly through the Ohio countryside. In the black of night, farmhouses appear as spots of light; stars on the ground. Allison gazes out of the window, lost in thought, nursing her third Manhattan. "Do you see those little farmhouses?" she says. "That was me growing up. Life out there is so quiet, so insular. So stable. Predictable. There is no war out there, save for whatever you hear on the radio, read in the newspapers, or see in the Movietone newsreels, and all that might as well be happening on the moon. There is only a set of chores to do beginning each day at sunup. And then supper, go to bed early and start over the next day." She runs her finger around the rim of her glass. "I'm not ready for this, Nathan," she says with a catch in her throat. "I'm not an Army boy. Or girl. I'm frightened."

"I understand. We'll be fine."

"How can you say that?"

"Because I have faith in the Army's planning. This will be a well-thought-out operation. General Groves will lay it all out for us tomorrow. Each and every step will be detailed."

Allison slowly shakes her head. "Every detail. Günther Snyder wants to defect. Maybe he does. At least our source thinks he does. And because he's in the inner circle of KWI, working side by side with Otto Hahn, Kurt Diebner, and Abraham Esau, he'll know exactly how close Germany is to building and deploying a bomb. At least we think he will. And he'll be anxious to tell us all he knows. Probably."

"That's right. And we need you to go with me, because when he passes the information along, I won't know what he's talking about. You'll know the right questions to ask."

"If he's defecting, why do you need me at all? He can tell you himself when he gets to Los Alamos, or Oak Ridge, or wherever they put him."

"He may not know all the answers, Allison. You'll ask him questions, and I assume he'll tell you what he knows, but what if he doesn't know? What if the information you seek is not within his experience, but is available for him in the KWI laboratories—in their records or in their studies? He may need to go back into the lab and retrieve that information for you."

"And he would do that?"

"Why not? He's asking us for asylum and a new career in America. I assume he'll do a lot for us."

After a minute of staring out the window, Allison says, "How do we know that Snyder will tell the truth? He's a German. Why wouldn't he purposefully mislead us? How do we know they're not planting him as a counterspy?"

"I think the hope is that you'll figure it out."

"What if the Germans discover that America has sent one of its nuclear scientists to Berlin; a woman who has knowledge of the U.S. program, just like you think Snyder has knowledge of the German program? What if they capture me? Have you considered that? Have you considered what they might do to me to find out about our program?"

"It sounds like you're having second thoughts."

"Second, third, fourth. I know I volunteered, and I was committed to this assignment, but now that we're on our way . . . I'm afraid. What if the Gestapo gets ahold of me?"

"We're not going to let that happen. The plan is to put you in a secure location. Nobody will know where you are. The Germans will never know you've come to Berlin. You're never going anywhere near the research facility. Look, we have to have faith; the Army knows what it's doing. They won't hang us out to dry. They'll have protection in place."

"In Berlin? Right." She swallows. "I must be out of my mind."

"I intend to complete this mission, Allison. I'm assigned to it. I understand if you don't want to go. You're not a soldier. No one can order you. But why don't you wait to decide until after we talk to General Groves? He might be able to put your mind at ease."

"I wish I had your confidence. I'm scared to death, Nathan." She takes the last sip of her drink. "If I do choose to go, will you protect me?"

"Damn right."

"Promise?"

"Cross my heart."

"Not good enough. Say, 'I promise.'"

"I promise to protect you, Allison Fisher. Every step of the way."

She brushes away a tear. "I think I need to go to bed. I'm feeling a little tipsy."

Nathan helps her to her feet. She turns to take one last look out of the window as the train whooshes through an intersection in some small Pennsylvania town. "Land of the free, home of the brave," she says. "I was brought up that way."

Visions of Brownshirts singing "Deutschland, Deutschland über alles" run through Nathan's mind as he leads Allison back to their compartment. He thinks: I was brought up that way.

10

DOUBLE IDENTITY

"Welcome back, Lieutenant," Molly says in her cheery voice. "General Groves is on a call right now, but I know he won't be long. And you must be Dr. Fisher. Welcome to New York."

"It's my first time," Allison says. "It would be nice to stay for a few days."

Molly's half-hearted smile says don't count on it, but her tone is cheery. "I hope so, too. Can I get either of you a cup of coffee? Tea?"

Nathan and Allison take a seat in the reception area. Allison spies a copy of *The New York Times* sitting on the end table. The headline reads 60 U.S. "FORTS" SHOT DOWN. The article goes on to say that sixty U.S. bombers, called Flying Fortresses, were shot down over western Germany on a bombing raid. Six hundred Americans were feared lost. The paper called it the "fiercest air battle ever fought." Allison reads the story with a pained expression. She taps the article. "This was a raid to take out a ball bearing plant?" she says. "Six hundred men and sixty planes lost for a ball bearing plant?"

"They need those ball bearings to build their Nazi bombers that wreak hell over England," General Groves says, entering the room. "We sent two hundred and ninety-one B-17 Attacking Fortresses on that mission. We lost sixty of them and fighter support as well. Altogether, along with the Brits, we lost more than ninety planes. Out of the twenty-nine hundred men on that raid, six hundred fifty did not return. It was a hell of a personnel loss, not to mention two hundred million dollars in hardware." He pauses and points his finger. "But, the Germans lost over a hundred aircraft and the use of three manufacturing plants." He makes a short affirmative nod. "It was a necessary raid, Dr. Fisher, and despite our losses, we consider it a success. We are making progress."

Allison swallows hard. The realization that this level of combat, this loss of men and equipment, represents just another page in the war, and that the general considers it "progress" is a shock to her. "That was just one raid?"

Groves nods. "It was. An area called Schweinfurt on the river Main. Our forces actually flew two hundred miles into German airspace. That's an incursion, Dr. Fisher. And I think we did considerable damage to that one roller bearing plant. Anyhow, come on in, Dr. Oppenheimer is already here."

"Dr. Fisher, a pleasure to meet you," Oppenheimer says, rising from his chair. "Leo continues to sing your praises."

"Very kind of him, sir."

"We're very proud of the work you're doing in Chicago," Groves says. "Dr. Oppenheimer is about to travel west and continue his efforts to engineer a weapon before our enemies do. It could bring an end to this war pretty quickly. I don't suppose you have any idea about Germany's progress in this regard, do you, Doctor?"

"No sir. How would I?"

"Oh, I don't know, scientists publish papers, communicate their findings to other scientists, that sort of thing."

"No sir. No one is publishing findings about the use of nuclear fission for military weaponry. I know our enemy has very talented scientists at KWI, and they've been working on fission longer than we have. That's where it all started. I would have to assume they are pretty far along."

"We've had some disturbing information just recently, Dr. Fisher." The general sits back in thought, pinches his chin, rocks forward, wags a finger, and says, "Let's assume that the Germans are just as far along in their nuclear development as we are, but they can only create a small amount of enriched uranium at a time—"

"Or plutonium, sir. That's pretty much where we are."

"Okay. My question is, what would be a bomb-sized amount of highly enriched uranium, or plutonium? Would it take ten to fifteen pounds?"

"Depends if it's uranium or plutonium. In a uranium fission bomb dropped from a plane or carried on a boat, I would think that a hundred and fifty pounds of enriched uranium could obliterate a city and cause multiple deaths. For a plutonium fusion bomb, it would take a much smaller amount of plutonium, but the housing would be much larger. Theoretically, of course."

The general continues. "Okay. Let's say there was a rocket capable of flying fifty, sixty miles with radio guidance that could carry a small amount of enriched uranium in its warhead . . ."

"No one has that, sir, not that I'm aware of."

"The Nazis might. They have a plant in Peenemünde where they have been developing a liquid-fueled rocket that they've named the Aggregat-4. We understand it has had more than a few successful flights."

"Which scientists are heading up that project?" she asks.

"A German officer and engineer, SS-Sturmbannführer Wernher von Braun."

"Are you serious?" Nathan says. "A guided rocket that can carry a warhead?"

"It's designed to do that, though we believe it is still in the testing stage. We received word through Austrian resistance that von Braun met with Hitler last month and told him that the project was nearly completed. He anticipated use of the rockets in six to ten months. We don't know what sort of explosives the Nazis are going to try to put in the head of those rockets. I only hope they aren't far enough along to mount a nuclear explosive in the warhead. My question to you, Dr. Fisher, is what if they could do it? What effect would it have if the warhead carried enriched uranium?"

Allison's jaw drops. "I'd have to make a lot of assumptions, General, relative to the critical mass, the development of a reactor to run their tests, the storage of the materials, the extent of their enrichment, not to mention perfecting a detonating device which would work within the rocket warhead, and the rocket would have to be very large . . ."

The general rolls his hand. "I get it, I get it."

"Assuming that they have engineered everything necessary to start a chain reaction in a rocket warhead, well, there's no doubt that the effect would be devastating. Launched from the French coast, those rockets could cause considerable damage in England."

"Not to mention what such a weapon could do to our expeditionary forces when we deploy in Europe," Groves adds.

Oppenheimer interrupts. "They would be significantly ahead of us if they have engineered small enriched nuclear warheads for guided rockets. We don't have those, and we aren't even engineering them. Our projected payload is a ten-ton bomb carrying one hundred fifty pounds of enriched uranium, dropped from a B-29. That is what we're working on."

Allison is stunned. She covers her mouth and whispers, "That would destroy Berlin and kill millions. Could we do that?"

"Not today," Oppenheimer says. "We're probably still a year or two away."

Allison shakes her head. "No, I meant, *could* we do that? Could the United States drop a bomb to annihilate a city of millions of people? Could *you* do that, Dr. Oppenheimer?"

"I'll do what the president asks me to do if it would end a war which is already killing tens of millions. And so should you. Realistically, having that capacity should act as a deterrent and end the war without ever having to use it. That's why we need to know the extent of Germany's program."

Groves nods. "All of this is hypothetical. We don't know for a fact that Germany has engineered a nuclear warhead for use in a rocket, or that it has the ability to launch and detonate a rocket. We are in the dark when it comes to Germany's nuclear progress. But, as you can imagine, those are things we need to know, and maybe Snyder can tell us. By the way, they are now calling their rocket the V-2. We need to know if there is anything going on at KWI to support the V-2."

"How do we know that Snyder possesses the information we're looking for?" Allison says. "Performing theoretical research often involves working alone, or in small groups. It's quite insular. He may not know what other physicists or other laboratories are doing or the extent to which they have developed their phase of the weapon design. He may be working on one small part of the project. Our nuclear physicists conduct their research in laboratories thousands of miles from Los Alamos where Dr. Oppenheimer is engineering a bomb. Speaking personally, I know about enrichment, I know about fission, I've seen the chain reactor operate at Chicago Pile-1, but I don't have information about engineering and detonating a bomb. Why would Snyder?"

Groves shrugs. "We don't know exactly what Günther Snyder is working on, or how closely connected he is with any specific project. We only know he is one of the many physicists working at the KWI laboratories in what they call their second *Uranverein,* whatever that means."

"It means uranium club," Nathan says.

"That's correct," Oppenheimer says. "Today it is a part of the Reich Ministry of Armaments and Munitions. Isn't that right, Leslie? You would know."

"That's right," Groves says. "Over the years the parent agency has changed, but now it is the Reich Ministry. They've had a lot of top scientists working for their club, including Otto Hahn and Günther Snyder."

"And my father," Nathan says.

"That's right. Now, Snyder wants to come over. Whether he knows what's happening on any given project is anyone's guess. He may not have all the critical information, but the hope is that he can get it."

"If Snyder's knowledge is too limited," Oppenheimer says, "it might be because he isn't given access. Maybe we should consider sending one of our own people into the KWI lab. That may be the only way to get an accurate assessment."

"That's impossible," Groves answers. "Günther is our only source."

"It's clearly not *impossible,*" Oppenheimer says flatly. "Like many projects, it's difficult, it may even be highly improbable, but it's not impossible."

"Okay, then, it's highly improbable. And what person do you propose we send into their lab?" Groves says. "I have no doubt Nathan is courageous enough, but he wouldn't know what he was looking at."

"No, he wouldn't," Oppenheimer responds. "It would have to be a high-level nuclear scientist."

"Are you volunteering?" Groves asks with a smile.

"I would certainly go, but do you really want to pull me out of Los Alamos? I don't think the president would appreciate that. Besides, I'm too well known. I would be instantly recognized. No, it needs to be a highly trained nuclear physicist, preferably one who has been working in the Manhattan Project. Someone who wouldn't be so recognizable. Maybe someone like . . ." Oppenheimer's head swivels to the right and stops at Allison. Her back stiffens. "Me?" she says. "You're suggesting that I go into the Nazi laboratories and spy on their scientists? Me?"

Oppenheimer shows no emotion. "Maybe Günther could arrange it. If you had access to the lab and its departments, it shouldn't take you too long to figure out how much progress they're making. I have no doubt."

Groves shakes his head. "Bold suggestion, Bob, but out of the question. The lab, the entire complex, is tightly guarded. They would never let Dr. Fisher through security. She wouldn't be allowed into the laboratory, even if she was with Günther Snyder. She has no credentials, and we're certainly not going to alert them that Dr. Fisher, an American scientist, is in Berlin. They would love to get their hands on her."

Allison looks at Nathan. "I told you."

Nathan responds, "It's not going to happen."

Oppenheimer is not convinced. "What if she wasn't identified as Dr. Fisher? What if she was brought in by Snyder as an additional resource, a nuclear physicist, to help him solve his equations?"

"They'll never believe that, and they'll never let her get close to the lab. A strange American female physicist that no one has ever heard about is going to suddenly show up and solve a problem for Snyder? Nothing personal, Bob, but stick to the science and leave the espionage to the OSS."

Oppenheimer raises his finger to make a point. "Don't dismiss this idea so quickly, Leslie. I've been thinking about it ever since I learned that Dr. Fisher was going to Berlin. Now, the Germans wouldn't let *Allison Fisher* get close to the lab, I agree. But what if Günther Snyder said that she was someone else?"

"Like who?"

"Like Irène Curie. What if Snyder told his staff that he was stymied and he had reached out to an old associate, a world-renowned expert who had agreed to help him with his research? Irène Curie is such a person. I believe that Snyder knows her. He did an internship at the institute in Paris. If he brought her, they'd welcome her with open arms, wouldn't they? Any laboratory would. Mine would for sure."

Groves shakes his head. "I don't know her. Is she a German?"

"No," Allison says in a dismissive tone, "she's French. She was the 1935 Nobel Prize winner in chemistry. It was she and her husband Frédéric Joliot in 1934 who made the seminal discovery that a stable element bombarded with alpha particles can create artificial radioactivity. She's a legend, and she wouldn't be helping the Nazis build a bomb."

"Right," Oppenheimer says, "she is a legend. And who can say what she would do when approached with a hypothetical problem? What if Günther was attempting to resolve a nuclear medicine problem? What if Günther told his fellow physicists that he was bringing in Irène Curie and asked that they be given full access, and of course, privacy?"

Groves is not convinced. "First of all, Dr. Fisher is *not* Curie. All these highly trained German physicists would know that in an instant. Hell, maybe some of them know Curie personally. Snyder apparently does. Bob, that's a crazy idea. Let's move on."

"Not so fast," Oppenheimer says. "I agree that the German physicists are bound to *know of* Irène Curie, but I'll bet very few, if any, have *met her*. She worked closely with her husband at the Curie Institute in Paris, the one named for her mother. Their work was highly confidential, and they permitted very few visitors. They remained isolated and they stopped their work altogether in 1939. If Günther said that he was friends with Irène, and that she had agreed to help him solve a problem in his work, what Nazi lab rats would object? If it was in our labs, if Leo brought Irène in, we'd welcome her and we'd stay the hell out of her way."

"No, we wouldn't," Allison firmly says, "because that is a crazy proposition. Irène Curie wouldn't just show up at our lab as a *favor*. She is a Nobel Prize winner with her own laboratory. If Leo had a problem, and if she agreed to help him, he would go to her, not the other way around."

"Where is Irène Curie now?" Groves asks. "Is she still in Paris?"

"No one knows for sure where she is," Oppenheimer says. "Rumor has it that she has been in a tuberculosis sanitarium in Switzerland. I heard that she has recovered, but still lives in the region. No one has seen her in a long time and who knows for certain what she would look like today?"

"Excuse me, Dr. Oppenheimer," Nathan interjects, "but I agree with Dr. Fisher. This is an insane idea. If you sent Dr. Fisher into KWI under this bizarre scenario, she would be checked out ten ways to Sunday. If, or maybe I should say *when,* the Gestapo finds out that it's really Dr. Allison Fisher, and not Irène Curie, they would torture her unmercifully. Who sent you here, they would say. What are your instructions? And then, they would turn the tables on her and torture her for information about our own nuclear program. And then they would kill her." He pauses and looks to his left at Allison, whose face has gone pale white. "Sorry, Allison, but I've seen what they can do. All that has to happen is that you make one little slip-up, or that someone recognizes you, or personally knows Curie and declares that you are not her." Nathan turns back to General Groves. "May I speak freely, sir?"

Groves chuckles. "You already have a good start on that, but of course, Lieutenant, speak your mind."

"Sir, I cannot take Dr. Fisher into Berlin under those circumstances. That's not what she signed up for. I promised her she'd be kept in a safe house to debrief Dr. Snyder. In the safe house and nowhere else. What Dr. Oppenheimer suggests is a death warrant. Respectfully, sir, if you order me to take Dr. Fisher into Berlin, knowing she will have to sneak into the Nazi lab, I will refuse that order."

Oppenheimer leans forward. "You would disobey a direct order from General Groves? It may be our best solution, but it's not *your* choice, it's *her* choice. And you will follow your orders, son."

Nathan looks across the room with a curled lip and venom in his eyes. "You don't give me orders, Dr. Oppenheimer." He turns to Groves and says, "I'm sorry, sir, I made a promise to protect Dr. Fisher and keep her safe, and I intend to keep that promise. Sending her into a Nazi lab with Günther Snyder on a make-believe charade would be . . ."

Groves holds up his palm. "All right, all right, let's hold on."

Oppenheimer sits back and crosses his legs. He exhales. "Just consider it, that's all I'm asking. It's not a bad idea. It's almost certain that none of the German physicists have seen Irène in many years, if ever. Irène is a sick woman, and besides, she has always been anti-fascist and anti-Nazi. She wouldn't have personally associated with any of them. She's stayed out of Germany."

"Exactly," Nathan says, "and they would know that as well." He turns to face Allison. "Dr. Fisher, don't do this," he pleads. "I've seen the Gestapo work; the way they investigate, the way they sniff out things. It's uncanny. Unearthly. It's like they receive messages from the devil himself. They'll want to know who this woman is who wants to get into the KWI lab. They'll find pictures of Curie. Hell, they'll find the real Irène Curie in Switzerland and they'll know you are a fraud. For all we know, they'll find pictures of you at Cal-Berkeley. And then these demons from hell will be at their worst. I can't let you do this. Please, Allison."

"Folks," Groves says, "I think we're getting ten steps ahead of ourselves. All this may not be necessary. If Günther Snyder has the information we need, it's a moot point. Why don't we take a break and meet again this afternoon? In the meantime, why don't you two check into your hotel rooms. You're at the Waldorf. I'll have my driver take you there. Rest up, get some lunch, and we'll see you back here at three o'clock."

11

TRAINLOADS AND TRAINLOADS

Nathan is enjoying a turkey club in the coffee shop when Allison walks up. "You look very seasonal," he says. She has a burnt orange sweater over a dark brown, pleated wool skirt. She feigns a curtsy.

"Thank you. You look very handsome yourself," she says. "I like that tweed sport coat, though I do prefer a man in uniform. Or in a lab coat."

He smiles. "It's the only sport coat I own. I haven't had much need for civilian clothes in the last couple years."

She slides into the booth. "How's that sandwich? It looks good and I'm hungry."

"It's great, want a bite?"

She chuckles. "No, thank you, I think I'll order a whole sandwich. It seems I'm always having what you're having."

"That will get you into trouble. What have you been doing this morning?"

She shrugs. "The hotel has a pool. What about you?"

"I took a nap. In a real bed. Not a chair."

"Sorry, but you could have slept in the upper berth, though I concede it would have been a little tight."

Nathan rolls his eyes, and then gets serious. "Look, I want you to know something: there's no way I'm letting you walk into a Nazi laboratory pretending to be some Nobel Prize winner, one who is a lot older than you are. Oppenheimer is crazy, it won't work. It'll get us both tortured and killed."

Allison looks at him with kind eyes. "I appreciate your sticking up for me, I really do. And I think you're right; it's a crazy idea and I'm not going to do it. It seems like no one bothered to ask me my opinion. I don't think it would work and I think I would probably die of fright. But I also don't want you to get court-martialed."

"I don't think they'd go that far, but I meant what I said. Oppenheimer is not a soldier, nor is he an intelligence agent. He is a scientist who has seen too many movies. Maybe he thinks you're Greta Garbo. It's a goofy proposition. I don't know what Curie looks like, but she's older than you and she's a French woman."

Allison squints an eye. "Well, she's only fifteen years older, more or less. I'll bet Garbo and I could pull it off. Sashay in there wearing a wide-brimmed bonnet and a thousand-dollar dress, grab all the secrets, and make a run for it." She smiles. "Seriously, do you think you could really tell the difference of fifteen years in a woman? Only fifteen years?" She pauses. "Don't answer that."

"Fifteen years? Right."

"In all the pictures I've seen of Irène, she does in fact wear a broad-brimmed hat that shadows half her face. And we really do resemble each other. I'm not kidding."

"You're only saying this because I've challenged you. Now stop it."

"Irène's mother was Marie Curie, the first woman to win a Nobel Prize and the only woman to win it *twice*. Marie discovered the element radium and coined the term 'radioactivity.' Irène followed in her mother's footsteps. I actually do know a lot about her. Any nuclear physicist would. Especially any female nuclear physicist."

"You're proving my point. All the more reason to reject Oppenheimer's dumb suggestion. I don't doubt that Irène Curie is a brilliant scientist, or that you are also a brilliant scientist, and that you might look like her, but you are not Irène Curie, and there are too many ways that such a stupid charade goes south with disastrous results."

"I speak their language, you know."

"You speak German?"

"No, silly. I speak atoms and molecules. I could be a member of their 'club.' And I do look like her, you know. If I curled my hair and wore a hat . . ."

"All right, that's enough of this nonsense."

She takes a bite of her sandwich and smiles. "Thanks for being my protector this morning. I think it was brave of you, and it was sweet."

"It was self-preservation, that's all."

"Can I ask you something?" she says quietly. "All this talk about uranium bombs, whether they are fifteen pounds or a hundred and fifty pounds, God forbid, does it make you lose sleep? How do you deal with participating in the Manhattan Project that is focused on developing a massive killing device?"

"I deal with it because I am a soldier, and we are making weapons to win a war. I trust the wisdom of my superior officers and my commander in chief. I am a soldier, nothing more. Like you said: Nathan the Soldier. I am part of the Army's Manhattan Project, and by the way, so are you. Your Chicago MetLab is funded and operated under the authority of the Army Corps of Engineers."

"I know that," she says with quiet resignation. "Growing up in Iowa, I was always taught to believe that America holds the moral high ground. That we are the good guys. Land of the free, home of the brave, and I do believe in that. I work at the MetLab and I tell myself that the Army wouldn't use a uranium bomb unless absolutely necessary to protect our country and defeat the enemy. But still, it is a massive weapon without a conscience, and it haunts my sleep."

"That's what makes our assignment so important."

"But Nathan, our assignment is to sneak into Berlin, meet with Günther Snyder, and help him defect, all with the purpose of discovering how close Germany is to using an atomic bomb. Shouldn't it be more?"

"Like what?"

"Like finding out how to stop Germany from achieving their goal; stop them from building a nuclear bomb at all."

"You mean flying bombers all the way to Berlin to destroy the Institute?"

"I'm not talking about bombing the KWI. That wouldn't do it anyway. Even if our bombers could successfully fly all the way into Berlin and blow up the Institute, we'd just be bombing college buildings, like you saw at the University of Chicago. It wouldn't deprive their scientists of their knowledge. They'd just move their lab and reassemble somewhere else."

"So, what are you suggesting?"

"It takes a lot to engineer and fabricate an atomic bomb. I'm sure Dr. Oppenheimer would agree with that. We know they have the science. We don't know how far along they are in their construction. Where do they get their materials? Where is the uranium dioxide coming from? Dr. Oppenheimer said that he contemplates building a bomb that would carry a hundred and fifty pounds of enriched uranium, remember?"

"Yeah."

"Well, think about separating enough of the U-235 isotope from the other ninety-nine percent of U-238 in the uranium ore; the process we call enrichment. To end up with a hundred and fifty pounds of enriched uranium, you would need tons and tons of uraninite ore. Do you understand? Trainloads and trainloads. Where is it all coming from? Not Russia, not Canada. Maybe Africa. Probably most from Czechoslovakia. And where is it all going? What route is it taking? Where is it being stored? Certainly not at KWI on a university campus in the middle of Berlin. I'm sure that the German operation is spread out like ours is. I don't know where they have their cyclotron or their nuclear reactor. It's certainly not in some office in the Institute. Where are they doing their enrichment? Where is their Los Alamos? Where is their Oak Ridge, Tennessee? What is the route of the material deliveries and more importantly, can we intercept them?"

"I understand. You're talking about stopping them from getting enriched uranium to the bomb factories, wherever they are."

"Not just the uranium. Remember, you need a moderator, those gray bricks you saw in the squash court. Where do they store whatever they're using for chain reaction moderators—heavy water or tons and tons of graphite? Where is all that coming from? It's all raw materials, Nathan, in huge amounts that has to be shipped one way or another. I'm thinking that's where our focus should be. In other words, how do we interrupt their supplies and their manufacturing process? How do we prevent the development of the bomb?"

Nathan smiles broadly. Allison sees his expression and says, "What?"

"I'm impressed. And you're right, that should be a focus of our mission. But what if the Nazis already have sufficient materials? What if they are already in storage and ready to be used? Isn't our assignment to find out whether they are, and how close the Nazis are to using them?"

Allison is not convinced. "Our discoveries have evolved slowly over the past several years. Unless they're way, way ahead of us, I doubt that Germany is anywhere near deployment of a workable atomic bomb. If they are, let's face it, the game is over, and it's a pointless exercise for us to go to Berlin. But I don't think they are, because if they have a workable bomb, they would have used it—without a second thought—on Moscow, on Stalingrad, or Kursk. There would be no Soviet Union left. No, they are not there yet, Nathan. Not close. We need to find out how far along they are, but we also need to find out how to stop them from getting any further."

"And if Günther doesn't know?"

"I suppose Oppenheimer would say we should send me into the lab to find out."

"That is not going to happen. You will be in a safe house far from the lab."

A few moments of silence pass as they finish their lunch. "You're staring," Allison says.

"I give you a lot of credit. You're a very brave girl."

"I'm not brave, Nathan. I'm terrified."

12

DRESSED FOR THE OCCASION

We had a discussion at lunch," Nathan says. "I think Dr. Fisher raised a very important concern. She believes that the focus of our mission should be broadened. We should be trying to find out about raw material supply lines and storage depots. For example, if we know where the Germans are getting their uranium ore . . ."

Oppenheimer sighs. "These are not novel concerns, Lieutenant. Supply lines have always been a focus, just not by our branch. As to the supply of uraninite, we believe it all comes from the Czech mines. At least, that's been our assumption for some time. You and Dr. Fisher have one job to do; connect with Dr. Günther Snyder, bring him back along with detailed knowledge of their program. Snyder's knowledge is invaluable. He will be a priceless addition to our scientific community. He will supplement our working knowledge with KWI's discoveries and applications. And he will be able to tell us how close the Nazis are to manufacturing and using a nuclear weapon. It's not your position to tell us what the scope of your assignment should be."

Groves reaches over and places a hand on Oppenheimer's arm. "Easy, Bob. Nathan has a point. Snyder may know about the supply routes."

Oppenheimer's impatience is evident. "We know where they mine the uranium. I'm only suggesting that the lieutenant keep his mind on his mission."

Nathan glances at Allison, drums his fingers on the arm of his chair. His lips are tight. "Tell me, Dr. Oppenheimer," he says curtly, "where does the uraninite go after it leaves Czechoslovakia?"

Oppenheimer looks to Groves and with a hint of a shrug says, "We're not certain."

"And if you don't know where it's going, then you don't know what route it is taking to get there, do you?"

"Of course not, but if you are suggesting that the Army has the military capability of interdicting supply lines deep in Germany, I think General Groves will tell you we do not."

After a pause, General Groves says, "Well, don't jump to that conclusion so quickly, Bob. Very soon, we'll know quite a bit more about our air capability. We might be closer than you think."

"That's my point," Nathan says. "Preventing the construction of a Nazi bomb should be our number one priority. Dr. Fisher correctly points out that the Soviet cities of Stalingrad and Kursk would have already been annihilated if the Nazis had a workable uranium bomb sitting in the belly of one of their bombers. Or on a warhead of a V-2 rocket. Don't discount Dr. Fisher; she's very sharp. She feels that we might have an opportunity to stop them, or at least delay them, from achieving that capability, maybe by interrupting their supplies or taking out their warehouse. That information should be a critical part of our mission."

Groves nods. "It makes sense to me, Bob. Our air force is making inroads every day. If Snyder knows how and where their raw material shipments are headed, that knowledge should be one of the goals of their mission."

"In that case, sir, we're anxious to go," Nathan says.

"Well, then let's talk logistics," the general says. "You leave tomorrow night. We'll try to land you on the Continent by the weekend. From there, you'll have to make your way to Paris. I think you are familiar with the French countryside, are you not, Ritchie boy?"

"Yes, sir," Nathan says. "We did quite a bit of map study at Ritchie. France and Germany."

"We'll provide you with the names and addresses of contacts and safe houses along the way. Bear in mind, it's a theater of war, routes may have to be modified. You might have to improvise, but isn't that also what you Ritchie boys have been trained to do?"

"In a manner of speaking," Nathan says. "Ritchie boys are being trained to accompany U.S. military divisions once the attack begins in earnest. We are trained to assist in prisoner interrogation and to advise squad leaders in navigating the terrain. You know, most of us came from Germany and are familiar with the German cities and customs."

"Exactly. That's why we've chosen you, Nathan. You'll navigate the terrain to Berlin and back again. Except, instead of a U.S. military division, you'll have a couple of professors in tow. In and out."

"Just like that?"

Groves smiles broadly. "Just like that, son. We'll give you new identities; passports, German IDs. You'll get a packet tomorrow with all the information. We believe the best option for you, Nathan, is to take the identity of a Wehrmacht officer. That should allow you to move about freely on the trains and through the towns. I talked to Colonel Banfill down at Camp Ritchie. They're sending up a couple of fancy uniforms for you."

"What am I to be?" Allison asks. "I can hardly be a German officer."

"We think it is best if you are Nathan's . . . how shall I say . . . female companion. You can travel about together and no one would think twice about a German officer and his lady."

"I'm to be his wife?"

"Well, no, not his wife. It's unlikely that a German officer would travel with his wife in the field. You would be . . . um . . . a girlfriend. Maybe someone he recently met. That would not be unusual."

"A pick-up? He's an officer, and I'm some easy pick-up?"

The general winces. "N-not a pick-up, per se. A lady. Nicely dressed. Maybe in an evening dress, or a . . . um, a cocktail dress?"

"You want me to run around Occupied Europe in a cocktail dress?"

Groves waves his hand back and forth. "Just nicely dressed, that's all, t-to compliment a German officer. You'll figure it out."

"I didn't bring those kinds of clothes."

"Then you have all afternoon to go out and buy them. You're in New York, for Christ's sake." He turns his head. "Molly," he shouts, "take Dr. Fisher shopping, would you please?"

The general stands. "That's all for today. Please be here at noon tomorrow, ready to go."

Nathan suppresses a smile, nods at Allison, and says, "I'll see you back at the hotel for dinner. Maybe you could wear a cocktail dress. Girlfriend."

She folds her arms and glares at him. "I hope you're getting a kick out this, Mr. Fancy German Officer."

"Kind of."

13

THE NIGHT BEFORE

Nathan rises from his seat as Allison enters the dining room. She is smartly dressed in a navy blue A-line, belted at the waist, with puffed shoulders. The salesman had assured her that the popular hourglass design suited her "elegant composition." Nathan's eyebrows rise in appreciation. "You look very nice," he says. "But I thought maybe I'd see you in your traveling cocktail dress."

"Very funny. Keep it up."

"Did you buy that outfit today?"

She has a guilty smile. "This and more. The Army outfitted me with a whole new wardrobe. They thought I should look French. Molly took me to Bergdorf Goodman, across the street from Central Park. I have never shopped at a store like that in my life. You wouldn't believe what they charge for a dress."

"Fancy, huh?"

"Oh, my yes. We were scanning the racks looking for French imports, for obvious reasons, but we couldn't find any dresses with French labels. So, we asked a salesperson, who said he was a 'style consultant.' He informed us that French imports would not be on the sales racks, and he led us back to a boutique area, which was a mistake because those dresses were for movie stars. Molly told him that I wanted to look like I had purchased my clothes in Paris, you know,

Parisian styles. He said that Bergdorf's didn't have any real French imports. Not since 1940. But he knew the styles and he showed us a number of gorgeous outfits. Can you imagine having your rich Uncle Sam taking you shopping? I mean, price was no object. I don't know who had more fun, me or Molly."

"We're going to be on the move, Allison. Walking, riding, who knows? You can't take a trunk with you."

"I know that. I only bought a few things, some casual. A couple of nice dresses. A suit. I can put them all in a small suitcase."

"No slinky cocktail dresses?"

"No! I did buy one evening dress."

"Shucks."

———

Dinner and drinks are served, and their conversation meanders in and around random topics, carefully avoiding references to what lies before them the next day and in the days to follow. Allison is talking nonstop. She recounts the sights and scenes of New York City that she experienced earlier that afternoon. As the evening passes, her narration quickens. Soon her words are firing out at breakneck speed, like bullets from a machine gun. Nathan watches her, and smiles.

"What?" she says, finally. "You're staring at me again."

"Take a breath."

"I'm talking too much, right?"

"You're nervous."

"No kidding! I'm scared to death, Nathan. I told you that." She lays down her fork. Her jaw is quivering. "It's not just the Nazis and going into Germany. I'm afraid of failing. I'm not a soldier, I'm not a Ritchie boy, I'm not a spy. I haven't been trained. I keep thinking, what the hell am I doing?"

Nathan is calm. "You're not being asked to be a soldier or to shoot a gun. Just to listen and ask the right questions."

"I know, but I am to do that in Berlin, in the center of a hornets' nest. I keep thinking, maybe it's a mistake for me to tag along? I'm bound to slow you down, or blow your cover. And why do you need me there anyway? Snyder is going to defect, and you are going to bring him back to the U.S., and he is going to tell everything he knows to Groves and Oppenheimer. They know the right questions to ask."

Nathan does not answer. He shifts his gaze down to his empty plate.

"What is it? What aren't you telling me, Nathan? I deserve your honesty."

Nathan takes a deep breath, nods his head, looks around the crowded room, and says, "Yes, you do. Let's take a walk."

The November night is cool, and Allison has a sweater wrapped around her shoulders as they head out onto Park Avenue. "Tell you the truth, I don't trust Snyder," Nathan says. "I don't know him very well, but I don't trust him. My father was twice as talented as that second fiddle, but Snyder got the promotions. I remember hearing my mother and father arguing one night. She said that Günther Snyder was taking credit for my father's discoveries, claiming they were his own."

"What did your father say?"

"He said it was no big deal, and he didn't want to cause trouble at the lab. Jews were losing their jobs all over Germany, and he still had his. Then my mother asked him why we were still staying in Berlin. Why shouldn't we leave like the other Jewish scientists did?"

"That's a good question," Allison says. "Einstein, Szilard, Meitner, Frisch, they all left. Was it because your father would have had to forfeit all of his assets?"

"I don't think so. He wasn't like that. He could have landed another position anywhere he chose."

"Then why?"

"I can't tell you for sure. Something else was keeping him there. In retrospect, I think he had made a deal for the protection of his family."

"So, you have a bad taste in your mouth when it comes to Snyder. Our job is to get information from him. If he has what we need, we take him and leave. If he needs more, he can go back in and get it from KWI, and then we'll leave. Am I right?"

"I won't know whether the information is correct and complete, that is why you are coming with me. He wants out. Maybe he'll give us bullshit information. You would know. He might have to go back into the lab and get the critical information you want. Only you can evaluate what he is offering."

"I worry that I will slow you down; that I will arouse suspicion as we travel."

"Believe me, you won't arouse suspicion. I'll be dressed as a Wehrmacht officer, and I can pull that off. You're just some French girl that I picked up."

Allison narrows her eyes. Taking note of her facial expressions, Nathan quickly says, "That didn't come out right. I meant to say, that I would be a German officer and you would be a fine French lady that I would be dating. An officer and his lady. That way, no one will question you in my presence. Groves told me that the safe house is a nice house in Charlottenburg, a quiet, upscale neighborhood in Berlin. You'll stay there, and I'll bring Snyder to you. You will question him. Thoroughly. We'll spend as long as it takes in the safe house for you to pry out every bit of relevant information about their nuclear program. Find out what he knows and what he doesn't know. Whatever he doesn't know, he can find out for you. If he can't provide the answers to your questions from his own knowledge, then he goes back into the Institute and gets the information. Or we don't take him. He gives us everything you want before we ever start his extraction."

"How do we know he'll be telling us the truth?"

"That's where Allison Fisher comes in. You'll know."

14

DC-3

Nathan stands at General Groves's window, wistfully staring at the small park across Broadway. There is a man in a fedora selling balloons, and a mother pushing a carriage. The leaves are falling, but the grass is still a deep green. Beyond the park is New York's City Hall where business is brisk. Everything seems so normal, so peaceful, so detached from a world where millions are engaged in deadly combat and weapons are being designed to kill millions more.

Nathan and Allison have just been handed envelopes. Inside are travel documents, passports, German IDs, and coded instructions for routes, contacts, and meeting places. Nathan opens his envelope and peruses the contents.

"So now I am to be Hauptmann Dietrich Froman, a captain in the Wehrmacht," Nathan says, holding his German passport. "Isn't that a stretch? I'm only twenty-eight years old. That would be a pretty quick rise in Hitler's army."

Groves shakes his head. "It's the war, Nate. Germany is suffering substantial losses in personnel, and field promotions are common. A bright young second lieutenant would step up to the position of captain of his unit right in the middle of the battlefield. Besides, you look older. According to Hauptmann Froman's birth certificate, you were born in 1912. Makes you thirty-one."

Nathan takes a deep breath. "Hauptmann?"

"It's a snap. As you travel about, you'll look real good in a captain's uniform. No one will hassle you."

Nathan looks over his shoulder at Allison. "Well, what do you know, I got another promotion. When I left Ritchie, I was just a sergeant. The general promoted me to second lieutenant last week. If I stay here much longer, I'm going to outrank him."

Groves laughs. "If you complete this mission, I'll sponsor you for bird colonel."

Groves gestures toward a dark green canvas suitcase. "That bag was delivered to me this morning by Chuck Banfill. Your dress uniform is inside. It has white epaulets on the shoulder with two medallions, green oak leaves, and triple bar insignias on the sleeve. Fold-back cuffs. Peaked cap. Shiny boots. Just what the snazzy German officer would wear traveling on an administrative assignment. You should receive appropriate deference in public settings. Your Wehrmacht orders authorizing travel between Paris and Berlin are in your packet."

Turning to Allison, Groves says, "And for you, Dr. Fisher, you have a French passport identifying you as Alicia Dumont, twenty-eight years old and born in Saint-Lô, a small town in the Cotentin Peninsula, along the route you and Nathan will probably take. Traveling with Nathan, you should be free from any questioning, but if one should arise, just say that you are a salesclerk."

"A salesclerk? Selling what?"

"You'll figure it out. Look, everything should go smoothly. We have people along the way to help you out. Places you can stay. The addresses, waypoints, and contacts are all in the packet—memorize them and destroy the information. Just be careful, you two. I would hate to have to go looking for another Ritchie boy and another nuclear scientist."

"Very comforting," Allison says.

Nathan examines the contents of his envelope. There is a timetable for train travel between Paris and Berlin. "How do I get to Paris?" he asks.

"In your packet you will find a suggested route from the coast through the French countryside. As I just said to Dr. Fisher, I believe that the plan is to place you ashore somewhere in the Cotentin Peninsula. The Calais coast is too well patrolled. The ultimate decision on where to land you will be left to our military command in England. I'm afraid we'll have to be flexible, both as to where you come ashore and how we will get you to Paris. Flexibility is the key."

Nathan turns to Allison. "That's Army talk for plans don't always work out. You know the term 'SNAFU'? Situation normal; all fouled up. Some would use a different F word." Turning back to Groves, he says, "How are we getting to London?"

With a mischievous twinkle in his eye, Groves glances at Allison and says, "You'll be taking the transatlantic tunnel. It's top secret."

"Oh, for goodness' sake," Allison says. "How gullible do you think I am?"

Groves grins. "Ah, nuts. It works some of the time, you'd be surprised. Truth is, we have a DC-3 waiting for you at La Guardia Field. You'll fly out this afternoon."

Allison's eyes widen. "I've never flown. Can you fly all the way from New York to London?"

"I hope so," Groves says with a smile. "You'll make a couple of stops in New Brunswick and Ireland. It shouldn't take more than eighteen hours. The plan is to get you to London by late tomorrow afternoon. You'll be met and driven to SHAEF headquarters at Camp Griffiss. It will be up to SHAEF to get you onto the Continent in the most efficient manner, but I believe the best bet is to put you ashore somewhere near Cherbourg. If all goes well, you'll meet with Snyder four days later at the Berlin safe house."

Nathan's forehead furrows. "I know it sounds so smooth and easy, but I barely slept last night. A couple matters have been troubling me. For example, who knows about our safe house? How safe is it? Who knows that Dr. Fisher is coming? Does Snyder know where we're going to meet? Does he know I'm bringing one of our top physicists to debrief him? If he does, he might spill the information. I've seen the Gestapo work. If he doesn't, and he sees Allison when he shows up, he might balk. I have to tell you, sir, I don't trust Günther Snyder. I never really liked him. I'm thinking this whole offer to defect could be a plot to lure Dr. Fisher to Berlin and turn her over to the Nazis."

"Oh, my God," Allison whispers. "Why didn't you tell me you were thinking that?"

"No, no, no," Groves answers. "No one knows Fisher's coming, and Snyder doesn't know the safe house address. He will be brought to the safe house by our contact. And he's not going to balk. He wants out of Nazi Germany. Look, no one outside of this room knows the identity of the person that is accompanying you. As far as anyone knows, she's Alicia Dumont, your girlfriend. I-I mean, your lady friend. Dr. Fisher's identity is secure.

"In your packet, you'll find the address of a house in Charlottenburg, a nice Berlin neighborhood just west of the Tiergarten. That is where you will go directly from the Berlin train station. It's all in your packet and all coded, but guard your packet carefully. Finally, if Snyder keeps his word and gives us the information he promises, we'll bring him back and he'll be a valuable addition to the Manhattan Project." Groves points at the packet. "You'll find new identification papers and a passport for Snyder under the name of Norbert Handron. Bring him back to Cherbourg, we'll pick him up there and send you both home with our gratitude. We have a pretty solid network all along your route, coming and going. So, are we all okay?"

Nathan nods.

"If there's nothing more, I wish you Godspeed, good luck, and have a safe flight."

Allison is transfixed as the DC-3 rises over the coastline. Her forehead is pressed against the window. The two-engine plane is large and noisy, and they are the only two passengers. Almost all of the seats have been taken out and the back half of the plane is packed with boxes, crates, and military supplies. The plane banks over the river and heads north at a speed of over two hundred miles per hour.

"Fascinating," she says. "What a way to travel. I thought we would be taking an ocean liner."

"That would take at least eight days. It took ten days for me to get to New York on an ocean liner from Hamburg in 1938. Besides, it's much more dangerous now. The waters are full of German U-boats. When I was back at Ritchie, I think the plan was to send us all to Europe on troop ships out of Baltimore Harbor, and we would be well guarded with destroyer escorts all the way to England. As for you and I, we're much better off in a plane. You seem a little nervous. Is it because this is your first flight?"

"I thought it would, but the flight doesn't bother me. Isn't that surprising? I'm not nervous about flying at all, it's lovely. I'm nervous about where we're going once we land. What did the general mean when he said it was up to SHAEF to get us to the Continent?"

"When I came here last week to meet with the general, when I was sitting in the reception area with Molly, I could hear Groves talking. He kept mentioning SHAEF. He was saying that Ike was moving the command headquarters from London to Bushy Park."

Allison's eyebrows draw together in an expression of consternation. "You lost me," she says.

"SHAEF stands for Supreme Headquarters Allied Expeditionary Force. Ike is Dwight D. Eisenhower, the commander of all Allied forces in the European theater."

"Expeditionary force?"

"Sooner or later we're sending our armies onto the Continent to pound those Nazi bastards. Down at Camp Ritchie, we've been training to go in with our troops, and the rumor is that it's only going to be a matter of months. Groves told us it would be up to SHAEF to get you and me onto the Continent. I think he meant they would arrange it. Probably through the Navy. I understand there is a large U.S. naval base at Portsmouth in southern England."

"Look!" Allison says. "Down there. Is that Boston? Cape Cod?"

Nathan nods. "Could be."

She sits back. "A horrible thought just ran through my mind. What if we were a German bomber and we had a uranium bomb in the belly of our plane? We could just open the doors, let it loose, and it would float down, and all that you're seeing would be destroyed. In an instant.

The time it takes for a chain reaction. All those people, Nathan. It's the devil's own design."

"We're not going to let that happen. We're going do whatever we can to prevent it. We're going to find out exactly where they're building their bombs and we're going to get precise information on their material supply routes and we're going to pass the information on to our military. We're going to learn how close they are to dropping that bomb and alert General Groves, who will take whatever steps are necessary to make sure they don't get any closer. Allison, we're going to do our job, and we're going to make a difference."

As the DC-3 drones on, Allison nudges Nathan and says, "Can I talk to you about something?"

"Sure. What's on your mind?"

"Well, you're going to be traveling through Europe as a captain in the German army."

"That's right."

"And I'm going to be a French woman traveling as your companion. And our assumed identities are meant to fool people as we travel together in public."

"Of course."

"Well, here's the rub. You speak German, and I do not. I speak French, and you do not."

"Correct."

"So, how do we talk to each other in front of other people? I'm your French girlfriend, how do you talk to me at a restaurant, or at a border crossing, or on the train to Berlin? Surely, we can't converse in English."

"Hmm. I could whisper."

"No."

"Do you have a solution?"

"I do. We have seventeen hours on this airplane. Essential French phrases only. Are you a good student?"

"Are you a good teacher?"

"I guess we'll find out. I also have another suggestion. My new name is Alicia Dumont. When you and I are talking, instead of calling me Allison or Dr. Fisher, I suggest you start calling me Alli. I'll respond to that; it was my nickname as a kid anyway. That way, in the heat of the moment, you won't say the wrong name."

"The heat of the moment?"

"Don't get any ideas. I'm talking about urgent, dangerous situations. I don't want you to refer to me as Allison by mistake."

"Alli. Okay. My new name is Dietrich Froman. What are you going to call me? You know, so you won't make a mistake in the *heat of the moment?*"

"I won't make a mistake."

"Oh, Miss Perfect. Well, you might, in the *heat of the moment.*"

She smiles. "*In the heat of the moment?* Well, in that case, I will call you *mon cher.*"

15

THE NANNY GOAT

Although Allison sat transfixed, staring out of her window the entire way from Shannon, across the Irish Sea and down into London, very little could be seen. The view was occluded by heavy fog and mist. The landing was rough. With her feet firmly on the ground, she finally exhales. Thirty-eight hundred miles in an airplane, who could imagine such a thing? The flight had been delayed in New Brunswick because of weather, and then again in Shannon because enemy aircraft had been sighted over the Channel. It is now evening, and Nathan and Allison stand on the tarmac with their flight crew waiting for their ride to SHAEF headquarters at Camp Griffiss.

"The Emerald Isle looked pretty gray to me," Allison remarks. "I couldn't see much. I suppose that cloud cover can sometimes be a good thing, especially if there are German planes in the air. They wouldn't be able to see us."

"Sometimes it's a good thing," the pilot remarks. "But bear in mind, we can't see them either. They're out there. They've been bombing England heavily for three years. Last week was quiet but you never know."

A black sedan pulls up. The driver exits, takes the luggage from Nathan and Allison and says, "Welcome to England. Let me get these into the boot and we'll be on our way. It's two hours to Portsmouth."

"I was told that we were to go straight to Camp Griffiss at Bushy Park," Nathan says.

The driver shrugs. "My orders say to go directly to Portsmouth, to the naval command post. They've been waiting for you since this afternoon. You blokes are late."

———————

The sounds of wind and waves and the chatter of seagulls announce their approach to the ocean. The driver looks over his shoulder and says, "We're just about there, it's right over that bridge. Portsmouth is actually on Portsea Island."

"It's pretty quiet here for a naval base," Allison says.

"It's a lot busier than it looks. They keep the lights off and the noise down. The damage done to this area by the German Luftwaffe has been substantial. Right now, there are over thirty naval ships docked hereabouts. If I knew anything, I'd say they were staging. A landing has got to happen sooner or later, right? But hey, I don't know anything."

Upon arrival at naval command, they are met by an ensign who ushers them down a walkway to the docks. "I didn't know whether you guys would make it tonight; weather and all," he says, walking quickly. "The seas are calm right now. You're in luck." He points to Nathan, who is dressed in his civilian clothes: wool slacks, cotton shirt, and his tweed sport jacket. "It might be cold on the Channel tonight, I'd keep that jacket on. Over there, that's the boat that will carry you to France."

Allison is surprised at what she sees. The *Nanny Goat* is a forty-foot wooden boat with a small cabin in the bow. "That looks like a fishing boat," she says.

The ensign smiles. "Yes ma'am, that's exactly what it is. We don't want to draw any attention. There are always lots of fishing boats in the Channel, including the *Nanny Goat*. You know, the Brits do love their fish and chips. The *Nanny Goat* will do just fine and won't arouse suspicion, and it just might catch you some lunch on the way."

Three hours later, in the black of night, the *Nanny Goat* glides into a small harbor east of Cherbourg and Nathan and Allison disembark. A silver Peugeot sits in the parking area and blinks its lights.

"Bienvenue en France," says a bony, angular man while he holds the back door open.

Allison acknowledges the greeting with a smile, a polite bow. "Un plaisir de faire votre connaissance," she says. "Mon nom est—"

"No, no," the driver says emphatically, wagging his finger back and forth. "Pas de noms. Pas de noms. No names, please. I take you to a place. C'est tout. I wish to know nothing more."

It becomes apparent to Nathan that the driver is avoiding the main roads. Occasionally he'll pass through a village, but it is the middle of the night, and the roads are empty. The French countryside is quiet and still. Very few lights are on. An hour into the trip, the Peugeot enters a small town, pulls onto a side street, and parks along the curb. The driver points to a red-brick building. "C'est là," he says. "Trente cinq." With that, the driver opens his door, exits the car with the motor still running, and starts to walk away down the street.

"Hey, where are you going?" Nathan says and starts after him. "You can't leave us here. What are we supposed to do with this car?"

With a flip of his hand, the man says, "Cette voiture n'est pas à moi. Adieu."

"What?"

Allison grabs Nathan's sleeve. "He says goodbye, the car isn't his."

"So, what does he expect us to do now?"

"The man pointed to this house and said, 'There it is, thirty-five.' I guess his chauffeuring job is finished. He brought us to our destination for tonight. As to what you should do now, I think you should turn off the motor."

Nathan hesitates. "This address was not in the packet. I memorized all of the contact points and addresses, and this is not one of them."

"You're right. We were supposed to be in Caen tonight."

"General Groves told us to be flexible. Something must have changed. Why else would the man have brought us here?"

"I don't like it," Allison says. "As he was running off, he said 'adieu,' not 'au revoir.'"

"So?"

"I know I only have college French, but one uses 'adieu' when someone is dying and you're not going to see them again. 'Au revoir' is the common way of saying goodbye. He said 'adieu' and that gives me the creeps."

Nathan shakes his head. "Four years of French." He chuckles. "Don't both words mean goodbye?"

"Yeah, but there is a difference, and . . ."

"Let's go in."

From the street, the small house looks dark and unoccupied. Nathan steps onto the front stoop and tries the door. It is unlocked. Standing in the foyer, Nathan whispers to Allison, "Call out. See if anybody's here." His right hand is resting on a pistol tucked into his belt.

"Y a-t'il quelqu'un à la maison?" she says loudly. "Hullo?"

A deep voice calmly answers, "I'm in the front room. Leave the lights off." His English is delivered with a heavy French accent.

In a dark corner of the front room, a man is seated by an empty fireplace. His legs are crossed, his hands are folded on his lap. A wide-brimmed fedora shades the top of this face. "The roads are crawling with Nazis tonight," he says. "The Germans are redoubling their presence in Normandy in expectation of an invasion. That's why the decision was made to bring you here to Saint-Sylvain tonight. It is a small out-of-the-way town where you are unlikely to be confronted. There are too many eyes in Caen." He points to Nathan's sweater and slacks. "It would be difficult for you to explain your presence in Caen, monsieur, especially in your civilian clothes. From now on, it is advisable to wear only your uniform." He gestures to a set of keys on the table. "Those are for the Paris apartment. One ninety-one, Rue Boursault, Seventeenth Arrondissement. There is a garage for you to park the car. Leave it there."

"Are you going with us?" Allison asks.

"No, madame. I have limited knowledge of your assignment, and that's the way we'll keep it. If I am questioned, I know only that a German officer and a female companion are traveling through Normandy to Paris."

"What should we expect along the way?" Nathan says.

"You are in Occupied France. You will see Germans everywhere, all up and down the coast. They are fortifying their Atlantic wall. You will see construction of concrete bunkers and pill boxes. In the larger towns you will see squads of uniformed soldiers. They've also sent the Gestapo, the secret state police, to sniff around and ferret out dissidents, spies, and what they like to call 'subversive elements.' To be sure, they are looking for those who will assist the Allies once the landings begin. In Paris, you will undoubtedly see contingents of SS. They are generally involved in the roundup and deportation of Jews, Gypsies, Communists, and other non-Aryans who fall into disfavor.

"On the roads between here and Paris you will encounter several checkpoints. Make sure you have a solidly rehearsed reason for being on the road and for wanting to enter Paris. You'll be quizzed. Even dressed as an officer, you'll be questioned, though a bit more deferentially. The guards are mostly young recruits, and I doubt that any of them will have the courage to challenge a German officer. Rehearse your story over and over in your mind before taking to the road."

Nathan nods. "I understand. My uniform patches indicate that I am a Hauptmann, assigned to an administrative division employed to discipline Wehrmacht soldiers for misconduct or desertion. My story is that I am leading an investigation into a squad of deserters and profiteers known to be working in western France. Will that fly?"

The man nods. "It should. It's doubtful they'll question a Hauptmann further."

"Other than the guards at the checkpoints," Nathan says, "are there other risks we should be aware of while driving through the countryside?"

"I suppose, in your uniform, you are a target for La Résistance, perhaps a sniper will put a bullet through your head and end your mission altogether." The man grins, and then shrugs. "After all, you represent a hated enemy which has mercilessly conquered our country. Two million French soldiers have been taken by the Germans. They are the sons and cousins of the people along your route. Most Frenchmen will detest you, but they will also fear you. And regrettably, there are those who blindly adulate ruthless power, and they will no doubt show you respect. In many ways, my country is divided.

"La Résistance grows stronger every day, and for that reason, the

Germans have greatly increased their surveillance. They are suspicious of everyone, even their own people. It is not uncommon for French citizens to be randomly confronted in the streets and accused. Often, they are beaten or verbally abused. I am sad to say that far too many have had their spirit broken. Their heads are down. They are starving, they are depressed. Many are ashamed of the French collaborators, but they resolve to go on about their lives as quietly as they can, awaiting the end, whatever that may be. They know that if they speak out, if they lift their eyes, if they show the slightest inclination to disobedience, the consequences will be swift and severe. Parisians have seen the Germans round up tens of thousands of Jews and send them in cattle cars to prison camps in Germany and Poland. Also, the Communists, the Freemasons, the Romani, all rounded up, held for a time in Paris, and shipped off to Germany and Poland. We have heard rumors that many thousands have been murdered in the Polish camps."

Allison swallows hard. "Bienvenue en France," she says softly.

"Maybe we should change our route to something less dangerous," Nathan says.

"You are in Europe. What is less dangerous?" is the solemn retort.

"What about Free France? Only part of France is considered occupied, isn't that so? Isn't the Vichy government in control of southern and eastern France? Would it be safer for us to travel through Vichy rather than Paris? Perhaps, we could go to Berlin through Lyon?"

"Lyon is no safer. When Marshal Pétain left Paris and formed his new French government in the town of Vichy, he did it with Hitler's approval. That should tell you everything you need to know. Vichy is Germany's ally and nothing more than a totalitarian state. Philippe Pétain holds total power unto himself: legislative, judicial, and executive. Sadly, it is a total rebuke of two hundred years of République française, two hundred years of democracy, and now a return to the autocracy of King Louis and the dominance of the Catholic Church. Lest anyone should doubt his design, he has replaced the French national emblem—Marianne, the young goddess of liberté, égalité, fraternité—with a statue of Joan of Arc: a symbol of subservience to higher authority. The new national emblem is a double-headed hatchet with the words 'travail, famille, patrie.'"

"Work, Family, Fatherland," Allison says quietly.

"Exactement, madame. Sounds quite similar to Germany, doesn't it? Pétain seeks to appease Hitler and courts his favor. Under Pétain's regime, more than fifty thousand Jews have been collected in Vichy and sent to Hitler's concentration camps. Pétain's police chief, René Bousquet, is as feared as any Gestapo leader, and he has organized several mass arrests. I do not think you want to go to Vichy."

The man stands. "I do not know what your ultimate mission is, monsieur, or why you are going to Berlin in masquerade. That is not my concern, and it is healthier for me that I do not know, though I wish you success. I strongly caution you to trust no one. Everyone is a spy; everyone is a collaborator. Sadly, under present circumstances, many would turn in a good friend for a loaf of bread."

Nathan nods his understanding. As if he has not made his point clear enough, the man adds, "I know that each of you has been given a cyanide capsule; that is standard issue. I only want to say that if you are discovered in France, do not hesitate. You will die anyway, and you may as well do it on your own terms." He walks to the table and taps a folded map. "Follow this route to your apartment in Paris. With that, I bid you bonne nuit and bonne chance."

Upon the man's exit, Nathan locks the front door, returns to Allison, and exhales. "Pleasant fellow. That certainly was a cheery welcome."

"Do I really have a cyanide capsule?" she says. "Since when?"

"It's in a matchbox in your valise, but forget about it. We're not going to take any cyanide. We are going to Berlin, finish our assignment, and return to New York. That's the plan. We should get some sleep and leave early in the morning."

"You sound a lot more confident of this mission than our mysterious Frenchman."

"Are you having those second thoughts again, Allison?"

"It's Alli. How many thoughts do I get?"

16

BOULANGERIE YVETTE

Shafts of morning sunlight illuminate the front room. Allison enters and stops short. Before her stands a German officer in full dress uniform, dark gray-green tunic belted at the waist, stiff black collar with double bars signifying the rank of Hauptmann, and bloused pantaloons tucked into mirrored black boots. A peaked cap sits on his head. In the center of the black hatband is Germany's symbol: a golden eagle holding a swastika in its talons. "Jesus," she says, "you startled me."

"You better get used to it," Nathan answers, "although, I have to admit, it makes my skin crawl."

"Is that what a German army captain would wear, a dark gray-green uniform like that?"

"The color is called *feldgrau*." He points to his shoulder patches, light gray with two gold sunburst emblems. "And it's *Hauptmann Froman,* if you please."

"What is the medal hanging from the red ribbon?"

Nathan smiles. "Groves thought of everything. As if the rank of Hauptmann is not prestigious enough, I am wearing an Iron Cross, awarded for bravery in the field of combat. He thinks that will give me an extra measure of respect. So, I'm not only traveling to Germany dressed as a Wehrmacht captain, but one who has been honored by Field Marshal Keitel."

Allison is impressed. "Well, you might as well be hanged for a sheep as a lamb."

"I don't care for the analogy, and by the way, look at you. Short flowery skirt, snug white top, ribbon in your hair, bright red lipstick. Not Allison's usual lab coat."

Allison nods. "Sheep as a lamb. If we're caught, we go down in style. And it's Alicia, remember, Dietrich?"

"Right, Alli."

"Is there anything in the kitchen?" she says. "I'm starving."

Nathan shakes his head. "Nope. Not even a tea bag. We'll have to get something on the road." He lays the map out on the table. "From what I can see, we should be able to reach Paris by nightfall." He traces his finger along the route. "There are a number of small towns along the backroads, the route we are directed to take. The trouble is, there is no straight-through highway, just these winding country roads. I hope we don't get lost, but I think we're okay as long as we keep going east."

Allison takes the map. "I'll navigate. Besides, you don't read French."

Nathan gets into the driver's seat, keys in hand, and stares at the dashboard. He looks left, to the right, at the gear shift console. After a few moments, Allison starts to giggle. "You don't know how to drive, do you? You've never driven a car!" She laughs harder. "You are supposed to drive us across France and on the streets of Paris, and you don't know how to drive a car!" Her laugh gets louder.

"We never had a car," he says with annoyance. "We lived in Berlin and my father could walk to his lab. On the bad days, he'd take a bus. But it can't be that tough." He turns the ignition key, the car lurches forward and dies. Allison struggles to conceal her laughter. He tries again and quickly kills the motor. "Shit!" he says angrily, and slaps the steering wheel. Allison has one hand covering her mouth and the other holding her side as she laughs convulsively. "You have no idea," she says between outbursts. "Not a clue. Oh, my side hurts. The most important mission in the world and no one bothered to ask if you could drive. Oops!" she howls.

"I suppose you know how to drive this car, Miss Smarty?" he says.

"I grew up on a farm," she says proudly, "I can drive a tractor and my father's Ford pickup. And I've been driving since I was fourteen." She gets out of the car, walks around, hands Nathan the map and says, "You navigate, I'll drive."

The golds and greens of fall paint the French countryside. Hedgerows separate the fields into orderly squares. The small, paved roads wind through picturesque villages, each of which seems to be anchored by a tall church. In the town of Sainte-Marguerite-de-Viette, Allison pulls the car over to the curb and shuts the motor. She points to a busy little shop. The sign reads BOULANGERIE YVETTE. "I need a pastry and a cup of coffee," she says.

Nathan nods, opens the door, and places his cap on his head. Allison says, "Wait, Dietrich. What will you say to the woman behind the counter?"

"I'll point," he says, with a bit of exasperation in his tone.

Allison shakes her head. She chuckles. "No, I'll go. What do you want?"

Nathan twists his lips and then says, "Whatever you choose."

Allison enters the shop and Nathan waits. And waits. After several minutes, Nathan decides that Allison has been inside the shop longer than necessary. He drums his fingers on the dashboard. Finally, he exits the car and walks into the shop. It is a small bakery and Allison is nowhere to be seen. He approaches the girl behind the counter. The sight of a German officer stiffens her posture.

"Wo ist die Fräulein?" he says to her sharply. With her eyes she indicates a door to her right.

There is some noise from behind the door, but Nathan hesitates. "Ist das Toilette?" he asks. She shakes her head. The noise behind the door increases and it sounds like a scuffle. Nathan tries the doorknob, but it is locked. The girl quietly says, "Soldat. Il est allemande." Then adds shakily, "Deutscher Soldat."

Nathan takes a step back and kicks the door open. Allison is pinned against the wall by a large man in the khaki uniform of a Wehrmacht infantry private. One of his hands is on her breast and the other is trying to get up the back of her skirt. Allison's lipstick has been smeared on her face. She is crying, but struggling.

The private turns, sees Nathan and snaps to attention. He throws his hand out in a Nazi salute and barks "Heil Hitler" with a smile. In a split second, Nathan backhands him across the face, knocking him back against a table. "You filthy pig," Nathan says in German. "You embarrass yourself, you embarrass the Reich."

The man swallows hard. "My apologies, Herr Hauptmann. But I have done nothing to shame the Reich. She is just a French street girl. There's a million of them. Probably nothing more than a prostitute."

"I see. Did she invite your affections, infantryman?"

The man shows a sheepish grin. He is easily two hundred fifty pounds. He is roughly shaven; his teeth are yellowed and he is sweating. "Not exactly," he says, "but she is just a street girl. What rule have I broken?"

Allison's face is red with rage. Nathan has one hand on his Luger and with the other, gestures for Allison to come closer. Every muscle is taut, her teeth are clenched, she takes a step. "Une prostituée?" she screams at the man. The private backs up a step and eyes the doorway. "Don't move an inch," Nathan says. "You're not going anywhere." Allison approaches. "Une prostituée?" she repeats, and spits in his face. "What gives you the right to touch me?" she screams in French. The man is not familiar with the words, but he gets the message. He stammers and shrugs, but he does not answer. With all her might, Allison slaps him across the face, knocking him to the floor.

Nathan points his gun at the private's head. The man pleads for his life. "Nein, nein. Bitte der Herr. Bitte." Nathan turns to Allison as though asking for permission to shoot. "So, Fräulein? Ja?"

Allison glares at the man sitting on the floor, sniveling. "Straßen-mädchen?" Nathan says to the man. "Street girl? If it pleases this *street girl,* I will blow your head apart." He nods at Allison.

She shakes her head. "Non."

"Lucky for you that the *street girl* is a lady who has decided to save your worthless life. Get up." The man rises slowly to his feet, his eyes focused on the gun. "What is your name and unit, soldier?"

"Rolf Tannings, 401st Infantry," he says, with tears running down his face. He is shaking like an aspen leaf. The front of his trousers is wet.

"What's the matter, Rolf Tannings?" Nathan says. "Does it bother you to have this woman see you whimper and cry and urinate on your-self? She is much braver than you are. She has character and you are a spineless worm."

"Bitte, bitte," the man pleads.

"Listen carefully, Private Rolf Tannings, I am now assigned to this region. If I hear that you've come anywhere near this bakery, or that you have been giving any woman any of your insults or unwelcome advances, I will personally take charge of your discipline. Now get out. Mach schnell!" The man turns, grabs his hat off the floor, dashes out of the room, through the shop and out into the street.

Nathan puts his arm around Allison. "Are you all right? Do you need medical attention? Did he hurt you?"

She shakes her head. "Not physically. No, I'm okay. I walked into the shop, and he was standing at the counter eating a croissant. He said something to me in German. I didn't know what it was. I ignored it and he became angry. Out of nowhere he grabbed me and pushed me into the storeroom. He was so strong, I couldn't . . ."

"It's okay," Nathan says softly. "He's gone now. Thankfully, he didn't harm you. Let's take a step into the shop, pick out pastries and a cup of espresso."

The woman behind the counter serves them but will not accept payment. "Tout est gratuit," she says. "Mon cadeau. Merci. Merci beaucoup."

17

L'HOTEL JOSEPHINE

It has been thirty minutes since they left the bakery, and the ride has been mostly silent. Allison is driving, Nathan is navigating. From time to time, Allison will brush away a tear. Near the town of Saint-Germain-d'Aunay, Allison pulls the car onto a farm road and shuts the motor. "I need a minute," she says.

She walks toward a stand of trees beside a stream and sits on a log. Nathan watches her from a distance. After a moment, she reaches up and buries her face in her hands, and for the first time since the assault, gives way to her emotions. After a bit, she looks up and Nathan is standing there. "My mother would say, I needed a good cry," she says, sniffling. "I'm sorry."

"Nothing to be sorry about. My mother would say, 'Let it out.'"

"The assault this morning was a total shock. Of all the dangers I perceived, all the situations I thought I might encounter on this assignment, I never anticipated anything like this. If you hadn't come into the bakery, if you had stayed in the car, if you hadn't come to rescue me, that man would have—"

"Don't do that, Allison. Don't paint pictures in your mind about what didn't happen. Don't create memories for things that didn't occur. It was bad enough as it was, there's no need to conjure up anything worse."

"Look, I'm not foolish, I'm not naive. I read the papers. I know what is happening here in Europe. I knew the risks before General Groves ever asked me to come. I prepared myself for any eventuality, including capture and death. I knew there would be danger. But . . ."

"Why did you agree?"

"Because, as much as anyone in the world, I know the power of an atomic bomb and what it can do to England, America, or any of our allies. If Germany is anywhere near to achieving criticality, I must do my part to stop it. My colleagues and I, the nuclear physicists of the world, must accept responsibility for the present danger. We must be held accountable. What was once initially the academic study of atomic structure, the identification of new elements, and ultimately the discovery of a new source of energy, has become a mad dash to develop the deadliest weapon ever known."

She stands and brushes herself off. "It was essential to me that I come on this journey even though the dangers are great. Preventing Hitler from possessing and possibly using an atomic bomb is essential to the future of mankind. Can you imagine the consequences if Nazi Germany actually possessed a workable atomic bomb? Just the *threat* of utilization, coupled with what everyone knows—that Hitler is mad enough to use it without a second thought—would give him unlimited power worldwide. No nation could responsibly stand up to a very real threat of total annihilation. He would answer to no one. He would become the world's Führer, a king who could impose his sick racial laws on the entire world. He would appoint his evil deputies to rule each subjugated nation. I must do whatever I can to prevent that scenario from happening, because I helped to create it."

When they resume their drive to Paris, Nathan says, "If you had it to do all over, would you work to split the atom? Would you help Professors Fermi and Szilard develop a nuclear reactor?"

"Knowing what we know now? Would I personally abstain, or would the profession? Are you asking if the entire study of nuclear physics should have been banned? Because once Lise Meitner split the atom, once the phenomenon was realized, the application of the science became inevitable. It was all a chain reaction, you might say. In many ways, the studies and the discoveries were fascinating, even intoxicating to me."

"You could say the same thing about my own father and his devotion to science. Intoxication is a good description."

"You haven't heard from him in a long time, have you?"

Nathan sadly shakes his head. "Not from him, nor my mother, nor my sister."

"I'm sorry."

"Although I don't know the situation, I was too young to judge, I fault him for not leaving. When other scientists were leaving Berlin, like rats from a sinking ship, he didn't go. My mother begged him to leave. We could have gone to America like Albert Einstein, or to England like Leo Szilard. Szilard urged my dad to go with him. We could have gone to Sweden like Lise Meitner. We could have all had new lives far from Germany if we had left early enough. But in the end, it was too late."

"Why do you think he stayed? Was it the fear of leaving all his money behind?"

"No. He didn't care about the money. It had to be his devotion to his work; that intoxication you talk about. He put it ahead of his family."

"Is that what he told you. Do you know that for certain?"

"No. It's what I surmise."

"You also don't know that your father, you mother, and your sister are missing, do you? I mean, they could still be in Berlin in your house, and they just haven't been able to communicate with you during the war."

Nathan does not accept that proposition. "They stopped writing to me in 1940. I don't know for sure what happened to them, and I intend to find out once we get to Berlin, but my gut tells me that they were put into a camp because they were Jewish, and if that's what happened, then I have to blame my father. It didn't have to be that way."

"Because he didn't take them out when they sent you to New York?"

"Maybe. I don't know. They probably didn't have the resources. Maybe by then it was already too late."

Toward the end of the afternoon, they stop at a small café in Dreux. The interior is warm, with dark oak beams and soft light from several chandeliers. They sit in a booth and order croque monsieur, the ubiquitous French ham and cheese sandwich, accompanied by glasses of Sancerre. They take their time, still unwinding from the morning's disturbance. Finally, Nathan pulls back the window curtain, peers outside, and says, "It's getting dark, we should be on our way. I think it's a pretty straight shot from here to Paris. We should get there later this evening. Are you okay to drive?"

"I'm fine," she says, "but if I said no, what would you do?"

"I would drive us as soon as I figured out how to stop killing the car. It can't be that tough. You drove at fourteen."

"Ah, but I'm exceptional."

As they approach Versailles, they are halted by a group of soldiers at what appears to be a checkpoint. One of the soldiers, his blond hair peeking out from beneath his round helmet, walks deliberately to the driver's window and taps on the glass. Allison rolls down the window and says, "Oui?"

"Dokumente, bitte," the young soldier says. His tone is officious. Allison hands the two passports and identification cards through the window. He examines hers, repeatedly looking back and forth between the passport photo and Allison's face, and then gestures for her to exit the car. Then he turns to Nathan's papers. With a look of surprise, he leans over and peers into the car. "Hauptmann, I beg your pardon, sir. I am required to search the car before letting it pass into Versailles. I hope I don't inconvenience you."

Nathan exits. "Of course not. Do your job."

The search was cursory and quick. "I am sorry to have detained you, sir," the soldier says. "Where are you headed this evening?"

"Paris," Nathan says. "May we pass?"

The soldier shakes his head. "I'm sorry, sir, but it's too late. Curfew in Paris is nine o'clock and they won't let you drive into the city. Not even you, sir. If I may make a suggestion, there is a nice hotel not far from the palace. They should have a room for you. Then, in the morning, you may leave for Paris. It's only an hour away."

Allison doesn't understand the conversation, but Nathan signals her to reenter the car. She gets behind the wheel and Nathan holds a finger up signaling for her to wait a moment. The soldier returns with written directions to the hotel. Nathan nods to Allison, she starts the car, and they are on their way.

"I take it we're not going into Paris tonight. I heard him say L'Hotel Josephine."

Nathan nods. "There is a curfew in Paris, and we wouldn't get past the gates. We'll go in the morning."

They park the car in front of L'Hotel Josephine and approach the desk clerk. "We need a room for the night," Nathan says in German. The clerk shakes his head. "Je ne comprends pas," he says. "Je parle français."

Allison steps up and in French declares, "My officer said we would like a room for the night."

"Mais bien sur," he replies with a broad smile. "Suite lune de miel."

With keys in hand, they proceed down the hall. "What did he say to you when he was grinning like a duck?" Nathan asks.

Allison chuckles. "I said my officer would like a room for the night, and he replied, 'But of course, the honeymoon suite.'"

"My officer, huh?"

The room is very French and very frilly in pinks and whites. The bed is a double with a gold, mirrored headboard. There is a side chair near the closet. Nathan hangs up his spare uniform and says, "I saw a little bar off the lobby. I need another glass of wine or two before I spend the night in that chair. Join me?"

In the small café, Allison takes a sip of Sancerre and sets her wine glass down. "Do you think someone is waiting for us in the Paris apartment, and he wonders why we didn't show up?"

Nathan shrugs. "It's possible, but I wouldn't worry about it. I have the train tickets in my packet and the address of the safe house in Berlin. Even if we bypassed Paris, we'd be all right. Remember, Groves said to stay flexible. I think we're okay. Do you want anything more, another glass of wine?"

"No thanks. I'm tired. It's been a long day. But I do have a suggestion. I think that first thing tomorrow morning, I should teach you to drive. What if something happens to me? Are you going to sit there killing the motor for an hour? How will we get back to the coast?"

"I suppose that makes sense." He stands. "I'm ready to call it a day as well. Do you want me to stay down here for an hour or so while you get ready for bed?"

"That's not necessary. Just give me a moment, and then come to the room."

The bathroom door opens, and Allison enters the room. She is wearing pink pajamas. "You match the room décor," Nathan says. He is sitting in the chair, and but for his cap and his boots, he is still wearing his uniform.

"Are you going to sleep like that?" Allison asks.

"You mean in my uniform, I guess so. I didn't bring pajamas."

"Well, I don't mind if you sleep in your boxers and a T-shirt. You do have boxers on underneath those pantaloons, right?"

"Yeah."

"Well, okay then. Don't sleep in your uniform. I was really asking if you intended to sleep in that chair. It doesn't look very comfortable. You didn't do very well in a chair on the Twentieth Century Limited, and that chair was not some Louis XIV replica."

"Well, I've slept in roomier chairs, but yes, that was my intent."

"Well then, bonne nuit," she says with a shrug and turns off the light. Eyes wide open, she lies there as the day's events play out in her mind. From time to time, she gazes over at Nathan, who keeps shifting position in his chair. Finally, she says, "You are never going to get any sleep in that chair, and you're going to keep me up all night worrying about you. You can share the bed with me."

"Are you sure? I don't want you to feel uncomfortable."

"I'm uncomfortable now watching you squirm in that chair."

"Thank you," he says, and he carefully lies on the edge of the bed on top of the covers.

18

LE VIEUX JUIF

The sun peeks through the split in the curtains and nudges Nathan from his sleep. He opens his eyes and looks around. Allison is not in the room. Nor is she in the bathroom. He puts on his shoes, grabs the key, and walks into the lobby. He would ask the desk clerk if he has seen her, but there is that language barrier. He walks outside. The car is in the lot. At least she didn't drive anywhere.

He orders coffee and a croissant and takes a seat in the lobby feeling very visible. *What must these French townsfolk feel about the Nazi invaders,* he thinks. *I know how I would feel. They nod and smile at me as they pass by, but I get the impression they would rather put poison in my coffee, or a knife in my back.* He checks his watch. Eight fifteen. He has been up for an hour. Is it time to sound the alarm?

Suddenly he sees her walking in the front door. "Where have you been?" he says quietly. "Is this a payback for my keeping you up all night?"

"You didn't keep me up. You were a sound sleeper. I went for a walk. It's only three blocks to the Palace of Versailles. I had to see it. And it's magnificent, at least it is from the outside. You can easily imagine Louis XIV in residence. I've seen pictures of the palace and the wonderful gardens in the back, but the whole property is surrounded now by an iron fence. There are at least a dozen German soldiers standing in front of the gate and there's a sign that reads, 'Museum is Closed.'"

"Well, I wish you would have told me that you were going for a walk," Nathan says. "I was worried."

"I left you a note."

"Where?"

"On the nightstand."

"Oh. I didn't see it. Do you want a cup of coffee?"

She shakes her head. "I stopped in a cute patisserie nearby. As I was walking, I could smell the bread a block away."

Nathan furrows his forehead. "You got all that done already?"

"You can get quite a bit done if you don't sleep the day away."

"Allison, it's eight thirty."

"Exactly. Time's a wastin'. Are you ready for your driving lesson?"

———————

That's it, that's it, not so quick, let the clutch up smoothly. Okay. Oops. Try it again." The car lurches forward and continues down the country lane that Allison has chosen for Nathan's lesson. Nathan shifts into second and grinds the gear. The Peugeot is proceeding forward, but in a spasmodic fashion. Nathan is clearly frustrated. Allison thinks the whole thing is a scream.

Finally, Nathan pulls over and says, "We need to get to Paris. I can drive just fine, I think I have it all under control, but I think I'll let you drive because I am definitely the better navigator."

The closer they get to Paris the busier the traffic. They stop at another checkpoint. The car in front of them is ordered to pull to the side and the guards rifle through the interior, throwing belongings out onto the curb. Nathan's ID is enough to get them through with just a wave.

At a second checkpoint, all of the cars are ordered to pull to the side and wait. After ten minutes have passed, two black Daimlers with German insignias speed by and Allison is then permitted to proceed.

On the western edge of Paris, in the town of Boulogne-Billancourt, the traffic is stalled at a stoplight. Three cycles have passed, and none of the cars have moved. There seems to be activity ahead involving a small group of young soldiers. A few onlookers are standing to the side. Nathan gets out of the car and approaches the group. They are laughing and screaming at an elderly man who is crawling on the ground on all fours. He has a worn wool overcoat with a yellow star sewn on the lapel. It reads JUIF. He crawls a few feet and one of the soldiers pushes him down with his boot to a round of laughter.

"What's going on here?" Nathan yells. The soldiers snap to attention and salute. The crowd of onlookers quickly dissipates. "I said, what's going on here?"

A young soldier gulps and answers, "Nothing much, sir. This Jew had gotten in our way and was causing trouble."

Nathan looks at the man sitting on the ground. He is clearly terrified. "What kind of trouble?" Nathan says.

The soldier looks to his companions, who divert their eyes and remain silent. "Well, a lot of trouble, sir. You know, Jews. They cause trouble."

Nathan bends down and carefully pulls the man up to his feet. "Your amusement is causing a traffic backup, private," Nathan says. "I'll take it from here. I'll see that he gets what he deserves."

"Thank you, Hauptmann," the soldier says with a salute, and his companions echo the phrase. "Heil Hitler," they bark, and walk away.

Nathan leads the man back to the car and puts him in the back seat. "Ask this man if he has somewhere safe where we can drop him," Nathan says to Allison.

The man's eyes are wide. "Anglaise?" the man says.

Nathan turns to him with his finger on his lips. "Shh."

"Where can we take you where you will be safe?" Allison says in French.

The man shakes his head. "There is no place in France where a Jew can be safe, but if you will drive another two kilometers, I will find my sister. I am deeply grateful to you, whoever you are, for rescuing me."

As the man leaves the car, he once again expresses his gratitude. "I will tell no one," he says. "God bless you."

When they enter Paris proper, the condition of occupation is immediately apparent. There are troops everywhere. Many of the streets are blocked by Panzer tanks and half-tracks. "It looks like I'm back at Ritchie," Nathan says. "If I'm not mistaken, that is the Ninth Panzer Division." As they pass the National Assembly building, Nazi swastika banners are hanging from the balustrades and rippling in the wind.

They proceed though the city, past enclaves of soldiers and French policemen. Nathan is uncomfortable. It seems to him that every eye is focused on his car. Twice they are flagged down at intersections while French policemen in their black uniforms and flat top caps peer into the car's interior. "Where are you headed?" one of them asks Allison brusquely. She looks at Nathan, who shakes his head. "Official business," Allison answers. The policeman tips his cap in acknowledgment of a ranked officer, and that seems to be sufficient.

They finally locate the apartment, but when they approach, there is a black car in the carport. "I thought our instructions are to park in that garage and leave the car," Allison says.

"They are. Something is wrong; pull around the corner."

She parks the car a half-block away, and Nathan stares at the apartment building. The unit is on the first floor and the lights are on. "Wait here," he says. Staying in the shadows, he approaches the building from behind, reaches the side window of the apartment, and peers in. He hears the sounds of conversation. He listens for a moment and his lips tighten. He rushes back to Allison. "There are people in the apartment. Three or four as far as I could tell."

"Are they our people? They might be our contacts," Allison says.

"I don't think so. They were speaking German, not English or even French."

"We spent a night in Versailles. Maybe they are our contacts and they've concluded that we were discovered, or that we'll be here later."

"Four people? Men and women? Does that sound like a safe house? Do you want to take that chance? Maybe our mission has been compromised. Or aborted. It doesn't feel right, and we don't need this safe house. We'll leave tomorrow morning on the train for Berlin."

"What are we going to do tonight? There's a nine o'clock curfew, remember?"

"We'll have to make other arrangements. We'll figure it out. Let's leave the bags in the trunk and take a walk."

19

THE CURIOUS SQUIRREL

In many ways, Paris resembles the Berlin I knew before I left in 1938," Nathan says to Allison as they approach the Tuileries. "Bright red Nazi banners everywhere you look. Groups of German soldiers and SS squads on the sidewalks as though they can x-ray everyone that walks by. You can feel the tension in the air."

They pass a newsstand and Nathan sees the same anti-Semitic clap-trap that was pasted all over Berlin. There is a poster slapped on the side of the hut warning of the "Peril Juif," depicting a grotesque monster with a menacing sneer, a nose larger than the rest of his face, and long sharp claws grasping a pretty French woman who is trying to get away.

Nathan points to a newspaper, and says in German, "I'll take a copy of the *Pariser Zeitung.*" The newspaper salesman shrugs and doesn't move. Allison repeats the request in French, and he nods, though he had to know the meaning of Nathan's request all along. As they walk away, Nathan says, "This is a paper written for German soldiers stationed in Paris. It may come in handy. Maybe it will recommend a place to sleep. We just need to make it until tomorrow morning. There is a train at nine forty-five."

Allison points at the Louvre. "Look, there are trucks in the plaza. They are removing pieces of art. In Versailles, the woman told me that Germans were confiscating and warehousing art in the Jeu de Paume museum, which is now closed to the public. I hope they don't destroy any of it, you know, declare it all to be depraved, like they did with books and music. The woman thought they are confiscating art in every city they occupy and storing it somewhere in secret. They claim they are protecting the art from air raids."

Strolling out of the Tuileries, onto the Place de la Concorde, they encounter thicker crowds, but they are mostly German military or French gendarmes. The French police salute Nathan as he passes. Nazi banners hang from many of the buildings. A street sign on a post points to the left and reads KOMMANDANT VON GROSS PARIS. "That sign points the way to the German High Command in Paris," Nathan says.

On either side of the Champs-Élysées, there are shuttered stores, and the famous Parisian cafés are thinly patronized. There is a line of people outside a closed boulangerie waiting for it to open, and knowing that the supply of bread will be limited. Due to a tight rationing of gasoline, there are very few cars and only an occasional bus on the boulevard. It seems like there are more pedicabs and carriages than motor vehicles.

Nathan and Allison continue walking down the boulevard, looking this way and that, when a uniformed Luftwaffe officer strides over and walks lock-step with Allison. He tips his cap and addresses her in broken French. "Bonjour, mademoiselle. Comme tu es belle ce soir."

She chuckles, but continues walking.

"Voulez-vous de la compagnie ce soir, jolie fille?" the officer says with a smile and an open hand.

Nathan looks at her for an explanation. She rolls her eyes upward. "Really," she says in French to the officer, "does that line actually work?"

He smiles. "Most of the time, mademoiselle. But it's innocent, I assure you. I only wish to know if you would like the company of a fine German airman this evening?" He points to the sky. "I fly airplanes high into the clouds and command squadrons to bomb our enemies." He feigns a pout. "But here on the ground in this city of eternal love, I am lonely tonight. With a pretty young Parisienne, I can be a lot of fun. Would you like to have a drink with me?"

Allison suppresses a giggle. "Well, monsieur, I am so flattered, but as you can see, I am in the company of Hauptmann Froman. He is a German officer, and he would not like it if I left him alone."

"Maybe he wouldn't mind."

Allison wrinkles her nose and shakes her head. "He is a *captain,* and he *would* mind, I can assure you. So, you don't want to get yourself into trouble, flyboy."

He smiles broadly. "I think I would not get into any trouble; I out-rank him. I am a major, and he will do what I tell him. But you know what, I do not wish to step on another man's toes. I am just looking for company. I know a very good bistro. I'll buy you both a drink. Come on."

Allison is in a quandary. Nathan does not understand French, but he is not clueless, and he picks up on the major's interest in Allison and her attempts to deflect his advances. He is unaware of the major's invitation, and Allison cannot explain it to him without speaking English. The major is beckoning them to follow. "Allez, allez," he says.

"Dietrich Froman," Nathan says and extends his right hand. "I don't understand French. Is there something I can help you with?"

The major takes his hand and shakes it heartily. "Otto Weber, guten Tag. I am with the Luftwaffe, and . . ."

Nathan interrupts. "You are a squadron leader." The major is impressed. "I recognize your patch and insignia," Nathan says. "A very brave and elite corps. I salute you."

Weber smiles and says, "I do not recognize your patch, Hauptmann Froman. Which division are you with? Where is your regiment?"

Nathan holds up his index finger. "I am currently on administrative assignment. I am not supposed to discuss my presence here. Special instructions from Field Marshal Keitel."

That seems to satisfy Weber, who smiles and emits a jolly laugh. He gives Nathan a slap on the back and says, "I have invited you two to join me this evening. I know a terrific bistro." Nathan nods and the three of them proceed down the Champs-Élysées. To ensure that the major understands the dynamics a little better, Allison links her arm with Nathan's.

"Let's go lift a beer or two. Bring your pretty French girlfriend who turned me down for the likes of you." He laughs again. "No accounting for bad taste. Ja?"

Weber leads them to a club called L'Écureuil Curieux, the Curious Squirrel, a block or two off the Champs-Élysées near the Arc de Triomphe. A sign in the front window causes Nathan to stop in his tracks. For the moment, he freezes. The sign has a red slash across it and reads LES JUIFS NE SONT PAS ADMISIER. Jews are not admitted. Weber looks at Nathan curiously. "What's the matter, Dietrich, you think that sign is meant for you? Are you a Jew?" Then he bursts into laughter and taps the end of his nose. "You sure don't look like a Jew." He then turns to Allison and says in French, "Did you know you were going out with a Jew? Maybe now you'll change your mind." More belly laughs. She joins him in the laughter. "Don't blame him," she says, "he doesn't speak or read French. And I don't speak German."

"That's an awkward combination," Weber says. "How do you two talk to each other?"

Allison smiles. "The language of love is universal."

Weber slaps Nathan on the back again. "You got some girl here, but my friend, you need to learn to read and speak some French if you're going to keep this fine lady. Come on, let's get a beer."

The noisy bistro reminds Nathan of a German sports pub during football tournaments. Music plays and the conversations are lively and loud. From the far corner of the room, a soldier sees Weber, stands and waves his arm. "Otto! Hier drüben," he yells above the clamor.

Nathan scans the room. It is filled with French girls and uniformed German soldiers. They appear to be from all branches of service: Wehrmacht, Luftwaffe, Kriegsmarine, and no doubt, a fair share of Gestapo, along with the French auxiliary of the Gestapo, the Carlingue. He has wandered deep into the lion's den.

They wind their way through the crowded room to a section filled with Wehrmacht soldiers in their gray-green uniforms. Evidently, they are all friends of Weber's, though not all from the Luftwaffe, and they greet him warmly. One man, powerfully built and dressed in plain clothes—a jacket and slacks—nods at Weber. He comes over and they exchange warm man-hugs. "Froman," Weber says, "this is Wolf. Henning Wolf. You don't want to be on his bad side ever." Then he whispers, "Gestapo." The two of them break into laughter.

Weber points at a couple of young noncommissioned officers and gestures for them to give up their seats. He then pulls a chair out for Allison and points to the adjoining chair for Nathan.

"Komeraden," he says, "allow me to introduce Hauptmann Dietrich Froman and his pretty friend . . ." He pauses, turns to Allison and says in French, "Mademoiselle, I am so embarrassed, I do not know your name."

"Allis . . . Alicia." she says. "Alicia Dumont." She smiles. dips her head coyly and holds out the back of her hand for a kiss. "*Enchanté,*" he says.

Weber signals for a waitress and says, "Boissons pour mes amis." She smiles and leaves to fill the order.

"So where are you staying while in Paris, Dietrich?" Weber asks.

Nathan shakes his head. "We just got here. I was supposed to stay with a friend of mine, but he must be out of town. I suppose I'll find a hotel room somewhere."

Weber chuckles. "Good luck, my friend. Hotel rooms in this city are scarce, and most are reserved for military units."

"We'll find something."

Weber raises his eyebrows. "All right, then. I like your style. Let me make a suggestion for my newfound friend and his *jolie fille*. The Luftwaffe command has taken over the Paris Ritz as its headquarters. It is located at the Place Vendôme and it's pretty posh. Although the hotel is packed with Luftwaffe personnel, I believe there are still vacancies. People get shipped in and out all the time. Ask for the desk clerk, his name is Henri. Tell him I sent you to him."

Mugs of cold beer are brought to the table and the men raise their glasses with a boisterous "Prost" and an obligatory, and less enthusiastic, "Heil Hitler."

In contrast to the general revelry of the room, an older officer sits quietly across the table. He is treated deferentially by the others. From his uniform insignias, Nathan knows that he is a colonel with the

Seventy-Fifth Infantry Division. As the drinks are being served, the colonel stares at Nathan, making him feel like he is being interrogated. The colonel raises his chin in Nathan's direction. "I haven't seen you here before, Hauptmann. What division are you serving with?"

Nathan shrugs in an attempt to brush off the question. "I just arrived in Paris, Herr Oberst. I haven't been in this bistro before."

"I see, but you did not answer my question. What division, Hauptmann?"

"Actually, sir, I am on a special administrative assignment, not attached to any unit."

The answer does not satisfy the colonel. He is clearly suspicious. "Who gave you this special assignment?" he asks.

Weber speaks up. "I believe it is a *secret* assignment, Herr Oberst. From the office of Field Marshal Keitel. Hauptmann Froman is very guarded about the subject of his assignment."

The colonel's lips curl down. "I see. Thank you, Major Weber." Turning back to Nathan, the colonel says, "What division were you with *before* the esteemed Field Marshal personally gave you this special secret assignment?"

Nathan smiles nervously. "I feel like I am under your intense interrogation, Oberst. I would hate to be your prisoner."

"No, no, not at all, Hauptmann. I am only trying to get to know you a little better. I like to know who I am drinking with. What division?"

Nathan is in a bind. He reaches back to his Ritchie training. What division would best answer this inquiry so that the colonel will cease his interrogation? "I was with the Fifty-Seventh Infantry Division," Nathan says at last.

The colonel nods. "Ah yes. Belgium. Quite a battle. Is that where you received your Iron Cross?"

Allison is watching this mind game. She senses Nathan's anxiety. Though her lack of German does not permit her to follow the colloquy, she knows that Nathan is being challenged.

"No, Herr Oberst," Nathan says, with a polite smile. "You are incorrect." The table is suddenly still. "The Fifty-Seventh Infantry fought bravely in Poland and then in Operation Barbarossa. We were part of the triumphant encirclement of Kiev where our brilliant army took six hundred thousand Russian prisoners. That is where I earned my Iron Cross."

The colonel forces a smile and sits back. His trap did not work, but he has been put down, and he has a clear distaste for Nathan. The evening's challenge is not over. "Hauptmann, I apologize for my confusion. As it happens, I was with Field Marshal Keitel last month, but he did not tell me of a special secret assignment. Perhaps, before the evening is over, you can tell me how this assignment came about."

Nathan sips his beer. "Of course," he says.

The colonel lifts his beer mug, and with a stiff arm points it at Nathan. "To the Führer!" he says confrontationally.

"To the Führer," Nathan repeats.

An outsider to the conversation, Allison is cognizant of the conflict and of Nathan's predicament. The body language is unmistakable. Nathan is a target. She decides something must be done to defuse the situation. She stands, grabs Nathan by the elbow and in a flirtatious manner says, "Dietrich, I'm bored with all this soldier talk. I want to dance."

Weber laughs. "You better dance with her, Dietrich. If you don't, I will."

Nathan takes her hand and the two wind their way through the crowded bar onto the dance floor. "Do we need to get out of here?" she whispers in his ear. "It looked pretty serious back there."

"We sure do. The colonel suspects something and I don't know how long I can hold him off. Thanks for rescuing me. That was quick thinking."

"Well, I remember back when we were on the train from Chicago to New York, you told me you cut a mean rug, and I said I'd put you to the test. I just saw my chance and took it, that's all."

They twirl away and dance to the lively swing music. The club is noisy, and the dance floor is packed. Allison's smile is infectious. "I'll hand it to you, Nathan, you do cut a mean rug."

"Thank you, but we need to slip out the door first chance we get."

"Where are we going to stay tonight?" she asks. "Are we going back to the apartment? Maybe those people are gone."

"I'm not taking that chance. Let's see if we can get a room at the Ritz. We'll get into the room, leave early tomorrow before anyone is up and about and no one will be the wiser. It's our best bet."

They make their way to the edge of the dance floor and then slide out the door. "Weber will think you took advantage of the moment and ran off with your pretty French sweetie," she says.

"And that's exactly what I've done. Great work back there, Alli."

To avoid making the same mistake twice, they walk arm in arm as would befit a loving couple on a Paris evening. When they return to the Champs-Élysées, Nathan taps on the back of a horse-drawn carriage. The driver nods and they get in. "Où allez-vous, monsieur?"

"L'Hotel Ritz, s'il vous plaît," Nathan answers.

"Ooh, my goodness, how suave," Allison says. "Imagine this: I am flown to Europe in a private airplane with a handsome captain. We stroll the Paris boulevards, dance in a bistro, and as the evening wanes, we ride together in a horse-drawn carriage down the Champs-Élysées to the Ritz Hotel. Am I in a movie? Is this every girl's dream?"

"You can cut the comedy. We could just as easily be discovered and shot."

"Stop spoiling my dream. Someday, years from now, I will have a hell of a story to tell."

"Let's hope so."

20

L'HOTEL RITZ

The Place Vendôme hearkens back to the days and the styles of Louis XIV. The Ritz itself was designed in the 1850s by the famed French architect Jules Hardouin-Mansart, with its sloping roof, dormer windows, and the midline of second-floor balconies. It is classic French architecture, but to Nathan, on this chilly Paris night, it resembles a hornets' nest. It is the center from which numbers of uniformed enemy soldiers are busily entering and exiting. Nathan has no desire to enter this building, but they need a place to sleep. They approach the desk and Nathan asks to speak to Henri.

A middle-aged man, smartly dressed in a tailored suit, smoothly approaches the front desk. "Did you ask for me?" he says in German. "I am Henri. How may I be of service to you, sir?"

"I'm looking for a room for tonight," Nathan says.

With a pained expression, Henri says, "I am so sorry. All of our rooms are spoken for. Have you tried the Majestic? That is where the Wehrmacht maintains its headquarters and where it provides rooms for its officers. Although they are very crowded, they may have a room for you. May I call ahead to inquire?"

Nathan raises a hand to make a point. "Major Otto Weber told me to ask for you personally, Henri, and that you might make an exception and find a room for us tonight."

"Major Weber?" Henri smiles the smile of a co-conspirator. "Of course. Let me look." Henri nods, picks up a large bound register, and flips through the pages. "Ah, yes. I think we actually do have a suite open on the third floor. Will that do?"

"Very nicely, thank you. And may I ask for a wake-up call at seven?"

"Mais bien sûr," he says and chimes the desk bell for a porter. "Charles will show you to your room."

The door to the suite is opened and Allison's eyes widen. The room is luxuriously accoutered. Fine linens, gilded mirrors, sculptured side chairs, all in classic French design to complement the hotel's character.

After the porter leaves, Allison says, "It all fits right into my dream. Do you suppose we could wait a few days before taking the train?"

"Do you have a death wish?"

She shrugs. "If you gotta go, you might as well go in style. I'm going to check out the bathroom and see if they have any of those fancy French soaps and creams."

Nathan peers out of the window onto the wide expanse of the Place Vendôme and at the tall spiraling column in the center of the square, built by Napoleon eighty years earlier to commemorate his victory. Nathan imagines how lively this area must be in more commodious times, but tonight he sees only the hornets. Allison reenters the room. "I would put some of those soaps and shampoos into my suitcase, if we hadn't left it in the car."

Suddenly they hear a loud knock on the door. Nathan and Allison exchange nervous looks. Nathan reaches for his gun. The voice behind the door announces, "Service de chambre."

"Room service," Allison whispers quietly. "Did you order something?"

Nathan shakes his head. The loud knock is repeated. "Service de chambre."

"Ja, ja," Nathan says loudly. He motions for Allison to go back into the bathroom. "Lock the door!"

There is a third knock. Nathan opens the door a crack and sees that there is a man in a white jacket pushing a small cart. On the cart is a bottle of Champagne in a silver wine bucket, a dish of choc-olate bon-bons, and an envelope addressed to Hauptmann Froman. With his gun behind his back, Nathan steps aside and the door swings open. The porter places the bottle, the glasses, and the chocolates onto a coffee table and says, "Puis-je vous servir?" Nathan nods. The porter asks, "Un ou deux?" Nathan signals two. The porter opens the bottle with a pop and pours into two flutes. He reaches his hand out for a tip, bows slightly, and leaves the room.

Nathan waits for a few moments, and hearing nothing, walks to the bathroom door. "It's all right, Alli. You can come out. It really was room service."

Allison reenters the room. She is shaky, her eyes are red. She throws her arms around Nathan. "I thought I heard a shot. Then the door closed, and everything was silent."

"No, it wasn't a shot, it was a pop. It's all okay. It's all fine," he says, smoothing her hair. "I waited for a moment to make sure no one was listening at the door, but it really was room service. The pop was the Champagne."

She exhales. "I feel so stupid. But to tell the truth, I'm pretty damn scared, Nathan."

"I know. I am too, but by tomorrow night we'll be in Berlin."

"And that is supposed to calm me down? I'll feel calm when we're back in New York. Do you suppose the Champagne is safe to drink?"

"You never know," he says with a grin. "Only one way to find out." He hands her a flute of Champagne and picks up the envelope. She takes a sip. "Ooh, that is heavenly. It also fits nicely into my dream!"

"This is a note from Weber," Nathan says. "It reads, 'Prost! Have a wonderful night, my friends. I hope to see you again soon. Colonel Zeist would like Hauptmann Froman to join him for breakfast tomor-row at the Majestic. He will send a car for you at eight A.M.'"

"Are you going to accept the colonel's invitation for breakfast?"

"That was not an invitation, it was an order. And hell no! He smells something. He tried to trap me back at the bistro. I'm not going to give him another chance. We'll be out of here long before eight o'clock."

She nods her head and takes another sip. "Are you going to make me drink alone?"

Nathan smiles at her. "I love how you can change my mood." He picks up his flute. "As some *belle femme* once told me, when it's your time to go, you might as well go in style."

———————

Nathan opens his eyes. It is predawn and the clock on the bed stand tells him it is only 5:45. On the other side of the bed, Allison is sound asleep, breathing deeply; perhaps she is in her dream. Their clothes are folded on a chair. She lies on her side in her night clothes, her curves alluring. Nathan lets the moment linger. It all seems so comfortable, so natural, and his mind pictures them together under more congenial circumstances. But this is not the time or the place, and he knows it.

He taps her gently. She lifts her head. "Good morning," she whispers pleasantly. She waits a minute, bites her bottom lip, and asks, "What time is it?"

"A little before six," he answers. "I think we should be going."

She shakes the cobwebs from her head and smiles. "Listen soldier, any time you want to fly me to Paris, take me for a ride in a carriage, get me a room at the Ritz, and ply me with Champagne, I'm your girl."

"I'll keep that in mind. But now, we have to go. I don't want to be here when Colonel Zeist or Major Weber comes by. We're not far from where we left the car. If it's still there, we can drive to the train station."

Allison scrunches her face. "Ah, phooey."

21

CHEMINS DE FER DU NORD

The Peugeot is right where they left it the day before. Their belongings are still in the trunk. Nathan glances over at the apartment across the street, the so-called Paris safe house. The lights are off. The garage is now empty and perhaps the occupants are now gone, though Nathan has no desire to find out. He will stay clear. Still, the mystery remains. If he was given the keys to the house, who were the others inside? Who else had keys? And why did they block the garage? Maybe they blocked it as a signal? Those questions will have to remain unanswered, and they enter the car.

His map shows the route from the Paris apartment to the Gare du Nord, and they are quickly underway. The early morning traffic is light. They approach the massive train station from the south on the Rue de Maubeuge, and the gracious Renaissance-styled masterpiece comes into view: a stone and cast-iron building, constructed nearly a century before. The Chemins de Fer du Nord was Europe's busiest railway before the war. Now, in November 1943, Nathan suspects that train travel in Occupied Europe is restricted and generally used for military purposes. Nathan directs Allison to turn down a side street and find a parking slot. Having no further need, they leave the keys in the glove box.

Allison and Nathan approach the station, an immense structure with Romanesque columns all along the perimeter. Up above them, and in each of the twenty-three large, windowed arches, sits a statue of a female on a pedestal, each one representing a European city served by the station.

Inside, Nathan's previous suspicions are confirmed. Most of the pedestrian traffic is military, but there is still a substantial number of business travelers. Nathan checks his tickets and the departure board. Their train to Berlin is on Platform 9, but it is not scheduled to leave for two hours.

With the morning trains preparing to depart, the station is gradually becoming more crowded. The Berlin train will be boarding in half an hour. A coffee bar in the corner of the terminal is open, and Allison and Nathan wait there for their train to board. A man in a long brown overcoat wanders over. He stands at the bar but does not order a coffee. He leans against the bar, stares at Nathan through the corners of his eyes, and finally says, "Where are we traveling today, Hauptmann?"

While Nathan does not want to offend the man, he also does not wish to engage him in conversation. This is not likely to be an accidental encounter. "Just traveling," he says with a shrug.

"Ja? Where?"

Nathan shakes his head and takes a sip of his coffee. He turns away from the man, but the man casually circles around and says, "Where are you going today, Hauptmann?"

Nathan eyes the departure board. There are trains leaving for several destinations in the next two hours. "Actually, I prefer to mind my own business, sir, but if you really must know, I am going to Munich," Nathan says and turns around to talk to Allison.

The man pulls a badge from his inside pocket. It identifies him as Geheime Staatspolizei, otherwise known as Gestapo. "May I see your papers, please?"

Nathan puts on a look of annoyance and frustration. He curls his lips. "Is it now the practice of the Gestapo to confront decorated Wehrmacht captains? Do you have cause to question me?"

"I assure you, Hauptmann, it is entirely routine. For all I know, you might be impersonating a German officer. May I see your passport?"

With a huff, Nathan takes out his passport, holds it open for the man to see, and says, "Are you satisfied?"

"There is no need for anger, Hauptmann." He holds out his hand. "May I have the passport, please?"

Nathan shakes his head and puts the passport back into his pocket. "No! I will not surrender my passport to anyone but my commanding officer. Those are the regulations. Now if you will excuse us, please, we are having a cup of coffee before we leave for Munich. And our discussion is private."

"Perhaps you can tell me why you ignored Colonel Zeist's instructions to meet with him this morning."

"I know of no such instructions. You are mistaken."

"Arrangements were made for you to meet the colonel. You were notified by letter. A car was sent to pick you up."

"I did not receive a notification, or any communication from Colonel Zeist. I was with him last night and he didn't say anything about a meeting. Obviously, I could not meet with him this morning because I have business in Munich that demands my attention. Please convey my regrets to the colonel. Tell him I will meet with him the next time I am in Paris."

"My advice to you is to put your so-called business on hold and go directly to the Majestic Hotel where the colonel is waiting."

"Thank you for your advice, but I have my orders and I am going to Munich."

The Gestapo agent then turns his attention to Allison. "Darf ich bitte Ihre Dokumente sehen?"

Nathan quickly places himself between the Gestapo agent and Allison. "She doesn't speak German. She's with me. We are traveling together. There is no cause to question her."

"I will determine if there is cause. She is not covered by army regulations. I wish to see her papers, as I have a right to do."

Nathan turns to Allison. "*Le passeport, mon cher.*"

Allison hands her passport to Nathan who holds it open for the agent to view. He reaches for it, but Nathan pulls it away. "She's with me."

"You will hand her passport to me. Now!"

"Or what?" Nathan says. "Look around. Do you see all those men in the feldgrau uniforms? They are infantrymen under my command, and they will follow my orders. Unless you stop this intrusive questioning, I will order them to take you into custody, and they will obey my orders. Understand, policeman?"

The Gestapo agent's face turns red. He clenches his teeth. "I will note this, Hauptmann Froman. You will answer to me for this insolence and to Colonel Zeist for your disobedience."

"Yeah, I'm sure. Now go away."

The agent hurries across the room to talk to another man in a long brown coat.

"Come on," Nathan says to Allison, "let's go stand with those soldiers. I told him those are my men. I don't think he'll bother us over there."

"I didn't get it all, but I heard enough," Allison says quietly. "You just defied the Gestapo and probably the colonel. Nobody does that. I don't think either one of them is going to forget this. We might be looking at a lot of trouble."

Nathan shrugs. "As you say, if you're going to go, you might as well go in style."

Allison places her hand on her chest. "Nathan, you are going to give me a heart attack."

Nathan shakes his head. "No, Dietrich is going to give you a heart attack. Nathan is nice to you." They remain standing with the infantrymen, every once in a while exchanging small talk, while the two Gestapo agents on the opposite side of the hall keep a watchful distance. One leaves and Nathan suspects that he has gone to make a phone call.

He checks the departure board. The Berlin train is now boarding. He takes Allison's hand. "Let's go." He starts walking toward the platforms.

She hesitates. "The departure board says that the train to Berlin is on Platform Nine. We aren't walking in that direction."

"I know," he says. "I told the Gestapo agent that we were going to Munich. It's on track twelve. Let's walk that way first."

"I didn't understand much of your conversation back there, but I heard you say 'Munich' a number of times," she says. "Now I know why." They quickly make their way out of the hall under the sign that reads *LES QUAIS 10–14*. "So, the agent thinks you are going to Munich?"

Nathan nods. "I hope so. I wouldn't be surprised if there was a welcome party waiting for me at the Munich station."

As soon as they are out of the agents' sight, they quickly traverse to Platform 9 and board the Berlin train. Their seats are together in a first-class car. The trip is scheduled to leave in thirty minutes. Without further complications, they should arrive in Berlin in nine hours.

Other passengers are taking their seats. Most of them are uniformed. More than a few give Allison, who is still dressed in her evening outfit, a flirtatious eye. She is careful not to return the look or encourage the men further. She stares straight ahead.

Nathan is nervous and he keeps watch out of the window, checking to see that no one is coming for them. Departure time is approaching but it seems like the minute hand is stuck. Finally, the train jerks forward, blows a whistle and starts to slowly pull out of the station.

He leans over and whispers to Allison, "Those two Gestapo clowns aren't going to let me slide. They had orders from Zeist. If they boarded and searched the Munich train, then they know that I lied, and they will look elsewhere to arrest me. They may call ahead. We have a passport check at the border, and they might be waiting for me there. If we see them, or anyone approaches us, you need to walk away. They don't care about you; you're just some French girl I picked up."

"I'm not leaving you."

"Don't be foolish. If someone comes to confront me or to arrest me, you need to go in the other direction and fast. If we're close to Berlin, go to the safe house. Otherwise, go back to Paris. Fade into the background and try to make your way back to Cherbourg."

"What about Snyder? What about our assignment? I can't abandon my duties."

"Then make your way to Berlin, but don't hang on to me if you see anyone coming. If they come for me, you walk away. Understand? Deal?"

She nods.

22

BORDER CROSSING

Reims will be the first stop. Reims," the conductor announces as he enters the car. The train is a half hour out of Paris on its way toward Luxembourg and passport control for entry into Germany. The conductor proceeds through the car punching tickets. "Billet, s'il vous plaît," he says to Allison, who smiles, hands him her ticket, and says sweetly, "Merci, monsieur." He looks at Nathan with a glare of disapproval that Nathan interprets as *Why would this nice French woman be traveling with a soulless Nazi officer like you?* "Zugticket, bitte," he says gruffly, and Nathan hands him his ticket.

Two businessmen occupy the seats opposite Allison and Nathan. Their faces are generally in their newspapers, but every once in a while, one of them will lift his head and smile at Allison. Between the two of them, they speak in German of meetings with bankers, about financing a couple of office buildings outside of Strasbourg. Nathan follows the conversation. Under normal times, such a conversation between businessmen would seem rather commonplace. To Nathan, however, at this particular time and place, in the midst of a savage and brutal occupation, the German business conversation turns Nathan's stomach. While people's lives are being uprooted and tossed to the wolves, these men discuss ways to increase their fortunes.

Like most of the passengers on the morning train, Allison and

Nathan are quiet. If they were to speak, it could only be in Nathan's rudimentary French, certainly not in English, and whispering would attract attention. Two soldiers walking through the car stop to smile at Allison. "Guten Morgen, schönes Fräulein," one says. Allison averts her eyes. They shrug and keep walking.

A woman carrying a tray of cigarettes and candy makes her way through the car. The man across from Allison buys two packs of cigarettes. He complains to his comrade about the shortage of "gute Zigaretten," and makes a sour face as he lights up the cheaper brand.

The train pulls into Reims and several of the passengers depart, including the two men who sat facing Nathan and Allison. The seat remains empty as the train pulls away.

After receiving more flirtatious looks, Allison leans over and whispers, "I'm going to go change my clothes." She takes her suitcase and heads to the restroom. A few moments later she returns dressed much more conservatively: a dark blue suit with a white blouse, accented by a colorful scarf, knotted at the collar. Her hair is pulled back and held with a barrette. "I'm tired of having these lascivious men eyeball me like I'm a cheap pick-up," she whispers to Nathan.

Nathan smiles warmly. "You are an attractive woman traveling on a train with all men. You are a rose in a barren patch of grass. What can I say? But I think you look just as attractive in your suit."

"Remich, Luxembourg, will be the next stop," announces the conductor. "Remich, Moselle Valley, German border. All passengers are required to disembark for passport and customs control."

When the conductor has passed, Nathan whispers, "It's possible that the Gestapo has called ahead and alerted passport authorities to detain me. I want you to walk ahead of me. You look very professional, and no one will question your traveling alone." Allison nods. Now with Nathan's warning, she is faced with the realization that she might actually be on her own, making her way across Germany, unable to speak or understand the language. She has only a memorized address in a Berlin neighborhood.

The train pulls slowly into Remich. Passengers are loudly ordered to exit the train and stand in single file. Through the window, Nathan sees uniformed guards with rifles marshaling passengers into a line. One of them has a dog on a leash. There are tables set before a gate near the end of the platform. Behind the tables are two observers dressed in civilian clothes that Nathan concludes are Gestapo agents. Are they here for him? Each passenger presents his passport and ID for examination before moving through the gate to enter the station or reboard the train.

"Time to go," Nathan says to Allison. "Get into the line, I'll follow behind in a few minutes. If you see anybody approach me, keep going and don't look back. Get to the safe house."

Allison takes a deep breath, nods, and steps down out of the car. Nathan watches her weave her way into the line. There is a lump of anxiety in the pit of his stomach. He mouths a short prayer for her safety, waits a moment, and exits onto the platform. Allison is ten people in front of him. He wonders what he will do if she is detained. He is in full uniform, there is a gun on his belt, but such a move would be foolhardy and would likely prove fatal for both of them.

While standing in the back of the line, Nathan is suddenly bumped hard by a chubby woman with curly hair carrying a cup of coffee. Apparently, the woman was distracted, and she stumbled, splashing her coffee onto Nathan's uniform. "Oh, I beg your pardon, Hauptmann," the woman says frantically in German. "How clumsy of me. I am so very sorry. I have soiled your tunic."

"It's all right," Nathan says brushing the coffee off his jacket. "It was just an accident." The passengers standing near Nathan are pressing their lips together and suppressing smiles. One passenger offers a cloth. Nathan waves it away. "No, thank you," he says, "I will be fine. Don't worry."

But the woman who stumbled is beside herself with shame. "No, no," the woman says, "I am such a fool. It is all my fault. I must clean you up, I insist." The woman takes a handkerchief from her purse and begins wiping Nathan's lapel. She unclips Nathan's name plate and vigorously wipes the pocket area. "Really," Nathan says, keeping one eye on Allison, who is now several more people in front of him. "It's fine. It's all fine. Really." Others in the line step around Nathan and move forward.

The woman continues to rub Nathan's jacket, repeatedly apologizing. "I am so, so sorry," she says, wiping the pocket area. "I hope you will forgive me, Hauptmann."

"You're forgiven," Nathan says. "You. Are. Forgiven. Really. But I have to go now."

"Wait," the woman says. "I'm almost done. It's almost all off your jacket." She pulls Nathan out of the line. Nathan notices that Allison is now approaching the passport table.

"It's just coffee," Nathan says. "I'll be fine. But I have to go now."

"Very well," the woman says. "Please accept my apologies, Hauptmann Strauss." Nathan wrinkles his forehead. "What?" he says. "Yes, of course. Whatever." The woman hands Nathan his name plate, which now reads Strauss, not Froman.

"There," the woman says, pinning the name plate on and patting Nathan's chest. "You are as good as new. A brand new man. I don't think your pocket got wet, so your passport should be just fine. Please hurry along. Catch up with your group, Herr Hauptmann Strauss." The woman smiles. "One must always be prepared for unforeseen situations." She nods sharply and walks away.

Nathan places his hand in his pocket and pulls out a German passport. It has his picture on it, but the name is Richard Strauss. Same birthday. What a coincidence.

Allison is now being questioned by the passport and customs guard. She looks nervous. Something is wrong. She keeps shaking her head. Nathan tries to inch closer. He hears her say in French, "Je ne connais personne qui s'appelle Hauptmann Froman." I do not know anyone named Hauptmann Froman. Nathan hears her arguing, saying, "Non, non, non." He hears the name of Dietrich Froman again and sees Allison shrug her shoulders and throw her hands up in total perplexity. "Qui? Froman? Non. Non. Je ne le connais pas." She does not know such a person.

She does not look back. She does not look around. Her chin is out. Her posture is strong. Finally, the guard waves his hand in defeat and lets her pass. She is cleared. She proceeds through the gate and starts to reboard the train. As she reaches the top step, she looks around, sees Nathan and sternly shakes her head. Then she is gone.

Several minutes later, Nathan reaches the passport officer. He tenders his new identification. The passport officer eyes Nathan carefully, takes the passport, studies it, looks at Nathan, and breaks into a chuckle. He elbows the examiner next to him, shows him the passport and says, "Look, it's Till Eulenspiegel." The other examiner rolls his eyes upward in annoyance at the stupid joke. The first examiner giggles and says to Nathan, "Hey, Till Eulenspiegel, how are your merry pranks going today?" Nathan is unsure how to respond and he is ready to make a mad dash. He feels the gun in his belt. He will not be taken into custody without a fight.

One of the Gestapo observers standing behind the table says to his companion, "It looks like him. It's definitely him," and shouts, "Halt." Everyone freezes. He walks over to Nathan and says, "Hauptmann Froman, come with me!"

"Nein, nein," says the passport officer over his shoulder, "er ist Hauptmann *Strauss,* nicht Froman." The Gestapo agent checks a paper he is holding in his hand and affirmatively nods his head. "Ja, er ist Hauptmann *Froman.*"

The passport officer shakes his head and holds up the passport for the Gestapo agent to see. The agent grabs the passport, studies it, looks at Nathan, stares at the passport again, and then hands it back to the officer. The Gestapo agent then turns to his comrade, shakes his head and says, "Nein, er ist nicht Froman." The passport officer then returns the passport to Nathan and says with a smile, "Apologies, Till Eulenspiegel," and waves him through.

Nathan is dumbfounded by the whole scene. It must be some kind of an inside German joke, he thinks, but nothing seems very funny right now. The morning's events are spinning in his mind. *How did Groves pull off that switch?* he wonders as he steps up onto the train. *That was a pretty smooth operation. How did they even know I was in trouble, and how did they react so quickly?*

He makes his way back to his car but does not sit next to Allison, who is shocked to see him. There is an empty seat a few rows ahead and Nathan settles in. For all Nathan knows, they might do a final check and discover the ruse. Best to stay apart for the time being.

———————

Two hours out of Remich, a man comes through the car pushing a cart, offering sandwiches, snacks, and drinks. Nathan takes the opportunity to change his seat and return to Allison.

"They were looking for you, how did you get through?" she says.

Nathan points to his name plate. "Somehow, someone in our network learned that we were compromised again. The Gestapo must have put out an alert for Dietrich Froman. One of the agents had my description on a piece of paper."

"When I approached the table," Allison says, "one of the Gestapo agents rushed over and said that Froman was traveling with a young French woman and I fit the description. They started asking me who I was traveling with, if I knew a Hauptmann Froman, and if I was at a nightclub called the Curious Squirrel in Paris yesterday. I denied the whole thing. 'I don't go to nightclubs,' I said with the haughtiest attitude I could manage. Then they asked me what my business was in Berlin and where I was staying. I said I was meeting family in Berlin. I didn't want to give them the address of the safe house, so I said I didn't know where I was staying, that my family was going to meet me at the train station."

"Smart," Nathan says.

"They were going to detain me anyway until one of the agents said that the report described me as a young woman dressed like she's going out for the night. Thank God I changed my clothes. They didn't think I was the type, and they waved me through. But I thought you were a goner. I didn't know you had a new passport."

Nathan explained the circumstances of his new identity. "It was really well done. Pretty smooth. I didn't have a clue and neither did any of the people standing around me. The woman gave me new IDs and a new name plate and walked away. All on the sly, without missing a beat. She was a magician. Really, Academy Award stuff."

"I wonder who tipped off General Groves? Who could have known about the Curious Squirrel and the colonel?"

"Or maybe the confrontation with the Gestapo at the Gare du Nord? I have no idea."

"Well, thankfully you're safe, and I don't have to go on without you. I have to tell you, the thought of my going it alone was terrifying. I don't know a word of German and I don't know how I would have made it to the safe house."

"But you would have."

"Well, I would have tried. I'm not a quitter."

"One thing I did not understand," Nathan says. "The passport officer looked at me, my passport, my Richard Strauss ID, started laughing and calling me 'Till Youla-shpeegle.' He asked me about my merry pranks. I didn't know what the hell that was all about, but he let me through anyway."

Allison laughs. "*Till Eulenspiegel's Merry Pranks* is a musical tone poem for orchestra composed by Richard Strauss. You are a famous German opera composer, Herr Hauptmann Strauss! You also composed *Der Rosenkavalier,* which I saw last year at the San Francisco Opera."

"Oh, that's great. This is Groves's idea of a funny joke. I don't know anything about opera. Is Richard Strauss in the German army?"

"I doubt it," Allison replies with a chuckle. "He's at least eighty years old."

23

BEGINNINGS

F rankfurt am Main," the conductor loudly announces. "Change trains for the Munich, Hamburg, Mannheim, or Nuremberg lines. This train will proceed to Berlin."

"I know this station well," Nathan says to Allison. He tilts his head back, closes his eyes, and lets the memories flow in. "I was born here in Frankfurt and spent the first fifteen years of my life here. I remember those years as good times, Alli. As a family, we were happy here. My father had a good job teaching biophysics."

"Was that at the Kaiser Wilhelm Institute?"

"No, that came much later. It was here in Frankfurt that my father got his start in nuclear physics. He was working with Professor Dessauer, who had been a student of Wilhelm Roentgen."

Allison knows the name. "Of course," she says. "He pioneered the application of radiation to medicine. X-rays are otherwise known as Roentgen rays. That was the beginning of nuclear medicine. That's a prestigious posting. Your father was a professor at the Institute for Nuclear Medicine?"

"Yes, he was. A full professor. It was called the *Institut für Physika-lische Grundlagen der Medizin.*"

"Even if I could pronounce it, I wouldn't know it by that name, but I do know the reputation of the school. There were some extraordinary discoveries there. How come your father left that post and went to Berlin? Wasn't he happy at the Institute?"

Nathan shrugs. "I was young. He seemed happy to me. He was a good father, but he spent a lot of time at the Institute. I guess that's the life of a scientist."

"Boy, don't I know it."

"My father was well regarded."

"Well, if he was happy and well regarded, it's odd that he left. Why do you suppose that happened? Why did he go to Berlin?"

"I believe the answer is Günther Snyder. Günther came to Frankfurt as a young research assistant and worked in my father's department under his tutelage. I remember my father talking about him. He would say that young Günther has talent, he's brilliant and he's eager, but he's a mite careless. He cuts corners. He was unwilling to put the time in to study and analyze a problem. You must understand, my father was a brilliant scientist, a perfectionist, and working for him was a humbling experience. But Snyder would push to get the top assignments, and then come to my father and beg for help when he couldn't finish them.

"Günther was young and free-spirited, but he was also full of himself. I remember him as an arrogant and boastful fellow. He bragged about how important he was, but in truth, my father taught him everything he knew and was always there to bail Günther out of his failures. One day, Snyder learned that a position was opening up at the University of Berlin in the chemistry department where they were doing cutting-edge work with atoms and particles. Those were heady times in Berlin. It was during the Weimar Republic, what people referred to as the Weimar Culture—an explosion of creativity. Art, music, literature, science. I'm sure you've heard of the cabarets, the night scene in Berlin?" Allison nods. "Well, Günther loved the night life. That was before the Nazis came to power, of course, and decreed that the Weimar Culture was decadent.

"Other than the night scene, it was easy to see why Günther coveted a posting at the Institute in Berlin. They were doing extraordinary work at the Institute. Identifying neutrons. Bombarding atoms. Making artificial radiation. My father called it the 'headwater of nuclear science.' Günther asked my father for a recommendation to the Institute. He came to our house for dinner that night, all excited about the work being done in Berlin and what an appointment there would mean for his future."

"I know all about the scientists who were working at the University of Berlin in the 1930s," Allison says. "I've read many of their published papers. It was indeed groundbreaking, and Snyder was smart to seek that appointment."

"I didn't say that Snyder was stupid. He is smart. He sensed that Berlin was going to be the epicenter of nuclear science and he wanted to get in on the ground floor. That lab eventually evolved into the Kaiser Wilhelm Institute.

"My father cautioned him that the position might be a little beyond Günther's experience or scholastic development, which was a nice way of saying that Snyder wasn't yet qualified. But he begged my father for the recommendation, and my father was a softy; he was fond of Günther and he gave in. Because my father was highly regarded, and on the basis of his recommendation, Snyder got the appointment."

"I understand," Allison says, "but it doesn't explain why Josef Silverman and his family left Frankfurt. How did your father end up transferring to Berlin?"

"Snyder. My father was right when he indicated that Günther was underqualified, and it didn't take long for Günther to return to Frankfurt and seek my father's help. He had talked his way into a very difficult research project at the Institute and found himself tackling problems way over his head. Once again, he needed my father to bail him out, but my father couldn't do it from a long distance. He had to travel to the lab in Berlin to resolve the problem."

"What was the problem?"

"I have no idea, but whatever it was, it was important. Günther had weaseled his way into a top secret atomic project working closely with Otto Hahn."

Allison raises her eyebrows. "Hahn is credited with splitting the atom."

"Right. Apparently, Günther had made some boastful representations about his experience, and the program director Abraham Esau assigned him to a project that Günther was totally unqualified to do. After a few futile attempts, Snyder came to Frankfurt and begged my father to accompany him back to Berlin and save the day. I guess you can figure out the rest of the story."

Allison nods. "Your father went back to Berlin, solved the dilemma, and so impressed Esau that he was invited to join the team."

"And what a team it was," Nathan says. "At that time, it was the foremost collection of nuclear physicists in the world—Strassmann, Meitner, Heisenberg, Szilard, Frisch, Einstein. This was before the Nazis came to power. Einstein was in the U.S. when Hitler came to power in 1933 and he never returned to Germany. Meitner, Szilard, many others left Germany as well."

"I know each of their stories. It's textbook stuff."

"Esau offered my father a large increase in salary, though the money was secondary to him. My mother was initially against it. She was happy in Frankfurt. She had her social group, and she didn't know anyone in Berlin. But it was during the Depression, it was a lot of money and very prestigious. So, my mother supported it. We moved to Berlin, and Rachel and I enrolled in public school. That was before Hitler and his racial laws closed the doors to Jewish students."

"So, that is how your father and Günther Snyder ended up at KWI working with Germany's top scientists. Obviously, Snyder is still there, and maybe your father?"

Nathan shakes his head. "That's the mystery, and I intend to find the answer. He was still working at KWI when I left Germany five years ago. Throughout Germany, Jewish professionals had been stripped of their licenses and their positions, but Josef Silverman did not lose his position at the lab. I assume it was because he was so valuable. If he is still there, I want to bring him home with Snyder. If he's not, Günther may know what happened to him. I have to believe that as long as Günther Snyder had a job at the lab, he would need my father to bail him out when he hit a wall. He may have become my father's protector. If my father is still alive, then I have hope for my mother and my sister. I know it's a long shot."

Allison smiles sympathetically. She is not optimistic, but she doesn't want to dash Nathan's hopes. "I suppose it begs the question: if your father is still alive and working at the lab, then why wasn't he the one identified by our contact? Why isn't he the one we're trying to get out of the country, rather than Günther?"

Nathan shrugs. "Well, the most obvious answer is that my father is not there. If he was available and willing to defect, he would be much more valuable than Günther Snyder. He would know everything, and his information would be more accurate and reliable. But our contact in Berlin made the deal with Snyder to defect, not Josef Silverman, and maybe that means that my father is dead."

"It could be that Snyder was more anxious to leave and sought out the contact," Allison says. "You've described him as that sort of person. And I assume it was all done in secret."

"But there are other explanations," Nathan says quietly. "My father may have been transferred to another location, maybe another nuclear lab. I've thought about it for a long time." Nathan takes a deep breath and exhales slowly. "If he did survive by the strength of his talent and wisdom, he may be a critical piece of the Nazi atomic program, too valuable to banish, but not loyal enough to leave alone. He may be heavily guarded, a captive scientist." Nathan twists his lips and shakes his head. "Hell, anything is possible. Maybe he still lives in our home with my mother and my sister and goes to work every day like he did when I lived there. I know that's far-fetched, but I'm not giving up hope until I know for sure."

"And you shouldn't," Allison says. "Maybe he *is* too valuable for them to deport to some labor camp. They'd be foolish to do that."

The train drones on and Nathan stares out of the window as though the dark countryside might hold the answers to his questions. He turns around. "We're fooling ourselves, Alli. The most plausible explanation is that they are all dead. This is Nazi Germany in 1943. The fate of Jews is well known. The bastards."

24

HOMECOMING

It is evening when the train pulls into Anhalter Bahnhof railway station in central Berlin. Even before the train comes to a stop, many of the passengers are standing in the aisle with their luggage. Nathan and Allison sit and wait until the aisle clears before heading out. "How will we get to our apartment?" she whispers.

"The house is on Aller Straße in Charlottenburg," he answers. "Twenty-five oh two Aller Straße. I know where it is. We could even walk there, but it is a little far. There should be taxis outside the station. At least that's how it was five years ago."

Anhalter Bahnhof is busy. Though there are only five platforms, trains are pulling in and out every few minutes. As they head down the platform, it feels like they are swimming upstream. Passengers are rushing past them to catch the trains in the final stages of boarding. Well-dressed men and women are pushing ahead, lifting their bags and quickly stepping up into the cars. The locomotives are steaming. Bells are clanging.

As the entrance to the station nears, Nathan stops short. There is a line of men, women, and children. Yellow stars have been sewn into their clothing. They are being ushered ahead, tightly guarded by uniformed men with rifles. They are being herded and funneled into the last three passenger cars of a departing train.

Many in the line are carrying cloth sacks, or pillowcases, holding their belongings. Though they appear to be a line of refugees, many are well dressed. The men are wearing cloth coats and fedoras, the women are wearing scarves. Like most Americans, Nathan has read and heard the rumors of forced deportations from Germany to Polish death camps, but this is visual confirmation, and it sends chills through his bones. And anger through his veins. He hears one of them, a woman, ask a uniformed guard where they are going. Such a question from someone standing in line to board a train, when viewed under ordinary circumstances, would be incongruous. One ought to know where they are going before boarding a train. But Nathan is well aware that these are not ordinary circumstances.

The guard does not answer the woman. She is invisible to him. He just waves his hand for the line to move forward. Nathan turns and approaches the guard. "Pardon me, Private," he says authoritatively. The soldier snaps to attention and salutes Hauptmann Strauss. "That woman asked you where they were being taken and you ignored her."

The soldier gulped. "Yes, sir, but she is a Jew, they are all Jews, and we are not supposed to talk to them, other than to order them to get onto the train and follow orders."

"Well, where are they going?"

"I believe they are all being relocated to the Theresienstadt Camp in Czechoslovakia."

Nathan raises his eyebrows. "To Czechoslovakia? In a passenger train?"

"Yes, sir. The ones that are being sent to Poland usually leave from Lehrter Station and are loaded into boxcars. These here folks are lucky," he says, with a grin, "they get to sit in a passenger car. But don't worry, sir, they will only be kept in the last three cars. They're not allowed in the rest of the train. The three cars will be uncoupled and transferred to another train in Munich before proceeding to Czecho-slovakia." The guard shrugs. "I believe that's the plan, sir."

Nathan eyes the line of passengers, finds the woman who asked the question, and says to her, "You are all traveling to a relocation camp in Czechoslovakia. I'm sure you will be all right. The man was rude not to answer you. I apologize for him." The woman is shocked but pleased, and she smiles. "Danke," she says nervously.

Nathan continues his walk toward the station. Others in the deportation line look at him contemptuously and turn the other way. To them, he is just a detestable Nazi officer, another Jew-hating German helping to carry out the oppressive treatment they have come to expect from the Third Reich.

So this is how they are treating Jewish families in Nazi Germany, Nathan thinks. Line them up, file them into a passenger car or pack them into a boxcar. Get them out of sight, out of Germany altogether. His mother, his sister, even his father could very well be in this line, or a line just like it. Hell, he could have been in this line himself had he not left Berlin in 1938.

The line shuffles forward. They know only that one foot must be placed in front of the other. Beyond that, they have no idea where their journey will take them, or what they could possibly have done to warrant this ordeal. Cause and effect has no application here. He wonders if any of the people in the line come from his neighborhood. Would they know him? Would they recognize him and call out his name? Prudence tells him he should hide his face, but he cannot help but stare at these helpless people who are his brethren.

He exits the station with Allison and walks outside into the night. Though it is dark, many of the buildings familiar to Nathan come into view. He is standing on Stresemannstraße, a busy thoroughfare. He could turn right, walk three blocks, turn right again and walk seven blocks, and he would be at his boyhood home. He would open the door, the lights would be on, and every piece of furniture would be right where he remembers it. The entire house would smell of roasted chicken. His mother would be in the kitchen at the stove, stirring a pot, smiling at him. His sister would be at a table doing her homework. Everyone would be waiting for Father, who is working late again at the lab. There was always so much love in that house, he would feel it the moment he opened the door.

He stops outside the station entrance, tears fill his eyes, and his breathing deepens. Allison senses what is going through his mind, and she patiently stands beside him. She places her hand in the crook of his arm. He looks down and she smiles warmly. The honk of a horn brings him back to reality. What an odd homecoming, he thinks.

Suddenly a voice calls out, "Hauptmann. Hauptmann Strauss!"

Nathan spins around to see a solid muscular man walking quickly toward him through the crowd and waving. "Hauptmann, I have a car around the corner," he says in German. He reaches out toward Allison, bends over, and says, "Here, let me take your suitcase, Miss Dumont," which he lifts with ease. "I can take yours as well," he says to Nathan, reaching with his free hand. Nathan shakes his head. "I'm okay."

"My name is Kurt," he says. "Kurt Renzel."

"Nice to meet you, Kurt. How did you know where to find us?" Nathan asks.

"We knew you were on this train. As long as you didn't get off the train after Remich, we knew what time you would arrive."

Twenty-five oh two Aller Straße is a brown-brick two-story home in the Charlottenburg section of Berlin. Allison observes that there are many beautiful homes in the area, and she likens it to the suburbs of Chicago, perhaps Evanston. Kurt has the keys, opens the door, and turns on the lights. "Make yourself at home," he says in English. "There is no one staying here but you. I've been told there are some eggs, cheeses, and other snack foods in the refrigerator. There should be drinks as well."

"Snyder's not here?" Nathan asks. "Where is Snyder?"

Kurt shrugs. "At his home, I suppose. I think a meeting with Snyder has been discussed for November twenty-third, but I'm not sure."

"That's days away. Is there anything else scheduled? Have plans been made for our return? What arrangements are being made? Our trip here was a little rough."

"I'm sorry," Kurt says. "I'm not the guy in charge. That would be Fred Gluck; he's the station chief. You'll meet up with him later. I hear from Fred that the arrangements are hard to make." He chuckles. "There's a war going on, you know." No one laughs. "I'm sorry," Kurt says. "Bad joke. I believe the plan is for you to return when you are satisfied with your questioning of Dr. Snyder."

"So, you don't know the plans for our return?"

"Not me. I'm sure there are plans, I just don't know them. My role in this project is limited. You might say I am helping with logistics. I picked you up at the station. I helped to arrange the apartment in Paris."

"The apartment in Paris? That was you?"

Kurt winces. "I take it the apartment wasn't up to your liking?"

"Up to my liking? There were three people in the apartment when we arrived and the driveway was blocked."

"Really? The driveway was blocked?"

"Yes, with a black car."

"Hmm. That's what we do when we don't want you coming in. Something got fouled up. You may have been followed."

"We left and slept at the Ritz."

"Oh, much better choice. That's really a nice hotel."

Nathan shakes his head like he's clearing a cobweb. "Kurt, can we talk to Snyder before November twenty-third? We're wasting several days."

"I'm not sure, I think I've been told November twenty-third."

"I take it you are not Günther Snyder's personal contact?" Nathan says with some degree of exasperation,

"Oh, hell no. I have never met the man. In fact, I don't even know what Dr. Snyder looks like. I guess he's an old scientist. But he is very cautious, as you can appreciate. I should say he's nervous. He speaks only to his contacts. Some time ago, this contact sent a message to us that Snyder was unhappy and would do anything to get out of Germany. Snyder offered to cooperate with the Allies and provide a lot of information about the German chemical laboratories at KWI, if they would take him out of here. The contact then relayed that message to the Austrian resistance and they passed it along to the OSS."

"Kaplan Maier's outfit?"

"That's right."

Allison is surprised. "You know about the Austrian resistance and a person named Kaplan Maier?" she says to Nathan.

Nathan nods. "I do. Part of my training at Ritchie."

"Our OSS office, mainly Fred Gluck, sent the information on to Washington," Kurt says. "And now you two are here." He smiles broadly.

"Exactly what is the OSS?" Allison asks.

"Office of Strategic Services, ma'am. It's our military intelligence-gathering branch. We have a small presence here in Germany that we call Berlin Station." He puts his finger to his lips. "Clandestine, you know. But none of us are in direct contact with Snyder. Sorry."

"Listen, Kurt, I've been made. The Gestapo is looking for me. There is a nasty Nazi colonel looking for me. A hard-drinking Luftwaffe major is probably looking for me as well, or maybe he's looking for Allison. I don't want to waste any time. I need to talk to the man who is controlling Snyder. Who is this person? We came here to rescue a defecting scientist, Dr. Günther Snyder, but only on the condition that his information is as valuable as he says it is. That was the deal. I'm not about to drag him all over Europe unless he gives us the goods. Do you get it, Kurt?"

"Oh yeah, of course I do. I'll pass the word on that you are anxious to set up a meeting."

"Right. We came to get answers about Germany's nuclear progress. If he doesn't give it to us, we don't take him out. Now, who can I talk to? Who is the contact?"

Kurt hesitates. "Um . . . you need to talk to Fred Gluck. He's the station chief. I can't make those decisions."

"Who was it that contacted Gluck? Who is Snyder's personal contact?"

Kurt holds up his hands. "I'm not supposed to release that information. I told you, my participation is very limited. I decided to come to the train station and meet you myself because I thought you deserved that. When I heard what train you were taking, I didn't think it was right for you two to travel all the way across Europe to Berlin and then have to take a taxi to the Charlottenburg house."

"Well, we sure appreciate that, Kurt. Now who is the contact? I'm going to meet him sooner or later anyway. Right?"

Kurt tips his head this way and that and finally says, "I suppose you deserve that too. It's Father Hannover."

"A priest?"

Kurt nods. "A Catholic priest. I believe he is the only one who speaks with Dr. Snyder."

"All right. How do I get in touch with Father Hannover? I have to make sure that all of our topics will be covered—supply routes, storage depots, operation of the lab—when we meet with Snyder. Where and when can I talk to Father Hannover?"

"It would be at the church. I think everything is supposed to happen at the church. Meetings and all."

"I thought all the meetings were going to be here at the safe house. I don't like the idea of Miss Dumont and me walking around Berlin."

Once again, Kurt shrugs and spreads his hands. "I'm sorry. Father Hannover is a fairly rigid man. He kind of calls the shots in this matter. That is the protocol here. If he wants to meet with you, he'll meet at the church at the time of his choosing."

Nathan stands. His fists are clenched. "You know what? Maybe I'm tired, but I'm getting more and more impatient with how this is being set up. We put our lives on the line for this damn operation. Is there a telephone here?"

Kurt closes his eyes and lowers his head. "I knew I shouldn't have stuck my nose in this. I actually *volunteered* to pick you up at the station and bring you here. The original plan was for you to take a taxi. You were given this address. There was going to be a message left for you here explaining the, uh . . . the protocol. I waited two hours at the station because I wanted to meet the man who had the courage to make his way across war-torn Europe, and then sneak a highly placed fugitive out of Nazi Germany. You're a damn hero, whether you ever make it or not. I didn't think it was right that you didn't have someone to meet you. But Hauptmann Strauss, or whatever your real name is, I am not the guy in charge. I am not in operations. Logistics, remember? I'm just a heavy lifter. And no, there is no telephone at this house. And I don't have Hannover's number anyway."

"I'm sorry," Nathan says, with an expression that conveys his regret. He holds out his hand. "I really do apologize. It's been a rough trip. I appreciate what you've done and the position that you're in. So, I guess I'm just supposed to sit and wait for Hannover to arrange an appointment with Snyder and the two of us?"

Kurt grimaces. "I think so. Or maybe you could go see him at St. Hedwig's. That's where he works." He shrugs again. "Wish I had something better to say."

Nathan exhales and nods. The lay of the land has just been explained. "A moment ago, you said that the house was stocked with drinks. I don't suppose that any of those drinks contain alcohol?"

"God, I hope so. Let's go see."

25

A PRIESTLY CONTACT

Nathan opens his eyes, stretches, and takes a moment to catch his bearings. Where is he today? Eleven days ago, he was leading a squad at Camp Ritchie in a training exercise and sleeping in his barracks. Since then, he has slept in a roomette on the Twentieth Century Limited, in a posh bedroom at the Chicago Palmer House, in a chair on the Twentieth Century Limited returning to New York, in a bed at the Waldorf Astoria, in a house in some small French town whose name he can't remember, in a hotel outside the Palace of Versailles, and a night of wishful fantasies at the Paris Ritz. Now he is in a strange bedroom on the second floor of a home in a quiet neighborhood just west of the Tiergarten, Berlin's five-hundred-acre central park.

There is an aroma. Something is going on in the kitchen. After a quick shower, he makes his way downstairs where Allison is frying eggs. There are a half-dozen empty beer bottles in the kitchen waste can. "Good morning," she says. "How did you sleep?"

"Pretty well," he says, pouring himself a cup of tea. "And you, Alli, how did you sleep?"

She shakes her head. "Not so well. My mind was way too busy. I want to get our interviews over, find out whatever we can about Berlin's nuclear progress and supply routes, get the necessary information back to New York, make our way across this continent to the French coast, and return to my peaceful daily profession of making atom bombs in Chicago."

That comment draws a laugh. "Is that all? Were you trying to wrap your mind around all that last night? No wonder you couldn't sleep. Maybe you should have stayed up with Kurt and me and had a few beers. You might have slept better."

"I was tired," she sighs. "I didn't have trouble falling asleep, but I woke up every half hour. I couldn't get my brain to stop churning. When I did sleep, I had weird dreams. I saw Colonel Zeist's face and his finger pointing at you, and then the Gestapo agent at the Paris train station was ordering me to surrender my passport. I couldn't calm down. It was a long night."

"You should have awakened me. Maybe you just needed somebody to talk to, somebody to tell you that everything is going to be all right."

She smiles. "Maybe. Probably. Anyway, I'm making scrambled eggs; do you want some?"

"Absolutely. Thank you."

"What is our agenda for today?" she says. "Are we just supposed to sit and wait for the rigid Father Hannover?"

"Nope. I'm going to pay him a visit at his church. I know Berlin and I know the church. It's not far. I don't like the fact that we're cut off, adrift. We have no way of contacting Father Hannover or anyone else for that matter, all of which I find disturbing. What if there was an emergency?"

She sets a plate of eggs and toast on the table. "If there was an emergency, you would handle it, Nathan. I have faith in you."

Nathan smiles. Someone believes in him, maybe more than he believes in himself. They hear a jangle of keys in the front door. Nathan jumps up, grabs his pistol, and heads to the foyer. The door opens and two men are standing there in suits and ties. "Easy, Lieutenant," one of them says in English, "we're on the same team. My name is Fred Gluck and I think you already met Kurt. May we come in, or are you going to shoot us?"

Allison pokes her head out of the kitchen. Gluck motions for her to come forward. "Have a seat, Dr. Fisher," he says in a friendly tone.

"Welcome to Berlin. We appreciate the sacrifices you are making in carrying out this important mission. Kurt told us that the two of you have expressed some urgency in setting up your meeting with Dr. Snyder."

"That's right," she says. "Time is of the essence. When can we meet with him here at the safe house?"

"I wish it were as simple as that," he responds with a pained expression. "Dr. Snyder is watched closely, as are all of the top scientists at KWI. They are not given as much freedom as you would think. He doesn't really go anywhere other than the lab, his home, and his church."

"So, are you saying we have to meet with him at the church?"

"I'm afraid so. Father Hannover will tell us when we can meet. He'll make the arrangements. I think he was talking about the twenty-third."

The answer doesn't sit well with Nathan. "We were told that the meetings would be here at the safe house. That is what we prefer," he says. "I promised Dr. Fisher that she would be protected, that she would be able to stay at the safe house until it was time to return. Snyder is the one who is begging to be rescued, why are we letting him call the shots? I have to be frank with you, sir, I don't trust Günther Snyder."

"I understand," Gluck says, "and believe me, Dr. Fisher is far more valuable to us than Dr. Snyder, but having him come over here for a meeting at this house would be too dangerous and would put us all at risk. If Snyder was walking around the streets, going to a strange house, the Gestapo would find out. It's very difficult to do anything in secret here in Berlin, especially for a valuable asset like Snyder."

"How do we know we can trust Father Hannover?"

"You'll have to take my word on that. I've known him for a long time. He tells me that Snyder has been a regular at St. Hedwig's for years. Several times a week. Then suddenly, his visits became less frequent. One day, Father Hannover asks him if everything is all right. Snyder breaks down. He tells Hannover that he is under enormous pressure at the lab. He's at the end of his wits, he can't take it much longer. Apparently, the military is making unreasonable demands. His work is being unfairly scrutinized by members of the administration. Even criticized! Science doesn't work like that, he tells them. You can't solve complicated equations just because Hitler says so. You can imagine their response; they did not like that answer. Snyder is now frightened to death. At one of his confessions, Snyder told Father Hannover that he would do anything to get the heck out of Germany." Gluck spread his hands. "We've worked with Hannover before. We'll ask if we can move up the date."

"So, Father Hannover will let us know when we can meet with Snyder? What are we to do in the meantime?"

Gluck looks at Renzel and shrugs. "Lay low. Read a book. I wouldn't advise going outside if you can avoid it. If you must, this is a quiet neighborhood and you are only a few blocks from the Tiergarten. Take a short walk, but remember, walking around in your uniform, you could be questioned. Why aren't you at the front? Where is your unit? You never know how well your identity will hold up. Obviously, on those days when you meet with Günther Snyder, you'll have to go to the church, but we'll try to have a car for you."

"I don't like being out of touch," Nathan says. "What if we need to contact you? What if there is an emergency? What if one of us becomes ill, or we think we are being watched? How do we get through to you? And how will you give us notice that a meeting with Snyder has been scheduled?"

Gluck hands a red envelope to Nathan. "There is a mailbox beside the front door. If there is an emergency, stick this envelope into the slot on the front. We'll see it."

"What about a shortwave radio?"

"Out of the question. The Germans monitor frequencies. Look, you'll have to do this our way. It's the safest for everyone concerned. We've done it before, many times. If we have a message for you, if Father Hannover gives us a date, we'll put a note in your mailbox." Gluck stands up to leave. "Just hang in there. We'll get it all done as quickly as possible and get you home."

The door closes and Allison is clearly disappointed. "This delay, this uncertainty, I didn't see this coming, Nathan. I was counting on an efficient operation. I expected Snyder to be here waiting for us. We'd interview him, get our information, and start our journey back."

"An efficient operation? You haven't been with the Army long, have you? Do you remember the term SNAFU? In General Groves's language, the polite term is 'flexibility.'"

Allison sighs. "So, we're supposed to read a book? Well, I don't see any English books around here and I forgot to bring one. Did you bring a book? *War and Peace*, maybe?"

Nathan smiles. "Take it easy. I did see a chess set and a deck of cards. There is a bottle of wine in the kitchen. We'll just have to make the best of it."

Nathan lies in his bed. It is the middle of the night, and his eyes are wide open. The uncertainties and insecurities of the operation are keeping him awake. He should have anticipated that the Nazis would be keeping close track of their top scientists, and that contacts with Snyder would have to be clandestine. It was naive to think that he would just walk into this house, interview Snyder, and be on his way. He knew that Snyder had a contact, but a priest? Secret meetings in a public church? Any number of things can go wrong.

Charlottenburg, a pretty neighborhood he has known for most of his life. He had friends that lived a few blocks away. Are they still here? He thinks about his family. His apartment is not too far away. Who lives there now? He doesn't hold out much hope for his mother, his father, or his sister, but he has to know for sure. Maybe tomorrow he will take a walk.

He thinks about Allison sleeping in the other bedroom. Did she bite off more than she could chew? Did she know what she was signing up for? It doesn't seem fair. He's a soldier, he's been trained to survive in enemy territory. He is mentally prepared. She is not military; she's a professor. How is she handling these uncertainties? She has confessed to him on a number of occasions that she is frightened, yet she doesn't back away. Is she able to sleep, or is she lying awake as well?

26

A WALK IN THE PARK

There is a white envelope in the mailbox. The note inside reads, *Your dental appointment is confirmed for Friday at 5:00 P.M.*

"That's tomorrow," Nathan says to Allison. She is standing at the stove, cooking breakfast. She turns and with a coy smile, says, "I hope that doesn't mean that getting information from Dr. Snyder will be like pulling teeth."

"Good one," Nathan says. "At least one of us still has a sense of humor. I'm glad we're moving forward. All I can say is 'Finally.' It's been a long two miserable days locked away in a safe house without a word."

Allison brings a plate of pancakes to the table. Nathan looks up into her face. It is kind and thoughtful. "Was it really all that miserable?" she says.

"That didn't exactly come out right. Let me try again. If it was my fate to be locked away in a safe house in Nazi Berlin in the middle of a war without knowing where or how or when we would get out of here, I'd say I was lucky to have you here," he says.

With the breakfast dishes cleaned and put away, Nathan announces, "I'm going to be out for a while today, Alli. Maybe a few hours."

"Can I ask where you are going?"

"I'm going to walk to my old neighborhood, to my home. Or what used to be my home. It's a starting point."

"Mr. Gluck said it wouldn't be safe for you to walk around. You could be stopped, and your identity could be challenged."

"I know."

"But you're going to go anyway?"

"I have to."

Allison grabs her coat. "Then I'm going with you."

Nathan shakes his head. "No, you're not. If I'm stopped, if I'm arrested, you can finish the mission without me. You are capable of interrogating Snyder, getting the necessary information and the map coordinates, finding out what Groves needs to know, and you and Gluck can send coded messages back to him. Gluck will get you home."

That answer doesn't work for Allison. She sets her jaw, and with a determined tone says, "*You* are going to take me home, not Fred Gluck. That was the deal! We will interview Snyder *together* and go back just as we planned. *Together*. With or without Snyder. And I'm not really comfortable sitting in this house alone. Besides, you swore to protect me."

"I have to find out about my family."

"Then we'll do that together. We are a team."

Nathan nods. "All right, we'll go together. We are definitely disobeying orders, but we will go together."

Allison shrugs. "Court-martial me."

That brings a smile to his face. "Wear your suit; people dress up in Berlin."

Other than the quick ride from the train station on the night they arrived, Allison has only seen Berlin in the Movietone newsreels. In her mind, the city was crudely painted in black and white. It was loud and unfriendly. A place where Hitler wildly waved his arms and shouted from a balcony. She expected to see hundreds of goose-stepping soldiers and lines of tanks proceeding down the Unter den

Linden passing crowds of people with stiff arms shouting, "Seig heil!" But on this November day, it is cloudy and quiet. Other people are out for their morning walk, though most of them seem to have a purpose. Perhaps they are businessmen. Perhaps they are shopping. As Nathan had predicted, they are nicely dressed.

"My parents' home is on a little street near Oranienburger Straße. They live close to the New Synagogue," Nathan says as they approach the west entrance to the Tiergarten.

To Allison's right there are lines of schoolchildren standing with their teachers at a gated entrance. The girls are all wearing red plaid skirts; the boys are in white shirts. "That's the Berlin Zoo," Nathan says. "They are all waiting for the zoo to open. I remember doing the exact same thing when I was a kid." Allison smiles at them. Everything seems so normal as they enter the park.

Once a royal hunting ground, the Tiergarten is hundreds of acres of woods, streams, meadows, and winding walkways. There is a peaceful pond with swans and ducks that Allison stops to admire. A young couple sits on a blanket with a wicker basket of food. A woman stands before an easel, skillfully capturing the cove in watercolors. Not knowing the German expression for "how lovely," Allison nods and says, "Mm hmm." The woman has a kind face. "Danke," she replies.

A few steps farther and they come upon a statue and an old woman tossing corn to pigeons. Allison stops. She takes a moment to sort out her thoughts. The incongruity of it all strikes her. She is an enemy combatant, sent to Germany to smuggle out a top scientist, to discover supply routes and coordinates to pass along to U.S. bombers, and to learn information to prevent Germany from achieving atomic superiority. The couple on the lawn, the artist, the old woman, the children at the zoo, and the ducks and swans seem to take no notice of what is going on in the world outside the Tiergarten. She looks to the side, where Nathan is lost in his thoughts.

He stands by the statue. There are tears in his eyes. He sees things from years ago. People he knew, people he loved. It was a place to walk hand in hand. His little hand wrapped in the big comforting hand of his father, who made a promise to always be there for him. His teenage hand finger-laced with Lena's, their arms swinging back and forth as they walked briskly on a summer day. The Tiergarten held those memories and played them back for him. Those were better days.

They exit the park on the east end and walk through one of the five passageways of the Brandenburg Gate. Its twelve columns call to mind the Acropolis. Atop the gate sits the quadriga—a chariot pulled by four horses, the symbol of triumph and victory. Allison has seen this structure in numerous newsreels but always in connection with a frightening military show of force, and it sends chills up her spine.

"I know what you're thinking," Nathan says. "What am I doing here walking in the footsteps of Nazi conquerors and murderers?"

"That's a fair description," she says. "I've seen this gate in the movies, and it's always a backdrop to every Nazi propaganda film— marching Nazi soldiers carrying banners and weapons, while some announcer talks about Hitler and his insane ambitions. I don't belong in this picture."

"We don't have much farther to walk. My home is six or seven blocks away on the other side of the river."

Nathan stands outside a three-story brown-brick building. It looks empty. They climb the steps to the second floor and the door is unlocked. But for a few odd pieces of furniture, the apartment is bare. A brass candlestick lies in the corner, and a scarf lies on the floor in one of the smaller bedrooms. There is a layer of dust throughout. He reaches into the back of a kitchen cabinet, withdraws his hand and shakes his head. "I was looking for my kiddush cup," he says. "That's where my mother kept it."

Allison stands to the side and gives Nathan his space as he goes from room to room. He sees things from long ago. They are still here; his mother is in the kitchen, his sister in her room with a girlfriend, his father is wrestling with a crossword puzzle and rattling the paper when a word escapes him. "What is an eight-letter word for *vorgeben*?"

There are tears in his eyes, and he leans against a wall. Allison comes over and offers her hand. There are no appropriate words. He squeezes her hand. "This is my home, Alli," he says. "Was my home. All gone." His words get caught in his throat. "What gives them the right, the Nazis? This was my family. Good people."

"That doesn't mean they're dead," she says softly. "They could have just decided to move."

Nathan points to a small, decorative silver cylinder attached to the doorpost. "My mother would not have moved and left her mezuzahs behind." He points to the bedroom doors also. "She would have taken them."

"Maybe they were forced to move quickly. Maybe they weren't given much time. It doesn't mean that they are dead," she says. "Let's keep our hopes up."

Nathan nods. "Thank you," he says. "You could be right." Though he doesn't believe it.

Stepping back out on to the street, Nathan spies a boy about to enter the adjoining building. "Excuse me," he says in German. The young man stops quickly. He has been addressed by a German officer. "Yes, sir," he says.

"Do you live in this area?"

"Right here, sir. For eleven years. My whole life."

"Do you know what has happened to the people who used to live in this building?" Nathan says.

"Why, they're gone, of course. The trucks have been through here. Months ago. You know, *Judenfrei*. The people in this building were Jews. They were taken away. Maybe you have been out of the city for too long, Hauptmann."

"Where did trucks take them?"

The young man shrugs. "They don't say. They took most of them a year ago. The people on the second floor, the Silvermans, they stayed longer. I knew them. They were nice, but they were Jews."

"Were you friends with the Silvermans?"

"Why would I be a friend of a Jew?" he says defensively.

"I'm not trying to trap you. I just wonder what happened to this particular family. I have my reasons. Official reasons."

"I only knew the daughter. Rachel. I would see her on the street. She was older, but she was nice to me. Sometimes we would talk. I would see her mother hanging laundry in the back. She was nice too, but they were Jews and as you know, Obersturmbannführer Eichmann ordered all Berlin Jews to be relocated. The Silvermans were among the last to go. They left last spring."

"What about the father?"

The young man shakes his head. "I haven't seen him in a long time."

"I heard he spent a lot of time at the New Synagogue. Do you think he might be there?"

The young man looks at Nathan sympathetically, as though Nathan's injuries may have affected him cognitively. "The New Synagogue is a storage depot, sir. You must have been away a very long time."

"Yes, that's true. All these Jews, do you know where any of them were taken?"

"No. You already asked me that. I'm sure you can get that information from the Reichstag. You're a decorated Hauptmann, for gosh sakes. They'll give you any information you want. But you know the rumors."

"What rumors?"

"About the camps for the Jews. No one comes home."

"Yeah, I guess so." Nathan turns to leave but stops and says, "One more thing; none of them were shot, were they?"

"Here, you mean? At this building? On this street? No, sir, not that I saw. When the trucks came, they left the building with a suitcase or a pillowcase full of stuff. I mean they really didn't have a choice. The soldiers had guns and those mean dogs. The Jews did what they were told and got into the trucks. Who wouldn't? I might be able to get you a little more information about the Silvermans, though. I can ask around."

Nathan smiles. "Thank you. I'd appreciate it. You know, son, they weren't all bad, like the papers say. Many Jews were fine people. Good citizens. Like you and me."

The young man shrugs. The war must have affected this poor

Hauptmann's mind. "I'll ask around; see if anyone knows about the Silvermans. How would I tell you, sir?"

"I'll be around. I'll look for you."

I'm sorry," Allison says as they turn to walk back to Charlottenburg. "I know you had hopes."

Nathan nods, but says, "Not really." He takes one last look at his apartment building and starts to walk away when a voice calls out, "Nathan? Nathan, is that you?"

27

CHANCE ENCOUNTER

Nathan spins around to see who is calling his name, although he knows without looking. A young woman strides quickly forward. Her blond hair is pulled back and to the side, held in place with a tortoiseshell clip. He feels that old pang in the pit of his stomach. She is biting her bottom lip as she catches up. "It *is* you!" she exclaims. "It really is *you*! What are you doing in Berlin, Nathan? Of all places?"

He reaches out and gives her a warm hug. Her body feels so familiar, just as he remembers it. For just that moment, it is ten years ago. "Hi Lena," he says with a catch in his voice. "You're looking great."

"So are you." She pats his chest. "Looking so handsome. But what in the hell are you doing walking around Berlin in a Wehrmacht captain's uniform? A Jew in a Wehrmacht uniform? Do you have a death wish? What in the world is going on?"

"I'm searching for my family. Do you know anything about my parents? About Rachel?"

She grimaces. "A little. You know I stayed in touch with your mother and your sister for a long time after it became socially frowned upon." She looks around uncomfortably. Oranienburger Straße, normally a busy boulevard with many pedestrians, seems extra busy today. "Why don't we get a cup of coffee? I can tell you what I know." She starts forward and then realizes that Nathan is not alone. He is with a woman. She extends her arm. "My name is Lena Hartz," she says politely with a smile. "I'm an old friend of Nathan's, though I haven't seen him in many years."

"Her name is Alicia Dumont," Nathan says. "She's French; she doesn't speak German."

Lena's expression changes. Her forehead wrinkles. Nathan has always been able to read Lena's expressions; they clearly convey her state of mind. Nathan has seen this look before. She is not buying the explanation. "You brought a French woman with you into Germany to help you find your parents? A woman who doesn't speak German?"

Nathan nods. "I guess that's right."

Lena shakes her head. "I know you better than that, Nathan. What else is going on?"

They reach a small café on a side street just off the boulevard and take a corner table. As coffee is being served, Lena smiles. "Nathan Silverman! Who would believe it?" She speaks quietly, though no one is in earshot. "I can't get over it—seeing you here after all these years." Her head tips to the side; Nathan recognizes it as Lena's expression of regret. "May I tell you something, Nathan? I've always been really sorry about the way things ended between us. I've wanted to say that to you for years. I never meant to hurt your feelings. You didn't deserve that. I know it seemed cold and uncaring, walking away like that, but you have to look at it from my perspective. I was young too, and I was getting so much pressure from my father and our friends. I felt like I was becoming an outcast." Now Nathan's feelings of fondness are giving way to his old feelings of resentment. Lena continues, "I mean really, how realistic was it for us to be planning a future at that time? We both knew it wasn't to be. But please understand that my feelings for you were always real."

Nathan casually nods again. "Thank you, Lena. What do you know about my mother and father? And Rachel?"

Lena purses her lips. "Well, they were Jews in Germany. I know that sounds blunt, but I don't know any other way of saying it. Jews were declared to be enemies of the state, you know that. Of course, *I've* never felt that way, but that's Germany." She takes a sip of coffee and shakes her head. "The last I heard, you were safe in America. Your mother told me that. Now, here you are, running around Berlin, dressed in a Wehrmacht Hauptmann's uniform, pretending to be someone named Strauss, with your French girlfriend, searching for your Jewish family. Excuse me, but that is so bizarre. Do you have any idea what will happen to you if you are caught?"

"I don't intend to be caught."

"You would be killed, Nathan, especially wearing that uniform. Where did you even get it?"

Nathan waves off the question. "What can you tell me about my family? Please, Lena, I'd like to know."

Lena looks first at Nathan and then at Allison. Her facial expressions are changing, her left eye is squinting. Nathan knows what that look means as well. She's suspicious. She's figuring things out. She was always smart and perceptive. That was one of the things he loved most about her. "When did you learn to speak French, Nathan? You never knew it when you lived in Berlin."

"I still don't. Alicia also speaks English."

"Then we should speak in English," Lena says, changing over to English. "It's rude to carry on a conversation that Miss Dumont doesn't understand."

"Thank you," Allison says. Lena smiles and nods.

There is silence for a moment, coffee is sipped, and then Lena lays down her napkin and says, "I feel like you two didn't come all this way just to look for your parents. There is something else going on, isn't there?" Lena gestures toward Allison. "Mademoiselle Dumont, if indeed she is a French woman, isn't really your girlfriend, is she? And I bet she speaks German just fine, don't you, honey?"

"No," Allison says quietly with an uncomfortable look on her face.

Lena shakes her head. "Whatever you two are up to, Nathan, I can't let you get me involved."

"First of all," Nathan says sharply, "Alicia does *not* speak German. She's smart, like you, Lena, and she can pick out some of the German words and interpret your body language. In that way, she can follow a little. And I'd appreciate it if you didn't call her 'honey.' Secondly, I didn't come looking to get you involved, you ran after me. Finally, whatever I am doing here in Berlin does not and will not involve you. But in fact,

I *am* looking for my family. You stopped me three blocks from my home."

That retort seemed to have its desired effect. "I'm sorry," Lena says quietly, "but give me a little leeway. You must admit, it's a shock to see you after all these years. And then, here you are, walking around Berlin in a Wehrmacht uniform with another woman. You couldn't have shocked me any more if you planned it. You knocked me back on my heels, Nathan. Seriously, whatever you're doing here, it's a mistake. You must have lost your mind."

"You're probably right. I'm sorry for the shock. Can I ask you to keep all this in total confidence? You didn't see me. I didn't see you. We're better off that way."

"Of course."

"Please, tell me what you know about my family."

"I'm afraid I don't have specific knowledge about what happened to your family. After we separated, I continued to see them from time to time. I always had a soft spot in my heart for your mother and Rachel. Even after you left the country. But every day it became harder and harder for me to socialize. The talk about the so-called Jewish question seemed to be on everyone's lips everywhere I went. There were all these terrible articles in the papers about Jews, their corrupt business practices, and the crimes they were committing. I know it was probably mostly propaganda, but things continued to get worse for Jewish people. Then, all of a sudden, there were these roundups. Mass arrests. Trucks came sweeping through the neighborhoods and taking the Jews—I mean the Jewish families. That started over a year ago."

"And my family?"

"Even throughout 1941, I would still see Rachel from time to time. She and your mother were still living here. It was odd because the other Jews in the area were gone. They were practically the last Jewish family left on the block. Personally, I think it was because your father was working at the lab. But then, he was never around when I came to visit. No matter what you think of me, I always loved your family and I made it a point to stay in contact with Rachel."

"What happened to my mother and sister in 1942?"

Lena shrugs. "I didn't see it, but I assume they were taken in a truck. They came for everyone. Every last Jew, that is."

"What about my father?"

"Like I said, for all I know, he could still be at the lab. Do you remember Franz Hagen from high school? He is an intern at KWI. He might know something about your father. I could reach out to him."

"That would be great, but be careful what you say."

"I know, Nathan, I'm not stupid. And it isn't like I don't care. I want you to know that before they left, I offered to hide Rachel in my apartment, but . . . in the end, I couldn't make it happen. It wouldn't have worked anyway. You know my family. My friends. The guy I'm dating now *never* would have stood for it. It wouldn't have been the right decision for Rachel either."

"Did you see the trucks take them, Lena?"

Lena slowly shakes her head. "First of all, I honestly don't know if they were arrested, I just assumed. I can try to find out and let you know." She points to a red-brick building. "I have an apartment over there at fourteen thirty Oranienburger. Where are you staying?"

Before he can answer, Allison digs her nails into Nathan's arm. Lena notices and opens her mouth in surprise. "Well, it appears that your French girlfriend doesn't want you to answer, do you, sweetie?" Lena says.

"She is a cautious woman, afraid of strangers. I'm sure you can figure that out."

"Okay, then that's the way it is. I understand perfectly." Lena folds her napkin and rises from her chair.

"Wait," Nathan says. "Don't be offended. We have something to do here in Berlin and it's private. If you can find out something, anything about my family, please, you have to tell me. We're staying in a house in Charlottenburg."

"Oh, fancy you. Classy neighborhood. Nathan and his girlfriend in a house in Charlottenburg. Well, what's the address?"

Allison grabs Nathan's arm. There is panic in her expression. She narrows her eyes and sharply shakes her head. "Don't do it, Nathan," she says. "You can't give out that address."

Lena's lips form a circle. "It sounds to me like your French girlfriend is really an American girlfriend. Or is she an American spy? Would that be right?" She flutters her eyebrows.

Allison looks at her without answering.

Lena turns back to Nathan. "I am sitting in this café as innocent as I can be, thinking I'm with my old boyfriend, but in reality, I'm having coffee with two spies. Why would you place me in such a position? Is this how you treat old friends?" Turning her attention to Allison, she says, "Well, don't worry, honey, I'm not going to turn you over to the Gestapo. No matter what Nathan told you about me, I am not a rat, and I am not an informant."

"I never told her anything about you, Lena, other than we had a serious relationship when we were young. At least I thought it was."

Lena stands, puts her purse on her shoulder, and pushes her chair back to the table. "I'll reach out to the sources I know. Discreetly. If I hear anything, I'll pass it along. How am I supposed to contact you?"

"Thanks, Lena. Really. I appreciate it very much. If you can find out anything about my family, please leave a note in my mailbox. We are staying at twenty-five oh two Aller Straße."

Allison closes her eyes. The wine has been spilt.

For several blocks, the return through the Tiergarten is quiet. Both of them know the reason why. Finally, Allison breaks the silence. "Why? Why did you give her the address of the OSS safe house? Why in the world would you do that?"

"I know on its face it seems risky, but I know Lena. Once we had feelings for each other. I'm sure she still does. She won't turn me in. Besides, how else would I get the information?"

Allison shakes her head. "Sometimes men are so damn empty-headed. I watched her expressions, the way she carried on the conversation. I know women. I didn't understand all of the German words, but they weren't necessary. I could see right through her. She is all about Lena Hartz and nothing else. She will do whatever profits her."

"I think that's unfair. I think she'll reach out and try to find out something about my father, maybe through her contact at KWI. She's not a threat. She may not love me anymore, maybe she never did, but she still cares about me and my family. She certainly did years ago and all of that could not have been fake. I would bet my life on the fact that she will not betray us."

"Well, in fact, you just did. In 1933, she made a choice and broke up with you. She may not be a Nazi, but she is a woman. And a German woman. She's living in a nice neighborhood; her father is an industrialist and Germany is her home country. She's comfortable here, and you are an enemy who threatens her way of life."

"I don't know if that's all true. I don't know how comfortable she is."

"Oh, come on, Nathan. Did you see her clothes? Beautiful knit suit. Gorgeous shoes. Matching purse. She's living the good life here in Berlin. She doesn't need Roosevelt and Churchill messing it up. Her Führer is doing just fine for her."

"She's not that shallow. She has ethics."

"Ethics? When the conversation centered around Jews and the Jewish question, she shrugged her shoulders. When she broke up with you, I'll bet she said she wasn't against the Jews, but she lives in Germany, so what could she do? Am I right? Did she say that? And when the racial persecution intensified, she looked the other way. Am I right?"

Nathan nods his head in resignation. "Something like that."

"Right. That's what they call the sin of silence, Nathan."

The walk is quiet again. They pass by the pond where the swans and ducks are swimming. A boy is fishing. There is thunder in the distance and the sky is getting dark. A light rain begins to fall. "We better get home," Allison says.

"I'm sorry you disapprove of what I did," Nathan says. "Tomorrow night we will meet with Snyder at the church. He'll give us everything we need, and we'll begin our journey home. With any luck, before we leave, Lena will leave me a message and I'll have some peace of mind. If she drops it off later, Fred Gluck can forward the message to me. It will all be okay; don't worry."

"I hope you're right."

28

THE SKY IS FALLING

On that afternoon, November 18, 1943, about the same time that Allison and Nathan were returning to the Charlottenburg safe house following their encounter with Lena Hartz, Britain's RAF Bomber Command received its orders to commence what would come to be known as the First Battle of Berlin. While Allison and Nathan were navigating the winding paths and gardens of the Tiergarten, 440 Avro Lancaster heavy bombers, fully loaded, were taking off from southern England and making their way across northern Germany toward Berlin. The rain was steady, the clouds were thick, and Allison commented that it was a "foggy day in Berlin town."

At eight o'clock, Allison and Nathan finally sit down to dinner. As Allison pours a glass of wine, the first air raid siren pierces the night. Allison's arm reflexively jerks upward, splashing her wine. "What the hell is that?" she says. The answer comes swiftly as a thunderous explosion sounds. The room shakes, the floor trembles. "We're being attacked," Nathan says. "I mean, *Berlin* is being attacked." He runs to the window and pulls back the shades. "I can't see anything, Alli, I'm going outside."

"Don't do that," she says with a touch of hysteria in her voice. "They're dropping bombs!"

Nathan steps onto the front stoop. Though the night is dark, and the clouds are low, flashes of light are visible on the horizon. He can hear the roar of the bombers and the rat-a-tat of the anti-aircraft guns. Another explosion shakes the ground. As far as Nathan can tell, he is standing at ground zero. Another bomb detonates a quarter mile to his left and a house explodes in a flash of fire. Debris is scattered everywhere. People dash in different directions, searching for shelter.

Allison stands behind Nathan and peers out into the neighborhood. She is awestruck, terrified. Suddenly she shrieks, "Oh, my lord," and points across the street. A young giraffe, dazed, confused, and disoriented, stumbles across a neighbor's lawn. It stops and looks around. An explosion sounds and it lopes away. Through the smoke, another animal appears, possibly a deer.

"The zoo," Nathan says. "Bombs must have hit the Berlin Zoo."

Nathan takes Allison's arm and quickly reenters the safe house. Lamps teeter on the tables. Dishes and windows are rattling. Another explosion, and then three more. Some are distant, others frighteningly close. The two hurry into the basement.

For a solid two hours, bombs continue to pound Berlin. The house shakes, the sirens scream, and dust, dirt, and insulation fall from the basement rafters. "Is this it?" Allison asks. "Is the Allied invasion on?"

Nathan shrugs. "They didn't consult me."

"Are we sitting in the crosshairs?"

"Sure seems like it."

At ten o'clock the explosions stop. The sounds of the huge Lancaster motors and the buzz of small Mosquito fighters fade away. Soon the "all clear" is sounded. The house is quiet again. Nathan and Allison carefully climb the stairs to see what remains of their safe house and the Charlottenburg neighborhood. The electricity is off, but the house is intact. The streetlamps are dark. There are people in the streets, dazed and walking aimlessly around, searching for reason. Smoke billows up from several locations.

The church on the corner has been hit and its interior splays open as though it were a dollhouse. Only the pulpit stands alone, ready for morning prayers. Rubble lies in bundles on the streets and sidewalks. A dog is barking. A woman is crying. A child is shouting for her mother. Nathan puts his arm around Allison. "A thought keeps running through my mind," he says. "This is the result of a conventional bombing raid. Just imagine if this was a—"

Before Nathan can finish his thought, a loud bullhorn interrupts. Blaring atop a half-track motoring slowly down Aller Straße, the bullhorn shouts, "The raid is over. We have defeated the enemy. All is safe. The raid is over."

Nathan and Allison continue to stand outside. Their safe house is undamaged, but their neighborhood is not. One of the grandest neighborhoods in Berlin has been injured. Allison turns to Nathan. "Will this invasion make a difference?" she says.

"I doubt this was an invasion; there are no troops. It was a volley. The Allies have made a statement. 'Attention Berlin, you are not as safe as you thought you were.' Maybe an invasion will come soon, but not yet. Thus far, Allied planes have never been able to reach Berlin, so this raid is bound to have some consequences, but will they make a difference? Will anything change Hitler's mind? Will he reposition his troop strength, his air defenses, to more effectively protect his capital? Perhaps he will recall some of his divisions from the coast? Was that the plan? Will the Allied incursion into heretofore untouchable Berlin intimidate Hitler or strengthen his resolve? Will he advance or fall back? Only time will tell."

———

Nathan opens his eyes, breathes deeply, and takes a moment to find his bearings. It is morning and he is in bed in the Charlottenburg safe house. Allison lies beside him. She had quietly entered his room not long after they retired. He saw her come into the bedroom and knew that she was frightened. He lifted the covers for her, and the two of them lay silently the rest of the night, though she did not sleep soundly. Her tossing and turning intermittently awakened him. Nightmares caused her to shudder. Sometimes she cried.

Allison rises and heads to the washroom. Nathan walks downstairs into the living room and stands by the window. He is soon joined by Allison, who says, "What's happening out there?"

"Cleanup. Crews are already in the street. There is damage, but not as much as you would have thought." Smoke still rises from some of the bomb sites. A white truck bearing the legend BERLINER ZOO travels slowly down Aller Straße. People are picking up the detritus of last night's indignities. They are talking to their neighbors. Their body language conveys their bewilderment. How could this have happened? How could our so-called beleaguered enemy strike so savagely when we have been assured of our supremacy?

"It's sad, isn't it?" Allison says. "I confess, I have mixed emotions. Is that strange? As an American, I applaud the attack on the heart and soul of our enemy, but I feel bad for the families who live here. Is it such a paradox to care about humanity? The women and children?" And Nathan agrees.

"If you're hungry, there is some bread in the drawer, but the electricity is still out. I can't make coffee," she says.

"I think there is a café around the corner," Nathan says.

She nods. "Give me a few minutes."

———

The café is busy, the tables are full, and Nathan and Allison wait for takeout. Allison is watching the customers. Some are silent, their heads are down; they have been sucker punched. Their Führer had assured them of their invincibility. Others are animated. Though she does not understand the words, they are clearly describing their harrowing experiences with their facial expressions, their hands, and wild arm movements.

"They're frightened," Nathan says. "Some are saying it was a onetime payback for the bombing of London. Others said the Allies were lucky—it was a fluke. Many are confident that the Luftwaffe destroyed the enemy's air fleet. Why else would it have been over so quickly? Some fear the worst."

"What do you think? Will they come back again?" Allison asks as they start back to the house. "Maybe even tonight?"

Nathan shrugs. "I'd be guessing."

"Of all the dangers you contemplated before accepting this assignment, did you consider being blown up by your own air force?"

"Hmph, no," Nathan answers. "Friendly fire. It's always something we considered in Ritchie training. After all, we were to accompany our expeditionary forces through France into Germany. But when I was given this assignment, I didn't think I would be killed by Allied bombs. In some ways, last night's air raid is heartening. Think of it, Alli; our job is to discover how far along their nuclear development has come, but we have agreed that, to the extent possible, it is also to disrupt it. Last night's raid means that we may be capable of penetrating deep enough into Germany to destroy their nuclear reactor and the supply routes."

"If we know where they are."

"Right, if we can get the coordinates, and maybe we'll learn that from Snyder this afternoon."

29

AFTERMATHS

The clock ticks slowly as Allison and Nathan anticipate departing for their afternoon meeting at St. Hedwig's Catholic Church. Nathan paces. Allison plays solitaire, but her concentration is somewhere else. Several thoughts run through her mind. Will it be safe to walk outside today? Have the attacks ceased, have the bombers truly been driven away, or are they reloading? Might there be further bombing raids today? Is the church still standing and is the meeting still on? Will Snyder show up? Will he cooperate? Will they get the information they seek and begin their journey home?

Allison voices her thoughts, and then says, "Do you think it's wise for us to walk across the city without knowing the answer to any of those questions?"

"I don't think I have a choice," Nathan says. "I have my orders and as far as I know, the meeting hasn't been canceled. I checked the mailbox and there were no notes in it, though I admit it would have been difficult to venture out in the middle of a bombing raid just to deliver a message. So, I have to go. You, however, are not going anywhere. You have no orders; you are not a soldier. You are here as a volunteer. It was always our expectation to debrief Snyder in this safe house. That's what I promised you. So, you will stay here, I will keep the appointment, and I'll bring Snyder here as planned."

"Since when did you become my commanding officer?" she says with her hands on her hips. "I'll decide what I'm going to do and when I'm going to do it. Besides, what if Snyder starts talking at the church? You don't have the background to evaluate him. You need me there."

Nathan is defiant. "Nope. If he shows, I'll bring him back here to be questioned. You are going to stay right here in this house. That was always the plan."

"I'm not comfortable staying in this house by myself."

"This house is a lot safer than walking around Nazi Berlin. And that was the deal we made in New York. You were to wait in the safe house."

"That was our deal before you gave our address to your old girlfriend. Not so safe anymore, is it?"

Nathan sighs.

Suddenly, there is a knock on the door. Nathan peels back the edge of the curtain, peeks at the front stoop and says, "It's Gluck and his partner."

Entering the living room, Fred Gluck has a friendly smile. "It looks like you two survived last night's fireworks. Everything okay?"

"Okay?" Nathan answers. "Hardly. Did you two know about the raid before last night? Did you know it was coming? Because if you did, and you didn't alert us, I'm pissed. Why didn't the OSS say something?"

"Hey, hang on, buddy," Kurt says. "We didn't know anything. It was all the Brits. All the bombers we could spare went on the joint raid over Schweinfurt last week, and we lost sixty Flying Fortresses. We didn't have any more to spare for this mission, so it wasn't us. The RAF went alone, and I understand they took heavy losses. Still, I hear they're proud that they nailed Berlin, so I wouldn't be shocked if they tried it again. They have a lot more equipment in Europe than we do."

"So, you're telling us you don't know whether there will be another bombing attack today or tonight?" Allison says.

"Nope, I sure don't. They don't check with me."

"Oh come on, Kurt," Nathan says, "are you telling me that the U.S. military isn't informed when the RAF is going to attack Berlin?"

Renzel shrugs. "The U.S. military? You mean General Marshall? And somehow that filters down to little ol' Kurt Renzel? I got news for you, pal, I'm just a pawn for OSS. Office of Strategic Services. Nothing more than a gumshoe in the field. I don't sit at the table, and Marshall doesn't share his information or strategies with me. But I can tell you this: Berlin got caught with its pants down last night. They scrambled their defenses, but not before there was plenty of damage, especially in the neighborhoods of the Tiergarten, Charlottenburg, Schoenberg, and Spandau. But I guess you already know part of that."

"We certainly know the Charlottenburg part; we spent a good part of the night in the basement. But it's hard to believe that the RAF flew all this way just to bomb a few neighborhoods," Nathan says skeptically. "What about the military installations, the airfields, German bases? What happened to them?"

Renzel shrugs. "I haven't heard that. I'm sure the Brits wanted to do more damage, but hey, they bombed Berlin. Give them a break; the imperious Nazi juggernaut took one in the nuts." He pumps his fist. "It was sweet. Bam!"

Gluck steps forward. "Settle down, Kurt." Turning to Nathan, he says, "In some ways, he's right, Lieutenant. The Brits inflicted some damage to downtown Berlin and hundreds of Berliners were killed or injured. There was no direct impact on any military installation that we know of, but there was heavy damage done to their collective psyche. The RAF took them by surprise, but as Kurt said, at a heavy price. They lost a lot of men and equipment. Still, whenever you can hit the enemy in its home, especially by surprise, it is a psychological victory."

Nathan huffs. "Well, they caught me with my pants down as well. It would have been nice to know it was coming. We are scheduled to go out late this afternoon and question Dr. Snyder, and we don't know if another raid is coming. To tell the truth, I don't relish the thought of walking around dodging British bombs. The least they can do is to tell us *when* the raids will occur. We're on the same damn team."

"Nate, we understand your predicament. I know your assignment has taken on additional risks, but as far as I know, your meeting is still a go for five o'clock this afternoon at St. Hedwig's."

"What does that mean: *as far as you know*?"

Gluck looks over at Renzel and back again. "It means that we haven't heard anything to the contrary."

Nathan is irritated and his response reflects it. "You mean you haven't heard *anything at all,* isn't that right?"

Gluck nods. "Yeah, I guess so, but maybe no news is good news in this case. I know that St. Hedwig's was not hit, and that Father Hannover hasn't canceled the meeting. I think he would have, if the plans had changed."

"Okay then. Allison and I will meet with Snyder this afternoon. If he's ready to go, if he gives us the information we're supposed to get, we'll bring him back here and start our journey home. And we'll have the full support and backup of the OSS, right?"

"Always have."

"Will you meet us at the church, or will you meet us here tonight?"

"The plan is to have a car pick you up at the church after your meeting with Father Hannover. When he calls, Kurt will come get you."

Nathan feels a bit better. "Is our passage back to England all arranged and secure? Safe houses and contacts all along the way?"

Now Gluck hesitates. He shifts his weight from one foot to the other. "We're studying the options."

"What is that supposed to mean?"

"There have been changes in the field. Because of the raid last night, the Germans have resumed shelling London and southern England, both with Messerschmitt sorties and some of those short-range rockets. The Channel is a fire box. Western land defenses have been strengthened. The usual passages may not be safe. We're working on taking you out alternative routes. That's all I can tell you."

Nathan hangs his head. "SNAFU."

Gluck nods. "We'll see you later. Good luck this afternoon."

———————

The walk from the safe house to St. Hedwig's is a retrace of the previous day: through the Tiergarten, down the Unter den Linden, and into the heart of downtown Berlin. This day, however, the scene is markedly different. There are no children in their uniforms waiting to enter the zoo. The Berlin Zoo has suffered massive damage and is cordoned off. Except for the ducks and swans, there is no movement in the Tiergarten. No couples with picnic baskets. No artists quietly capturing the idyllic convergence of woods and ponds. No other people strolling the paths.

Many structures that did not suffer a direct hit show collateral damage: broken windows, shattered store fronts, buckled walkways. Cars and wagons lie askew or overturned. But as Gluck had mentioned, the damage was not widespread. A building here, a building there, in no particular pattern.

The Unter den Linden, Berlin's picturesque boulevard, had suffered hits and some of the foreign embassies lay in ruins. The famed Kaiser Wilhelm Church was badly damaged. But to Nathan, it all resembles a prizefight. The challenger has delivered a powerful uppercut that seems to have come out of nowhere, dazing and staggering Berlin. But the heavily favored boxer has shaken it off and remains upright, dancing and swinging, every bit as menacing as before the punch.

Taking measures to show strength and unity, the Nazi Party has staged more than the usual number of parades up and down the major thoroughfares. A regiment of Brownshirts—storm troopers, named the Sturmabteilung, the SA—passes in formation before Nathan and Allison on the Unter den Linden, arms extended in the Hitler salute. People standing on either side of the boulevard cheer them and return the salute.

As a decorated Hauptmann, Nathan nods and tips the bill of his cap. He whispers to Allison, "Stick out your arm. It's mandatory."

"The hell I will," she says, with as much distaste as she can muster.

"Then turn your back and pretend you didn't see." In past years, Nathan has seen SA break formation and assault a person who did not return a salute.

On Friedrichstraße, a young group of army recruits march behind a military band. Behind them are four half-tracks, beeping their horns, and behind them are six uniformed men carrying red swastika banners on ten-foot poles. As the soldiers pass by, the Berliners thrust their arms out in salute. Nathan nods and offers the kind of half-hearted salute one might expect from a battle-weary officer. Allison turns her back.

———

At Bebelplatz, in the center of Berlin, in the area referred to as the Mitte, they finally reach St. Hedwig's Kathedrale, seat of the archdiocese, as yet untouched and unharmed. Built in the eighteenth century and modeled after the Roman Pantheon, its six Corinthian columns and six thirty-foot archways form a classical entrance to the copper-domed cathedral behind. While the Mitte is relatively quiet this evening, the church plaza is crowded. A five o'clock mass has been scheduled, and lines of people wait to enter the church. Without a doubt, there are more worshippers than usual this evening. War has come to visit them in person.

It is 4:30 P.M. when Allison and Nathan climb the steps and meld into the crowd moving through the Gothic doorway and into the church. Despite the massive rotunda's generous seating space, the pews are all full and many attendees stand along the walls.

Nathan stops at the foot of a rococo fresco and takes a deep breath. "It's time to meet and greet the eminent Dr. Günther Snyder. Are you ready?"

Allison smiles. "Born ready."

30

ST. HEDWIG'S KATHEDRALE

Nathan walks directly down the center aisle of St. Hedwig's nave and taps the shoulder of an usher who responds by holding up a wait-a-minute finger. He is apologizing to an elderly man, explaining to him that there are no empty seats available for this special service. He suggests that the man stand at the back or along the wall. The usher turns, takes notice of Nathan's uniform, rank, and Iron Cross, and quietly whispers, "I'm sure I can find seats for you and your wife, Hauptmann. Just be a bit patient."

Nathan shakes his head. "That's not necessary, thank you. I would like you to direct me to Father Hannover. I have a meeting with him."

The usher is puzzled. He looks at his watch. "Now? You want to meet with him now? Father Hannover is about to serve mass to these three thousand people, Hauptmann. In fifteen minutes."

"I understand. Where might I find him?"

The usher sighs. He is weary of Nazis like Nathan swinging their arrogance around. "All right, then," he says, "through that doorway over there. The black door on your right will be his study. No doubt he's in there preparing for *this mass*." He spreads his arms. "I'm sure you can appreciate how important that is today, with last night's bombing attack. This is a specially scheduled mass and I'm certain he doesn't want to be disturbed, and I'm also certain—"

"Thank you," Nathan says, and with Allison on his arm, walks forward through the crowded assembly.

Yes?" is the response Nathan hears after knocking on the study door several times. "What is it?"

"Father Hannover, please," Nathan says to the closed door.

The door swings partially open. An elderly man with snow-white hair, dressed in a highly decorated, ankle-length green and gold chasuble, stands at the door with one hand on the doorknob. He is clearly irritated. "What can I help you with, Hauptmann? As you can see, I am terribly busy. Do you suppose that the Reich can wait until after I serve five o'clock mass?"

"I am here to see Dr. Günther Snyder."

The priest shakes his head. "Who? I know of no such person."

"Are you Father Hannover?"

"Certainly."

Nathan lowers his voice. "We have come a long way to meet with Dr. Günther Snyder. I have been sent by a mutual friend to talk to Günther about his travel plans."

Father Hannover waves an angry hand of dismissal. "I am not acquainted with any doctor named Schumacher, and I could care less about his travel plans. I am sure you can find many fine doctors in Berlin. Now if you will leave me alone, I have the Lord's business to attend to."

Though she does not understand all the words, Allison is following the discussion just fine, and she is stunned. This incredible journey, the risks they have undertaken, the essential, critical information they have come to obtain, has it all been for naught? What are they to tell General Groves? President Roosevelt? That somehow, the information about a top German nuclear scientist seeking asylum was a ruse? A blunder? That there is no viable contact person in Berlin? This is not merely a SNAFU, this is a total disaster.

But Nathan is not dissuaded, and he does not intend to give up. He stands in front of Father Hannover like a middle linebacker, blocking the doorway. "Look, Father, I didn't come all the way here into Nazi Germany to get brushed off. I think I'm in the right place and I am going to take a chance, because I have a feeling that you are who I think you are. I'm going to put my neck on the line and level with you. I am not Hauptmann Strauss. I am not really a German officer. I am, in fact, an American soldier. Our mutual friends have arranged a meeting for us with Dr. Günther Snyder. Right here. Right now. You know it and I know it. I have been told that you are his contact person, and I believe that to be true. Now unless there are two Father Hannovers at this church, you know darn well what this is about."

"What *mutual friends* would those be, Mr. American in Hauptmann's clothing?"

Nathan takes a breath. He cannot reveal OSS identities. That is against all regulations. Hannover eyes him with suspicion waiting for an answer. Nathan figures, *in for a dime, in for a dollar.* He will go halfway. "Their initials are FG and KR, and you know who I mean. Now stop playing with me."

The priest takes a step back. "All right, come in," he says. "Forgive me, but you can never be too careful these days in Berlin. The Gestapo is hiding in every corner. I don't know you, and I am not comfortable placing my trust in strangers, but if Fred or Kurt sent you, that's good enough. May I ask who this young lady is and why she is here?"

"I prefer that you don't. She is here for a strategic reason, and she has been appointed to this assignment by the highest authorities. When might we expect to meet with Günther?"

The priest shuts the door and speaks in a whisper. "I have not heard from Günther today. The meeting was previously arranged for five o'clock. That was before Berlin was attacked last night. Whether he comes in or not is anybody's guess. If he does, you may use my study to conduct your business." He leans forward. "I have known Dr. Snyder for many years. He is a devout Catholic, and like many of us, he is critical of the current leadership. Some weeks ago, Günther began to raise the subject of leaving Germany. I'm not sure that it is all politically motivated, he may have other reasons, but I know he detests Nazi authoritarianism and the effect it has on his day-to-day life."

"What effect, Father?"

"Günther is a highly placed scientist who works in a top secret laboratory. What they are doing, he wouldn't tell me, and I didn't ask. But I sense that he is unhappy with his co-workers, or his supervisors, I don't know which. So he has decided to leave, and I assume he could be of value to the Allies. In any event, he asked me if I could help facilitate his defection."

"Why did he come to you? How did he know that you were in contact with the OSS?"

The priest shrugs. "I don't think he knew. He came to me for help because I would sympathize with him during his confessions, he felt safe, and he surmised I had contacts. As I said, we have known each other for years. So, at his request, I was able to put the necessary pieces together. I made the contacts, and I was informed that an initial screening meeting would be necessary before the U.S. would undertake a mission to smuggle him out of Germany. Against my better judgment, I agreed to let Günther and Fred meet here at the church. I trust them both. I did not know about you or this young lady."

"I understand, Father. We have been sent to meet with Günther to do the initial screening. To determine his usefulness and honesty. If we decide it is all legitimate, we will accompany him back to America."

"Very well, if Günther shows up today, use my office, conduct your screening, and if he passes, take him and be gone. Godspeed. If he doesn't, then I ask that you leave without drawing any attention to me, my network, or St. Hedwig's. Please be conscious of the precarious role my church is playing in this matter, and take care not to expose us."

"Of course, Father, and I thank you. It is nearly five o'clock. Do you know of any reason to believe that Snyder won't show?"

The priest shrugs again. "Hard to say. His nerves are on edge. He has been very anxious recently, more so than usual. There is great pressure where he works." The priest stands and walks to the door. "Now I must leave. There are many congregants waiting for words of comfort tonight. Friends and neighbors of theirs have been killed by Allied bombs. These are tumultuous times. Many would say Godless.

I would not. I would say challenging, and they need faith to get them through it all." He starts through the doorway, stops and says, "You may stay here to wait, but keep the door closed and be mindful what you do and say. Do not compromise this church or my network. We have helped countless souls escape the Nazi death squads. Don't expose our operation because of one scientist no matter how highly placed he is."

Alone in the study, Allison asks, "I missed a lot of that. Did Father Hannover give us any new information?"

Nathan shakes his head. "Not really. He called Snyder nervous and anxious. That sounds to me like the Günther Snyder I used to know. He said that Günther's desire to leave Germany was not necessarily political, and to me that means Günther feels unappreciated. Father Hannover said Günther was under a lot of pressure at the lab. I don't know what that means."

"So, we sit and wait?"

"We sit and wait."

31

A HASTY COURTSHIP

The two-hundred-year-old St. Hedwig's Catholic Church is sturdily built with solid concrete walls, but the music and prayers of the mass permeate the structure and can be heard in Father Hannover's study. Though it was a hurriedly called Friday evening service, it seems more like a funeral mass for those that died in the Thursday night air raid. For Allison, sitting behind the closed door to the priest's study, it feels claustrophobic, and the wait is interminable. She fears that at any moment the door could burst open and someone could enter the room. Yes, it could be Snyder, but it could also be the Gestapo. It wasn't supposed to be like this. The plan was to wait for Snyder at a safe house.

Back in New York, the concept of a safe house seemed a lot safer to Allison than the little two-story in Charlottenburg, especially since Nathan has given the secret address to his old girlfriend. Just an ordinary house in an ordinary neighborhood. How much do Gluck and Renzel really know about it? Who are the neighbors? Do they work for the government? The police? The Gestapo? The house didn't seem very safe last night while British bombs were blasting the city. As far as Allison is concerned, the sooner they get out of Germany, the safer she will feel.

From what she can hear, it sounds like the mass has ended. The choir has stopped singing. No one is speaking through a microphone. Now what? It is 6:30 P.M. How long are they going to sit and wait for Snyder in Father Hannover's study?

Suddenly the door opens. It is Father Hannover, and he is alone. "I take it Dr. Snyder did not appear," he says, removing his vestment and hanging it in the closet. He is much thinner than Allison imagined. Nathan shakes his head. "No, he didn't. Is there any way for you to contact him?"

The priest nods. "I have his telephone number, but I don't see the purpose of placing a call. He knows about this meeting; it isn't like he forgot. I didn't see him at mass. He is either detained or he has changed his mind. If he has been compromised, a call would place my operation in jeopardy."

"Do you know where he lives?"

"Are you thinking of going to his house?" Father Hannover shakes his head. "That would be very unwise."

"Does he live far?"

"Walking distance, but that is a foolish idea. He has chosen not to come, and the conclusion seems obvious. If he will not speak to you here, he will certainly not speak to you at his home, and in such a case, he may have you arrested. Or shot. I do not counsel it."

"I have my orders, Father. He has information that I am obliged to learn. One way or another. Where does he live?"

"He lives in a multi-unit apartment building. But such a foolhardy venture would place you and this young woman in grave danger."

"She is not going. She will stay here until I return."

Allison jumps to her feet. "The hell I will! If you're going, I'm going."

"No, you're not. You are going to stay right here with Father Hannover. If I don't return, Father Hannover will get you to Gluck and Renzel through his network and they will get you home. Am I right, Father?"

The priest nods. "She may stay here with me. She will be safe, and should you not return, I will make sure she finds her way to your network."

Berlin's streets are surprisingly busy this Friday night, as though the bombing was a singular aberration. Berliners have rallied behind the confidence of their leaders who assure them that the city is well fortified. Nathan joins a sea of pedestrians, making his way through the Mitte, toward Snyder's building. He is proving General Groves's hypothesis that in a German officer's uniform, he will become invisible. Indeed, there are many uniformed men out and about this night. Gray uniforms, brown uniforms, feldgrau uniforms, all out and about, and Nathan is just another tree in the forest.

"Hey Froman," someone shouts from behind. "Froman. Dietrich Froman, hold up."

Nathan instantly recognizes the voice. It is Major Weber. What a stroke of bad luck. How the hell did this happen? He quickly unclips his Strauss name tag and puts it in his pocket. Weber catches up and slaps him on the back.

"You rascal," Weber says. "You know you are in deep trouble. Colonel Zeist is looking for you." Weber laughs. "He sent a car to pick you up and found out that you had ditched him." Weber laughs heartily. "The colonel doesn't like being stood up. You better hope he doesn't catch up with you."

Nathan shrugs. "I had enough of the old man's questions. I didn't like him, I'm not under his command, and I didn't need to spend my social time drinking with him. I had better things to do that day."

"I know. I met her. Ooh-la-la. Where are you headed? I'm going to meet some friends at a very chic club where your knowledge of French will come in very handy. Come with us. I won't take no for an answer!"

Nathan equivocates. "I . . . I don't think I can. I was, uh . . . planning something else."

"Nonsense. It's Friday night. I insist!" He leans over, bites his bottom lip, and says, "There will be some fine ladies, French ladies, a veritable pastry cart, if you know what I mean."

Nathan is in a bind. He has to figure something out and fast.

"Stop stalling," Weber says. "This is a direct order!"

Nathan sighs. "I'll join up with you later, but I have to make a stop first."

"Oh no, you don't. I know that Froman trick. I saw it in Paris. I'll go with you to your stop, and then we'll go the cabaret together. I told you I won't take no for an answer. I'm not letting you out of my sight."

"Really, Major, you don't want to come with me. It's a long walk and—"

"Comrades in arms. I'm going with you."

Nathan knows he can't take him anywhere near Snyder's. An idea pops into his head. *I could use her, and I don't think she'll let me down.* Still, it's long shot. "Very well," he says, "come along." They turn left at the corner, walk a couple more blocks, cross the river, and arrive at 1430 Oranienburger Straße. Nathan hopes she is at home.

With Weber at his side, he knocks on the door. They wait. He knocks again. Lena opens the door, and her face freezes. She's staring at a Hauptmann and a major, one of whom she knows to be a fake. A million thoughts race through her mind, but before she can say a word, Nathan grabs her in a passionate hug and kisses her. He whispers in her ear, "My name is Dietrich Froman. I'm in trouble. Play along with me."

Lena steps back and takes a breath. Her cheeks are flushed. "Well, Dietrich, how lovely to see you. Um . . . as usual."

Weber chuckles. "Froman, you dog. You just had to make a stop?" He bows slightly to Lena and takes off his cap.

"Lena, this is my friend Major Weber. Otto, this is my fiancée, Lena Hartz."

She looks at Weber and offers the back of her hand. "An honor to meet you, Major."

Weber takes her hand and politely kisses it. "I insist that you two lovebirds accompany me tonight to the cabaret as my guests. As Dietrich will tell you, I do not take no for an answer."

Lena looks at Nathan, who covertly squints his left eye. She immediately pouts, sticking out her bottom lip. "Oh, Dietrich, you promised. I was making such a nice dinner for just the two of us. Like we planned."

Nathan shrugs. "Sorry, Otto, but it looks like this time you will have to take no for an answer. I can't disappoint my fiancée."

Weber nods. "Ach, I wish I had such a beautiful lady to come home to. You are a lucky man, Dietrich Froman."

"Oh, you have no idea," Nathan says.

Weber tips the bill of his cap, turns to leave and says, "We'll make it another time, Froman. Have a smashingly good night." He turns to Lena. "Guten Abend, Fräulein."

The two smile, wave goodbye, and step back into Lena's apartment. She shuts the door. The smile is gone. She is peeved. "What do you think you are you doing? You can't get me involved in your espionage. I could be shot."

"I'm sorry, I had no choice. It was an emergency."

"Emergency? To accompany Major Weber to a nightclub? And this was your only choice? To come to my apartment? You owe me an explanation, Mr. Nathan Silverman. Would you like to tell me what in the world is going on here?"

Nathan nods. "All right, all right, sit down." She sits on her couch, folds her hands, and tips her head in a fashion that Nathan has always found alluring. He takes a deep breath. "You saved my ass tonight. I know you must have figured out by now that I didn't come to Berlin, masquerading as a Wehrmacht officer with a French woman, just to go off searching for my family."

"From the very beginning."

"I'm sorry for being dishonest with you. The flat-out truth is this: I am a soldier in the U.S. Army, and I have been sent here to interview a man and help him escape to America."

"What man?"

Nathan shakes his head. "That's all I should really tell you. You don't want to know the details. It would only put you in jeopardy. The less you know the better."

"I'm already in jeopardy. Major Otto Weber now knows my name and my address. And more importantly, that I am connected with you. How do I explain that? If and when you're caught—and knowing

German intelligence, chances are pretty good that you will be—they'll be breaking down my door."

Nathan apologetically hangs his head. "I'm so sorry, Lena. It was a spur of the moment decision. I didn't plan to put you into danger."

"Well, that may not have been your plan, but you did. I suppose I could blame myself. I didn't have to play along. I should have said, 'Hello, Nathan Silverman.'"

"But you didn't."

"No, I didn't. I wouldn't."

Nathan slowly shakes his head in regret. "I know it was stupid. I should have figured some other way out of my dilemma."

"What about your French girlfriend, the charming Mademoiselle Dumont? Is she a spy as well?"

"She's not my girlfriend. She's not even French."

"No kidding. What role does she play in this espionage?"

"She's a scientist, that's all. She is going to interpret the scientific information from the man I am to meet later today."

"And that's where you were going when Weber met up with you? To meet with a man and get the information."

Nathan grimaces. "In a manner of speaking."

"So obviously, this man you are going to meet, he is a scientist as well, isn't he?"

Nathan nods again. He is being grilled by a gifted interrogator.

Lena throws her hands in the air and walks to the other side of the room. "Your mission is to help a top German scientist betray his country, provide top secret information, and defect to the West. Am I right?"

Nathan stands silent.

"And I, a loyal German citizen, have knowledge of the plot. If I don't call the police or do something to stop you, I am committing treason."

"No, you're not. You don't know anything, and no one can prove that you do. All you did was date a man you thought was Hauptmann Dietrich Froman. What is the crime in that?"

Lena doesn't buy it. "A Dietrich Froman who doesn't exist? How long has this fictional Dietrich Froman been in Germany, Nathan? Two days? Three days? A week maybe? If they checked with immigration and passport control, when would the records show that you crossed the border into Germany?"

"A few days ago."

Lena shakes her head in disbelief. "I suppose the story is that during these *few days* I met you, dated you, fell in love with you, and became your fiancée? Right? And, as your fiancée, I am totally ignorant of who you are and what you are doing here in Germany? Oh, I'm sure the Gestapo will see it all just like that. Especially after you sneak off with one of our top scientists."

"What do you want me to do, Lena? I can't undo what just happened. You could say you've been dating me for years and that wouldn't be a lie. Look, as of right now, nothing has gone wrong. No one is looking at you. No one has captured me. No one is checking up on Dietrich Froman. There is no reason for you to be frightened."

"Easy for you to say. Once something goes wrong, even a little bit, then your whole scheme unravels, and they trace it back to me. You don't think things through, Nathan. You never have. Suppose you go out now and Weber sees you walking alone on the street, without me? How would you explain that when we are supposedly having a romantic dinner for two?" She feigns a pout, sticks out her lip, and sarcastically whines, "Oh Dietrich, you promised." She pops her finger on his chest. "How would you bumble your way through that one?"

Nathan shrugs. "I wouldn't have to. If I know Weber, he will be drinking the night away in some cabaret, and I'll be long gone before then. It will only take me an hour or two to finish up my business. I've seen Weber drink and I've seen him chase women. He won't be on the streets for hours, probably not until tomorrow morning. Nothing can go wrong."

Lena rolls her eyes. "Oh, mein Schatz, you are so wrong. So much can turn upside down. Did he mention the name of the cabaret?"

"No, but he said my knowledge of French and my experience with the French ladies would come in handy."

"Hmph. *Nuits Parisiennes.*"

"What?"

"That's where he's going. It's a popular club on Torstraße. So, stay away from the northeast side. Please, whatever you have to do, do it quickly and leave as soon as possible." She grabs Nathan's arms. "Please, both for your sake and mine. It's dark tonight; there's no moon and many of the streetlamps are out. Stay out of sight, do your spying and go home. Then, if anyone asks, I'll say you were called up for duty."

Nathan nods. If anything were to go wrong, her life would be on the line. She knows that and still, she is supportive. "I will," he says softly. "I can't thank you enough."

She nods. He reaches for her and they hug, but Nathan realizes that the endearment isn't there anymore. She ends the embrace and steps back. It brings back memories of the talk on her father's porch. The lump he felt in the pit of his stomach that night. He knows that what he once believed was there between them was only in his mind. Now she is merely kind to him, and for that he is grateful.

32

CONTACT

The address Father Hannover provided turns out to be a brown-brick apartment building in a quiet neighborhood, northwest of the Mitte and similar to the one Nathan knew as a child. Unlike Charlottenburg, this section of the city was unharmed in the air raid. In many ways the walk through the Lichtenberg neighborhood is nostalgic. In Nathan's mind, it could very well be 1936. Harold's house was near that corner. Reynard's house was over there. *These were my people,* he thinks, *we grew up together.*

Dressed in his uniform, Nathan is frequently given a second or third look by passersby. A nod. A slight wave. A smile. People are kind. After all, he is there to protect them. Commonfolk. It's hard to think of all these people as the enemy. He's known them all his life. They're good people. So, how do they justify following Hitler's racial madness? Why, as a country, do they adhere to a national policy of hatred of their fellow German citizens? How do they go to sleep at night? Maybe they are like Mr. Hartz. Business is good, it's just politics. After all, the policies didn't affect him. Turn your head and talk about other things. What Allison called the sin of silence.

Günther's apartment is on the second floor. Nathan knocks on the door. He waits. There is no answer. A woman on her way to the third floor says, "Dr. Snyder doesn't come home at this time of day. At least not recently. He usually arrives after nine o'clock." Nathan thanks her and checks his watch. It's 8:15. Rather than take a walk around the neighborhood and risk being recognized or questioned, he takes a seat on the floor.

It is ten after nine when Snyder climbs the stairs. There is a bag in his left hand, most likely a carry-out dinner. He stops cold on the first-floor landing. "Excuse me," he says, "but you are sitting in front of my door. Is there some purpose to your presence, Officer?"

Snyder has changed very little in five years. Perhaps a few more pounds on his frame. His cheek jowls have puffed out. What curls are left on his head are starting to gray. Nathan stands, and with his cap pulled low on his forehead, he is a powerful figure. He says, "Are you Dr. Günther Snyder?"

"I am. What is your business here? I don't have any reason to expect a visit from the military. I insist that any professional contacts occur at my office at the Kaiser Wilhelm Institute."

"I understand. This is more personal, Dr. Snyder. May we step inside your quarters for a moment, please?" Nathan says in an officious tone.

Snyder sighs. "Yes, I suppose, but *only* for a moment. It has been a long and stressful day and I am tired." He quickly walks up the remainder of the stairs and unlocks the door. As he passes Nathan, he says, "You look vaguely familiar. Do I know you?"

They enter the apartment and Nathan looks around. It is evident that Snyder lives alone. The place is a mess. His clothes are strewn about, pants thrown over the backs of chairs, socks on the floor. Dirty dishes are on the table and in the sink. There is a stale odor. It is hard to believe that such a slovenly man is a nuclear scientist. Nathan removes his cap. "Do you recognize me now, Dr. Snyder?"

Günther squints and studies Nathan's face. He shakes his head. "As I say, you look familiar, but no, I don't. Should I?"

"I am Josef Silverman's son."

Nathan's response evokes shock. Snyder is taken aback, and he blinks several times. Then he snorts sarcastically. "A Jew has a son who is a decorated Nazi officer? I don't think so."

"It's true," Nathan says with a steely expression. "Where is my father?"

"You're serious, aren't you, Hauptmann? You really want me to believe you are the son of Josef Silverman. Why? What are you doing here at my apartment?"

"Where is my father?"

Snyder exhales and shrugs. "How the hell should I know? You think I have him hidden in my apartment? Do you want to check the closet? The last I knew, he was still working for the lab. Ask Dr. Esau; he's in charge. Silverman's not my responsibility."

"Esau's not here right now. I'm asking *you*, Dr. Snyder. You worked with him every day. He got you your job at the lab. Where is he?"

"I haven't seen him in a long time. Truly." Snyder tries to act complacent, but he is unsettled. He stares at Nathan. "If you really are Josef's son Nathan, then what are you doing disguised as Hauptmann Strauss, confronting me at my residence?"

"You asked for me. I came for you."

The blood begins to drain from Snyder's face. "Me? What have I done? I have harmed no one. Why are you after me?"

"You want to defect to America? I am here to take you. And I want to find my father."

"You? I was supposed to meet with an American. I thought it was a scientist. I didn't know it was you."

"Now you know. You need to come with me. Again I ask you, what has become of my father?"

"I don't know where he is. How many times do I need to tell you? I never did anything to hurt your father. I was his friend."

"A moment ago you said he's not your responsibility."

"No, no, Nathan, you misunderstand. I only said that because I thought you were a Nazi officer. Maybe Josef did something culpable, and they've come to me because Josef and I were good friends. And we *were* good friends. We still are, I hope. I only said that to distance myself from Josef in case you really were a Nazi Hauptmann and thought I was culpable. Nathan, I dined at your house many times, don't you remember? I knew your mother and your sister. I respected your father enormously."

"So, where is he now? Is he at the KWI lab?"

Snyder shakes his head. He is tiring. "No. He left our unit almost two years ago. More or less. One day he was there, the next day he was gone. No explanations. We were working on many of the same algorithms, we were a tight-knit group. Then, without any prior notice, Josef is gone. When we inquired, we were told that he was transferred."

"Why would they transfer a brilliant man like my father?"

Snyder spreads his arms. "Why do the Nazis do anything they do? Begging your pardon, I could assume that he was removed from the KWI because he was a Jew, but I don't know that for sure. That's only speculation. If that's what they did, they were fools. He is brilliant."

"Was he sent to a concentration camp?"

"I don't know that. I don't know anything. If he was, that would have been a waste of talent. The Nazis aren't that stupid. We were told that his analytical skills were needed on another project. That's all we were told."

Nathan curls his lips in disbelief. "So, no one knew where Josef Silverman went? He just vanished? Disappeared? Is that what you're saying? There are no records?"

"Hmph. Hardly. In this country, there are records of everything and everyone."

"And those records, would they be located at the KWI labs?"

Snyder shrugs. "Personnel records? I would assume so. I don't know. I'm not given access to that department." He stands and walks to the door. "Now, young Mr. Silverman, I've told you all I know. I don't know where your father is, and I don't know where they sent him. I don't have the information you seek."

Nathan doesn't move. "One more question, Günther. Why didn't you show up at St. Hedwig's this evening?"

Although he tries to disguise it, Snyder is stunned. He has no retort.

Nathan continues firing questions like a prosecutor. "You had a five o'clock appointment at St. Hedwig's and you failed to appear. I was there. Father Hannover was there. Where were you?"

"Who said I had an appointment?"

"Oh, so now we're going to play games. Father Hannover, the man who gave me your address, the man who set the meeting for you that you failed to attend, he told me. Listen, Günther, I have risked my life coming all this way to meet with you. Others have risked their lives as well. You're the one who seeks asylum. You're the one who begs to be transported to America. Now, what's it going to be?"

Snyder stands in silence. Nathan can hear the clock tick on the wall. Finally, Snyder says, "You have no idea. It was impossible today. We are under enormous pressure at the lab. Like we are wizards who can wave a magic wand and come up with a nuclear weapon. Poof! And it's ten times worse after last night's bombing. Because of that attack, the Reich Ministry of Armaments decided to put extra pressure on us. Reichminister Albert Speer, a thug, who knows little of nuclear science, wants to know when the bomb *will be ready*? How is that for a question? Not what hurdles remain for us to achieve such a break-through result, but *when will it be ready*? Like he is ordering spaetzle for dinner. He has been in and out of the Institute for weeks and weeks, always pushing us to finish and present the Führer with a workable nuclear bomb. Even worse since the Allied bombing. He knows nothing of science. You can't rush this project.

"Hahn met with him, Esau met with him, others have met with him. He demands meetings every day. 'What are you doing?' Speer says. 'What is the holdup?' They told him there is no way to know exactly; this is a new science, it's not like building a tank. We hope we are making steady progress, but we need more money. Speer scoffed at us. 'What am I to tell His Excellency, Der Führer? That our finest scientific minds can give us no answer and have nothing to say other than we need more money?' He says, 'Many in the Ministry think that the Reich has spent too much money and directed too many resources to get nothing in return.'

"Dr. Hahn was furious. He stood up for us. 'Who are you to come into my laboratory and criticize my work? I split the atom. These are all dedicated men, geniuses, who are working as hard as they can, applying principles that you could not possibly understand. Now, get out of my lab and leave us alone! Tell Der Führer if he wants answers, he should come here himself and ask questions.' I thought that Speer would shoot him on the spot, but he shut up. He stayed all afternoon and evening lurking about, watching us like a hawk and making notes, but he kept his mouth shut. I am sure you can understand that there was no way I could sneak out of there and keep a five o'clock appointment with Father Hannover. I will make an effort to break away and meet with you tomorrow evening at St. Hedwig's."

The answer doesn't satisfy Nathan. "Why not come with me right now? We came a long way to learn about Germany's nuclear program and to help you escape. If you want to defect, let's go right now. There is no reason for us to wait until tomorrow. Just grab your coat and we'll go to our safe house where we can talk."

Snyder scoffs. "I will be happy to answer any questions about the KWI and the work that I am doing. That was the arrangement with your contact here. If my information is valid, then I am to be transported to America. But frankly, Nathan, you are not qualified to evaluate what I have to say. You are not a scientist. Much of what I say will be way over your head."

Nathan grins. "No doubt you are correct. I'm not the one who will evaluate your information. A brilliant nuclear scientist will question you. Believe me, she will understand anything you tell her. She will ask you how close Germany is to fabricating a nuclear weapon. What has been done; what remains to be done? Where do your raw materials come from? Where are they stored? Where do you keep your enriched uranium? Where are your engineering sites? Where is your reactor? Where are—"

"Okay, okay. I understand, and I will tell her what I know. That was the deal. But Nathan, I do not have all that information. I work in a section of the lab that is rather insular. We concentrate on our part of the project. I am not privy to information from other sections or other laboratories."

"But you can get it."

"Some of it."

"Excellent. Go back to the lab tomorrow, get as much of that information as you can and meet us at St. Hedwig's at five o'clock."

Snyder takes a deep breath. "That may be a problem. If there are watchdogs again, it will be very hard to get out at five o'clock. But there is another problem, and it is a big problem."

"What big problem?"

"If I leave with you tomorrow, and I don't come back to work on time the next day, they will send out someone to find me. They'll come to my apartment, and when I'm not at home, they will immediately conclude that I am defecting, and they will alert all of the border crossings. The whole country will be looking for me."

Nathan smiles. "Maybe the whole world, huh? I admire your self-regard, Günther. So, let's build in a little time before they send out the dogs. Give your colleagues at KWI a reason that you might not come into work. Pretend to get sick tomorrow. Go to the bathroom for a while. Then when you don't come to work for a couple of days, no one will be suspicious. So, get all the information you can and meet us tomorrow evening at the church."

33

IN RUINS

Nathan is halfway back to St. Hedwig's and feeling good. He made contact with Günther Snyder, he outlined the information they will need, and they made plans to meet tomorrow at five o'clock. Gluck will drive them to the safe house, where Allison will debrief Snyder and find out what she needs to know. There is a spring in his step and a smile on his face, and at just that moment, on the evening of November 19, 1943, the sirens sound again. Those who are out walking on this Friday night freeze and then scatter in every direction. Moments later the thunder starts, and the ground begins to shake. Nathan picks up his pace. He left Allison at the church several hours ago, and she is on her own. She won't know where to go. He is responsible for her. He swore to protect her, and she is alone in the middle of an air raid.

The roar of British Lancasters and the drone of German Messerschmitts fill the air. Bombs explode in random sequence, and this time the strikes aren't restricted to the Charlottenburg neighborhood. Some are close by and rattle the earth. He nears the Mitte, a few blocks from the church, when the ground shakes so hard it knocks him off his feet. He hits the ground hard, gets up, and continues running. He turns the corner and sees that the entire front entrance of St. Hedwig's is in ruins.

People flee the area. A few maintenance workers scramble out of the church. Nathan fights through a fleeing crowd, swimming upstream. He dashes inside. While the nave is partially destroyed, the transepts and altar are intact. As he enters what is left of the sanctuary, a man shouts, "Don't come in here, the building could collapse at any minute." Ignoring him, Nathan makes his way through the sanctuary and into the back corridors. He has to find Allison. He is just this side of frantic.

The back corridors are dark. He stumbles on things he cannot see. Finally, he reaches Father Hannover's study. The door is open, but the study is empty. "Allison?" he shouts. "Allison?"

A deacon passes him and urges him to leave the building. From the outside, more explosions rumble. "Where is Father Hannover?" Nathan asks. The deacon shrugs. "Try the basement, but if I were you, I'd get away from the church as fast as you can, go to somewhere safe. I think the church is a target."

"How do I get to the basement?" The deacon gestures to a door and a staircase.

Nathan descends the stairs and finds that several groups are huddled in corners. "Where is Father Hannover?" he asks. "Where is the French woman who was with him?" People shake their heads. No one seems to know. After looking around the dark basement, Nathan decides to return to the main floor and search the classrooms. As he reaches the stairs, a child's voice says, "She went home."

"Who went home?" Nathan says.

"The French woman," says the little girl. "The lady with the black hair. The one who was with Father."

"How do you know she went home?"

"Because Father Hannover told her to. He said, 'Go back to the house.'" The little girl is no more than eight, her hair is in pigtails, and she has her church clothes on.

"Are you sure?" Nathan says, bending down. "Is that what he said when the bomb fell on the church?"

The little girl nods most affirmatively. "Yes, he did. I saw the woman nod and use some French words. And then she ran. Father told me to stay in the basement."

"Thank you," Nathan says, patting her on the shoulder. "You should stay in the basement like you were told. Everything will be all right soon."

"Are you going to stop them?" the little girl says, pointing at the sky. "You're a soldier. Go and stop them from dropping bombs."

"I'll do my best, darling," he says, and turns to climb the stairs.

What a sweet little girl, Nathan thinks. *She is no different from these nice, innocent people who are now forced to huddle in the basement to shelter themselves and their loved ones from deadly bombs. I grew up with and lived among these people. They are not warmongers, they are peace loving. They don't deserve to be slaughtered. And yet it is the Allies,* my Allies, *that are killing them indiscriminately. How do I morally justify my participation?*

Nathan wanders out of the church and onto the street. He is overwhelmed by the incongruity. Conflicting thoughts cloud his mind. He walks slowly, aimlessly. Bombs explode in every direction, but they don't snap him out of his fog. The deep roar of bombers and the whirring sound of fighters continue, but Nathan is dazed, and he doesn't seem to hear them.

A little boy, running with his mother, stops to salute Nathan. After all, he is Hauptmann Strauss. Nathan returns the salute. He is a soldier and there is war all around him. And Berlin is right smack in the middle.

He looks around the Mitte and his thoughts return to his family, his neighbors, his schoolmates. They were peace loving as well. They did nothing wrong. But they were Jewish, and most of them had been rounded up and sent to death camps for no reason other than their religion. The specter of his mother appears to him. There are tears in her eyes as she offers her wedding ring and kisses him goodbye. "Sell it when you get to America," she says.

It is all madness. He shakes his head to clear his mind. *Who am I?* he asks. And he answers, *I am a soldier, an American soldier. I am fighting criminal insanity, and I must do my part to bring it all to an end.* He rushes to get back to the Charlottenburg safe house, praying that Allison has made it there unharmed.

The lamplights are out, and the streets are empty in the Charlottenburg neighborhood. Following orders broadcast on the radio, houselights have been turned off and will stay off until the all clear is sounded. The menacing buzz of the aircraft has faded away. The bomb blasts have ceased. Turning the corner onto Aller Straße, Nathan can see no evidence of additional damage to the neighborhood. He opens the safe house door and immediately shouts, "Allison?" He waits and listens. His heart is racing. "Allison?" There is no response.

She left the church. The little girl said so. If she isn't here, he has no idea where she might be. Perhaps she took a different route, a slower route from the church. Perhaps she became confused, even lost. He will not allow himself to consider the other alternatives.

Whatever has happened to Allison, it is his fault. He promised to protect her, and he left her. He takes a seat in the living room in front of the window. He will wait for her, no matter how long it takes. In his mind, he reviews his operational protocol. None of his plans prepared him for this. No contingencies were designed for an Allied air strike. None of the plans had considered the destruction of St. Hedwig's. But it doesn't matter: a soldier must adapt. And a soldier doesn't leave a comrade in the field. He will find Allison.

Nathan decides to contact Gluck and Renzel. They might be able to help. The safe house doesn't have a telephone. Even if he had one, or if he was able to use the pay phone at the corner drugstore, he doesn't know any phone numbers. The only way to contact them is by inserting the red card into the mailbox and hoping that sooner or later Gluck or Renzel will notice it. As he places the card into the mail slot, the all clear sounds. The attack is over. Nathan returns to his window to stand vigil for Allison.

Time passes slowly, and Nathan's nerves are on edge. Suddenly, from behind his back, a voice says, "When did you get here?"

Nathan spins around to see Allison standing there. He rushes over, throws his arms around her, and squeezes her tightly. "You're safe," he says. "You made it. I was so worried about you. I had no idea where you were." He hugs her again.

"Well, you could have checked the basement," she says with a shrug. "That's where you took me last night."

"The basement!" Nathan says, slapping his forehead. "I came into the house, I called your name, but there was no answer. The house was dark and quiet. Why didn't I think to look in the basement?"

She smiles. "I'm okay." She brushes the hair back from his forehead. "Oh, my God, look at your head," she says. "You've been injured."

"I'm okay," he says. "I fell on the sidewalk."

"Well, there's some blood. Let's get you cleaned up."

Allison dabs at Nathan's forehead with a washcloth. "How did you get back?" he says.

"I remembered the route."

"I was so worried. I thought . . . it doesn't matter, you're safe. That's all that matters."

She continues to clean the wound. "There aren't any bandages here, but I think you'll be all right. Did you ever find Günther Snyder?"

"I did. I talked to him in his apartment. He says he didn't show up at the church because the lab was being closely watched by ministry officials. He's going to meet with us tomorrow night at St. Hedwig's, or what's left of it."

"What did he tell you about KWI's nuclear readiness? Where are the materials stored? Where is their reactor? Where are they getting their graphite or heavy water? How do they transport it?"

"Hold on, Allison, hold on. He didn't tell me those things. I didn't ask him. I didn't want to get into the details. That's your job."

Allison shakes her head. "It figures."

"I don't think he knows all those things anyway. He says his group is insulated from the rest of the project. I told him, in general terms, what we wanted to know, and he is going to find out what he can and meet us at five o'clock at St. Hedwig's. I hope."

Allison quickly turns her head. "Did you hear that?"

Nathan nods. "There's someone at the door." He places his hand on the grip of his pistol and cautiously approaches the door. To his surprise, it swings open and Gluck is standing there. He sees Nathan and holds his hands up in mock surrender. "Don't shoot, don't shoot, I'm innocent," he says with a laugh.

"I'm glad to see you, but why did you come here tonight?"

Gluck is puzzled. "Didn't you put the panic card into the mailbox? That wasn't you?"

"Of course it was me. But I just put it in a little while ago. I didn't think you would come so quickly."

Gluck shrugs nonchalantly. "I live around here. The all clear sounded, so I took a walk." He narrows his vision. "What happened to you?"

"A blast knocked me over. I'm okay. Nurse Fisher has tended to me."

Gluck hands the red card back to Nathan. "What's on your mind, Silverman, other than Churchill dropping bombs?"

"Snyder didn't show at St. Hedwig's. I asked Hannover for his address, and I went to his apartment to wait for him. He showed up a little after nine and we talked for a while. He said there was a lot of pressure being exerted at the lab. Especially because of the Allied bombing. Despite my suggestion, he didn't want to leave with me tonight. He wanted to gather further information. He thought he could get it. Then he wants to create an excuse for not going back to work. He is going to pretend to be sick tomorrow afternoon, so they won't miss him for a few days. He promised to meet me tomorrow night at the church, or its remains. He still wants to defect."

Gluck nods. "I heard that the church got hit tonight. Snyder might not show tomorrow, either. Or he might be late. It's not wise to sit outside the church in a car for too long. Use the church phone to call me if he shows. Hannover knows the number. I'll come and get you and we'll debrief him here at the safe house."

"There's a good chance the church phone is out," Nathan says. "The place is in pretty bad shape."

"You could be right. Okay, I'll drive by at six. That will give you an hour. Look for a white VW."

There is a knock on the door. "Busy place tonight," Gluck whispers.

"Are either of you expecting someone?" Nathan and Allison shake their heads. "All right," Gluck says, "step out of sight, into the kitchen, and I'll take care of it."

Gluck opens the door to see an attractive woman in a camel hair overcoat. Gluck says, "Can I help you, madam?"

The woman is perplexed. "I . . . I'm sorry," she says, "I think I was given the wrong address. Please excuse me." She turns to leave.

"Wait," Nathan shouts and darts out of the kitchen. "Let her in. That's Lena Hartz. I know her."

Gluck steps aside and Lena enters the room. Lena eyes Allison and vice versa. There is a palpable air of distrust between them. Gluck turns to Nathan and says, "You gave her this address?"

Nathan nods. "It was the only way she could get me a message about my family." He turns to Lena. "Why are you here?" he asks. "Do you know something about them?"

Lena looks at Gluck with cautious eyes, and then back at Nathan. "It's all right," Nathan says, "you can speak freely. Fred is a friend."

She hesitates, then exhales and says, "It's not about your family. I came to warn you. I think Major Weber might be coming here. And he's not alone."

"How would Weber know where I am staying?" Nathan says. "I never . . ." He stops short. "You told him?"

She bites her lip and nods. "I didn't have a choice," she says. She lifts her blouse. There are red marks below her ribs. She rolls up her sleeves. There are bruises on her upper arms. "He forced me. He was physical with me. He showed up at my door with two other soldiers. He said he wanted to talk to Hauptmann Froman. I remembered that was the false name you gave him. I said you weren't there. He gave me a snarly look. 'I thought you two were having a romantic dinner. Isn't that what you both told me earlier this evening? Did you say that just to brush me off, or did you just plain lie to me?'

"'Oh, no, I didn't lie,' I said. 'Dietrich had to leave. He had to go home.' Well, that was the wrong thing to say. Weber got a mean expression on his face. I could tell that he didn't believe me. 'Oh yeah?

Where is his home? What is his address?' he said. I didn't want to give up your address, so I said, 'I don't know.'"

Nathan shuts his eyes. "Oh, Jesus."

"Right," Lena says. "He didn't believe me at all. 'Froman is your fiancée,' he snapped, 'and you don't know his address? Is that what you're telling a German officer?'

"I said, 'I know it, I just can't remember it. You make me nervous.' Then he grabbed me by my arms, squeezed real hard and shook me back and forth. I fell into the corner of a table." Tears were flowing from Lena's eyes. "Then he said, 'Lady, you have no idea how nervous I can make you. If you don't tell me his address, right here, right now, I'm going to take you to where we can get real friendly. And pretty soon, you will tell me everything I want to know. That, I promise.'"

Lena swallows hard. "He continued to shake me back and forth, and he pulled my hair back. I though my neck would snap. And then, then I told him your address."

"What happened next?" Gluck says.

"While he was there in my apartment, the bombs began to fall, and the air raid siren went off. Weber said to the others, 'Shit, it's starting up again.' His companion said, 'We have to get back to the airfield. We gotta go.' Then he looked at me and he said, 'We'll come back later.' And they left." Lena presses her lips tightly and breaks into tears. "I'm so sorry," she says.

Allison quickly steps up and puts her arm around Lena's shoulders. She walks her to the couch and sits with her. "You were very brave," Allison says.

Gluck pulls Nathan into the kitchen where the two can talk in private. "The all clear has sounded. The emergency is over. Weber is probably relieved of duty. He could come at any minute. We can't stay here. It was a real dumb move to give this woman our address."

"I know. I was hoping she could find out something about my father. She said she'd try. I told her to drop a note in the mailbox. I didn't expect to meet up with her later in the company of Major Weber. It was all a mistake."

"To say the least. You blew a safe house."

"I know. But what should we do about Lena? Now I've put her in danger. When Weber comes over here, as he's bound to do, he'll find the place empty. Then he'll go back to Lena."

"Frankly, I don't give a shit. She can't hurt us anymore. Unless she knows about Snyder. Does she?"

Nathan lowers his head. "She doesn't know his name, but she knows the operation."

"Oh, you dumb bastard."

Nathan nods. "I was an idiot earlier tonight, but I was in a bind. I was on my way to Snyder's when Weber saw me. He remembered me from Paris where he made us follow him to a bistro. Tonight he insisted that I go with him to some French nightclub. So, I used Lena as an excuse. We pretended that we were engaged, and we were going to have a romantic dinner for two. Weber believed it and went on without me. After he left, I told her what I was doing and why I needed her. She wanted honesty. I thought it was the right thing to do."

"Not good," Gluck says. "Not good at all. She's a liability now, and this mission is too important."

"You don't have anything to worry about," Nathan says. "She won't say anything about the mission. She won't tell anyone; you can trust me on that. I mean, she came here to warn me tonight, didn't she?"

Gluck shakes his head. "How long did it take before she gave up this address? Ten minutes? Five minutes? How tough was it for Weber to get her to talk? How long do you think it'll take him to get the whole operation out of her? She's a liability, Silverman. Plain and simple."

"What does that mean? Exactly what does that mean: 'she's a liability'?"

Gluck turns and walks out of the room.

Nathan chases after him. "What does that mean, Fred? I won't let anything happen to her. It's not fair. If it wasn't for her, I wouldn't have met with Snyder tonight."

Gluck turns and confronts Nathan with an angry expression. "Then what do you suggest, Lieutenant Silverman? How do I protect this mission, which has top priority, now that you've gone and screwed it up?"

"I'll talk to her."

Gluck shakes his head. "That's not going to do it. She'll promise to stay silent and then crack like an eggshell when Weber or the Gestapo gets hold of her."

"Then she can come with us."

"Absolutely not. Arrangements are made, papers are prepared, transportation is arranged for just the *three of you*. Besides, I doubt she'd go anyway. She lives in Berlin, her family is in Berlin, her friends are in Berlin. She had a comfortable life as a woman of *German blood*. That is until tonight when they turned on her. That's what the Germans don't get. They are playing footsie with a snake."

"Let me talk to her. I'll figure something out."

Gluck looks at his watch. "Be quick about it. The all clear sounded over an hour ago. Weber and his buddies could show up at any minute."

34

LENA'S DILEMMA

Nathan returns to the living room. Allison and Lena are sitting together on the couch. Lena dabs at her eyes with a handkerchief. "She is a very brave girl," Allison says. "She tried to stand up to that Nazi major. She has bruises on her arms and her stomach to show for it. For all we know, she has a cracked rib. And she risked her life coming here."

"I know," Nathan says. "I appreciate it very much."

"Well, it's not as easy as that."

"As easy as what?"

"As easy as, 'Thanks for your help, ma'am, see ya around.'"

"I'm not saying that."

"She's afraid, Nathan. She knows too much, and she's afraid that Weber or some other inquisitor will torture her for information."

"I was just talking to Gluck about the same thing. He also agrees they might pressure her to tell them what she knows."

"Exactly, so we can't let that happen. I offered to take her with us, back to America."

"And she wants to go?"

"Well, she's not sure. She afraid to stay, but her whole life is here."

"I suggested that to Gluck a moment ago, and he immediately rejected it. He says that arrangements are made for three, not four."

Allison narrows her eyes. "Which arrangements? Are there only three seats on a fishing boat? Is there no room for an extra woman on a cargo plane?"

Nathan swallows. "He was talking about papers, having to prepare identity papers."

"She's German, Nathan. She has all the papers she'll need."

Nathan presses his lips and shakes his head. "I know, but Gluck says no. He was firm."

Allison mocks him. "'Gluck says no. Gluck says no.' Well, who the hell is Gluck to tell us what to do? He's a facilitator. He gets his orders same as us. Let *me* talk to Gluck."

"I'm right here," Gluck says, walking into the room. "We can't do something that will compromise this mission. The orders come straight down from General Groves."

"And do the orders say, 'No extra woman allowed'? Not even one who put her neck on the line to save this mission and our asses? Is that right? I'd like to see those specific orders, Mr. Gluck, because they don't exist. Look, Weber is already suspicious of Nathan. He will undoubtedly contact the Wehrmacht to inquire about a certain captain named Dietrich Froman. He will quickly learn that Dietrich Froman does not now exist and never has existed in any German army records. It will then be assumed that Nathan is a spy. And then, we both know what will happen. Weber will go straight to Lena Hartz to find out what she knows."

Gluck stands with his arms crossed. He quietly listens with no signs of disagreement.

Allison continues. "If we leave Lena behind, there's a good chance she'll be questioned. In the eyes of the Germans, she'll be condemned as a traitor for helping a spy. They will squeeze her until they get all the information she knows, including *your* name, Fred Gluck, and then they will kill her." Allison directs her attention to Lena. "Sorry, dear, but that's the way it is."

Nathan is impressed by Allison's logic and her forceful delivery. He looks directly at Gluck, who stands speechless. "Allison is one hundred percent correct, Fred, and you know it. Lena Hartz has put her life on the line for this mission. This mission would have stumbled to a stop unless I was able to connect with Snyder, and Lena made that possible. So I consider her a part of the team. We're not leaving a member of our team behind."

"Does she *want* to be a member of your team?" says Gluck. "Did you ask her? You two signed up for a very dangerous mission. Maybe Lena doesn't want to sign up. Maybe she doesn't want to put herself in harm's way. Or maybe she likes it just fine here in Berlin." He addresses Lena: "Do you want to help a German scientist defect to the Allies and help him escape through active fields of combat?"

Lena swallows. "Not necessarily. Truth be told, I don't want to leave my home, but I don't know how I can stay here. I'm worried that sooner or later, either Weber or some Gestapo agent will come after me. They'll want to know about Hauptmann Froman, who they will have determined is an imposter. I could tell them that I didn't know his true identity. That I'm just a dumb girl, and he fooled me too. But I don't think they will believe me."

"Not a chance they would believe you," Allison says.

"Oh, I don't know," says Nathan. "As far as Weber knows, Dietrich Froman is just an imposter. He doesn't know that I'm an American. He doesn't know what I'm doing. He really doesn't know anything. Why would Lena know any different? She wouldn't take up with a spy; she's a solid Berliner. Her father is an important industrialist here."

Gluck shakes his head. "Nathan, you are naive. So what if Froman isn't *American*? He's running around in a Wehrmacht officer's uniform. That is a crime in and of itself. Whatever you're doing, it's punishable. The Nazis are great detectives. It's only a matter of time before they put two and two together and find out the date when a man calling himself Dietrich Froman entered the country disguised as a Wehrmacht captain. They'll ask why would he do that? What is his purpose? And then they'll realize that a few days later a top KWI scientist defects to the West. It won't matter who Lena's father is. And I think we have to consider your phrase, 'solid Berliner.' I'm sorry, but she may not be as trustworthy as you believe. What if she changes her mind? What if her patriotism gets the best of her? What if she wants to help Germany where her father is an *important industrialist?*" He looks at Lena. "I'm sorry, Miss Hartz, but these are circumstances we have to consider."

"I understand," she says.

"I trust her," Nathan says. "As far as I'm concerned, she's trustworthy. She wouldn't be sitting here right now if she didn't want to help me."

"How can I agree to this?" Gluck says. "How do I respond to headquarters? Leaving her behind in Berlin, with what she knows, creates an unacceptable risk. Our entire mission could be blown—all the information we will learn about Germany's nuclear program, not to mention the future scientific assistance Dr. Snyder will render to our country. She can't stay, and we have no authority to take her out. You got me in a real fix."

"If she wants to go, she goes. Allison and I won't leave her behind. You can tell headquarters that we didn't give you a choice."

Gluck is beaten, and he knows it. He shakes his head in regret. "She can't stay here. She knows too much. She can go with you, but we have to vacate this safe house. We'll debrief Snyder at a different address, which, if you don't mind, I'll keep to myself until absolutely necessary. I'm going to get my car and drive us all to a different location. I'll be back in a few minutes."

———

I really made a mess of things, didn't I?" Lena says through her tears.

"No, you didn't," Nathan says. "It's all on me. I came to you for help and you bailed me out."

Allison looks sympathetically at Lena. "Nathan's right. It's not your fault. At what point would you have done something different? No, Lena, you are a hero, and we are indebted to you."

"I agree," Nathan says, "but Gluck will be back in a few minutes. We have to get our things together."

Nathan and Allison leave for the upstairs bedrooms to pack their things. Lena goes into the kitchen to make a cup of tea. *It might calm me down,* she thinks. Suddenly, there is a knock on the door. She peeks through the side curtain. It is Weber and another man! She freezes. Weber knocks louder. She has to answer the door or he'll break it down. And she has to get rid of him.

She swings the door open. "Major Weber," she says loudly enough for Nathan and Allison to hear. "What a surprise. What are you doing here this late, as if I didn't know. But you're out of luck, Dietrich is not here. He's gone out."

"Where is he?" Weber says firmly. He takes a step into the house and looks around. "Froman!" he hollers. "Where are you? Come on out."

Listening in the upstairs bedroom, Nathan puts his hand around the grip of his gun.

"I told you, he's not here," Lena says calmly.

"I don't believe you."

"Well, you can look around if you want to," Lena says nonchalantly. "Go on, look all over, but he's not home. He said he had an important meeting." She shrugs. "If it makes any difference, I'm not very happy with him either. He invited me to come over, we spent a whole five minutes together, and some of his army buddies came by to pick him up. So, he gives me a kiss and says, 'See you later.' Really, that's the way it was."

"What friends came by to get him?"

Lena shrugs. "Could have been any of them: Paul, Fritz, Alfred, Dirk." She shrugs again. "You tell me. They don't come in; they honk their horn and out the door he goes."

"When did he tell you he would be going out?"

"When the car horn honked. Pretty shitty, isn't it. I get roughed up by you, I come over here for some companionship and some comfort, and he leaves me for his buddies. And I'm supposed to marry him? I've about had it with him."

"He didn't say where he was going?"

"He didn't say anything except, 'See you later.' Do you want to grab my arms and shake me side to side until I cry? That's your way isn't it?"

Weber stands quietly. He looks around the room. In the upstairs doorway, Nathan is fingering the grip of his pistol.

"Major," Lena says, "I'm the fool here. It's embarrassing to me. He's gone out and I'm making a cup of tea by myself so I can just sit here and cry. You want a cup?" She points to the kitchen.

"No, I don't want any tea," Weber says, "I want Froman."

"Then stick around and wait for him because he said he'd be back later. He always comes back, but it's usually late, and he's usually drunk."

Weber's companion speaks up. "She's lying to you. There's no way any woman puts up with that crap. You know how to get the truth out of her, Otto. Be firm."

Nathan takes a step out of the bedroom door, pistol drawn, but Allison grabs his arm. "Wait. Sounds like she's in control."

Weber sighs in resignation. "When do you think he'll be home? I need to talk to him."

"He didn't say. He never says." With that, Lena starts to cry, sits down on the couch, and buries her face in her hands. "I don't know why he treats me like this, I don't deserve it, and I don't know why I put up with it. Would your girlfriend put up with it?" She shakes her head. "He can be so sweet, and then he can be so callous. He does this all the time: runs out, leaves me alone, and then he comes back. And like a fool, I take him back. Why do I do that?"

"I don't know, Miss Hartz. What time does he usually come home?"

"Late: two, three o'clock. And he expects me to wait up for him. He tells me that a fiancée has certain relationship responsibilities, and I should wait for him. What a damn fool I am," she says, and sobs loudly.

Weber speaks quietly. "Look, I need to speak with Froman. There's probably some things you don't know about him. Maybe after this, you should rethink this engagement."

"Maybe I will. I don't know. I can tell him that you came by looking for him."

"No, no, no."

"Well, then you should come back in the morning. He'll be here. That's for sure. Sleeping it off." She continues to sob.

Weber looks at his companion. "Let's come back later, Henning." He turns to Lena. "Miss Hartz, don't say anything to Froman about our being here. Just go along as usual. But you're a nice girl, so maybe you should rethink this whole thing."

Lena nods. Weber leaves and shuts the door behind him.

After a few minutes, Allison and Nathan come down the stairs. "Wow," Allison says, "back in my hometown, we'd say that was an Academy Award–winning performance."

Lena is shuddering. She grabs the arm of the couch and falls onto the cushions.

We had an unexpected visitor in your absence," Allison says to Gluck.

He furrows his forehead. "Really, who was the visitor?"

"Major Weber," she says, and Gluck quickly scans the apartment with his eyes.

"Don't worry," she says, "Lena got rid of him. Pretty much as deftly as any femme fatale I'd ever seen. Nathan whispered to me what she was saying to Weber and it was just like Rita Hayworth."

Nathan chuckles. "I'd say Gene Tierney. Maybe Garbo. For sure it was a stellar performance."

"What are you two talking about?" Gluck says.

Allison takes a minute to explain it all to Gluck.

"Do you think you might change your mind and stay here?" Nathan says. "It may not be so urgent for you to leave. Apparently, Weber believes you and feels sorry for you. I think he might leave you alone now."

Allison shakes her head. "Only because Weber doesn't know the whole story. When he finds out, he'll feel foolish for not being more aggressive and he'll blame Lena. Come with us to the new safe house."

Lena nods. "I need to get my things first. I can't leave without my clothes, my makeup, you know. I think I'll be all right for tonight. He's not going to come back until tomorrow morning. But there's no doubt that I should get out of Berlin for a while. I can always come back after the war. So, I'll go home, pack up some things, and meet up with you at the church tomorrow evening."

"That's not a good idea," Gluck says. "What if you're followed?"

"Well, where is she supposed to meet us?" Nathan says. "We're not coming back here."

Gluck grouses, twists his head this way and that, and finally says, "Meet us at four fifty-two Bredower. It's in Falkenhagen. *Please,* can I ask you to keep the address secret?"

"Of course. I know the area," she says.

"Okay then, let's go," Gluck says to Nathan. "My car is out front."

"How is Lena supposed to get home?" Nathan says. "It's the middle of the night."

Gluck closes his eyes and shakes his head. "Come on, I'll drop you off."

It is 2:00 A.M. and Nathan lies in bed. His eyes are wide open. Several scenarios play out in his mind. Now there is an extra person to smuggle out of Germany. Where will she go? She doesn't know anyone in America. Doesn't have a home, doesn't have a job. Maybe she'd be better off staying in England. She'd be close to her family once the war ends. If it ever ends.

There is a noise. Footsteps. He looks to his right and Allison is standing in the doorway. She is quivering, her lips are tightly pressed together. "Do you mind?" she says. He lifts the covers, and she slips into the bed. "It's okay," he says. "It'll all be over soon."

35

FALKENHAGEN

Construction barriers block the main entrance to St. Hedwig's. At Father Hannover's insistence, the church has not and will not be closed. God's house will stay open. Entrance to the central part of the chapel is permitted through a door on the north side of the church. Damage to the exterior of the church has been considerable, especially on the south side. Signs are posted warning of loose and unstable concrete, but a good portion of the sanctuary has been cleaned and set for services. The electrical system has been damaged. It is evening in late November and the interior is lit solely by a supply of candles. Attendees filter in slowly tonight. Notwithstanding, Father Hannover will serve his flock and he will hold daily mass.

"I'll be back in an hour and a half," Gluck says to Allison and Nathan as they exit his VW on the street in front of the church. "I'll be right here at six o'clock."

As they make their way back through darkened hallways, past the broken pillars and piles of plaster, Allison shakes her head. "Senseless damage. Dropping a bomb on a church."

"What do you think a uranium bomb would do?" Nathan says. "Isn't that what this assignment is all about?"

"Partly," says Allison, "it's about preventing Germany from getting a uranium bomb. The other part is delivering Günther to the Manhattan Project."

Father Hannover sits in his study. He sees Nathan and raises his hand. "Look what they've done to my church. The house of God. Your Allies. My alleged friends. The people I'm supposed to be helping."

"I'm sure they weren't aiming for your church, Father," Nathan says.

"Then tell me, at what are they aiming when they dropped their bombs in the middle of a city? Do they see tanks, airfields here? Or are there just people. Just families."

"They see an enemy; a country that has invaded other peaceful countries, that has sent thousands of peaceful families to their deaths in concentration camps."

Father Hannover hangs his head. "I don't accept it. Kill an enemy battalion in the field, I can understand. Kill children in a city and you are monsters."

"Do you think that Dr. Snyder will know to come directly to your study?" Allison asks.

"He's been in my study many times. He knows to meet with me here."

"I think he'll want to stay out of sight," Nathan says. "He plans to tell his co-workers that he is ill and has to leave work early. He presumes that his employer won't be suspicious for a few days. For that reason, he doesn't want to be seen talking to people in the church."

At five thirty, Günther Snyder enters the study carrying a large valise. Though the weather is chilly, he is sweating profusely. "I did it," he says. "I left. I told them all that I was feeling ill and I had to go home." He wipes his forehead. "It wasn't easy. Albert Speer himself came to the laboratories today to look over everyone's shoulder." Nathan translates Snyder's words for Allison, which annoys Snyder.

"Who is Albert Speer?" Allison asks Günther through Nathan.

"Whoa ho, who is Albert Speer? Now there's a question," Snyder answers. "Is there a person on this planet who doesn't know who Albert Speer is? You might as well be asking who is Heinrich Himmler, who is Hermann Goering?" Snyder says with a snarky laugh. "Speer is a member of Hitler's cabinet. He is reichminister for Armaments and Munitions. As such, he has authority over the entire German war industry. He's the man in charge of war materials, acquisitions, and production. That means weapons and bombs. He's supremely interested in the development of nuclear weapons. As you may imagine, KWI is under the auspices of the Ministry and Albert Speer. He was there all day, snooping around the lab, asking a million questions."

"I understand."

"No, I don't think you do. He's the money! KWI needs more funding and that means convincing Speer that we are close to an operating nuclear weapon. We can't produce sufficient enriched uranium without a lot more money. We need money for our reactor. We need money for heavy water, for uraninite, for transportation, for our supplies, for everything we do. So, we are all on our toes when he comes in. If Speer reports favorably to the Führer, we'll get increased funding. Everyone's nerves are on edge worrying about how to impress Speer with our progress."

"How is that going?"

Snyder shrugs. "Could have been better. We have some problems that we're working on. Solutions aren't coming easily. But all in all, I think it wasn't too bad. The closer we are to a workable bomb, the better our chances of greater funding. To tell you the truth, our theories are correct, our methods are sound, we just haven't put them to a trial."

Allison turns to Nathan and says, "Ask Günther what problems he's working on? What can't he solve? After all, why am I here?"

Snyder hears the question and looks at her with disdain. He doesn't wait for a translation. He immediately responds, "You wouldn't know if I told you, miss."

"You speak English?" she says. "I didn't know that."

"Hmph. Apparently, there's a lot you don't know. I speak English, French, and a little Russian, though not too much. I lived in Paris for two years." He points at Allison. "Who is this woman? Why is she here questioning me?"

Nathan raises his eyebrows. "She's your ticket out. She's the person you need to dazzle if you want to make it to America. And for the time being, as far as you're concerned, her name is Alicia Dumont."

Snyder sits back. "Oh, I am sorry. It is nice to meet you, Miss Dumont. You are the nuclear scientist I am to meet with?"

"Bingo."

"So, you ask what problems are we having? Broadly speaking, we can't put our theories to a test, though we are sure they are right. We cannot conduct trials. We don't have a dependable supply of adequate materials: heavy water, graphite, uraninite. We're having problems calculating the critical mass for the delivery devices the military has in mind, but we have theories. We've yet to engineer remote detonating devises but it's not far off. The diffusers used to separate the isotopes are slow and unreliable. We have problems, Miss Dumont, but they are problems you encounter when you are growing. All in all, we're not that far off."

Allison is unimpressed. "Some of those are entry-level problems. They cannot possibly be delaying the project. Where is your enriched uranium stored?"

Snyder shrugs. "I don't know. I'm sure there are records at the Institute, but it's out of my department."

"Where is the graphite stored?"

"At the moment, we don't use graphite. Graphite, which is carbon, was discarded as a moderator for the reason that the neutron absorption coefficient value for carbon, calculated by Dr. Walther Bothe, was too high, probably due to the boron in the graphite pieces having high neutron absorption."

Nathan looks at Allison. "Do you know what he's talking about? Does that mean something to you?"

"Of course."

Günther continues. "Dr. Hahn and I have had our doubts about the validity of Walther's conclusions and we have been working on our own calculations. But up to now, the Institute has followed Dr. Bothe's recommendation and we use heavy water, which is also expensive, difficult to transport, and impossible to store in sufficient quantity."

"Dr. Bothe concluded that graphite is ineffective?"

"That's correct. We use heavy water, but it is in short supply, and as I said, we have transportation hurdles to overcome."

"The heavy water, where does it come from, how is it transported, and where is it stored?"

Again, Snyder shrugs. "I have no idea. Again, that's out of my department. Other KWI members are working on that side of the equation."

Allison shakes her head. She's not getting the information she needs. "What is the project's concentration: uranium or plutonium?"

"Listen, Miss Dumont, my work has been theoretical, and only with uranium. I don't know what progress is being made with plutonium, if at all. That's in a separate office on the floor above me. Some in my group have been concentrating on developing a chemical trigger. I don't have all the answers to your other questions."

"Evidently. Most importantly, Dr. Snyder, has Germany been able to reach critical mass on a reactor?"

Snyder shakes his head. "If we have, I am unaware of it. But I think we'd be close if we were able to conduct live trials with a reactor. In my opinion, our delay is due to a lack of substantial funding. If Speer is convinced of our success, he will increase the funding. He's coming back tomorrow and that is why everyone at the lab is on pins and needles. We need the money."

"Where is your reactor?" Allison asks.

Snyder shrugs. "I don't know. I heard that there was an incident in June last year."

"What sort of incident?"

"They're not saying. I know that some of the physicists had plans to move ahead with actual trials, but they have been put on hold until the incident, whatever it was, is cleared up. Again, that is not under my authority."

"Under whose authority would that fall?"

"Well, certainly under Dr. Hahn and Dr. Esau, but I think Dr. Clusius would also know."

As Snyder finishes his sentence, Gluck comes running into Father Hannover's study. "My car is outside," he says. "We should go now."

Gluck drives into a quiet residential neighborhood. Nathan stares out of the window and furrows his forehead. His eyes narrow. "What's the matter?" Allison says.

"This is not Falkenhagen," he answers softly.

After a few minutes the car comes to a stop in front of a small, two-story frame house. "Why are we stopping here?" Nathan asks as they exit the car.

"This is where we are staying tonight," Gluck answers. "You'll do your examination here this evening, and if everything is in order and Dr. Fisher approves, you three will leave tomorrow night."

"Wait a minute," Nathan says, "you told Lena Hartz the new address was four fifty-two Bredower in Falkenhagen. What the hell are you doing? Are you pulling a switch on her?"

"I can't have her blowing another safe house, Lieutenant. She already spilled the Aller Straße address. And because of that, Weber and some Gestapo goon showed up at the door. You were there. That house was useful to us, and now it's trash."

"Yeah, I was there, and because of Lena Hartz, Weber went away without looking for us. Lena saved our lives. You can't leave her out in the cold. She's on our side and she's planning on coming with us."

"Well, those plans have changed."

"You son of a bitch," Nathan said through clenched teeth. "You have no right to make that decision."

Gluck tightens his lips in an unmistakable show of derision. "Back off. I'm in charge of the Berlin Station and I will make that decision if I think it's right and it protects our section. This is where we're staying tonight. And Fräulein Hartz is not invited. You heard her, Lieutenant, she thinks she'll be fine here in Berlin with her father and all his money. Besides, you witnessed it, she had Weber twisted around her finger. He told her to rethink her relationship, for Christ's sake.

She put him off beautifully, remember, Academy Award stuff? She'll have nothing to fear."

Nathan pulls his gun. "Give me the keys to your car, Gluck. I'm going to get her. I don't give a shit what you say or who you think you are."

"Oh, put your gun away, Nathan. You're not going to shoot me."

Nathan sighs and puts the gun into his holster. "I gave her my word, Fred. If you don't give me the car, I'll take a taxi, but I'm going to get her. She's coming with us. My word means something and I'm going to keep it."

"Wait a minute, Fred," Renzel says. "He's got a point. She's done a lot to protect Nathan and Dr. Fisher. Give her some credit. How does it hurt to bring an extra person along? I'll drive Nathan over to her place and we'll bring her back. She doesn't know this address, so she couldn't have blown it, and she won't have an opportunity to divulge it to anybody before she leaves Berlin tomorrow. I think she's tougher than you believe. She played along as Nathan's fiancée so that he could ditch Weber and meet up with Snyder. She came over to Aller Straße to warn us that Weber knew the address, and she stood up to Weber and his Gestapo friend when they showed up. She put herself in a world of trouble to help us out. I think we owe her."

Gluck hesitates and then nods his head. "All right, all right."

"Thank you," Nathan says. "Let's go pick her up. C'mon, Allison."

Allison shakes her head. "I don't need to go, Nathan. I'm needed here."

"I told you I wouldn't leave you alone anymore."

"I'm not alone. Fred is with me. No one knows about this address. I'll be fine."

"Listen to her," Gluck says. "Her time is better spent debriefing Snyder."

"All right," Nathan says, a bit reluctantly. "Let's go, Kurt."

Renzel glides into a parking space a half block from Lena's apartment at 1430 Oranienburger Straße. "She's in the red-brick building," Nathan says, as the two walk together, one a hulk of a man in a poplin jacket and the other in a Hauptmann's uniform.

As they approach, they notice that the door to Lena's apartment shows damage. The wooden frame is splintered at the hinges and at the lock. "Looks like someone forced the door," Renzel says.

Nathan nods. "It could have been the other night when Weber confronted her." He knocks. They wait a moment, but no one answers. Nathan tries the doorknob, and the door opens without resistance. They rush in and Nathan calls out, "Lena? Lena, are you here?"

Hearing nothing, Nathan walks around the apartment and comes back shaking his head. "She's not home," he says. "Maybe she went out to pick something up. Maybe she needs something for the trip; medicine, toiletries, or something, I don't know? Maybe she decided to go directly to the Bredower address. Gluck shouldn't have given her a phony address. But she's not here."

Back in the car, Nathan says, "Do me a favor, Kurt. Drive over to four fifty-two Bredower. Just in case she might have gone there. After all, that's where Gluck told her we were going to stay." He pauses. "I'm worried about her. I dragged her into this mess. She was doing just fine living in Berlin until I came back into her life."

Renzel turns the car around. "I can understand why you'd want to protect your old girlfriend and bring her to safety. Probably still a lot of feelings."

"No. It's not like that. When I first saw her, I thought maybe we could strike up our old relationship again, but the truth is, those feelings aren't there. Not for her, not for me. My goal now is to get her out of harm's way. That's it."

Renzel nods and drives on.

As they approach Bredower, Nathan asks, "Why did Fred give us the address of four fifty-two Bredower? What's there?"

Renzel flips his hand. "Oh, it's just a vacant unit that we use from time to time."

The street is dark when Renzel arrives. There's no place to park and Renzel says he will wait in the car. Nathan jumps out and hurries to the door. The lights in the house at 452 Bredower are out, but the front door is open.

As he enters the house, the lights come on and Nathan freezes in his tracks. There is Lena, tied and bound to a wooden chair in the middle of the living room. Numerous bruises and cuts discolor her pretty face, arms, and legs. There is a pool of blood beneath the chair, but she is still alive. Sitting across from her on the couch is Major Otto Weber. A sickly grin is on his face. In his hand is a standard-issue Walther P38, pointed directly at Lena. Beside him is a large hunting knife.

"I figured you'd come looking for her, Froman. Or whatever the hell your real name is, she never would tell me. Now, slowly take your gun out of your holster and lay it on the floor. Keep your hands where I can see them. Don't be stupid enough to make a move or she dies."

"Don't hurt her anymore, Weber," Nathan says, as he lays his pistol on the floor. "Just let her go. It's me you want."

"That is true. Kick the gun over here," he commands, and Nathan obeys.

"Let her go," Nathan pleads. "You've got me. She hasn't done anything wrong. Just let her go. She needs medical care."

"Indeed, she does. I believe she is bleeding pretty badly," he says nonchalantly. "Probably doesn't have much time left. But then, what does she deserve? She collaborated with the enemy. She assisted you in your espionage activities, though she tried hard not to tell me anything about them. It took a lot of persuasion just to get this address out of her. This address and a little more. She was tough, your girlfriend. Or should I say, your fiancée?"

"She didn't do anything, Weber. She doesn't know anything. She has no idea what my activities are."

Nathan looks at Lena; her blue eyes are partially closed. Her breathing is shallow. She faces Nathan. "I'm sorry," she says, in a whispered voice.

"What is your real name?" Weber asks Nathan. "Where do you come from? England?"

Lena looks at Nathan. She shakes her head. "Don't tell him."

"I'm German," Nathan says. "She needs a doctor right now. I'll cooperate with you. I'll tell you what you want to know. Just let me take her to a hospital. You can follow me. Or come with me."

Weber snorts. "Well, you will cooperate, that is for certain. The only question is whether you'll make it easier for me and easier for yourself, or whether you'll be sitting in a chair like your fiancée. Either way, your cooperation is assured."

"I'll do whatever you want, just let me get her some medical care."

"No," Lena says in a breath. "Don't do it."

"What kind of man are you to let this woman suffer like this?" Nathan says.

"You're right, Froman. I've spent enough time with her. And since I have no further need of her, I'll end her suffering." He stands, walks over to Lena, and shoots her point-blank in the chest. The force of the bullet knocks Lena and the chair over backward.

"You filthy bastard!" Nathan screams. "You murdered an innocent woman. A German citizen."

"Yeah, I know. A wonderful citizen. You're breaking my heart. She's a rotten spy, like you. Turn around and head out the door. There is a car waiting for us. One funny move and I'll lay you out next to your bitch."

They step out onto the stoop, and a shot rings out. Then another. Weber's body stiffens, he drops his gun, stumbles forward and falls to the ground. Renzel is standing beside the doorway. He drags the body inside the house, looks around, and then back at Nathan. "I'm really sorry, Nate. She was a good lady. But we better go now before the police arrive."

"Give me one minute," Nathan says, walking over to Lena's body. He unties her, lifts her gently onto the couch, kneels, and kisses her lightly on the forehead. "Oh Lena, what did they do to you?" he cries. "Why did I bring you into this? Why did I ever involve you? This is all my fault." Tears run down his cheeks. "She was so kind, so innocent, so lovely. Always a lady, a dignified lady. And she's lying here because of me."

"We'll take care of her, Nate. I'll see to it. I'll send a crew over here right away. They'll treat her with honor. We'll take her to a mortuary

I know. The story will be that she was found outside her apartment building and the logical explanation is that she was mugged. They'll clean her up and we'll make sure she gets a proper burial."

Renzel walks outside and returns, dragging another body. "That's Weber's sidekick. He was waiting in his car for you two to come outside. I had to take care of him as well."

"Thanks, Kurt. I appreciate your handling the funeral arrangements. Lena's father has to be informed," Nathan says, with a catch in his throat. "He deserves to pay his last respects to his daughter."

Renzel agrees. "I'll have the mortician contact him. I've known the man for a long time, he'll handle it correctly. We'll figure it all out, Nate, don't worry. I'm sorry, bud, truly I am."

36

PLANNING FOR THE MASQUERADE

Allison knows the moment that Nathan walks into the house. She can see it in his face. His eyes are bloodshot, his uniform is bloodstained. She covers her mouth with her hand. "Lena?"

He nods. "She's gone. Weber murdered her. He beat her, tortured her, and then he shot her through her heart, right in front of me. He took her to the Bredower address and held her as bait for me."

Allison rushes over and puts her arm around him. He buries his head in her shoulder and cries as she leads him to the couch. "I'm so sorry," she says. "I know that you had deep feelings for her."

He nods. "When I was younger, we had plans to get married one day, or so I thought." He stares into Allison's eyes. "It doesn't matter, does it? Now she's dead and it's because of me."

"No, Nathan, she's dead because of Weber. She's dead because an evil, hateful man who serves an evil, hateful empire took her life."

Nathan continues to wipe away his tears. "She wasn't a soldier. She wasn't a traitor. She didn't possess any secret information. She wasn't even in this fight, not until I showed up. I dragged her into it, Allison. I had no right to enter her life. But I did and there is no denying that I am responsible for her death. I had no right. Do you understand me?"

"Yes," she says quietly.

Nathan hangs his head. "She had a comfortable life, one she had built for herself. She didn't kill anyone, she didn't deport anyone, she didn't expose anyone. What right did I have to barge into her life un-invited and bring pain and death? What right, Allison? Tell me!" He shakes a few tears from his eyes. "I killed her."

"No, you didn't! Weber killed her! You cared for her. She was killed by a cold, heartless Nazi soldier. Weber, Hitler, the Nazis, they bear all of the responsibility. They started this war and so many have sense-lessly died because of it."

They sit in silence for a while, until Nathan turns to Gluck and says, "Why did you give her a bullshit address? If she had come here instead of going to Bredower, she'd still be alive. I could have pro-tected her."

Gluck answers quietly. "I think it's obvious; you just don't want to concede it. When morning came, Weber went to the Aller Straße safe house. Finding it empty he went back to confront Lena. With his Ge-stapo buddy, he confronted her, demanded information and a new address. She couldn't hold out. Plain and simple, Nate, he tortured the address out of her. If I had given her this address, Weber would have come here with his Gestapo goon. As it was, he probably went to Bre-dower, found an empty house, and realized she didn't have the right address. You can figure out the rest. He used her to set a trap for you. He was looking to take you in, and he would have, if it hadn't been for Kurt. I know how these guys work; it's just what I feared. That's why I didn't give her the right address. I only hope that she didn't reveal the rest of the operation, but I'm not confident of that either."

"It's the Nazis, Nate," Renzel adds. "It ain't you. They care nothing for human life. Don't blame yourself."

Gluck adds, "It's a war. Good guys die. Just imagine if Germany manages to produce a workable nuclear bomb. How many millions more will die. Hitler has no conscience. We need to finish our mission and get the information back to Washington."

Allison turns to Nathan. "Why don't you take a few minutes, take all the time you need, get yourself together, and whenever you're ready, I'll tell you what I've learned from Günther."

Nathan sits on the bed trying to clear his head. But the doubts keep coming.

Why couldn't I have anticipated the consequences of my actions? Why am I so shortsighted? Am I the wrong man for the job? Maybe so, but here I am. I left Allison Fisher alone at the church during a bombing raid. Hell, I could have lost her too. Everything has happened so damn fast since I left Camp Ritchie. I can't catch up with it. Things just spin out of control so quickly.

In a little while, Allison walks into the bedroom and sits beside him. She holds his hand and kisses him softly on his forehead. "I know what you're doing, but you have to stop taking the blame. You were sent here to do a job and that meant meeting Günther secretly, outside the presence of the Nazis. You did what you had to do to get rid of Weber. Had Weber seen you with Günther, had he followed you to Günther's apartment, had you missed meeting up with Günther, had any of those things happened, the entire operation could have failed. You are a soldier in a war, remember? Nathan the Soldier. Gluck is right; there are casualties in war, and sometimes they are people we love. You're a good man. There isn't another soldier in Uncle Sam's army that I would want to serve with. But we have a mission to complete and it's going to save a lot of lives."

Allison and Nathan return to the front room and take a seat next to Günther. Gluck and Renzel are seated across the room. Gluck looks at him sympathetically and says, "Are you all right?"

He shakes his head. "No, not really, but we have a mission. I need to finish my work. Let's go over what Allison learned from Günther. Did we get everything we need? Do we head back tomorrow?"

Allison shakes her head. "We can't. We got everything Günther could give us, but it's not close to what we need. His work at KWI has been focused on calculating a critical mass, but he's never actually witnessed a chain reaction. He's quite sure that there is a nuclear reactor somewhere, but he doesn't know where. He heard that there was an incident with a reactor, but he doesn't know what it was. He is unaware of the source of the raw materials or where they are stored. Others may know, but not him."

Nathan has a troubled expression. "Despite all of our efforts, despite Lena's tragic death, we're falling short. Günther isn't able to tell us if there is a working reactor or if Germany can produce a chain reaction. Or whether a reactor is being used to produce plutonium. He's not even aware of what progress is being made by his colleagues. And he doesn't know the supply routes. We can't go home yet. We're lacking critical information. Given what's happened, I don't want to quit early in this mission. And to tell the truth, Günther, I just don't understand why you don't know more than you're disclosing."

Günther huffs. "It's not my fault. You have to realize, it's all secret stuff, Nathan. They don't let the left hand know what the right hand is working on. I'm pretty sure that there is a reactor, but I don't think it is a working reactor. Otherwise, I would be right there testing out my calculations."

Allison interrupts. "Go easy, Nathan. Günther hasn't given me everything, but he has given me a terrific overview of Germany's nuclear program, and that will help us to understand how far along they are, and what more we need to know."

"What did he tell you?"

"Well, starting before the war, even before Albert Einstein wrote his letter to President Roosevelt, there were communications sent to the German hierarchy describing the potential of a uranium bomb. Remember, it was the Germans that discovered nuclear fission in December 1938, right here in Berlin.

"In April 1939, a top secret meeting was held at KWI. The purpose of the meeting was to plan the development of a uranium research program, with emphasis on consideration of a nuclear weapon, though the scientists were not actually told to build a weapon, just to continue perfecting nuclear fission. After the meeting, Paul Harteck, a German chemist, wrote a secret letter on his own behalf to Germany's War Office, describing the explosive properties of nuclear fission and suggesting that creation of such a weapon was theoretically achievable."

"And my father was in on that?" Nathan says.

"No," Günther says. "Your father was all about peaceful application. Harteck never spoke to me or your father."

Allison continues. "In September, the month that Germany invaded Poland and started this war, Kurt Diebner brought several German scientists together to discuss atomic fission. Diebner was really the heart of the program. Still, the meeting was not about developing a bomb. As I said, the original group of scientists were only researching fission in terms of nonmilitary uses. It was all about the value of nuclear energy. That group included your father, Fritz Strassmann, Werner Heisenberg, and Otto Hahn, who is currently running the lab. That was the inception of the Uranium Club. Subsequent to the meeting, and probably because of the recommendation of your father, Günther was transferred from the lab in Frankfurt to Berlin. He remembers all of the early discussions: pile design, isotope separation, and neutron fission. Günther insists that the initial meetings were just about nuclear energy and not about a weapon, though the explosive properties of nuclear fission were known."

Nathan agrees. "That sounds right to me. I'm sure my father would not have willingly joined a program to develop a nuclear weapon. He was against war."

Allison smiles warmly. "I'm sure that's the case. Of course, as you know, research on nuclear fission, even for peaceful purposes, requires a large amount of uranium—enriched uranium. Remember what I told you in Chicago?"

"I think so. Uranium ore is ninety-nine percent U-238 which is not fissile. It will not cause a chain reaction when bombarded with a neutron. You have to separate out the isotope U-235 if you want to achieve nuclear fission."

Allison beams. "You would have made a great scientist."

"No thanks."

Allison continues. "Well, to Günther's knowledge, Germany has never been able to produce any significant amounts of enriched uranium. If it has, and he doubts it, it is outside his sphere and stored somewhere secret. It seems, though Günther cannot be sure, that most of the isotope separation work is being done by the thermal diffusion method, which we in Chicago know to be very inefficient. He also believes that KWI has yet to achieve critical mass with a pile, essential to a chain reaction and the development of a weapon, but again he cannot be sure because the scientists are not in constant communication with each other. In fact, he believes that is what your father was working on."

"Development of a weapon? He believes that?"

"No. Pursuit of a chain reaction. Günther has never witnessed a chain reaction, though his work has concentrated on calculating a critical mass, the amount needed to sustain a chain reaction. That may be because Günther and the rest of the scientists at KWI are working in silos, very independently, and because they were never given access to a nuclear reactor to prove their theories.

"In 1938, 1939, and 1940, when Germany conquered countries in Europe—Belgium, France, Czechoslovakia—it gained access to a plentiful supply of uraninite, or, as it's called, pitchblende, remember?"

"I do."

"Germany took all the natural resources it wanted from the conquered lands, especially uranium ore and whatever they are using for moderators in order to construct a pile."

"When you say 'pile,' are you referencing the pile Fermi and Szilard built at the University of Chicago, the one you showed me?"

"Exactly."

"The ones in the squash courts under the football field."

"Right."

"As I remember, the rooms were stuffed with hundreds and hundreds of graphite bricks that served as moderators to control the speed of the neutrons in a chain reaction."

Allison smiles. "Good memory, but not just hundreds. The reactor was stuffed with forty-six thousand blocks of graphite to act as neutron moderators. There were piles of graphite and uranium bricks. That's why Dr. Fermi gave them the name 'piles.' We're talking about a reactor here. A large, insulated underground structure, obviously not

located in an academic building like the KWI. Günther believes it has
been built, but he really can't provide any further information. He's
sure that the scientists are making and keeping records—notes, mem-
oranda, sketches, daily dairies—but they are not shared. They are all
stored in a different room under the supervision of the program's director, Dr. Abraham Esau. To assess their program, we need to see
those records. Actually, *I* need to see them."

"Why do *you* need to see them?" Nathan asks. "Why can't Günther
go into the lab and read them himself?"

Günther scoffs. "If I asked to see records of other scientists, they
would ask me why. What reasons would I have to poke around in
other scientist's records? Oh, I could make up some excuse, tell them
I wanted coordination with a colleague's findings, but odds are they
would know something was up. Second, my work concentrates on calculating a critical mass. Have you ever played marbles?"

"Of course."

"Think of a circle of marbles on the floor. Tightly together. When
I flick a marble into the circle, what will happen? It will cause all the
marbles to bang into each other. In some ways, that is a chain reaction.
Now think of the marbles as fissionable uranium U-235 atoms. When
I fire a neutron into an atom, that atom will absorb the neutron and
in turn release more neutrons to slam into more atoms, and in turn release more neutrons to smash into more atoms. Get it? All that smash-
ing creates a great deal of heat and energy."

Nathan nods. "Got it. A chain reaction."

"Yes, but how many marbles do I need for a sustained chain reaction? How close together do they need to be? What happens when
they spread out a bit? What happen if we slow down the shooter?
Does that facilitate the chain reaction or impede it? And, very importantly, using my marble analogy, what sort of medium do we need for
this chain reaction to take place? A wood floor, a tile floor, a carpet? I
don't know what the others are doing, but I am working on calculating a critical mass in varied mediums."

"Well done, Professor," Allison says.

Part of this secret operation seems illogical to Nathan. "You mean the notes and memos of your colleagues are off limits to you, a KWI scientist, who's been working since the program was started?"

"Well, not entirely. I can interact with my colleagues and discuss critical mass and isotope separation, but when it comes to the nuclear reactor, or a detonating device, or how and where materials are shipped, that's totally out of my realm, and no, I would not be able to see those notes."

"It's hard to believe," Nathan says. "Why couldn't you ask for permission to enter the file room and review the documents to find out how close you are to testing your critical mass in a working reactor? Aren't you entitled to know? After all, aren't you all working to achieve the same result?"

All eyes turn to Günther, who is noticeably sheepish. He shrugs his shoulders. "This is Germany. Everyone is suspicious. Everything has to be controlled by a leader. In our case, that person is Professor Esau."

Allison leans forward. "Günther, tell me, is a reactor being used to produce plutonium-239? Is that research being carried on here at KWI? That is of utmost importance."

"That is one of the goals, but I can't tell you who would be working on that. Maybe Dr. Clusius. I have never been involved on that side of the research."

Allison stands. "Then I should be the one to go into the file room. I have experience in levels above Günther, especially in isotope separation, critical mass, chain reaction, and production of plutonium. You want me to view the records."

Nathan shakes his head. "Well, no I don't," he says. "How are we supposed to get you into the lab? They're never going to let some unknown woman, who doesn't even read or speak German, come in and review their German records. How are you supposed to carry that off? Are you and Günther supposed to sneak in during the middle of the night?"

"Hardly," Günther says, "the lab is well guarded at all hours."

"Then I don't know how you figure you're going to do this."

Allison raises her index finger. "Okay, here we go. Do you remember

Dr. Oppenheimer's crazy idea? We poo-pooed it at the time. Well, Allison Fisher cannot get into the KWI lab, let alone the file archives, under any circumstances. *But,* Irène Curie could. What if Günther brought her to evaluate and help solve some of Günther's problems in calculating critical mass? Remember when we discussed this in New York? Günther could say Dr. Curie is offering herself as a resource to Günther and his colleagues."

"Oh, no you don't," Nathan says. "I remember very well that we talked about that in New York and we all rejected it as a crazy idea. Even if you look a little like her, and you speak a little French, would Curie just show up at the KWI lab to help Günther build a bomb? Seriously?"

"No, she wouldn't. She's going to come at Günther's invitation, and not to build a bomb, but to improve the progress of creating nuclear energy. Remember, Günther studied in Paris. He even visited the Curie Institute and met Irène. Knowing Günther, I'm sure he's boasted about that."

Günther nods. "I have. I did meet her, and we had a very nice conversation one afternoon."

"Well, the presumption is that Günther requested his 'longtime friend Irène Curie' to help him solve his problems, not for a bomb but for peaceful nuclear energy."

Nathan is confused. "Where is the real Irène Curie?"

Allison shrugs. "I don't know. In Switzerland, I think. I've heard she's sick. The word is that she has tuberculosis, but I've also heard she has radiation poisoning."

Nathan shakes his head. "This is insane. I can't imagine this sideshow could be successful, and I'm not going to let you do it. It's too easy to get caught and the Gestapo are merciless. You know what they did to Lena."

"Calm down. Hear me out. Günther will tell his superiors that he's run into a roadblock of sorts. He can't proceed without testing his algorithms under actual circumstances in a reactor, and he has been unable to conduct such trials because of the so-called incident. But Irène could look at his calculations and know from her experience whether they would prove out. Nathan, she won the Nobel Prize for her synthesis of new radioactive elements and her discovery of artificial radioactivity. She could evaluate Günther's work and correct any errors."

"Irène Curie?"

"Sure. Hahn knows that Günther lived and studied in Paris. He is in a position to greet Irène, grant her access to the facility, and guide us through the labs."

"And how would you set this up?"

"Günther can call Hahn and say that he invited Irène to review his work a few weeks ago, that she agreed. In fact, she's planning on coming into the lab with Günther on Monday morning. Hahn knows this will benefit the entire program. He will gladly find a way to have the necessary authority issued through the program's director for her to enter the lab."

"This is nuts. You are not Curie. Curie is in her forties and she's ill."

Günther wags his finger. "Don't dismiss it so quickly, Nathan. I think it will work. Everyone is in awe of what Irène accomplished in Paris at her mother's institute. I always brag that I studied there, even though I was only there on occasion. I have also boasted that Irène and I are friends." He looks at Nathan with a guilty face. "You know me; sometimes I bend the truth a little. I figured it would get me additional prestige. Anyway, I will say that I contacted her and told her that I was working on a nuclear energy project at KWI, the second-most respected lab in the world next to hers—solely for peaceful purposes, of course. A nuclear power plant to generate electricity. But I have come to an impasse. I can't test it. I will say that, after much begging, she agreed to come to Berlin and help me out, and she's coming to Berlin tomorrow."

Nathan stares at Allison. "And that's you, of course. You are going to play Irène Curie."

"I can do it. I can be her. I'll go into the lab, review Günther's work, and I'll say that I see the problem. In order to make sense of his calculations, I'll need to evaluate his colleagues' findings, the other pieces of the puzzle, and how well they fit together in the overall project. I will say I can fix it, but I need to go into the KWI files. I will need to know about their reactor. How is it constructed, what are they using for a moderator, where are they getting it, and where are they storing it, and especially the notes of their successful chain reactions. If Günther is right, and they tell me they haven't done any of those things, then they are way behind. Isn't that what General Groves needs to know?"

"Yes."

"But Günther could be wrong. KWI has a collection of some of the world's foremost physicists and chemists. I have to believe they are making solid progress. Günther says they are looking for a way to increase funding. Tell me they wouldn't welcome the input of Curie to impress the intractable Albert Speer."

"Hmm. You make a point."

"So, they will give me—I mean Irène—access to everyone's notes, all the files, and believe me, I'll find out what I need to know."

"I think you are dreaming."

"Oh, I believe Hahn will happily arrange for Irène—I mean Allison—to access the files if it means increased funding," Günther says. "Especially if she impresses Albert Speer. As I said, Speer is always there, always whining, 'Where's the weapon? Where's the bomb? Why are we even bothering with all of you?' He's always criticizing our work. 'The Reich Ministry is growing impatient,' he says. 'There is talk of shutting this whole money pit down.' If Curie can save the program, you better believe that Esau and Hahn will let Irène in. They want Speer to increase the funding, not cut us off."

Gluck likes the idea. "If a Nobel Prize–winning scientist is brought in to assist on the project, they will roll out the red carpet. Esau will jump at that opportunity and Hahn will approve it. I think it's a great idea and I think it's going to work."

Nathan shakes his head. "That's your opinion, Gluck, because it's not your ass on the line. If they figure this out, if someone actually knows Curie and that she is terminally sick with tuberculosis and cannot travel, then we have lost both Allison and Günther."

"Well, we wouldn't lose her," Günther says. "We'd just leave."

"Right. And the guards would let you walk out the door?"

Günther shrugs. "Why not?"

"I don't like it," Nathan says. "Allison has been brought here to do a job—to find out how close the Nazis are to developing a nuclear weapon, and I think she's done it. She's interviewed Günther, and she can transmit her information to Washington. As far as I'm concerned, she is not going out of this house. She is not Irène Curie. It's a crazy plan. Curie is twenty years older than Allison, and she's sick, and she's not going to come to KWI from wherever she is just to help Günther convince Reichminister Speer to increase funding. That is nuts. It's way too easy for something to go wrong. We lost one woman tonight and we're not going to lose another."

"Just think about it," Allison says. "It could work. Just a few hours inside the KWI labs. Günther is also studying isotope separation, and that is exactly what Irène received the Nobel Prize for in chemistry. Günther has never seen a chain reaction. In fact, to Günther's knowledge, no one at KWI has. But Irène Curie surely has. She could look at his calculations and make corrections. Maybe she could see other records to verify them. Then Günther would boast to Speer about how close they are to achieving nuclear fission, and that Irène could make the difference."

"But we don't want the Nazis to have increased funding," Nathan says. "Why would we send Irène—I mean Allison—into their labs to correct Günther's calculations and convince Speer?"

Allison rolls her eyes. "Nathan, I'm not going to build their bomb. I'm not going to provide the secret formulas, even if I could. Anything I provide will fall well short of useful. I will look at Günther's work and assure them all that I can help, and I will get access to how far along they are."

Nathan is still not convinced. "Alli, you are not Irène. You are too young. You are too healthy. Something is going to go wrong with this masquerade. And I'm going to lose you."

Allison affectionately smiles. "Aww, that's sweet, but you won't lose me. It worked for you. Talk about masquerades, Mr. Hauptmann Froman, or Strauss. The fact is, I look a little like Irène, at least I can make myself up to look like her. I can style my hair with short curls. I can wear a dowdy long dress. I speak French pretty well, and I know a lot about Irène's mother, Marie Curie. I know the science; I can speak the language. Would you know the difference? Would Speer know? Dr. Oppenheimer thought it was a good idea, and he's met Irène Curie. I can do it, Nathan, I know I can. Just give me a chance."

"How are you going to go into a German lab and look at German records written in German, when you don't read or speak a word of German?"

"I read chemical formulas. I speak mathematics. I can understand chemical records, and what I don't understand, Günther will translate for me, in French."

"What about me?" Nathan says. "Am I supposed to walk you into the lab as a German officer? Why would she need a German Hauptmann to accompany her into a chemical lab?"

"She would not," Allison says. "You're not coming."

"Oh no, I'm going. I'm not letting you out of my sight."

"I agree with Allison," Günther says. "There is no reason for a German Hauptmann to enter the lab. Speer would know something was amiss and would confront you immediately. But you needn't worry, Nathan, I'll be with her."

Nathan's eyes roll upward. "Oh right. Günther the bodyguard. With all due respect, Dr. Snyder, she isn't going anywhere without me."

"Now hold on," Renzel says, "this is a pretty good plan. I like it, let's make it work. Given the fiasco with Hauptmann Froman, the Gestapo might be on the lookout for a fake Hauptmann. That could kill the whole thing. He needs to be someone else."

"Kurt's right," Gluck says. "Nathan's identity has to be solid. If Nathan is exposed, Allison and Snyder go down as well. What are your thoughts, Nate? Can she go? It's your operation. You call the shots. What do you want to do?"

"Come on, Nathan," Allison says, "we've come this far, we've all risked our lives, and we don't have a lot to show for it."

Nathan knows he is defeated. He slowly shakes his head. "If all of you believe it will work, I'll go along with the plan. But I don't want Allison going in without me. So how do I fit into this scenario?"

Gluck paces in the center of the room. "Well, you can't go in as a military figure. We know that when Lena Hartz was tortured, she gave up the Bredower address, but we don't know how much more she told Weber. She knew that Nathan's job was to sneak a top scientist out of Germany, and we have to allow for the possibility that she told that to Weber as well."

"But Weber's dead," Renzel says proudly. "I took care of that myself."

Gluck shakes his head. "He wasn't working alone. He was usually in the company of another guy, probably Gestapo. When he first confronted Lena at her home, he had a man with him, we presume Gestapo. When he came to the Aller Straße safe house the other night, he was with a different man, again presumably Gestapo. I have to believe that one of them was present when they tortured poor Lena to death. So I think it's reasonable to assume that the Gestapo knows about the planned defection of a top scientist. It wouldn't surprise me if there are agents on the lookout at the KWI lab."

"I never told Lena who the defecting scientist was," Nathan says. "She didn't know it was Günther, and they won't know to watch Günther. As I remember, KWI is located in a large building with several floors. Are they going to have Gestapo watchmen on each floor? In each office?"

"Who knows?" Gluck answers.

"So then Nathan doesn't go in as a Hauptmann," Allison says. "He goes in plain clothes. Suit and tie."

Nathan furrows his forehead. "And why would I be going to the lab? Me in a suit and tie?"

There is silence in the room. Heads turn from one to another looking for an answer. Finally, Kurt says, "Hell, you could be her lover."

Nathan laughs. "She's taking her lover to a nuclear lab? That's what we call a hot date! Besides, Curie's twenty years older than me, and I don't speak French. Sorry Kurt."

"How about her brother?" Günther says.

Allison shakes her head. "Marie Curie had two children, both girls."

"How about a cousin?" Renzel says. "He could be Irène's cousin who made the trip with her because she's been sick and he's taking care of her as she makes her journey."

"Marie had sisters, but they were all Polish and lived in Poland. I don't know if they had children, but if they did, they would speak Polish. None of us know how to speak Polish."

"What about Irène's father? Did he have a brother or a sister? Who would know? Nathan could be a cousin."

"Irène's father is Pierre Curie," Allison says. "I don't know anything about Pierre's brothers or sisters or their children. Irène is married to Frédéric Joliot. In fact, when they married, they both changed their legal names to Joliot-Curie. Irène Joliot-Curie is her legal name, although she just uses the name Irène Curie in everyday matters. Frédéric has a brother."

"There it is," says Gluck. "Nathan Joliot."

Renzel agrees. "If Nathan pretended to be Irène's brother-in-law, he'd be taking a chance that someone would actually know and discover his disguise, but it's workable."

"I think we could carry it off," Günther says. "No one at the KWI lab is going to know the Joliot family."

"I'll concede, it's definitely more credible," Nathan says, "but we're stuck with the same problems. Frédéric's brother would not be twenty-eight years old. And I don't speak French."

Gluck steps up. "We could make you look older. A little gray in your hair, a little face makeup. It takes a theatrical makeup artist, and I know just the girl who can do it. In fact, I've dated her off and on. She's worked for the Berlin theater for fifteen years and she hates the Nazis. She can make you look a hundred years old if she wants to. Let me see if Hanna is available and if she can get here before Monday. As for the French language, just don't speak at all. Maybe there's something wrong with your throat."

Nathan shakes his head. "This gets crazier by the minute. My total wardrobe consists of two Hauptmann uniforms and a tweed jacket. I didn't bring a suit and tie."

"Hell, I'll loan you one of mine," Renzel says.

Nathan laughs. "Two of me could fit into one of your suits."

"Maybe Hanna has a white shirt and a tie in the theater wardrobe," Gluck says. "Let me give her a call. Is everyone okay with this?"

Allison smiles. "Well, are you in, my brother-in-law? Will you take care of your poor sick sister-in-law?"

Nathan closes his eyes, nods his head, and inhales deeply. "Yeah, I'm in."

37

CURTAIN CALL

Early Monday morning, before sunrise, Gluck pulls his car up to the curb and parks in front of the new safe house. He and Renzel exit and hold the door open for a woman in an ankle-length cloth coat and a knit cap. She carries a large bag and a white shirt on a hanger. She is introduced as Hanna Weiner.

"Thank you so much for coming out so early," says Allison, who is dressed in her dark wool suit and heels, the ones she bought in New York with Molly.

"I brought pastries," Renzel says proudly, waving a white paper bag back and forth. "Do I get a thank-you?"

"Thank you," Allison says. "And there's coffee in the kitchen. Hanna, were you able to find a large hat?"

"Yes, I was," she answers, pulling a wide-brimmed felt fedora out of her bag. "It looks like the one Irène Curie wore in the photo. But Irène's hair is much shorter than yours."

"The hat is great, it will hide much of my face, but there's not much I can do about the length of my hair at this time."

"I can cut it any size," Hanna says with a smile, but then she gets serious. "May I be blunt, Dr. Fisher?"

"Of course."

"You intend to impersonate Dr. Irène Joliot-Curie, a forty-six-year-old Nobel Prize winner?"

"Yes."

"Whose physical appearance, while not as recognizable by some, is still well known."

Everyone in the room stops and quietly listens to Hanna's reasoning.

"And as I understand it," Hanna says, "she has recovered from a severe bout of tuberculosis, which required a long stay in a sanitarium. She is weak and feeble, but you, Dr. Fisher, are young and fit. Very fit, I might say. Perhaps when Dr. Curie was also young and healthy, you bore some resemblance, but not now."

"Are you saying that it is a mistake to pose as Irène Curie? I don't think we can pull this off otherwise."

Hanna shakes her head and smiles. "No. I am saying it will take some work to make you look like present-day Dr. Curie."

"And . . . ?"

Hanna shrugs. "That is what I do. Pretty much every day." She turns to the rest of the group. "Gentlemen, if you would give us some privacy, please, we have a transformation to perform, turning one woman into another."

Ninety minutes later, Hanna calls the group into the bedroom. Standing next to her is a forty-six-year-old woman in very poor health. She has a pasty white, sickly complexion and dark circles beneath her eyes. Her back is bent, and she steadies herself with a cane. The blue suit is gone, replaced with a floor-length, long-sleeve, formless print dress. Her high heels have given way to laced boots. There are wrinkles and age spots on her face and neck. Her hair is a mousy brown with gray streaks. As Allison requested, a wide-brimmed hat hides a good portion of her face.

Nathan, Günther, Fred, and Kurt stand mesmerized with their mouths wide open. "Oh my God," Kurt says. "Do you need to sit down, Dr. Curie?"

Hanna holds up a white shirt and a thin red tie. "This is for you, Nathan. It's the best I could do on short notice. I also brought a hat for you, a fine gray trilby, a favorite of gentlemen in Berlin. And I have been instructed to put some years on you as well. Twenty to twenty-five, am I right?" Nathan groans and nods.

"Let me get started," she says. "If you're going to be at KWI by nine o'clock, I have a lot more work to do."

"Oh, don't worry about the time," Günther says, "we're not expected until ten."

"So then, you were able to reach Dr. Hahn last night?" Nathan asks.

"Yes, I was. I woke him up. At first, he was cranky with me, but then I told him I was bringing Irène Curie, and his attitude changed like Berlin's weather in the spring. Otto knows I've been having trouble with my calculations. I keep getting different results and he knows that I am frustrated. We all are, especially with Speer looking over our shoulders."

"Exactly how did you explain the presence of Irène Curie?" Hanna asks. "It is known in some circles that she is a sick woman."

"Otto asked me the same question—how was I able to get her to come to Berlin? I told him I've known Irène for years, going back to the time I worked and studied in Paris. I told him that I reached out to her and practically begged her for help. I said my job was in jeopardy. Could I come to Switzerland and consult with her on my work? She asked me what I was working on. I told her I was working with Otto Hahn and that we were running into problems calculating critical mass. I told her that I feared for my position.

"I know it wasn't exactly true, but Reichminister Speer has been coming quite frequently, and he complains about our lack of progress. So, I told Irène that I wanted to bring my notes and some of my files to Switzerland for her to review, and to my surprise, she said that they would be better viewed at the lab. That way, if she had any questions about how well my calculations integrated with my colleagues', she could get them answered."

"And Hahn believed all that?" Allison says.

Günther tips his head. "I'm a pretty convincing liar. I told him that she took an overnight train, and she will accompany me to KWI, examine my work, offer whatever suggestions she has, and then return home. And then I added, 'And by the way, Irène is very anxious to meet the famed Otto Hahn who split the atom.'"

"And he believed the whole story?" Nathan says.

"Oh yeah. He kept saying, 'Really? Really? Did she really say the *famed* Otto Hahn?'"

"I feel a little sorry for him," Allison says. "You tricked him."

Günther shrugs. "What else could I do. How else am I going to get into the lab with you?"

"She reputedly suffers from tuberculosis," Nathan says. "How is she able to travel?"

"I believe she has recovered from the tuberculosis some time ago," Allison says, "but she is still weak. She rarely goes out. She also reportedly suffers from radiation poisoning. In any event, she would need help to travel."

Günther holds up his finger. "So, her brother-in-law has come along with her and will help her every step of the way. Isn't that the plan?"

"It is," Nathan says with a sigh, "but why are you dealing with Hahn when Esau is in charge of the Institute?"

Günther waves him off. "Esau defers to Hahn. Abraham is a respected scientist, but he is more of an administrator. Hahn is a genius. He is the heart and soul of Germany's nuclear chemistry. After Irène's discovery of artificial radioactivity, Otto Hahn and Lise Meitner discovered the radioactive isotopes of radium, thorium, and uranium. They discovered nuclear fission! We are talking about gods here. Anyway, when I told Otto about Irène, Otto was beside himself. He's so concerned about Speer cutting back our funding. I asked him to make sure there were no problems getting through security and into the labs. He assured me that he would be there to greet us when we arrived at ten o'clock and he would smooth the road. I asked him not to tell anyone it was Irène Curie, unless absolutely necessary. I don't want them to have time to check out the story. I don't want them trying to reach her sanitarium in Switzerland, if indeed, that is possible. Anyway, he agreed to anything I asked."

"Sounds perfect," Allison says. "I'm sure that Hahn will want Speer to know that Irène Curie has come into his lab. She adds credibility to the project and can vouch for the progress you are making."

"If she—I mean you—can fix our problems and praise our progress,

Hahn will make sure that Speer knows, but I will try to delay that discussion until the end of the day."

"Good thinking, Günther," Nathan says.

————————

Gluck walks into the room with a cup of coffee. "We are making arrangements to take you three out of Germany tonight," he says. "We have new identification cards and passports for all three of you. We have your train tickets and your connections. Get what you need to know, Allison, come back to the house and we'll put you three on a late-night train. You'll be in Paris tomorrow."

"What if we can't get all of our information in one day?" Allison says. "You're asking quite a bit. We're not getting there until ten o'clock."

"You have to get it done," Gluck says. "The longer you are in the lab, the greater the chance of your exposure. At some point, the Gestapo will want to verify your identities. If they can't get it done during the day, they'll damn sure do it overnight. Try to get as much as you can as quickly as you can and get out."

————————

As the group is leaving the safe house, Nathan pulls Allison aside. "You're not really planning on praising KWI's success for Speer, are you? If Speer thinks they are getting close, he'll pour more money into the program."

"I'm not stupid, Nathan. I'm going to make sure Speer knows that Germany is miles away from manufacturing a workable uranium bomb. If anything, he'll postpone funding."

"Good. I was worried. One more thing. You have to find a way to get into the personnel records. Make up some excuse. I have to find out what happened to my father."

"I understand. I'll do what I can. By the way, you look very distinguished in your coat and tie and your gray hair. A la Cary Grant, you know?"

"All right, all right, let's get over to the lab."

38

KWI

The Kaiser Wilhelm Institute for Chemistry, a stately four-story building, sits alongside a divided boulevard. It is an imposing structure with four Roman columns at the entrance, cylindrical turrets on the south and north corners, and a line of attic windows poking through a gabled roof. Gluck glides the car to a stop a half block north of the Institute on the opposite side of Möllhausenufer Boulevard. "I'll be right here the whole time," he says. "If anything goes wrong, if anything feels funny, get the hell out of that building and run to the car."

Günther, Allison, and Nathan exit the car, cross the boulevard, and walk slowly toward the Institute precisely at ten o'clock. "Home sweet home," Günther says.

"Reminds me of the MetLab," Allison says.

There are two uniformed security guards on either side of the front door. Günther knows them well and nods hello. One of them points to Nathan and Allison and waits for Günther to explain. "They are here with me today," Günther answers. "They are guests of the KWI."

The guard narrows his eyes. "Do they have credentials?" he asks. "You know I can't let them in without credentials."

Günther smiles. "They surely do. Top credentials. Dr. Hahn will be down in a moment."

They step away from the door to wait. For a late November day, the weather is pleasant. A sparrow chirps on the branch of a tree. A woman is out strolling with a baby carriage. Despite the peaceful setting, everyone's nerves are on edge. No one knows whether British bombers will return tonight. Allison peers out from under her wide-brimmed fedora at Nathan and suppresses a smile.

"What's so funny?" Nathan asks.

"You're actually not Cary Grant. You look more like my father. With our makeup and our costumes, I could swear it's a Halloween party. Trick or treat. Remember?"

"We didn't have Halloween when I was growing up in Germany."

―――――――――

Günther, Günther, it's wonderful to see you all this morning," announces a distinguished man in a charcoal suit, white shirt, and narrow black tie. He rushes up to greet them. Dr. Otto Hahn is in his sixties. His receding hair comes to a widow's peak in the center of his forehead. He has a small brush of a gray moustache over his upper lip and bushy eyebrows over deep-seated dark eyes. A wide grin animates his face.

Günther quietly says, "Good morning, Otto. It is my pleasure to introduce to you Dr. Irène Joliot-Curie and her brother-in-law, François Joliot."

Hahn, ever the gentleman, does not reach for a lady's hand uninvited. He knows that if she wants a formal greeting, she will extend the back of her hand. Which Allison does. Hahn bows, kisses her hand, and says, "Enchanté." He turns to Nathan. "François, a pleasure to meet you, sir." Hahn extends his arm for a hearty handshake.

"Günther, as you have requested, and for your privacy," Hahn adds, "name tags will not be necessary. Your identities will not be broadcast."

Allison, who does not understand a word that Hahn says, looks to Günther for translation into French. "He says that he will respect your privacy and not reveal that you are here," Günther says. Allison smiles and says, "Merci."

She looks at Hahn, but says in French for Günther to translate, "It is my wish that it not become public knowledge that I have come to assist Günther in Berlin. Some may take it the wrong way, that Günther lacks competence and needs the assistance of an expert. I prefer that the truth be told; that I have come to Berlin to add my knowledge and experience to assist in the development of a nuclear energy project." Allison's speech is delivered weakly, in a labored manner, and she intermittently stops to cough.

Hahn steps back a bit and turns his head, being careful not to get too close to Allison. "Of course, of course," he says. "I'm quite sure no one here would come to such an erroneous conclusion."

Allison continues. "I am not a political person, Dr. Hahn, and these are political times. Again, I do not want people to come to the wrong conclusions. I am here solely in the interest of science. Many will know me, but please, no newspaper or magazine photos." She watches as Günther repeats her statement in German.

"Most assuredly," Hahn says.

Allison is not through. "Perhaps some of the scientists will not recognize me, and it may become necessary to introduce them to me if they can provide necessary information for my evaluations. I trust that will not be a problem."

Hahn spreads his hands. "Dr. Curie, we appreciate the time and efforts you have so graciously provided. We welcome any contributions that will enhance our program. Feel free to roam about and ask your questions, but I must tell you that you are going to find a bit of chaos going on here. We have just begun the process of moving."

"The Institute?"

Hahn nods. "Because of the bombing raids, all of our research, indeed all of our work here, is at risk of being destroyed. We have no choice. We are relocating our laboratories outside of Berlin to a more remote location."

"What?" says Günther. "When was this decided? Where are we going?"

Hahn leans forward and speaks in a whisper. "It's all very quiet. Dr. Esau proposed it a few days ago when the bombing began. We must get our labs out of harm's way. Of course, it will take a while, but you will see that some men are already packing, and some are beginning moving preparations. We hope to be out of here before the end of the year."

"And go where?"

Dr. Hahn looks around as if someone might be listening. "We are going to a city in the Black Forest region. Top secret."

Günther is dumbfounded. "The Black Forest? Why in the world are we going there?"

"It's far from here," Hahn replies. "And far from the bombs. Maybe nine hundred kilometers away where no one will know we are working."

Günther is astonished, but Hahn is calm. "Günther, relax; you may like it. It's in a beautiful area, almost all the way to Strasbourg."

"Leave Berlin?" Günther says with a pained expression. "Live in the Black Forest?"

Hahn shrugs. "We're not setting up in a forest, Günther. You're smarter than that. It's in a city in the far western regions. Near France. And it's charming. Think of Hansel and Gretel. Snow White. They'll be your neighbors." He chuckles. "Like it or not, that is where we are going and remember, it's all very top secret."

Allison quickly glances at Nathan and raises her eyebrows and gives a conspiratorial nod.

Günther shakes his head and says, "Well, we better get started. We don't want to have Dr. Curie standing around more than she has to."

"Of course, of course," Hahn says. "And please tell her that I've heard about her illness and I'm so glad that she has recovered so well. And I very much appreciate her traveling here today."

After the translation, Allison says, "Well, my brother-in-law is a great help to me."

Hahn nods. "So, shall we go in? Abraham has given us free rein."

Snyder translates and Allison smiles broadly from beneath her floppy hat. "Entrez-vous, François," she says to Nathan with a wink.

They enter the stately building and proceed up a wide marble staircase to the second floor and into Günther's laboratory. Allison takes her time and rests intermittently. Hahn bows slightly from the waist and says, "I'll leave you three alone. I have some work I need to attend to. If you need anything at all, Günther knows where to find me."

Günther takes several notebooks out of a drawer and lays them on the table. Allison sits down and begins to read. Nathan quietly says to Günther, "Where are the personnel records kept? I need to know when and where my father was transferred."

"To my memory, your father was transferred quite abruptly in the spring of 1942. I don't know where. I assume the transfer records are in the administration office. That is Dr. Esau's domain. We can't exactly walk in there and shuffle through the records. Irène Curie would have no business looking through personnel records."

"Then I'll go in there myself," Nathan says firmly. "I have business. Maybe I can get in and out without anyone noticing."

"Entirely impossible," Günther says. "Several women work in clerical posts in that office, and they would stop you and ask you what you are doing."

Allison looks up from the records and says, "He's right. Besides, François Joliot doesn't speak German. If you walked in there and start perusing the personnel records, if you could even find them, you'd blow the whole operation."

Nathan presses his lips. "Can't you dream up some reason that you would want to see employment records? Can't you think of one?"

Allison takes a deep breath. "I'll try. I know it's important to you."

Nathan turns to Günther. "By the way, I have an idea where KWI is moving. If it's in the Black Forest region near Strasbourg, then it might be Haigerloch. That town wasn't far from where I grew up. We used to go hiking around there. It's a small town with a lot of caves and limestone gullies. Maybe they're trying to hide their laboratory there. Hahn is right; it is pretty. It's not far from the Rhine River and eastern France."

Allison is deeply studying Günther's notes. She taps her finger on a notebook and turns to face Günther. "Dr. Snyder, this is really very good! Really great work! Your calculations on the time variations necessary to reach critical mass are most impressive. It is no wonder that Dr. Oppenheimer wants you on his team."

"Thank you," Günther responds. He turns to Nathan with raised eyebrows and says, "I guess Josef Silverman is a pretty good judge of talent."

Allison continues, "While your work on critical mass is most impressive, as far as it goes, it's incomplete. There are no notes of actual trials."

"Well, you know I've never had access to the reactor."

"And you have no idea where it is?"

Günther shrugs. "It's obviously not in this building. I assume it's underground somewhere, but probably not in central Berlin."

"Who would know? Who is managing the reactor? Who is working on achieving a chain reaction?"

"That would be Dr. Werner Heisenberg. He has been in charge of the reactor for a long time. But he doesn't work here in Berlin."

"I know of Dr. Heisenberg," Allison says. "I know his reputation."

"I'm sure. He received the Nobel Prize in physics in 1932. In those years, he worked very closely with Albert Einstein. In fact, he taught Einstein's theory of relativity at the university. For that reason, Himmler called Werner a 'White Jew' who should be made to 'disappear.'"

"Is that why he is not working here? Did they send him off to some camp?"

"Goodness no. He's too valuable. I'm sure he's off somewhere working on a reactor. That's his expertise. I worked with him briefly when I first came here, and he talked about building a reactor. He knows what he's doing, but I don't know where he is. He hasn't been at KWI for a couple of years or more."

Allison continues to study Günther's notebooks when Hahn returns. "Oh, I'm glad to see you, Dr. Hahn," she says, through Günther's translation. "First of all, I would like to say that even though Günther and I are friends, I can objectively comment on his work. It's very well done. Quite expertly. And I feel sure that I will be able to contribute my experiences and advance his theories even further.

That said, although his work is very well done, it is incomplete. His calculations are as yet unproven. I mentioned that to Günther and he told me that he has not had any access to a reactor to test any of his theories. In fact, he does not even know where the reactor is located. Frankly, for such a sophisticated lab, it is hard to understand the logic of tying the hands of brilliant scientists by denying them access to the proof of their calculations. How does he go from one step to the next? Why is he kept away from the reactor?"

Hahn nods and looks around the room again, as though someone might be snooping or listening. "He's not being kept away from a working reactor, Dr. Curie. Our one reactor, L-IV, is under the supervision of Dr. Werner Heisenberg in Leipzig. It was originally built for peaceful purposes, to produce electricity for the region. Werner hoped that this achievement would be a model for the world. When it was finally completed, in the first quarter of 1942, results from trials of the L-IV indicated that the spherical geometry, with five metric tons of heavy water and ten metric tons of metallic uranium, would be able to sustain a fission chain reaction. Everyone was thrilled! Especially those who perceived its application for weaponry, I'm sorry to say." Hahn shrugged again. "But I'm afraid something went amiss and the reactor was shut down."

"What happened?"

"I'm not entirely sure. There was a mechanical incident. Something went wrong. But ever since June 1942, we have been unable to access the reactor for any experimental purposes."

Nathan elbows Allison. She nods. "So this problem happened in the spring of 1942?" she says.

"I don't know precisely what happened in Leipzig in June of '42. I just know that there is still a temporary hold on further use of the reactor. And as you may imagine, that has crippled our progress in that regard," Hahn says. "But it's being worked on."

"June of 1942; wasn't that about the time that Professor Josef Silverman was transferred from this facility?" she says.

Hahn tips his head in thought. "No, I believe it was before that. How do you know about Josef Silverman?"

After translating for Allison, Günther says, "She knows because of me. I was very close to Josef for many years. He is the reason that I was brought to Berlin. I'm sure I mentioned him to Dr. Curie. She would like to know whether the incident with the Leipzig reactor was the reason that Dr. Silverman was transferred."

"No. I think he was transferred at Dr. Heisenberg's request, and that was well before the incident that temporarily shut down the reactor."

"Would the personnel records provide information about his transfer?"

"Perhaps."

"Would you be so kind as to check those records while we are still here?"

Hahn shakes his head. "I'm afraid not. That would be a time-consuming activity and my time is better spent elsewhere. Besides, what difference could it possibly make? Dr. Silverman was transferred from here many months ago, and that's all we need to know."

Hahn has a suspicious look on his face. Allison sees it and waves her hand dismissively. She speaks and Günther translates. "Dr. Curie agrees that we are wasting time. She would like to know who else is involved with the nuclear reactor. Perhaps she might offer her help. As you have said, having our theories tested and proven seems to be the stumbling block to our progress here."

Hahn doesn't like to hear the words "stumbling block," especially with Albert Speer lurking in the hallways. "I will take you to Dr. Clusius," Hahn says. "He is a brilliant physicist who is doing remarkable work with isotope separation and heavy water production. He was very involved with the L-IV."

39

ACCUSATION

As Allison, Nathan, Günther, and Hahn climb the steps to the third floor and to the laboratories of Dr. Klaus Clusius, they nearly run into Berthold Konrad Hermann Albert Speer, Minister of Armaments and War Production. Speer is thirty-eight years old and a powerful member of Hitler's inner circle. He is also universally despised by the scientists at KWI. He hovers over them as they work and puts enormous pressure on them to develop a nuclear weapon. There is another man in plain clothes walking with him.

Hahn's group tries to brush past him, but Speer holds up his hand and says, "Good morning, Dr. Hahn." He waits for a response, which comes nonchalantly, with barely the tip of his head in recognition. "Good morning to you, Reichminister Speer."

Speer focuses his eyes on Nathan and Allison. "I do not recognize your companions, Dr. Hahn. You might have the courtesy of introducing me."

Hahn shrugs. "They are esteemed visitors who are kind enough to help us with our research. They are of no importance to you."

A sly smile creeps onto Speer's face. "One can never be sure what is important to another man, no?" He leans forward. "Please."

"This is Dr. Irène Curie, recipient of the Nobel Prize in chemistry in 1935 for her discovery of artificial radioactivity. The gentleman beside her is her brother-in-law François Joliot. I think you already know Dr. Günther Snyder. Now if you will excuse us, Dr. Curie's time is most valuable."

Speer wags a finger back and forth. "Please, give me a moment to express my sincere appreciation that such a renowned chemist should see fit to come to our laboratory to assist in our research."

After translation, Allison smiles and lightly nods.

Speer is ready to leave, but his companion's eyes are fixed upon Nathan. He narrows his vision and stares intensely. Then he leans over and whispers something to Speer. "Hmm," Speer says. "Mr. Joliot, would you mind removing your hat?"

Nathan stands still, as though he doesn't understand the odd request.

"He speaks French," Hahn says. "And frankly, I don't understand your request for him to remove his hat. That is hardly an expression of your 'sincere appreciation.' It seems rude."

Speer's facial expressions are taut. "I don't require your understanding, Dr. Hahn." Then to Nathan, Speer says, "S'il vous plaît, Monsieur Joliot. Le chapeau. Maintenant." With circular hand motions, he gestures for the removal of Nathan's trilby.

Nathan shrugs, timidly removes his hat, and holds it at his belt. Nathan's hair is mostly gray. He has age spots and lines in his face. Speer looks to his companion, who stares, shrugs, and then shakes his head.

"Well, carry on," Speer says. "Perhaps Dr. Curie will accomplish what you have thus far been unable to do, Dr. Hahn." As they proceed down the stairs, Speer's companion turns and stares at Nathan again. He whispers to Speer and they turn around the corner.

"That man with Speer," Nathan whispers to Allison. "I think I've seen him before."

"You have," she says, "it's Wolf. Weber's friend. He's Gestapo."

———————

Dr. Klaus Clusius is sitting at his desk staring through a glass partition and making notations in a notebook when the group enters his lab. He is a surprisingly young man, considering the advanced degrees achieved in Poland, England, and Germany, and his extraordinary accomplishments in isotope separation. Günther makes the introductions. Clusius is pleased to meet the celebrated Irène Curie and to learn that she has come to lend her assistance to KWI's staff. She looks through the glass enclosure behind Clusius. Günther points out a large glass and metal cylindrical capsule that sits in the enclosure. He explains, "That is the 'Clusius-Dickel Thermodiffusion Isotope Separation Tube,' which Klaus has used with uranium hexafluoride."

"Bravo," says Allison with a smile and a slight bow, though she knows from her days with Professor Lawrence at Cal-Berkeley that purities achieved with electromagnetic separators are far superior to those from a diffuser. She is not about to share that information.

"I understand that you are somehow involved in the restoration of the reactor in Leipzig," Allison says.

Clusius is shocked. "You know about that reactor? And the incident? Somebody told you? That's highly confidential."

Hahn interrupts. "Really, Klaus, she is here to help us. We feel comfortable in sharing that information with her. Esau has approved. Please feel free to speak openly in her presence. Now if you'll excuse me, I have to show my face at a conference. I'll try to catch up with you later."

Clusius shrugs. "Okay, then. My current connection with the L-IV reactor project is to coordinate and deliver heavy water for the moderation. As Otto knows, I favor graphite, but Dr. Bothe was more persuasive, and he prefers heavy water. Graphite is cheaper and more available, but," he spreads his hands, "it was not my call. So, we use heavy water."

Allison signifies her understanding with a nod. "I assume that the heavy water production facility is close by, is that correct?"

Clusius chuckles. "If you consider Norway close by. Our heavy water comes from the Norsk facility in Telemark. Near the town of Tinn. It is stored in barrels and shipped by boat across the North Sea to Denmark. It is then transported by train through Denmark and south all the way to Leipzig, where it is put into storage." He smiles. "Now you tell me, is that more efficient than graphite bricks which can be manufactured locally? But, who am I to argue with Bothe?"

Clusius's attention is drawn back to his diffuser. He studies it and makes certain notations in his papers. Allison takes the momentary pause to whisper to Günther. "Find out exactly where he directs shipments of the heavy water. Then we will know the precise location of the reactor in the city of Leipzig."

"If the barrels of heavy water are shipped all the way from Norway, through Denmark and Germany on a train, the reactor site must be close to the train yard, no?" Günther says. "Otherwise, it would be very clumsy to take those barrels back and forth to the facility."

"You are exactly correct. The reactor is adjacent to the Leipzig-Wahren freight yard in an old yellow, concrete warehouse. The heavy water is stored there as well. But now, with our relocation, I am told to redirect the heavy water shipments to a city in the western provinces." As he says that, he taps on a piece of paper sitting on his desk. "This place." The paper has latitude and longitude coordinates.

"Haigerloch?" Günther says.

Clusius is shocked. "How did you know? They're not telling anyone."

"Well, they told you."

"I know, but I have to manage the shipments of materials. I'm just surprised that you know, that's all." As he says that, he quickly picks up the paper on which the coordinates are written.

"Well, they certainly depend on you for quite a bit, Dr. Clusius," Allison says. "I'm most impressed."

"I appreciate that very much, coming from such an esteemed scientist," Clusius says.

Allison looks at Günther and raises her eyebrows. "I've learned quite a bit today and I think I could be very helpful, but I'm getting awfully tired," she says weakly. "I think I would like to rest for a while. We could come back later. Perhaps we could find a café somewhere and I could get some soup."

"Of course," Clusius says. "There is a very nice café just up the street. I have had the chicken soup there. It is very good."

As they enter the staircase, Allison whispers to Nathan. "Jackpot. Everything we wanted to know. We just have to get all this information to General Groves."

But Nathan is hesitant, and Allison notices it. "I know what you're going to say," Allison says. "You want to try to get into the personnel records before we leave and know for certain where your father was transferred."

"That's right. If he was transferred to Leipzig, maybe my whole family is down there with him. According to Lena, they enjoyed protected status while he was working here."

"We're not going to get into the personnel files," Günther says. "Otto told you as much. But it's pretty obvious that Josef was transferred down to Leipzig, isn't it? That was his specialty and he left right about the time that they were having issues with the reactor."

"You want to go to Leipzig and see if your family is there," Allison says, "am I right?"

Nathan nods. "I don't see how I can leave Europe without checking that out. I don't expect you to go with me, this is my concern. Gluck will find a way to get you and Günther back to New York. I'll tackle this part on my own."

"The hell you will, Nathan. Or François, or Hauptmann Whoozie-coots, whatever your name is now. You swore to take care of me. If you're going to Leipzig, so am I. Besides, I—I mean Irène—should take a look at the reactor and determine if it is actually usable, or how soon it can be put into service. Günther accompanying Irène Curie to the Leipzig reactor is a good cover for our travel. We'll all go together. Are you okay with this, Günther?"

"Yes, of course."

Nathan leans over and gives Allison a kiss on the cheek. "Then, off we go, the Three Musketeers. Gluck is waiting in the car."

As they descend the staircase and reach the landing between the second and third floors, the group once again runs into Reichminister Speer and his companion. Günther nods and walks past him. Nathan and Allison tip the brims of their hats to shelter as much of their faces as they can, but Wolf can't take his eyes off Nathan. Nearing the bottom of the stairs, Speer calls out, "Dr. Snyder, would you hold your group there for just a moment please?" Speer and Wolf quickly descend the stairs.

Speer walks over to Nathan and says in German, "Monsieur Joliot, I'm sure that you've noticed that Herr Wolf has been staring at you. It's really quite innocent. Really. He thinks he knows you." He gestures for Günther to translate to French.

Nathan wrinkles his forehead. "Non. Impossible."

Speer continues. "No, he is *sure* he has seen you before. Perhaps in Paris."

Nathan cannot respond in English or German, and he knows little French. When Günther translates Speer's request into French, Nathan spreads his hands, shrugs his shoulders, and says, "Hmm, comme si comme ça à Paris. Avec Herr Wolf?" Nathan shakes his head. "Mais non."

Günther translates it into German. "Monsieur Joliot is saying maybe yes, maybe no, like anything could be possible in Paris, but he was not there with Herr Wolf."

Wolf steps forward and points an accusatory finger at Nathan. "You're lying. I saw you at the Curious Squirrel with Major Otto Weber and Colonel Zeist. It was you, only you were in a uniform. A Hauptmann's uniform. I am sure of it."

Günther translates and Nathan laughs. "Curious Squirrel? Non, non, non. Impossible."

Günther turns to Speer and says, "Monsieur Joliot denies any such contact. Perhaps he resembles another man. I suggest you reach out to Major Weber. Ask him to describe the man at the so-called Curious Squirrel. Ask him straight off who he was with. Better yet, have Major Weber come over here and take a look at Monsieur Joliot for himself. Do it right now. See if he can identify him. I'm sure that Major Weber would deny any knowledge and would clear up this absurd accusation. In fact, I insist you bring Major Weber here instantly."

Speer snarls. "Dr. Snyder, you do not give me orders. However, I will do just that. I happen to know that the major is in Berlin, and I know where he is staying. I saw him just the other day. But I am the one who will do the insisting. Until Major Weber gets here and clears up this discrepancy, Dr. Curie and Monsieur Joliot shall be my guests in the security office on the first floor."

"Outrageous!" Günther says. "You can't lock them up. They have done nothing wrong. Monsieur Joliot and Dr. Curie are esteemed guests at this facility. They are *my* guests. Monsieur Joliot is caring for his sister-in-law, Dr. Curie, whom you can plainly see is weak from illness and strenuous travel. She is not a well woman. Locking her in a security room is injurious to her health."

Speer shrugs his shoulders. "What am I to do, Dr. Snyder? Their identities have been challenged. As a cautious man, I must take all reasonable steps to verify who they are. After all, you have given them free access to a top secret facility."

"I work here, and I vouch for these fine people."

Speer slowly shakes his head. "I'm afraid that will not do. They must be detained until we locate Major Weber and he confirms that he does not know them."

Günther will not back down. "I know that Dr. Hahn and Dr. Esau will be furious that you have seen fit to lock up a Nobel Prize winner on the scant memory of one man. In fact, Dr. Curie was and is in the midst of helping us improve our methods and move our project forward. Isn't that what the Reich Ministry of Armaments desires as well?"

Speer considers the request. "But, Dr. Snyder, if this man is indeed an imposter . . ."

"And if he is not, then you have insulted him, and you have prevented Dr. Curie from advancing our program. I am sorry, sir, but you would be made quite the fool on the basis of Herr Wolf's wild accusation. Don't let Herr Wolf's reckless allegation blemish your career."

Speer sighs. "Hmm. Very well, then, I will not lock them in the security office. But for the time being, they are not allowed to leave the building. I will post a guard at the door. They may not leave until Major Weber arrives and has an opportunity to clear up this accusation, which I imagine would be no later than this afternoon. That should satisfy you. She may continue with her work while I contact Major Weber."

Günther agrees. The group then proceeds into Günther's lab and closes the door. "Nice work, Günther," Allison says, "but what do we do now?"

Günther is pleased with himself. "He certainly won't find Weber this afternoon, will he?"

Nathan pats Günther on the back. "Very clever. But Weber is not our problem. The risk is Colonel Zeist. When Speer fails to contact Weber, he will no doubt reach out to Zeist, and if he shows up, that's trouble. Zeist suspected I was an imposter when we were at the Curious Squirrel."

"I feel that Speer won't contact Colonel Zeist until he's convinced that he cannot contact Weber. The colonel is an important man and a scary individual. I doubt he will contact Colonel Zeist before tomorrow or even the next day."

Nathan agrees. "He'll keep trying to look for Weber, at least for a while. Then ultimately, he'll reach out for Zeist, but I think you're right. It won't happen today."

"He won't keep us here beyond the end of the workday," Günther says. "When everyone goes home tonight, he'll have to let us leave."

———

True to Günther's expectations, there is a knock on his lab door at 4:00 P.M. Speer and Wolf are there. "I have been unable to reach Major Weber today," Speer says. "I left word at his command post, and I left word at the airfield. He is momentarily out of touch, but they are sure he will check in later today or early tomorrow. In any event, you may leave for the day, but I command you to return promptly tomorrow."

Günther nods. "Of course. I come to work every day, Reichminister, as you well know. I will see you tomorrow. I shall ask that Dr. Curie and her brother-in-law postpone their departure until then."

Speer turns to Allison and asks in French, "In the event I am able to reach Major Weber later this afternoon, we should speed this up. Where are you and your brother-in-law staying, Dr. Curie?"

Allison is speechless. She cannot give the Aller Straße address; it has already been compromised. As a Gestapo agent, Wolf probably knows that Weber confronted Lena Hartz at the Aller Straße house. Allison doesn't know the address of the current safe house, but even if she did, she wouldn't divulge it. She is in a quandary, and she knows it, but before she can answer, Günther interrupts. "Dr. Curie and her brother-in-law are staying with me, of course. I am honored to have them as my houseguests."

"Very well then, until tomorrow," Speer says, and he motions for Wolf to follow him out of Günther's office. Before leaving, Wolf takes another long look at Nathan, smirks, and says, "I know it's you. You were at the Curious Squirrel. I'd bet my life on it."

40

CHANGE OF PLANS

The group leaves KWI as quickly as possible and walks directly to Gluck's car on the other side of the boulevard. As he pulls away, Gluck says, "So, how did it go? You were there all day."

"Very well," Allison says. "I obtained most of the information I was seeking. There is no need to go back to the Institute."

"That's great," Gluck says, "because your train leaves for Paris in four hours."

After a moment of silence, Nathan says, "Change of plans, Fred. We need to go to Leipzig. As soon as possible."

"Leipzig? Are you serious? That's not part of the mission. Nate, we're getting too far afield. You were sent here to help Dr. Snyder defect. Dr. Fisher was sent to interrogate Snyder and learn whatever she could about the German nuclear program. That was all supposed to take place in the safe house. And then you were all going back to England. All those arrangements were made. The documents are all prepared. Going into the Institute was not part of the mission. Dressing up like Irène Curie was not part of the mission. Killing and disposing of Major Otto Weber was not part of the mission. Hell, bringing Lena Hartz into the picture was—"

"That's enough, Fred," Nathan says. "We all know what the mission was. Günther didn't possess all of the information we needed. We learned a great deal about Germany's program at the Institute, and we need to get that information back to Washington. But there's more to be learned in Leipzig, and we're going there."

"Does it have anything to do with finding out about your family? Is this a personal mission, Nate, or is it in the interest of the United States? Going to Leipzig is out of the question."

"We're going to Leipzig, Mr. Gluck," Allison says. "There is critical information to learn. For all we know, there is a workable nuclear reactor there."

"I agree," Günther says. "We need to examine the nuclear reactor and we need to talk to Werner Heisenberg. The condition of the reactor is an important piece of the puzzle. That is reason enough to go to Leipzig, but if Josef Silverman is also there, that would be a blockbuster. He is a far better scientist than I am, and worth two Günther Snyders to the U.S. program. He taught me everything I know. If you could help us get him out of Europe, you'd be a hero. If Nathan's family is also there, we need to bring them out too. We're going to Leipzig, Fred."

Back at the safe house, Gluck is furiously making phone calls trying to arrange for the group to travel: new identity cards, fake passports, train tickets. He even considers changes in their appearances, which would require Hanna. Allison is in the living room drafting a message to be sent by code to General Groves. It contains brief summaries of the information she has learned and her estimate about the current state of Germany's nuclear program. She specifies that the Norsk hydro plant in Tinn, Norway, is the source of the heavy water. It is shipped through Denmark and sent by rail to Leipzig. She reveals that KWI is leaving Berlin because of the bombing and will relocate somewhere near Haigerloch, Germany, along the eastern border near Strasbourg. Signs point to plans for construction of a new reactor in that area. She suggests that the Haigerloch area should be an important destination for the ALSOS team, once the Allies land on the Continent. Finally, she summarizes the deficiencies that are slowing down

Germany's success: failure to achieve a chain reaction, lack of a stockpile of enriched uranium, presumed lack of a serviceable reactor, and an inability to test their theories. But she warns, with a high degree of caution, that KWI has the scientific talent, and that achievement of a nuclear weapon is only a matter of time. She ends by noting that her group is headed to Leipzig tomorrow to determine if a reactor exists and whether it is operable.

She hands the draft to Gluck, who has just reentered the room. He reads it carefully and nods. "I will get this transmitted tonight, but you cannot leave tomorrow. I am trying to manufacture new identities for you, and they will not be ready by tomorrow. There's something else to consider. When you don't show up at KWI tomorrow morning, Speer will throw a fit. He will immediately send a squad to Günther's apartment, and finding it empty, he will issue a warrant for your arrest or detainment, and then he will issue an alert. Every train station, every bus station will have your name and description. The Gestapo will be combing the country looking for you three. We need new identification papers and new passports for each of you, but most importantly, we need to consider a new safe route back to New York."

"A *safe* route?" Nathan says sarcastically. "We're in central Germany; is any route safe?"

"Hmm," Gluck says. "You have a point. Let's say less dangerous. Speer suspects that Nathan was the phony Hauptmann Froman at the Curious Squirrel in Paris. He will believe that Paris is your destination on your route back to England. If it hasn't already, the entire operation will reveal itself to him: Günther Snyder is the defecting scientist, and the woman who disguised herself as Irène Curie is an espionage agent, and she is smuggling scientific intelligence to the Allies. Finally, Hauptmann Froman is a military spy: American OSS or UK MI6. All of that will become clear to Speer and to Colonel Zeist. They will make every effort to stop you."

Nathan seems unfazed. "Hopefully, we will have completed our mission in Leipzig and taken your so-called safe route out of Germany before that happens. For the moment our disguises should allow us to enter the reactor facility and evaluate their L-IV reactor."

Gluck shakes his head. "As of tomorrow, the characters of Irène Curie and François Joliot will be public enemies number one and two. We should have Hanna come here and change your appearances. Give you new identities. And that goes for you as well, Dr. Snyder. You are probably public enemy number three."

Günther shakes his head. "I don't care for that plan. How would we get into the reactor facility in Leipzig? It will take my credentials and Allison's disguise to get us inside."

"He's right, Fred," Nathan says. "Give us a day or so in Leipzig, then we'll return here. Hanna can work her magic on new identities after we return."

"A day or so?" Gluck says. "Are you all dreaming? Time is critical. As soon as you don't show up at KWI, arrest warrants will be issued. Everything will become clear to Speer. He didn't get to where he is by being stupid. They'll alert the Leipzig facility. If you're not arrested when you get there, you'll be taken into custody as soon as they get the message."

Günther stands and, in a professorial posture, pulls up his trousers. "Fred, your time estimates may be a little off. You don't understand the scientific community. Everything works slowly and methodically. I know how they do things at KWI. Nothing is instantaneous. Nathan, Allison, and I are supposed to show up first thing in the morning. That means maybe nine, or maybe ten. They'll wait until eleven before ringing the panic bell. Then they'll send some guards out to my apartment. That will take an hour or two. Then they'll make some phone calls and finally, sometime in the mid- to late afternoon, they'll realize we're not coming and they'll issue an alert. Now, where would that alert be sent? Like you said, to every train station and bus station. But not to an inoperable reactor site in Leipzig. They don't know we're going to Leipzig. I guarantee you they won't contact Dr. Heisenberg or any of the scientists at the Leipzig facility. They'll think we're making our escape and heading west. I know how these people think. We'll have time to review the reactor site and return here."

Nathan nods. "Dr. Snyder makes a good point, and I agree. After the alert is issued, and maybe in the midafternoon, train stations are taboo. We can't take the train tomorrow, especially in those disguises, unless we can complete the whole thing in the morning and take a return train to Berlin in the early afternoon."

Gluck shakes his head. "The trains to Leipzig don't run that often."

Allison asks the obvious. "So, if we can't take the train, how are we supposed to get to Leipzig and back?"

Gluck groans. "Only one solution I can think of; I'll have to drive you. It's only a couple of hours. I already scheduled Hanna for early tomorrow morning, when I thought you were going to change your identities. But we can still use her. Your age spots are smearing. And she can take your measurements and prepare new costumes for the following day. So, have some dinner, wash your faces, get a good night's sleep. She'll freshen you up in the morning, and I'll have you to Leipzig by ten."

As if on cue, the door to the safe house bursts open, and Renzel walks in with a large paper bag and an ear-to-ear grin. "Look what I have," he says. "Roast chicken and dumplings, and two chilled bottles of Moselle."

When they are all settled around the table, Nathan raises his glass. "I propose a toast! To the OSS, the Berlin Station, and, most importantly, our friends Kurt and Fred, who have made this whole operation possible . . ." Just at that moment, at precisely 7:55 P.M., the air raid sirens sound again. The group dashes quickly into the basement and huddles together while explosions boom and the ground shakes. "I didn't know about it, I swear," Gluck says. Allison grips Nathan's hands as tightly as she can. Nathan tries his best to reassure and calm her, but she is just this side of hysterical.

Surprisingly, the attack lasts only a half hour, and at 8:25 the bombing ceases. Minutes later, the all-clear horn sounds. During that half hour, seven hundred British bombers dropped two thousand five hundred tons of bombs on the city of Berlin, primarily in the city center and in the western sections. The devastation is severe and not limited to residential areas. Among the targets were Albert Speer's private office, the War Industry Ministry, Hitler's private train, and the Naval Construction headquarters. Speer is unharmed.

Gluck, Renzel, Nathan, Allison, and Snyder wait another half hour before ascending from the basement. Their nerves are jangling, but their safe house is undamaged. Their neighborhood has been spared. "Providing the roads are passable, nothing changes," Nathan says. "We go to Leipzig tomorrow. We finish our mission and get the hell out of here." Everyone agrees.

Gluck is on the phone. He is receiving information from OSS. He turns to Nathan and nods. "Leipzig is unharmed. We go as planned."

Renzel opens the second bottle of Moselle. "Anyone need a drink? I'm not going to let this Moselle go to waste," he says, filling the glasses. Nathan raises his and revisits his toast.

Despite the glasses of Moselle, Nathan cannot sleep. He tosses and turns and squishes his pillow. He is thinking about his visit to Leipzig and his father. Will he see him tomorrow? If he is alive, why is he still working for the Nazis? Did he make a deal with the devil to keep his wife and daughter alive? If Nathan's mother and sister have been taken away in a truck, like Lena suspected, then there's little hope for them. They would have perished in a concentration camp. Could they have taken his father as well? Maybe he's not in Leipzig at all. But if he is alive, and he is in Leipzig, how could Josef Silverman keep working for the Germans at a nuclear reactor site? Why would he work for the betterment of Nazi Germany? That would certainly not be the Josef Silverman that Nathan remembers.

Nathan's thoughts turn to Allison Fisher, who lies beside him, intermittently weeping. Actually, he thinks about Allison all the time. She's an extraordinary woman: a brilliant scientist and a fearless spy. She is so strong, so powerful. She may cry, but she doesn't back down. Even in the midst of a bombing raid. She can put her fear to the side when necessary, but she comes to him at night for comfort. For security. He holds her when she shivers. When he was first told he would be taking a certain Dr. Fisher along to Germany to assist in the defection of a top German scientist, he envisioned a white-haired, feeble old man. Why else would they need a Ritchie boy to shuttle him around Europe? Of course, that was foolish and naive. But he never expected a woman like Allison Fisher. And there is no denying his growing affection for her. He's never known anyone quite like her. If the circumstances were different, if they were together in a different place at a different time . . .

A llison also cannot sleep either. When Leslie Groves first approached her for this mission, her assignment was to meet Günther Snyder, assess the strength of his knowledge and abilities, and if, in her judgment, he would be a positive contribution to the Manhattan Project, then she and some army guy were going to help him defect. Would Günther fit in with the likes of Robert Oppenheimer and Enrico Fermi? She must admit, at first she was doubtful. Now she is confident. There is a likeable quality about the chubby old man, and there is no doubting his brilliance.

Allison's thoughts turn to Nathan, who lies beside her. What will happen after Leipzig, after their return to America? Will she go back to the MetLab in Chicago, and will he go back to Maryland? He swore to be there for her and to protect her. And he has. But, of course, that was just during the mission. Would he make that promise again, maybe in a forever way? She's never known anyone quite like him. She looks to her right. Nathan is awake. They smile at each other. If only it were a different time and place, but right now they are in Berlin, they are public enemies number one and two, and they will be headed off to Leipzig in the morning.

41

THE LEIPZIG REACTOR

The group piles into Gluck's VW for the one-hundred-mile journey from Berlin to Leipzig. Hanna was kind enough to come very early in the morning to redo their facial makeup. Neither her neighborhood nor the Berlin Theater were hit, but she confessed to being "scared to death." As far as she knew, the roads south were passable.

She worked her magic, and once again, the aged, sickly Irène Curie and her timid, wrinkly brother-in-law are on their way with Dr. Snyder to another KWI laboratory, this one in Leipzig.

Wartime Leipzig is a bustling city with over seven hundred thousand residents. Because of its location in central Saxony, it is also a transportation and commercial hub. The Leipzig-Wahren freight yard, commissioned forty years earlier, is one of Germany's main marshaling yards, where coupling and uncoupling freight cars goes on all day and night. Numerous warehouses line the edges of the yard, and Gluck has to drive the area twice before spotting what would fit Clusius's description of a faded yellow warehouse.

"Do you think it's large enough to house a reactor?" Gluck asks before pulling into a parking area.

"The reactor would be underground," Allison answers. "The warehouse sits on more than enough land for the reactor and for the storage of materials."

Allison, Günther, and Nathan exit the car and walk through the gravel yard toward the warehouse door. Nathan says, "Are you ready, Dr. Curie? Can you repeat the act?"

"You better believe it, brother-in-law."

There are two armed guards at the door to the warehouse. They are in black uniforms, which Nathan does not recognize. They are not military, and Nathan presumes they are security forces. Günther shows his KWI credentials to the taller of the guards. "I am Dr. Günther Snyder, and this is Dr. Irène Curie," he says. "We have come directly from Berlin to meet with Dr. Heisenberg."

The guard ignores the credentials, and quickly responds, "You have the wrong address. There is no Dr. Heisenberg here."

Günther thrusts his KWI identification forward so that the guard can more clearly see it. "Is this a KWI facility, or not?" Günther asks confrontationally. "Where is Dr. Heisenberg?"

The guard pushes Günther's arm away, shakes his head, and says, "There is no Dr. Heisenberg here. Now leave."

The other guard walks over. "What is the problem here, Karl?"

"This man keeps asking to see a Dr. Heisenberg. I told him that he has the wrong address."

"Look, mister," the second guard says with his hand resting on the barrel of his rifle. "This is a freight warehouse, not a medical facility. There are no doctors here. And frankly, I don't recognize your identification card. Is there anything else we can help you with, Dr. Günther Snyder of KWI?"

Günther is frustrated and is getting more aggravated by the minute. "Who is in charge here?" he demands.

"As far as you're concerned, I am. Now leave before I call the police."

Günther turns around and faces Nathan. "Maybe Clusius was wrong. Maybe there is another faded yellow warehouse at this freight yard."

Nathan has had enough. "Horseshit." He reaches into his pocket, pulls out his Hauptmann Strauss identification card, steps up to the first guard, and in a no-nonsense tone says, "Do you recognize this identification? I am not in uniform, but I'm a captain in the army accompanying this esteemed physicist. And I'm tired of listening to your disrespectful crap. Now let us in, and take us to Dr. Heisenberg."

Without another word, the guard opens the door and beckons the group to follow him.

The warehouse is surprisingly quiet. If not for the guards, one might think the building is deserted. They walk down a narrow corridor. But for a few bare light bulbs hanging from the ceiling, the area is dark and quiet. Certainly nothing like Nathan imagined for a nuclear reactor facility. The guard leads them to a door, knocks, and from behind the closed door, a man says, "What is it?"

The guard answers, "I have three people here who say they have an appointment with you."

"I have no appointments scheduled," says the voice.

"Yes, you do," Nathan says loudly. "You have an appointment with Dr. Günther Snyder, Dr. Irène Curie, and a Wehrmacht captain who is losing his patience."

The door swings opens, and an older man says, "Hello, Günther, it's been awhile."

Günther clasps Heisenberg in a friendly hug. "It's good to see you, Werner. This is Dr. Irène Curie and Hauptmann Richard Strauss."

Heisenberg turns his attention to the guard at the door. "Thank you, Karl. You may go now. Please shut the door."

"What is this all about, Günther?" Heisenberg says. "You show up here unannounced with a military guard and a woman who says she is Irène Curie?"

Günther clears his throat. This charade is quickly falling apart. "We have come from Berlin where Dr. Curie has graciously been reviewing our work at the lab. As you may know, I have been working very hard on calculating critical mass. Dr. Curie has been helping me. She has also met with Otto and Klaus and is offering her expertise to further our progress. This has all been cleared through Dr. Esau. We came here to review the progress of the restoration of the Leipzig reactor and—"

"You can stop right there, Günther. This woman is not Irène Curie.

I visited Dr. Curie last year in Switzerland. Shall I get her on the phone? What is going on?"

Günther's jaw is wobbling. "Oh, I can assure you that this is Dr. Curie. Although she has been ill in Switzerland, she came to Berlin with the help of her brother-in-law to help me with my work. We spent valuable time in Berlin and now she would like to assess the readiness of the reactor."

A laugh escapes Heisenberg's lips. "The brother-in-law who is also a Wehrmacht Hauptmann? What kind of nonsense is this? Even if she were Dr. Curie, and she could analyze our reactor problems, we don't require her help. And this woman is not Irène Curie."

"Werner, if you don't believe me, ask her a question. A complicated scientific question. You'll see that she is a brilliant scientist."

Heisenberg rolls his eyes from face to face. "I have no doubt that she is a brilliant scientist, Günther, but she's not Irène Curie. So, do you want to tell me what is going on?"

"Just what I said. We want to inspect and evaluate the reactor."

"For what purpose?"

Nathan has heard enough of this banter. He pulls his pistol from his coat pocket. "Take us to the reactor, please, Dr. Heisenberg."

Heisenberg smiles. "Well now, the truth surfaces. What a collection you three are. A KWI physicist who is thoroughly out of his element, a woman—perhaps a brilliant scientist—who pretends to be Irène Curie, and a quick-tempered man who says he is a Hauptmann in plain clothes. And you all want to see my reactor. Or what, Hauptmann? Will you shoot me?"

Heisenberg stands up and sighs. "What do we really have here? Three people who are not who or what they say they are, off on a mysterious venture. Perhaps to find out how ready we are to manufacture a nuclear weapon? Is that not so? It doesn't take a scientist to see right through you three. Put your gun away, Hauptmann. I am not your enemy. I'll take you to the reactor, for all the good it will do you. But you will see for yourself, that we are not anywhere close to manufacturing a nuclear bomb."

Heisenberg leads the three down another corridor and to a pad-locked door that leads to an antechamber. "Put these on," he says, pointing to a rack of white full-body suits. "I'm not entirely sure, but there may be particle radiation still present, and these garments will protect you from contact."

Thus attired, the four leave the anteroom and enter a large room cordoned off with yellow steel rails. Heisenberg flips on the light switch and there in the middle of the floor, behind several circular rails, is a concrete and steel well, built deep into the ground. Perhaps twelve feet in diameter. "Oh, my God," Allison utters in English. "That is a large reactor. Much larger than the Chicago Pile."

Heisenberg raises his eyebrows. "Does Irène Curie now speak English, as well as French and Polish? And does she come from Chicago?"

Allison takes a few steps forward. She leans over the rail and peers deep into the well. The metal encasement is inside, but the pressure lid is off, exposing the interior of the reactor.

"Looks like a giant pressure cooker," Nathan remarks.

"Indeed it is. Don't get too close," Heisenberg says.

"Excuse me, Dr. Heisenberg," Allison says in English. "Do I see traces of powder burns, cracks in the sides of the concrete?"

Heisenberg nods. "Yes. you do. Now all of you, back away please, there is likely to be residual radiation present."

In the anteroom, they dispose of their protective suits by throwing them into a large steel container, and they return to Heisenberg's office.

"They are not working to restore this reactor, are they?" Allison asks. "It's beyond repair, isn't it? You're going to seal it, aren't you? What happened here?"

Heisenberg looks at Günther. "She asks a lot of questions, doesn't she? She's not Irène, but she is indeed a knowledgeable scientist, and one with experience in nuclear reactors. There aren't many like her in the world." He turns to Allison. "Are there? I'm thinking of one who may work with Leo Szilard." He lifts an eyebrow and says with a large smile and a wink, "But you are much too *old* to be her. All that gray hair and wrinkles. Actually, you are much too old to be Irène Curie, but that's another matter."

Allison ignores the jokes. "What happened here, Dr. Heisenberg?"

"To whom am I speaking?"

Nathan grabs her arm and wags a finger. "Don't."

Allison brushes him away. "You are speaking to Dr. Allison Fisher, the physicist from Chicago."

"Hmm. Say hello to Arthur Compton. And Leo, if he's still there. We attended a seminar together." Heisenberg takes a deep breath. "By the spring of 1942, we had constructed—I should say, I had constructed—a working nuclear reactor. Filled with heavy water and uranium powder, the Leipzig L-IV pile—to use Enrico's description—demonstrated the potential for neutron propagation. The reactor was capable of generating enough electricity to light the whole state of Saxony at a ridiculously low economic cost. Of course, it was also capable of producing weapons-grade plutonium. In its trials, it was marvelously successful. But KWI's Kurt Diebner and Robert Döpel took hold of the project, saw the enormous potential for weaponry, and brought in the Ministry of Armaments."

"Albert Speer."

"Right. It was Döpel's plan to fund the reactor with money from the Ministry. He said it could then have a dual use. Nonsense, of course. Peaceful energy operations were bound to give way to military applications. That's Nazi Germany. I couldn't allow that to happen."

"You sabotaged the reactor?"

"Not by myself. I had help from another peace-minded scientist whom I shall not name. Certain internal controls were compromised a bit, I won't say exactly how that happened, but it was really quite brilliant. It was designed to prevent the rapid development of an atomic weapon, but after the war, the deficit could be corrected, and the reactor used for peaceful electricity.

"Then, on June 23, 1942, during a supposed check on the reactor's operations, it was detected that there were blisters on the gaskets. Naturally it was slowing down our progress. Döpel insisted that the machine be opened during the operation and—"

Allison's hand shot to her mouth. "Oh, my God."

"That's right. Air leaked in, the uranium powder was ignited, the heavy water was raised to a boiling point. Enormous steam pressure ensued, and uranium powder was shot twenty feet high, hitting the ceiling. It generated so much steam that the unit itself was cracked in several places. Sadly, four people died."

"Is it being repaired?" Günther asks. "That's what we are being told at the KWI."

"Do you see anyone working on it? It's contaminated. It's not serviceable now or ever, but we allow the myth to continue at the instruction of KWI leadership. It will be ready soon, they say, just give us more money. I am sitting here in this facility to lend credibility to the project."

Allison looks to her companions and shrugs her shoulders. "Okay then. We won't trouble you any further. Our business here is completed."

Heisenberg raises his finger. "Just a moment, Dr. Fisher. Although this reactor is history, they plan to build another. They have asked for my help, but I said I was too busy here in Leipzig restoring this reactor." He shrugs. "I fear that my excuse will not last long and they will order me to build the new one."

"Where are they building the second reactor?"

"I'm really not sure. They mentioned it once, but I can't recall."

"Haigerloch?"

"I think that's it. They're building it deep in some limestone formations in or around Haigerloch. In fact, Otto told me that all of KWI is moving to the hills of Haigerloch. Especially, since the bombing."

Allison nods and holds out her hand. "Thank you, Dr. Heisenberg. I appreciate your help more than you can imagine."

Nathan steps forward. "One more thing, Dr. Heisenberg. I had heard that Dr. Josef Silverman was transferred here at some time in 1942, before the accident. Is that so?"

Heisenberg is surprised. "Who wants to know?"

"I do. Nathan Silverman."

A light goes on in Heisenberg's head, and he slowly nods. "You are Josef's son?"

"I am. Is he here?"

"Officially, he is here. Officially he comes in every day and is helping me rebuild the reactor. Otherwise . . . well, he is a Jew, and he would be taken away. So officially, he is here, and we say that he is indispensable to the Reich's nuclear program. But in truth, he doesn't come in that often. He's not well."

Nathan's heart leaps. "Then he's alive? You're saying he's alive, but he's ill?"

"Correct."

"When can I see him? Where does he live?"

"In Leipzig, of course. I will give you the address."

"And my mother and my sister, do you know of them?"

Heisenberg shakes his head. "I do not believe they are with him. It is not something that Josef ever discusses with me." Heisenberg writes out an address and hands it to Nathan. "I believe you'll find him here. He is home most of the time."

Nathan shakes Heisenberg's hand. "Thank you. I appreciate it."

"Good luck, Nathan Silverman, and to you as well, Dr. Fisher. Peace be with you, Günther."

42

REUNION

It is late morning when Nathan, Allison, and Günther return to Gluck's car in the parking lot. "How did it go?" he asks. "Did you find out about their reactor?"

"It's badly damaged," Allison says. "It doesn't look like they are in the process of restoring it anytime soon. Heisenberg said they are planning on building another reactor in Haigerloch. You may report all that back to General Groves."

Gluck starts the engine. "Great. Let's get back to Berlin and work on your return."

"Wait," Nathan says, handing a folded paper to Gluck. "Please take us to this address."

"What's there?"

"With any luck, it's my father. That's what Dr. Heisenberg said."

Gluck shakes his head. "We need to get back, Nate. I don't even know this street."

"Dr. Heisenberg told me that you head into the city center, turn left at the Altes Rathaus, go three blocks, and turn right. It is the third building, a two-story apartment house."

"Dr. Snyder, Dr. Fisher, are you okay with this delay?"

"Absolutely," they say in unison.

Gluck grumbles and fires up the car. He enters the city center at lunchtime and street traffic is heavy, not only with cars and trucks, but with a number of horse-drawn carts. The Altes Rathaus is located on the east side of a large market, which is jammed with pedestrians and carts.

"I don't see how I'm going to drive through this," Gluck says. "We have to park and walk."

He finds a spot two blocks away and the group heads off in the direction of 112 Petersstraße.

Allison and Nathan find themselves unconsciously walking arm in arm. She leans over and quietly asks, "When we find your father, what are we going to do? Are we going to take him with us?"

Nathan shrugs. "Heisenberg said he is ill. If he's not too sick to travel, then yes."

"I'm with you," Allison says. "If he wants to go, we'll take him. I don't think Fred is going to be too happy about it. That's an extra set of IDs, passports, and tickets."

Nathan smiles. "I know. He'll grouse, but he'll do it."

They walk through the Marktplatz toward the Altes Rathaus, a five-hundred-year-old building, built in the style of the German Renaissance. A walkway with more than twenty arches forms a rectangular perimeter around the ground floor. A tall clock tower sits in the center. Altes Rathaus is German for "Old Town Hall," and true to its name, the building used to be Leipzig's city hall, but by the time Nathan and Allison pass by, it serves as the city's most popular museum.

Günther stops and says, "Wait." He quickly walks into the market, buys a bag of apples, and returns, which brings chuckles to the rest of the group. "What's wrong?" he says. "I'm hungry."

They arrive at the Petersstraße address and Nathan says, "Why don't you three stay down here. Let me go up alone. I don't know what's wrong with my father and a large group might upset him. He doesn't know we're coming."

Gluck and Günther agree, but Allison says, "I'll go up with you. I have a little medical training. Maybe I can be of some assistance."

There is no answer when Nathan knocks on the door. They wait a moment and knock again. When there is no answer the third time, Allison says, "He doesn't appear to be home."

"Maybe. But maybe he's afraid to open the door. He's a Jew and we could be Jew hunters. He might open it if he knew it was me." Nathan knocks and calls out, "Papa, es ist Nathan. Ich bin Nathan. Papa, es ist dein Sohn."

The woman on the first floor opens her door and sticks out her head. "Was ist das?" she says. She yells at Nathan that he is making a racket, disturbing the whole neighborhood. Nathan waves her away and repeats his knocking.

Finally, the door opens a crack. Elderly eyes peer out. "Papa, it's me. I know I don't look right, I'm wearing a disguise, but it's really me: Nathan." The door opens a bit more and Josef says, "You are not Nathan."

Nathan answers with a catch in his throat. "It's true, Papa. Es iz Emmis. It's your boy Nathan. We lived on Grovner Street in Frankfurt. You, me, Mama, and Rachel."

The door sweeps open, and Josef throws his arms around him. Tears are flowing, and in Allison's eyes as well, as she stands to the side. "Come in, come in," Josef says. He looks at Allison and smiles. "Is this your wife, Nathan?" Nathan blushes. "No, no, Papa," Nathan answers, patting his father's back. "She is a very close friend. Her name is Allison."

Josef lifts his chin. "Mm hmm. A close friend? That's all?" Allison is smiling broadly. She doesn't understand German, but she gets the gist of the conversation.

Nathan is a bit befuddled. "Look, Papa, it's a long story. Allison is also in disguise. She's really a young woman, my age, and very pretty. She is a scientist."

Josef turns to Allison and gives her a warm welcome, and a hug. Allison smiles and nods.

"Papa," Nathan says, "she doesn't speak German."

Josef pouts. "No? How about Yiddish?"

Nathan shakes his head. "She's from America, Papa, and she isn't Jewish."

Josef pauses for a moment, shrugs, and says, "Well, that's okay with me, as long as you like her and she likes you."

Nathan knows he is losing control of this conversation. "Papa, we don't have a lot of time. We have to return to America, and we want to take you with us. What about the rest of the family: Mama, Rachel?"

Josef's head tips forward and he stares at the floor. Then he lifts his eyes and sadly shakes his head. "Your mama, God rest her soul, is gone. She was taken from me last year. They promised to protect Mama and Rachel as long as I worked for them at the lab, but then . . ." Josef stops. He is struggling. "They told me it was all a mistake. She wasn't supposed to be taken. Mama was at the market. They came in with trucks and swept them all away. Whoever had a star. When she didn't come home, I went looking for her. I asked the local prefect. Even Abraham Esau made a call on my behalf, but it was too late."

"And Rachel? Did they take her too?"

Josef stands silent. His lips are pressed together.

"Papa, did they take Rachel? Tell me."

Very quietly, almost in a whisper, he says, "Rachel is alive."

"Where is she?"

"After they took your mother, I hid Rachel. She is safe."

"Good. I will take you both home with me."

Josef shakes his head. "And how will you get home from Leipzig? Rachel is safe where she is."

"Nothing is safe in Germany. The Allies are bombing German cities. We had to hide in a basement when they bombed Berlin. Thousands will be killed before this war is over. This whole country will be a battlefield sooner than you think. Let me talk to Rachel. Let her make her own decisions."

While Josef ponders the proposition, Nathan takes a moment to fill Allison in on the conversation. "He has a point, Nathan," she says. "It is a risky trip back for us. It's anything but safe. But I agree, Rachel should be the one to make her own decisions. What about your father? Is he coming with us?"

"Papa," Nathan says, "I want to take you and Rachel back with us. But we have to make a decision immediately. Where is Rachel?"

"She is hiding at a church, like a nun in training. But I don't think you should go there."

Nathan shakes his head. "Don't worry about it. We have credentials, fake identities. I don't have to go as Nathan Silverman. Let me bring her with us to America. And Papa, Günther is coming with us too."

"Günther Snyder?"

"Yes, pack up now, get ready to go, and I will go talk to Rachel."

"She is at the St. John's Catholic Church on Kolpingweg. It's in the southwest part of town. She is always there; she doesn't go outside. I have visited her on occasion; it is all very secret. She is safe and she is happy. Be very careful what you do."

"Go with me and we'll both talk to her."

Josef nods. "It's a long bus ride."

"We have a car. Get your coat and we'll drive over there. But we have to hurry."

Josef cautions, "Don't walk so fast. I'm moving a little slower these days. I'm not feeling so good."

———

Gluck sees Nathan, Allison, and Josef approaching his car, and he starts the motor. "Hop in, everyone, we have to get back to Berlin before they start setting up checkpoints to look for you."

"We have to make a stop at a church on Kolpingweg," Nathan says. "My sister is there, and I need to talk to her. She may go with us. My father will give you directions."

"Getting pretty cozy in this car," Gluck says.

While they are driving across Leipzig, Nathan leans over and asks his father, "I thought you were working at the KWI lab in Berlin. How did you end up in Leipzig?"

"Werner Heisenberg had me transferred. The Leipzig L-IV reactor was nearly completed, and we both knew it would only be a matter of time until KWI physicists achieved a chain reaction. Given German technology with guided rockets, we knew that nuclear missiles were only months away."

"I don't understand. If the reactor was nearly completed, why were you brought here?"

Josef sighs. "*Tataleh,* you're not following me. The reactor was ready to be put into use. We couldn't let that happen."

"Wait a minute. Are you telling me that you and Heisenberg sabotaged the Leipzig reactor?"

"Not just Werner and me. We had the help of Paul Rathje and Fritz Strassman. Unfortunately, Paul was killed in the explosion. And the explosion is what's killing me."

"What do you mean?"

"The radiation. I have cancer, son. It's fatal, I'm afraid. That's why I can't go with you. I don't have the strength, and I don't have the stamina. And I don't have the time."

Nathan's heart sinks. "The doctors can't help you?"

Josef shakes his head. "No. I'm sorry, Nathan."

"You could still come with us," he pleads. "For whatever time you have left, we could spend it together. There are great doctors in America."

Josef pats him on the knee. "I love you, my son, but I would slow you down. And besides, I'm needed here in case they try to restart the reactor. I go in every other day."

The car pulls to the curb in front of the Gothic structure that houses St. John's Catholic Church. "Here we are," Gluck says. "Please make it snappy."

43

A TOUGH DECISION

Josef and Nathan get out of the car in front of the church. Nathan walks around to the driver's window and says, "Allison, I'd like you to come in with us."

Gluck wrinkles his forehead. "Does that make sense? She doesn't know Rachel Silverman, and she doesn't even speak German."

"I think Rachel might be comforted by the fact that another woman is making this journey. Allison is wise and she can answer Rachel's questions. She doesn't have to speak German. She speaks common sense."

Gluck shrugs, turns to Günther and winks. "Comforted. I'm sure. Seems to me like Nathan doesn't do anything without Dr. Fisher."

Günther nods. "Agreed."

They enter the nave of the large church, which is empty of parishioners. There are no services in progress and the church is quiet. Josef knows where to go. He leads Nathan and Allison to a business office which is occupied by an older woman in ordinary attire. "Hello, Ruth," Josef says. "I came to see Gerta Felds."

Ruth wrinkles her forehead and her eyes land on Nathan and Allison. "He's my son, Ruth. My son, Nathan and his . . . his girlfriend."

"Of course," she says, and she leaves the office. Moments later she returns, accompanied by a young woman dressed as a novitiate: black skirt, black sweater, and a white cloth bonnet. The older woman leaves and shuts the door, leaving the group alone. Rachel stands by the door. She sees her father, but she doesn't recognize the other two people with their wrinkles and age spots.

"It's me, Rachel," Nathan says quietly. "I'm in a disguise. For safety reasons." Like a light switch, Rachel suddenly recognizes her brother, and runs over to hug him. "What are you doing here?" she says. "Have you lost your mind? Why did you come back?"

"I was sent here on a mission with the U.S. Army, but now I've finished and I'm getting ready to go home. I came here to talk to you about coming to America with me," he says. "This is Allison Fisher. She is also on the mission and she will be coming with us."

"When?"

"Now. Right now."

"Really?" Rachel narrows her eyes. "What arrangements are there for such a bold journey, Nathan? The borders are all closed. There are military checkpoints on all major highways. You can't drive a hundred kilometers without showing your papers. The train stations are filled with Gestapo. Do you have some magic way of getting out of Europe?"

"We got in here, didn't we?"

"For what purpose, what mission?" she says testily. "You weren't sent here by the U.S. Army just to rescue me and Papa. What was it? What's going on, Nathan?"

Allison senses the tension building between brother and sister. She taps Nathan on the shoulder, and says, "May I please speak to Rachel, and would you please translate?"

Once again, Nathan recognizes that Allison has a better handle on this situation than he does. "Sure, but my sister is a little hardheaded."

Allison smiles and invites Rachel to sit with her on the couch. She speaks in a soft and friendly way. "What we say here, stays between us. Okay?"

Rachel nods.

"We were sent here by the U.S. government to assess the level of

KWI's nuclear readiness. I am a nuclear scientist. Like your father. Your brother is a soldier."

"Nathan is a soldier?"

"Yes. We have also come here to assist a nuclear scientist who wants to defect and escape to the West. You know him. It's Günther Snyder."

"Günther is here?"

"Yes. Günther is sitting in a car in front of the church. Nathan and I have finished our assessment. We are ready to go home, but your brother wouldn't leave without trying to find you. He insisted that we find both you and your father, and take you back with us. That is, if you want to go."

Rachel slowly turns her head from side to side. "Nathan the soldier!"

"And a damn good one."

Rachel smiles at him. "So, how will you get us out of Europe?"

Allison continues. "New identification papers are being prepared for us by the American intelligence agency OSS, the Office of Strategic Services. We came here by train, but I don't know how we're going back. They haven't told us. Look, Rachel, there is no way of soft-pedaling this; it's as risky as it gets. Your brother and I visited the KWI lab with Günther, pretending to be other people."

"That's why you are in costume?"

"Yes. Günther Snyder is now missing from the lab and they will presume he is defecting. They already suspect that your brother and I were imposters who spied at the KWI and they'll be on the alert for us as well. I know this is a lot to throw on you, but we are leaving, and you need to make a decision right now. Do you want to go with us?"

Rachel turns to face her father. "Are you going too, Papa?"

He shakes his head. "I can't, and you know why."

A tear runs down her cheek. "You could go too, Papa. You could have more than six months. No one knows for sure."

He shakes his head. "They know."

"If I leave with Nathan, who will take care of you when your sickness gets worse?"

Josef walks over and takes her hand. "*Bubbeleh,* think of this: when

I die, any promise they made to me for your protection would be null and void. The nurses will take care of me."

She turns her head. "I can't. I'm sorry, Allison, but I don't feel right about going. Leaving him alone in his last days. They don't know I'm at the church. I use the name Gerta Felds. I wear the clothes of a novitiate."

"I understand," Allison says.

Nathan nods. "I do too."

Josef waves his hands back and forth. "Oh, no. No, you don't. You're not going to stay here on my account. You do what's best for *you*. You have years in front of you. If you want to go, considering all the dangers, then tell your brother right now. But don't think it is safe here. Especially for you and me. You know what happened to your mother. They've cleared us all out; there's no one left. It's *Judenfrei*."

"In Leipzig too?" Nathan says. "It's so hard to believe."

"There have been Jews in Leipzig for eight hundred years," Josef says. "Before the Nazis came, there were thirteen thousand Jews living here; leaders in every profession. Then came the armbands and the roundups. One by one they were taken away. The last eighteen Jews still living in Leipzig were deported to Auschwitz in June. They let me stay because of the reactor. When I'm gone, Rachel will be the only Jew left in this city. It will be *Judenfrei,* just like Hitler wants it."

"I'm safe, Papa," Rachel says. "I know that someone could turn me in, but only a couple people know that I'm Jewish." She turns to Allison. "I'm torn. I want to stay for my papa, but . . . What should I do, Allison? What would *you* do?"

Allison's lips are tightly closed, and she shakes her head. "I can't make this decision for you."

"Before I decide, I want to talk to Mother Superior. She has been a Godsend for me, and she's very wise. Can you give me five minutes?"

———————

When Rachel returns to the office, she is carrying a bag. "I told Mother Superior as much as I could without breaking our agreement," Rachel says nervously. "And she said she shouldn't make the decision for me either. But I pleaded. I said, 'I just don't know what to do,' and she closed her eyes, and she made two fists, and she said, 'Lord, help this girl.' Then she opened her eyes and said, 'Go!' So here I am."

Allison, Rachel, Nathan, and Josef leave the church and return to the car. "Oh, my goodness, do you think I'm driving a bus? Are you sure there's nobody else you want to pick up?" Gluck says, with a laugh.

"My father's not going with us. We have to drop him at his apartment. He's going to stay. Then we can go back."

"You could stay the night with me," Josef says. "I have two bedrooms and a big couch. It would be one extra day with my Rachel. Who knows when or if I will see her again?"

"It would be dangerous for you, Josef," Gluck says. "There is a warrant out for these three public enemies. And we need to get them on their way back to the States."

A tear comes to Josef's eyes, and he kisses his daughter. "I understand."

44

MEASURING FOR THE LONG JOURNEY

The drive back to Berlin is uneventful. No roadblocks and no questions. It is late in the evening when Gluck pulls up to the safe house. "Make yourself comfortable, folks," he says. He checks his watch. "By now Speer has no doubt concluded that you are all runaways. Travel will not be so easy tomorrow."

"What do you mean by that?" Rachel says.

"I mean that locations which customarily check identification papers will have been alerted and notified to detain Nathan, Allison, and/or Günther. Presumably they don't know about you, Rachel. That means train stations, bus stations, automobile checkpoints. Certainly, all border crossings."

Nathan adds, "I assume that also means they are looking for Hauptmann Froman, Hauptmann Strauss, Irène Curie, and François Joliot."

"Don't forget Alicia Dumont, who danced the night away at the Curious Squirrel," Allison says with smile.

Gluck nods. "They're not dumb enough to think that you will continue to use those identities. They'll stop anyone, regardless of the name, who fits any of your physical descriptions."

"Does that mean we can't take trains at all?" Allison asks. "How else do we get to Cherbourg?"

"You'll have to take the trains, and I think it's logical for the Gestapo to believe that you are going to retrace your route and return through Paris. That's where Weber and Zeist saw you."

"We'd have to drive back through the Cotentin Peninsula," says Nathan. "We were stopped at several checkpoints on the way to Paris. Will the checkpoints be alerted?"

"Probably. You were identified at several stops along the way to Berlin. All of those stations in between will be heavily watched. Especially the passport control in Luxembourg, the Paris Gare du Nord, and of course the Berlin Anhalter Bahnhof."

"What about driving all the way?" Allison says. "Maybe different routes?"

Gluck grimaces. "It's over a thousand kilometers and a couple dozen checkpoints from Berlin to Cherbourg. And, to tell the truth, I wouldn't be surprised if the Gestapo has alerted gas stations along that route. But I suppose it is an option."

"What about a small plane, like a crop duster?" Nathan says. "I saw that in a movie once. They made an escape in a crop duster."

"Do you fly? Are you a pilot?"

"No."

"Well, neither am I. To my knowledge, OSS Berlin Station doesn't own a plane, let alone a crop duster. And personally, though I am not a farmer, I think it would be unusual to crop dust in late November. And even if we had a small plane, it would probably have to refuel three or four times on the round trip, and that would mean stopping at small airports where they would check identities. And of course, there is always the opportunity to get shot down in a British bombing raid. But, you know, it's an option."

"All right, all right, take it easy."

"Well, let's get serious. You're probably limited to taking a train. We'll have to decide where and when."

Günther is visibly nervous. "Frankly, I have to say, it scares me that the Gestapo is looking for us. And by 'us,' I mean 'me.' They have my physical description, and I'm not so easy to hide."

"You're right," Gluck says. "Our number one priority tonight is to find a new route back. Number two is to change your identities and your appearances. I have called Hanna. As you know, she's an artistic director and she'll have ideas for each of you. Once you settle on a new identity, she'll make you an outfit, and we can print up your travel documents. In the meantime, I'm going to contact OSS in Washington. It's morning there and they can get a head start planning your return."

It is 8:00 A.M. when Hanna arrives at the safe house. She stands in the foyer and brushes the snow off of her coat. "You'll never believe what's going on out there," she says. "It's at least half a meter, already over my boots."

"Then there'll be no bombing raids tonight," Renzel says.

She looks around the room. "Okay," she says, "where are my Most Wanteds?"

Allison and Nathan respond "one" and "two," respectively. Günther stands and bows. "Number three reporting for service."

Hanna takes a tape measure out of her bag, looks across the room at Rachel, still dressed in her novitiate's uniform, and says, "Don't you have a number, sweetheart?"

Rachel smiles. "I don't think they know about me. I'm Gerta Felds, also known as Rachel Silverman, Nathan's sister. I've been living in a church convent for the past two years."

"And no one knows you are traveling with this group?"

"Nope."

"Well, honey, you don't need a costume. Just wear what you have on," Hanna says, and then points at Günther. "Dr. Snyder, could you come over here, please. I have a delightful idea." Hanna measures Günther, backs up, and says, "It will take some effort on your part, Günther, but I think you can pull it off. First of all, let's face it, preparing a disguise for you is a challenge. You are a heavy man: what are you, one hundred fifteen, one hundred twenty kilos? People know you by your silhouette. You have curly hair and a recognizable face. No doubt your KWI picture is on every Gestapo agent's desk."

Günther shrugs. "Thanks for the flattery. You know, I could try to lose a little weight."

Everyone laughs. "We don't have that much time, Günther," Hanna says. "But standing here looking at Rachel, an idea came to me. It will take a day or so to put it all together, but we're going to dress you up as a nun, and you're going to travel with Rachel by your side."

Günther shakes his head. "Oh no. Not a chance. I can't travel around as a woman, let alone a nun. I don't think I could carry that off. Maybe something more manly. I have a reputation to uphold. For the rest of my life, I'd always be known as the guy who escaped in the guise of a nun."

"Are you serious, Günther?" Nathan snaps. "Are you worried about your masculinity? Your reputation as a he-man? I think it's a damn good idea, and you'll help to protect my sister."

Hanna spreads her hands. "Why not, Günther? The habit will hide your figure, the cowl will hide your hair and a good portion of your face. And who is going to look closely at a nun traveling with a novitiate?"

"I like it," Renzel says, and Allison adds, "Me too."

"Good. Let me take measurements for each of you. I'll get back to the theater and work on your costumes." She approaches Allison, who says, "What do you have in mind for me? Am I to be a nun as well?"

Hanna shrugs. "You could, but since you're going back to Paris, it's more logical . . ."

Gluck enters the room and interrupts. "Paris is out. Washington OSS has intercepted messages alerting the Gestapo to be on the lookout for Nathan, Allison, and Dr. Günther Snyder. Hanna is right when she says that Günther's KWI picture has been distributed, along with very accurate descriptions of Allison and Nathan. They assume you three will be traveling by train, and that you will most likely take the route through Frankfurt, Luxembourg, and Paris on your way to the coast. Apparently, the Gestapo has also increased personnel at the stops on the route through Brussels and Calais. OSS considers it too dangerous to travel by train along those lines."

"Then what are we going to do?" Allison says. "Cars are out, planes are out, and now trains?"

"Not all trains. Washington thinks it's less dangerous to travel south. Munich to Milan, then to Marseille. From there they have taken people out through Lisbon. We've had success there before. Casablanca could be an alternative, but that's a stretch."

"Ooh, I don't know about Casablanca," Allison says. "I saw that movie last spring. It had a real sad ending. It made me cry."

Gluck smiles. "You mean because the couple broke up at the end. Is that the reason you don't want to go to Casablanca?"

Allison blushes. "Oh, cut it out. It's because there were Nazis in Casablanca. It was very dangerous."

Gluck can't stop chuckling. "Yeah, I think you meant it was sad because Bergman left Bogart. You think Casablanca is a place where couples break up. That's why you don't want to go there. Allison leaves Nathan? Nathan leaves Allison? Hmm?"

"Stop it," Allison says. "Nazis, that's what I meant."

Gluck laughs. "Casablanca is safe now. There is a large American air base there. Roosevelt and Churchill met in conference there almost a year ago."

Hanna, who is getting a kick out of this conversation, says, "I'm going back to the theater now. I have a lot of work to do."

"What about Allison and me?" Nathan says. "What are you thinking about for us?"

"I need to make you very different from the two old scientists that went into the KWI. No wrinkles, no gray hair. And different from the Hauptmann and his French girlfriend who walked the streets of Paris. I'm thinking for Allison, a Marseille girl—young and sassy. Short black hair. Young twenties."

"That's kind of what I was in Paris," Allison says.

"No," Nathan says. "You were a vamp. Slinky evening dress. Dancing in a nightclub. High heels."

Allison sighs. "Can't I just be a boring, brilliant nuclear scientist?"

"Definitely not. For Nathan, I think a young man as well. Let me ponder it and see what we have in the theater wardrobe. I'll try to finish up and get back tomorrow, but it might be the next day." She puts on her winter coat and furry hat, stares out of the window at the blizzard, and shakes her head. "I wish it was me who was getting out of this storm and going to Lisbon. Good night, Fred." She turns to Allison, suppresses a giggle, and says, "Good night, Ilsa. You'll always have Paris."

"Nazis. That's all I meant."

45

THE NIGHT BEFORE

Day breaks on a foot-deep blanket of white. "This might actually be a good day to travel," Gluck says to Nathan in the kitchen, as the two drink their coffee. "Vision will be limited, people will be all bundled up; collars pulled up, hats pulled down. There won't be much face to see."

"I'm worried about the Berlin train station, the Anhalter Bahnhof," Nathan says. "No matter how clever Hanna is, no matter how well she prepares our costumes, they know we have to take the train, and they know we have to leave from Berlin. There will be more agents than passengers inside the Bahnhof. I guarantee that Henning Wolf will be standing at the gates."

Gluck nods. "I've been thinking about that as well. Anhalter would be a tough departure spot for you folks. What if I drove you south and we met the train in Dresden? You could board it there. It's about two hundred kilometers and the weather is shitty, but it might be our best plan."

Nathan agrees. "I'd rather take my chances on a snowy road than the Berlin station, but what if we're stopped? You have a car full: a nun, a novitiate, a young, sassy girl, and me. A car full of Germany's Most Wanted, one through three."

"You're right."

"Still, I like it," Nathan says. "Should we go at night, and should we all be armed? If we are stopped, and if there is the least bit of suspicion, or any discussions of a detention . . . well, I have a gun, and you have a gun. I think you should also give one to Allison. I'm not going to be taken alive by these sons of bitches, and you saw what they did to poor Lena Hartz."

"Agreed. If Hanna can get her costumes done by this afternoon, we'll leave early in the morning. You know, I'd be willing to drive you all the way to Marseille, but mountain passes might be closed, and I know we'd never get across the borders. You're much better off on the train. My advice to you is not to travel as a group. They're looking for a group. Once we get to Dresden, split up. Your sister can ride with Günther, but you and Allison should be separated. Ride in different cars. The two of you shouldn't be seen as a couple."

"Understood. What about our new IDs and passports?"

Gluck brushes the question away with a smile. "That's no problem. Kurt will handle it. We print those things every day."

Allison is in the living room talking with Rachel when Nathan walks in. "We were just discussing what Rachel is going to do when she gets to America," Allison says. "Her English is pretty good. She wants to go to school. Maybe she could go to the University of Chicago, and I could keep an eye on her. It's not such a bad town; maybe you should think about it too," she says with a smile.

"Pretty sure I'm going back to Ritchie," Nathan says. "That's where I was before I was transferred to Groves. By the way, Fred says we're changing our travel plans. He is going to drive us to Dresden, and we'll board the train there. The Berlin station is too risky."

"I thought it was too dangerous to drive," Allison says. "Fred said there would be roadblocks and checkpoints."

"That may be true, but there are some advantages to driving early in the morning in a snowstorm. They're not expecting a car full of people, our disguises may fool them, and no one wants to hang around outside in this nasty weather. Maybe the roadblocks will be unmanned, or inspections will be hurriedly processed. Fred will take a back road out of Berlin and it's a three-hour drive to Dresden."

"If that's what you want to do. I leave it up to you."

Nathan walks over and takes her hand. "I know this wasn't the way it was all supposed to go down when we discussed it back in New York, and I feel bad. We were supposed to meet with Günther in the safe house, question him about Germany's nuclear progress, and make a quick return trip to New York with him in tow. We weren't supposed to have half the Gestapo on our tail."

Allison looks up at Nathan. There is a loving look in her eyes and Nathan can see it. "And we weren't supposed to find your father and rescue your sister. And we weren't supposed to get into the KWI labs in disguise and discover their progress firsthand. And we weren't supposed to see Germany's nuclear reactor and learn that it had been sabotaged. But we did, we did all those things, Nathan, and I'm damn proud of it."

Nathan sighs. "Do you know how to shoot a gun?"

"I grew up on a farm. I've fired my daddy's shotgun several times, and bagged my share of doves, but I never have shot a pistol."

"Well, a trigger is a trigger. Point and shoot. Fred is going to give you a pistol. Use it if you're threatened. You know what those bastards did to Lena. If it looks like they're going to arrest us . . ."

Allison reaches up and places her finger on his lips. "I know."

It is late afternoon when Hanna arrives. She brings in two large bags. "There's a nun's outfit out in the car," she says, "along with a couple of coats and some scarves. I just couldn't carry it all."

Nathan and Gluck go out to fetch the clothes and return to grousing about the weather. "It's terrible out there," Gluck says. "Wind, swirling snow. Here's your habit, Günther."

He takes it and holds it up. "I hope it fits. You know, I'm rather large-chested."

Hanna rolls her eyes, turns to Allison, and says, "Dr. Fisher, please come with me. We have some work to do."

Hanna and Allison return to the living room. Allison's hair has been dyed black and cut short. She has on a leather jacket, tight in the waist, over black slacks. She is holding a long winter coat and a knit cap. Nathan whistles. "You do look sassy, that's for sure," he says.

"But do I look like Alicia Dumont, the vamp who ran around Paris? Would Speer's buddy, Wolf, recognize me?"

"Nope."

Günther stands. "How do I look?"

Hanna is not pleased. "You are one sorry-looking nun." She walks over, straightens the cowl, and fits the veil to his head. She shows him how to wear his beads. She takes out a pair of rimless spectacles and hands them to him. "Wear these at all times." Then she says, "Where are the shoes I brought? I brought you black-laced shoes."

Günther frowns. "I didn't like them."

"Put them on," she commands, "and then go shave; you have a shadow. I brought some pancake makeup. It'll hide your shadow and provide a little color to your pasty white cheeks. Keep it on your face for at least twenty-four hours, then reapply it."

She walks over to Nathan. "Your turn. I want to color your hair. I'm thinking Nordic blond. Young German businessman look."

When they return to the room, Allison says, "Wow, right off the Scandinavian rowing team." Nathan is wearing a gray suit, a long, heavy cloth coat, and a white scarf wrapped around his neck. He holds a black, flat cap with earflaps.

"My idea is that you cover as much of your face as possible," Hanna says. "Wrap those long woolen scarves around your neck like this, and over the lower part of your face. Pull your hat down as low as it goes so that all that shows are your eyes."

Gluck comes in with papers in his hand, looks at the group, and smiles. "I like it. All bundled up, I can't tell who's who. Great work, Hanna." He reaches out and hands IDs and passports to each. "These are your new identities. Here you go, Sister Angelica." Günther groans.

Nathan's German passport identifies him as Kurt Holzer. Allison is to become Paula Leiber. Rachel Silverman will remain as Gerta Felds.

"The train to Munich boards in Dresden at nine A.M.," Gluck says. "We need to be there a little early, but not so early that you're standing around. We should leave here by five. That will give us the cover of night for most of our trip. Let's all get a little sleep and be ready to go at five."

46

A WINTRY DEPARTURE

Gluck assembles the four travelers earlier than expected. "The snow has deepened," he says. "The roads are bound to be hazardous. Maybe even impassable in spots. I fixed chains to my tires, but even so, it will take much longer to get to Dresden. You might want to think about postponing the journey."

"I would agree," Günther says. "In the interest of safety, we should delay the return until the roads have been cleared. I suppose one should consider whether it is foolhardy to drive at all."

"Look, I don't want to take anyone against their will. This safe house is here for you as long as you want to stay."

"How long will that be?" Rachel says. "Winter travel in Germany is treacherous even when there's not a snowstorm. It could be weeks or months."

"We can't wait weeks or months. I have information that I need to deliver to General Groves," Allison says. "Detailed information. Everything that I saw, every paper I reviewed. It's all right in here." She taps her head. "And the Manhattan Project needs Günther's expertise. Every day we stay in Berlin is a day we can be caught. I vote we go."

Gluck raises his eyebrows and looks at Nathan. "Feisty one, isn't she?"

"Oh, you have no idea," Nathan says with a smile. "About the storm, it may actually benefit us in some regard. It's just as tough for the Gestapo to get around. It'll take that much longer for them to alert their agents along the routes out of Germany. How are they going to get that information to soldiers at roadblocks and checkpoints? When the snow clears and the roads are open, it will be that much easier to spread the word about our escape. I agree with the feisty one."

"I stand with my brother," Rachel says. "Germany's roads can be horrible in the snow, but it's horrible for everyone."

Everyone turns their attention to Günther. He squints one eye. "How good a driver are you?" he says to Gluck. "Can you manage these conditions?"

"I grew up in Montana, Dr. Snyder. It can snow three feet in one night. I'm comfortable."

"Then we go."

All right, I've warmed up the car," Gluck says. "Günther, you sit up front with me. That way if anyone should look in the window, they'll see a big fat ugly nun sitting there. That might dissuade them from looking any closer."

Günther gives Gluck a dirty look. "Oh, you are an unpleasant fellow. I just happen to be large-chested, that's all."

They start off into the night with Gluck's windshield wipers slapping back and forth. He says over his shoulder, "The latest VW. Factory-installed wipers and defoggers, along with factory heat, but I advise you to keep your coats on. The heater doesn't work all that well."

They leave Berlin's city limits and head out through the countryside where the snow is deep. The car slides now and then, but Gluck manages to maintain control. "How does a Montana boy speak German so fluently and get assigned to OSS Berlin Station?" Nathan asks.

"You grow up on a ranch with German parents. When the war comes, you join the State Department and volunteer for whatever Uncle Sam decides you're suited for. And you, Nathan? You're a U.S. citizen?"

"Not yet. I grew up in Berlin. My family is Jewish. My parents sent me to live in New York in 1938. When the opportunity arose in 1942, I enlisted. Same as you."

"Look," Günther says, pointing at a light in the distance.

"I see it," Gluck says. "It's a fire pot. It'll be a checkpoint."

Gluck slows the vehicle. An orange and white pole sits on two cones and stretches across the road. There is a small wooden hut off to the side. A metal garbage can is blazing. A snow-covered half-track sits beside the hut. There appear to be two helmeted men dressed in field gray double-breasted great coats with dark green collars and shoulder straps standing by the fire pot. "Infantrymen," Nathan says. One of the two soldiers starts waving his arms, signaling Gluck to stop.

"Should we blow through?" Gluck says. "I can outrun them."

"They'll have some sort of communicator or shortwave, won't they?" asks Nathan.

"Probably."

"Then they'll radio ahead. Someone will be waiting for us down the line."

"Possibly. The costumes might get us through. Your call."

"I believe we should stop," Nathan says. "Let's bank on the costumes." Nevertheless, he pulls his handgun from his coat pocket and holds it out of sight.

Each of the two soldiers, rifle in hand, walks slowly to the car. One of them taps on the driver's window with the tip of his rifle. Gluck rolls the window down and says, "Guten Morgen."

"Ja," the snow-covered soldier says. "Ja, good for nothing. Papers, please." He peers into the car, first at Sister Angelica, then at Rachel, Allison, and Nathan.

Everyone tenders their IDs and passports to Gluck, who hands them to the soldier. He examines them and peers into the car once again. "Where are you going," he says, "that requires you to be out in the middle of the night in a snowstorm?"

"I am taking Sister Angelica and a novitiate to the St. John's Church in Dresden. They are required be there for early morning mass."

The soldier narrows his eyes. "And the other two? Are they also required to be in church for early morning mass?" The soldier motions for his companion to come over. "Jodl, look in the back seat; the man and woman. Do they match the descriptions we received?"

"Maybe. Ja, maybe the man. Maybe he is Froman. And the woman, maybe is the girlfriend."

The first soldier nods and with a stern expression, commands, "Everyone out of the car! Hands up! Now!"

Gluck shrugs, tips his head to Nathan, and calmly says in English, "I'll take the one on the right."

The back door and the driver's door fly open simultaneously, the handguns fire immediately, and each of the startled soldiers falls to the ground. Additional shots ensure they are dead.

"Let's drag these two into the woods," Gluck says. "The snow will cover them up."

———

The group resumes their ride to Salzburg. The car is quiet. No one is making small talk. Rachel is weeping. Allison puts her arm around her. "It's all right. We had no choice. It had to be done."

———

Dresden, capital of the German state of Saxony, is one of the larger cities in Germany. A classic beauty along the River Elbe. The train station itself is an architectural landmark. Gluck parks the car and walks with the others toward the station. At his suggestion, Nathan, Allison, Rachel, and Günther slip into an adjoining coffee shop and take a booth in the corner until boarding begins for the Berlin-to-Munich train. "I'll go buy the tickets," Gluck says, "and I'll come get you when it's last call for boarding."

Fifteen minutes pass, then twenty, and Gluck has not returned. "Something's wrong," Nathan says. "I'm going to go check it out."

He exits the coffee shop, enters the terminal, and sees Gluck talking to a man in a long black leather coat. Gluck catches sight of Nathan out of the corner of his eye and gives a quick shake of his head. Nathan backtracks and rapidly returns to the coffee shop. A few minutes later, Gluck joins them.

"The man I was talking to is named Uwe. He didn't say, but I am sure he is Gestapo. He was continuously scanning the terminal and making eye contact with another guy in a leather coat." Gluck chuckles. "They might as well wear signs: 'Gestapo on duty.' Anyway, when I went in to buy the tickets, he was standing near the gate for the Nuremberg train. I decided to engage him. Maybe I could learn something about their surveillance. I took out a pack of cigarettes to have a smoke. I saw the way he looked at the pack—they're French, the ones you get around here are shit—and I offered him one. So, while we're sharing a smoke, I asked him if he knew what track the Berlin-to-Munich train was on. I was supposed to meet someone. He told me it was canceled. Probably had something to do with the storm. He was also trying to meet someone. Actually, he was looking for a group of people."

"Jesus, the word sure got here fast," Nathan says. "They're already monitoring the Dresden station. How many are there?"

"I only saw the two. Uwe said the next through train to Munich wasn't coming until tonight. I asked him what he was going to do, and he said he was going to take the train to Nuremberg. From there he could get a train to Munich and he'd wait for his group there. Then I asked him if the group was family, and he laughed. He said, 'If they were my family, I wouldn't be standing around. If I don't catch up with them in Munich, I'll meet them in Strasbourg. I know where they're going.'"

"The Berlin-to-Munich train doesn't come through until tonight?" Nathan says. "We can't wait here that long. And when we do get to Munich, Uwe and his friend will be there waiting for us."

"I know," Gluck says. "We could put you on that train to Nuremberg and then on to Munich. You'd get there earlier than tonight, but you'd be riding with Uwe and his partner. I think we need to reroute, and I have an idea. They all think you're going west to the French coast, and that's where their concentration will be. Uwe's probably covering the route that goes Munich to Strasbourg to Paris to the coast."

"But we're going to Marseille."

"Right. That's where our agents will be waiting for you. We can circumvent Munich and get to Marseille a different way. There is a train that leaves for Prague in thirty minutes. They're not looking for you to go east."

"What are we to do in Czechoslovakia?" Nathan says. "What trains do we take from there?"

"I'm not sure yet. We need to get you from Prague to Marseille." He checks his watch. "Let me make a couple of quick phone calls. Stay here."

In a bit, Gluck returns with a handful of tickets. "This is the result of our collective judgment," he says, as he distributes the tickets to each member of the group. "Dresden to Prague is a quick train ride. Less than two hours. You have separate seats. You'll go through customs in Prague, but we don't think there will be a problem. Change trains in Prague for Salzburg."

"What is the layover time, and do we have an OSS agent in Prague?" Nathan asks.

"We do, but I haven't been able to reach him yet. You shouldn't need him. Washington is alerting agents along the way, but we don't think Prague will be a problem. The train to Salzburg leaves an hour after your arrival. Find the gate and board. Your seat assignments are on your tickets. You will arrive in Salzburg between five P.M. and six P.M. Austrian passport control is notoriously lax. You shouldn't have a problem there either. Your train to Milan leaves at seven P.M. and arrives the next morning."

"Border control in Italy?" Allison says.

"Practically nonexistent," Gluck says. "Four-hour layover in Milan, and it's a straight shot to Marseille." He hands a folded paper to Nathan. "Here is the name and address of our contact in Marseille in case anything happens." He checks the time. "Prague is boarding now. Other than Günther and Rachel, you should stay separated. Remember the checkpoint guard said he was looking for Froman and his girlfriend, and Uwe is looking for a group. Stay separated. All right, are you ready?"

They put on their coats and scarves. "We're ready."

"Günther and Rachel, you two go first. Wrap those scarves to cover your faces, try not to make eye contact with other passengers." He watches as Sister Angelica and her novitiate walk regally into the terminal.

Gluck turns to Allison. "Your turn." He gives her a hug. "I have to say I'm going to miss you guys."

"I'm going to miss you too," Allison says. "Thank you so much for everything you've done."

"Part of the job. It's all for a good cause. When this war is over, when we've disposed of this mad paper-hanger, someday we'll all get together and lift a few steins."

"Are you ever coming back home?"

"God willing." He leans over and whispers, "And when I do, I'll come visit you and Nathan and all your little Silvermans in Chicago, or wherever you two end up."

"Oh, you think that's what's going to happen, do you?"

"I do, and so does anyone else who's lucky enough to spend time with the two of you."

Allison blushes, gives him a kiss, and heads off into the terminal.

Gluck turns to Nathan. "You take care of that little girl," he says. "She's a keeper."

"I know."

"Stay apart until Marseille. They'll be looking for a couple. I booked your seats close together, but a few rows apart. From Salzburg on, you're all in different compartments, but within the same car. Stay alert."

Nathan nods. "I'm sure everyone understands, and I think we'll be okay."

"Remember, Hanna's costumes only go so far. You are the most recognizable. They are looking for Hauptmann Froman, and they have a pretty good description. I'll walk you to the platform in case my buddy Uwe is still hanging around."

47

CUSTOMS

Nathan's seat is toward the rear of the car. From there he has a clear view of Allison, six rows up and on his left. She is sitting in the window seat next to a woman who is knitting. Rachel and Günther are farther up, near the front of the car. It is a smooth ride to Prague, even though the snow continues to fall. The only people to come through the car are the conductor taking tickets and a woman selling candy and cigarettes.

Customs and immigration in the Prague station go smoothly as well. The line to examine passports moves quickly. When Günther and Rachel approach the agent, Günther smiles, nods at him, and makes the sign of the cross. *He is hamming it up pretty good,* Nathan thinks. Allison also walks through without a second look. When it is his turn, Nathan lays his passport on the table. The agent takes his time scrutinizing the passport, then nods his head, stamps it, and slides it back to Nathan. One down, two to go.

The seats on the train to Salzburg are similarly situated. Nathan is toward the rear of the coach, Allison is in the middle, and Günther and Rachel share a seat in the front. The snow has lightened up and Nathan is able to view the striking Austrian countryside. Once again, nobody stands out as a German intelligence officer or a Gestapo agent, and Nathan is breathing easier. Perhaps this roundabout way of getting to Marseille was an excellent idea after all.

In the calm of the ride, Nathan allows himself to daydream. What will he do when this assignment is all finished? He expects that he will return to Camp Ritchie, join up with his squad, and prepare to accompany the Allied Expeditionary Force when it lands on the Continent next spring. He wonders whether he will get all the way back to Berlin. Will he meet up with Fred Gluck or Kurt Renzel again? Or will he meet up with Henning Wolf?

Then it occurs to him that he has been transferred to General Groves and the Manhattan Engineer District. Will he remain on the general's staff? Will he be given assignments in the Manhattan Project? He may not get back to Europe at all.

He wonders what will become of Allison. Will she return to Chicago? Or will she accompany Günther to whatever Manhattan Project location he is assigned: Chicago, Oak Ridge, Tennessee, or Los Alamos? Someone will have to shuttle him around at least for a while. He will probably be a fish out of water in America. A large fish.

Late afternoon, and the train begins its ascent into Salzburg. Nathan leafs through a travel magazine. Oh, if times were different and he could just tour the city: the birthplace of Mozart, six-hundred-year-old breweries, baroque architecture. Wouldn't it be fun if he and Allison could jump off the train in Salzburg and explore the city together?

———

Gluck was right; the Salzburg station is quiet this evening. As in the other border crossings, passengers line up to pass through customs and passport control. WELCOME TO SALZBURG, the sign says. To be more accurate, Nathan thinks, perhaps it should say, WELCOME TO NAZI-OCCUPIED AUSTRIA.

Standing toward the back of the line, Nathan watches as Günther and Rachel wait to have their passports examined. There is a man standing behind the passport agent, looking over his shoulder. He is dressed as a civilian in a herringbone jacket, white shirt, and tie.

Perhaps he is a supervisor. Perhaps he is training a new passport agent. Sister Angelica and her novitiate present their passports. The agent smiles, stamps the passports, slides them back, and waves them through. Several more passengers proceed, and it is Allison's turn. Nathan watches closely. He nervously fingers his gun in the pocket of his coat.

Allison tenders her passport. The agent routinely stamps it and waves his hand but the man in the herringbone jacket says, "Halt." He picks up Allison's passport and compares it to a piece of paper in his hand. He says something to the agent. No one is moving. The man seems to be studying Allison's features intensely. Her face, then the paper. He is taking way too much time. Nathan knows he must do something, and do it quickly.

"Hey, what the hell is taking so long here?" Nathan hollers from the back of the line. "Do we have to wait all day? I have a train to catch." His voice gets louder. "Why isn't this line moving? You have a simple job to do and it takes you all day long to do it? What's the matter with you? I'm going to complain to the authorities."

The commotion draws the attention of the passengers. People in the line step aside. The conversations grow louder. Some of the passengers agree with him, and add their voices in discontent. Some tell Nathan to be quiet and stop raising a fuss; it's slowing everything down. The man in the herringbone jacket gives Allison's passport back to the agent and hurries out to stop the commotion. "Calm down," he says to everyone. "Things take time. Everyone will be served in order." To Nathan he says, "You must stop this behavior or we will temporarily shut down customs."

"Well, it's just taking a long time," Nathan says calmly. "I don't know why it has to take so long."

"Passport control is serious business," says the man. "If you can't behave, I'm not going to let you through."

Nathan nods. "I'm sorry."

The supervisor hurries back to his post behind the customs agent and tells him to resume the examinations. The agent hands Allison her passport and waves her through. She looks back at Nathan, nods her head, and follows Günther and Rachel into the terminal toward the Milan platform.

Nathan continues to wait in the line. Some of the passengers are having difficulty. There is something amiss with a man's passport. One woman can't find it in her purse. The man standing behind the examiner helps him resolve discrepancies as they occur. Günther, Rachel, and Allison are long out of sight. Finally, it is Nathan's turn. The agent eyeballs him and shakes his head. He waves his finger back and forth. "You must learn patience." But then he smiles. "Passport please, Mr. Impatient One." Nathan tenders his passport. The agent looks at it and hands it back to the man in the jacket. "Finally your turn, eh Herr Holzer?" the man says.

Nathan nods. "Finally."

The supervisor studies Nathan's passport and compares it to the paper in his hand. Then he does it again. And again. He nods to a uniformed guard who walks over, rifle in hand. "Herr Holzer," the man says, "would you come this way, please." He gestures to an office door.

"Not another delay," Nathan says. "Don't you care that I have a train to catch? I have only a short layover. What is the problem?"

"This way, please," the man repeats. Nathan feels like making a run for it, but sighs and follows the man. Perhaps it can be cleared up quickly. Maybe this is payback for making noise. Nathan reasons that if the man were Gestapo, he wouldn't say please.

They step in front of a door to a back office. Suddenly, pointing his rifle, the uniformed guard says, "Hands up, Herr Holzer." Nathan is quickly searched, his pistol found and confiscated. The door is opened and Nathan and the supervisor enter the small office. There is a desk and two chairs. The man gestures for Nathan to be seated, and the door is closed.

"What is the problem?" Nathan says again. "I don't want to miss my train to Milan. What's wrong with my passport?"

The man is polite, but firm. "I am sorry, Herr Holzer, I truly am, but we have our orders here. While there is nothing untoward with your passport, even the possession of a handgun, it is your facial features that concern us. You strongly resemble a man that the authorities desire to question."

Nathan's heart is sinking. "Question for what? What man? What am I accused of doing?"

The man shrugs. "I do not know, Herr Holzer. I have been told to detain any person who resembles the man in this picture." He places a wirephoto on the table. It is a rough picture of Nathan in the lobby of the Ritz Hotel, posing as Hauptmann Froman. Allison is behind him and to his left, but her image is not quite as sharp. Maybe that was the reason the man took a long look at Allison.

"I don't know the man in that picture," Nathan says. "That's not me. How long am I to be detained? I have to catch my train. It leaves in a few minutes."

The man nods sympathetically. "Once again, Herr Holzer, I apologize for the delay. I have sent for the German authorities, and I expect they will be here before long. There is another train to Milan tomorrow."

Nathan slaps the table. "This is outrageous. I can't wait until tomorrow. I have an important meeting in Milan. You can't hold me on some bizarre suspicion that I am somebody else. You have no right. Where is the legal process?" He stands. "I'm leaving." Nathan opens the door, but the uniformed guard is standing with his rifle and his hand on the trigger. He is blocking Nathan's passage and calmly shakes his head side to side.

"Please come back and sit down, Herr Holzer," the supervisor says again. "We must follow the rules. You might as well take off your coat. We may be here for a while."

One hour passes, and then another. Nathan wonders what will become of his sister, Günther, and Allison. Will they make their way to Marseille? They have train tickets, but once they arrive in Marseille what will they do? They won't know where to go. The name and address of the OSS contact is on a piece of paper in Nathan's pocket. How will they find their way to Lisbon? There is panic boiling inside Nathan's veins, and he struggles to hold it all together.

Finally, Nathan snaps. "Look," he says as he stands and faces the man. "You have no basis to hold me here. I have broken no laws in Austria. So what if I look like that picture. Am I supposed to stay in this room forever? I have important business in Milan."

The man calmly answers, "I have contacted the authorities and I'm certain they will be here soon. I do beg your forgiveness for the inconvenience. I am only doing my job."

Nathan remains standing and paces the floor in the little room. His thoughts return to Allison, Rachel, and Günther. By now they will have figured out that he didn't make the Milan train. They might wait in Milan for a while, maybe until the next train arrives from Salzburg. But that would be foolhardy. Hanging around the train station only invites attention. They will have to complete their journey to Marseille. But then what? Maybe the OSS agent will look for them. Or maybe he will figure that the mission has been blown. And damn it, it has!

Around midnight, there is a knock on the door and a tall man in a black sweater enters. "What do you have here, Villi?" he asks. "Why did you call us?"

"I believe I have Hauptmann Dietrich Froman," the supervisor replies. "Look at the picture."

The tall man stares at Nathan, picks up the picture, stares at Nathan again, and shakes his head. "Very similar, but you made a mistake, Villi. This man isn't Froman. They caught up with Froman yesterday in Munich."

"But, sir—"

"Look. The man in the picture has dark hair. This man is blond. And you see the hair line? Even if his hair was dyed, the lines are all different. Really, the whole face is different. Villi, you were about to make a fool of yourself."

"Oh, my goodness. That would have been embarrassing. What am I to do with this man here?"

"Don't worry, Villi, I'll handle it for you. Let's keep it quiet."

"Oh, thank you, sir. Thank you so much."

The tall man picks up the passport, looks at it and says, "Kurt Holzer. German citizen. Hmm. Pick up your coat and come with me, Herr Holzer. Don't blame Villi here, he's just doing his job."

They walk out of the room and into the station. The tall man holds out his hand. "Bremer."

"OSS?" Nathan asks.

"Don't know what you're talking about. I'm just doing a favor for an old friend. Glad I could straighten out your mess. You can exchange your tickets for the next train."

"What about the people I was traveling with? Do you know what happened to them?"

Bremer shakes his head. "Nope. Why don't you have a seat over there until the morning. Train boards at six."

"Can you get word to Milan? There are three people—"

Bremer holds up his hand like a stop sign. "I did a favor. I settled a debt. Just have a seat over there, Herr Holzer. Train boards at six."

48

MARSEILLE

The ten-hour train ride from Salzburg to Milan seems like twenty hours to Nathan. He shares a compartment with an elderly couple who speak infrequently. Having had little or no sleep the night before, Nathan is able to doze now and again. When he does sleep, he has nightmares. When he is awake, he is immersed in self-recriminations. How could he have left Allison unprotected again? He did his best to divert attention from her. The Gestapo agent was studying her. He had to make a commotion. It is Allison he worries most about. Rachel and Günther seem to have their roles perfected. They are together. Allison is alone, she doesn't speak German, and she doesn't know where to go. Can't this train go any faster?

If they don't make it, he will have failed in every aspect of his mission; everything he was sent to do. He was sent to bring Günther Snyder back to the Manhattan Project, and he has lost contact with him. Allison was to gather detailed information about the German nuclear program, and she did, but it's all in her head, and now he has lost track of her as well. He promised to protect her and he failed again. He talked his little sister into traveling with him to America, and he has left her unprotected, too. All in all, he couldn't feel any worse.

It is late afternoon when the train pulls into Milano Centrale. Because Italy is an active theater of war, there are German soldiers everywhere. After all, the Allied forces are now on the peninsula and they have their sights set on Rome. Mark Clark and his U.S. Fifth Army are approaching from the west, and Bernard Montgomery and his British Eighth are approaching from the east. Northern Italy, especially the areas around Milan, remain German strongholds. Nevertheless, to Nathan's surprise, Italian passport control is predictably lax, and Nathan enters the terminal without a hitch.

Once in, Nathan scans the terminal. Hundreds of passengers are hurriedly walking from one location to another. Everything is in kinetic motion. It is foolish to think that he will spot Allison or Günther. It is also foolish to think that they decided to stand around the Milan terminal to wait for him. Although Günther might be prone to panic, Allison is stable and resourceful. She is a leader. She will take command and shuttle them forward to Marseille. He is convinced that the success of this entire mission is now in Allison's hands.

Nathan checks the departure board. There is an 11:00 P.M. train to Marseille that arrives at 9:30 A.M. He has a six-hour layover. He decides to leave the terminal and find a less conspicuous location to wait. Nearby is the Duomo di Milano, the giant six-hundred-year-old church that has been described as being "intensely and enthusiastically Gothic." The nave is immense, with four side aisles and forty pillars. Nathan takes a seat in a side chapel to wrestle with his guilt, and to pray for his lost companions. From time to time a nun or a young pastor will inquire. Is he all right? Does he need something to eat?

At 10:30 P.M., Nathan reenters the terminal and walks briskly toward the Marseille platform. Suddenly, someone taps him on the shoulder. A woman says, "Mi dispiace, signore, credo che tu abbia lasciato cadere questo." She hands a folded white paper to him, gesturing that the paper has fallen to the ground, and indicating that Nathan had dropped it. She smiles and walks away. Nathan opens the paper; it reads, "MARIE MONTROUX, 46 Rue Sainte Françoise, Vieux-Port." Nathan doesn't understand, the note was obviously meant for Marie Montroux. Someone else dropped this paper. He tries to locate the woman and tell her that he didn't drop the paper, but she has disappeared. He stuffs the paper into his pocket and boards the train.

Sitting in his seat he takes the paper out of his pocket and looks at it again. Marie Montroux? A French address. Is this in Marseille? It then occurs to him that the last time he was bumped by a stranger, it was to intentionally deliver a message. *You are a little slow on the uptake today, Nathan,* he says to himself. When he gets to Marseille, he will check out the address before doing anything else.

Morning in Marseille, the biggest city and only functioning port in the Unoccupied Zone of France. Nathan leaves Gare St. Charles terminal and flags a taxi. He shows the driver the folded piece of paper. The driver nods and says, "Bien sur." After a short ride through densely crowded back streets, the taxi pulls up beside a brown-brick three-flat. The driver says something in French that Nathan does not understand. He pulls a few Reichsmarks from his pocket and tenders them to the driver. The driver nods, takes the money, and drives away.

The front door is locked, and Nathan knocks on the door. Then he knocks again. A hefty woman in a blue ankle-length housedress answers. With her hand on the door frame, she says, "Oui?" Nathan is in a bit of a quandary. Does he answer in English or German? After all, wouldn't this be a safe house? Does he dare ask for Allison or Günther? What if this folded paper wasn't meant for him after all?

He decides to show the paper to the woman. He holds it up for her to see and says to her in English, "I'm looking for some friends and I wonder if they are here." She examines the paper. "My name is Nathan," he adds.

"What are the names of your friends?" she asks, also in English. Nathan shakes his head. "I'm sorry, but I don't know you, and I cannot divulge the names of my friends to a stranger."

She smiles. "But you want to come into my house? Do you expect this stranger to let you in?"

"If my friends are here."

"Hmm. Are they refugees? Do they come from the Occupied Zone? Are they Belgians, Czechs, Poles, anti-fascist Italians, Communist Spaniards, anti-Nazi Germans, or are they just Jews? Because I have housed them all, Monsieur Nathan. So, do your friends have names?"

Nathan takes a breath. "Sister Angelica, Gerta Felds, and—"

"And Dr. Allison Fisher?"

Nathan's heart pounds in his chest. His response catches in his throat. "Yes."

"They are staying here, but right now they are around the corner at Basso's. Having lunch. Welcome to Marseille, Nathan Silverman."

Basso's is a crowded bar on the Vieux-Port. The moment Nathan enters, before he has had a chance to look around, Allison sees him, runs to him, and throws her arms around him. "I knew you'd make it," she says. "I knew it! I told them all you'd make it. Wait a couple more days, I said. He'll be here."

"I was so worried," Nathan says, embracing her tightly. "They sent our photo by wire to who-knows-where? I was afraid someone would recognize you."

"Then Hanna's disguises did the trick, because we didn't have any trouble."

Then Nathan warmly embraces his sister. "How are you, Rachel? Did you take good care of Günther?"

"He's a funny guy. If you have to ride three days on a train with a nun, I'd recommend Günther anytime." She laughs.

Nathan shakes Günther's hand. "Where's your habit, Sister Angelica, and how did they ever mix you up with an angel?"

Günther waves his finger back and forth. "Now, now, you watch your tongue, young man, or I'll send you to the headmistress. That's what the nuns used to say to me when I was in parochial school."

Nathan addresses Allison again. "How did you know to come to Marie Montroux? Did someone hand you a piece of paper?"

"Piece of paper? No. We were met at the train the moment we arrived. They told us you had been arrested in Salzburg. They feared that the Gestapo had either sent you back to Berlin or had you executed, God forbid. But I said no, they're not going to take down Nathan the Soldier."

"Didn't they tell you that they rescued me at the Salzburg station? They sent a man to tell my captors that Dietrich Froman had already been arrested. That I wasn't Froman at all, and they let me go."

Allison shakes her head. "I don't think OSS knows about that. That wasn't something that they set up. They didn't send someone to rescue you. They were sure you were dead."

Nathan pauses. "But this man came in and rescued me. He was a German officer, I think. He said his name was Bremer. I thought for sure he was OSS. But he said no."

"I don't think he was OSS. They kept urging us to move on because you were presumed dead," Allison says. "I told them no. I told them to wait. I knew you'd come."

Nathan leans over. "What next?" he asks quietly. "What are they telling you? When do we leave for Lisbon?"

Allison shakes her head again. "We're not going to Lisbon. You see all these people?" She gestures to the people in the crowded bar. "They're all planning to go to Lisbon. The city is packed full of people waiting to go to Lisbon. That is, as soon as they get their visas, which they may never get. This town is a bouillabaisse of people trying to escape. Besides, there is a backlog of people in Lisbon waiting to board the few planes that take off from the Lisbon airfield."

"Then how are we getting home?"

Allison lifts her glass, tips it in Nathan's direction, and says, "Here's looking at you, kid."

"Casablanca? That's how we're getting home? Casablanca is a thousand miles away."

Allison shrugs. "Lisbon is over six hundred miles through the mountains."

Nathan is dazed. "I've studied French terrain. There is no direct way to get from Marseille to Casablanca. Are we going to take another fishing boat for a thousand miles? Take trains though France and Spain to Gibraltar? I don't know if I can handle another thousand-mile train ride. We'd all have to get back into our costumes and . . ."

Allison is laughing. "No trains. The Army is going to fly us. We're taking a ferry to Corsica and a plane to Casablanca."

"Corsica?"

"We've had an Army base there since September. General Groves has ordered a plane to fly us directly from Corsica to the Army base at Casablanca, and then home. Private planes all the way. They're sparing no expense."

49

MANHATTAN ENGINEER DISTRICT REVISITED

A fresh dusting of snow covers the park in front of New York's City Hall. Wreaths hang on the lampposts, festive lights twinkle in the trees, and a majestic blue spruce sits in the middle of the park, gayly decorated. Postmaster Albert Goldman warns New Yorkers to get their Christmas mailings out now in order to ensure their timely delivery. It is Monday morning, December 6, 1943, and New Yorkers are out and about, busily heading here and there, in the center of the universe.

Today's *New York Times* reports heavy fighting in the European theater. The Fifth Army is suffering casualties but making strong headway in the hills south of Rome. American planes are attacking German fortresses on the coast of western France. British Lancasters continue to drop thousands of tons of bombs on Berlin and surrounding cities. The *Times* reports devastating damage in Germany. President Roosevelt is headed home after a clandestine meeting with Churchill and Stalin in Teheran, where the three pledged their support to their multifront alliance, and agreed to implement a "peace to eliminate tyranny."

Across from the park, a taxi pulls to a stop in front of 270 Broadway, and three people get out. One of them, a chubby man with curly hair, looks around in wonder. "So, this is the New York operations center," he says. "It looks like any other office building."

"This is where it all started," Nathan says. He is dressed in his U.S. Army uniform, identifying him as Lieutenant Silverman, freshly cleaned and delivered to his room at the Waldorf. He assists Allison from the cab and they walk toward the entrance hand in hand. The elevator opens on the eighteenth floor and they head to the office labeled ARMY CORPS OF ENGINEERS, MANHATTAN ENGINEER DISTRICT.

Molly has a broad smile. "Welcome back, Dr. Fisher, Dr. Snyder, and Captain Silverman. General Groves is waiting for you."

"You mean Hauptmann Silverman," Nathan says. "Or Froman or Strauss, take your pick."

Molly's eyes are twinkling, and she shrugs her shoulders in a playful manner. She opens the office door and General Groves rises. "Welcome back," he says. Standing next to him is a man in a white shirt and tie. His thick black hair is combed to the side.

"Hello, Leo," Günther says. "It's good to see you again. What has it been—ten years?"

Szilard nods. "I left in 1933."

Leo turns to Allison. "Hello, Dr. Fisher. Welcome back. May I applaud you for the wonderful work you have done? We received your coded messages, and we are most anxious to talk to each of you in more depth."

"I have seen and witnessed a wealth of material," Allison says. "Thanks to Günther, I was allowed access to several of their top scientists, and I can pretty much lay out what they are working on. Speaking summarily, they are many, many months behind us, but they do have qualified personnel. There is a lot of talent at KWI. Of course, much less since Günther has left, but they have a brain trust there, as you well know. What they don't have is a solid commitment from their government."

"That is correct," Günther says. "My feeling is that Reichminister Speer will not devote the necessary resources, and the development of a bomb, if at all, will be slow."

"I understand you saw their reactor," Szilard says.

"What's left of it," Allison says. "It was severely damaged in an accident. It is inoperable."

"In truth, it was sabotaged," Günther says, "by Werner Heisenberg and Josef Silverman, Nathan's father. It will not be rebuilt."

"But you told us in your message that they were moving the entire KWI operation to Haigerloch," General Groves says. "Aren't they planning to build a reactor in their new location?"

"They are," Nathan says, "but construction hasn't started and may not for several months. Actually, we spent time with Klaus Clusius, a brilliant young physicist who is attached to that project. He says it will be built in the caves and valleys of Haigerloch, east of Strasbourg. He had a piece of paper with the actual coordinates, but I couldn't get my hands on it, and I didn't have a pencil to write it down."

"Damn, that would have been nice to have," Groves says. "When and if we move on Germany, we could take it out, but we need to know the geographic coordinates."

Günther clears his throat. "48.3667 degrees north, 8.7920 degrees east. Thank you very much."

"You memorized the coordinates?" Nathan says. "We only had a few seconds to look at it."

"What can I say? I have a photographic memory. Clusius said the heavy water comes from Norway, the Norsk facility, but I don't have the coordinates for that."

General Groves smiles. "That information was conveyed to us in the coded message. We know where Tinn, Norway, is. British fighters have been doing quite a bit of damage to their heavy water production facility there."

Nathan steps forward. "Sir, I have read in the *Times* that Leipzig was heavily bombed. My father is there. Have you heard anything? Can you tell me about it?"

Groves sadly shakes his head. "I can't tell you about your father, but the city center was virtually destroyed. Fifteen hundred tons of bombs were dropped on Leipzig. The Royal Air Force took out the entire downtown area. It was flattened."

Nathan is stunned. There are tears in his eyes. Allison quickly steps up and squeezes his wrist. "He could be okay," she says gently. "We don't know. Maybe he survived. But thank God we got Rachel out."

"Hmm," Günther says, "where is my young novitiate? Where is Rachel today?"

"She's applying at Columbia," Nathan says, "and moving into Aunt Gertrude's. Thank God she made the choice to leave Leipzig. But we should have taken my father with us as well."

"It was his choice," Allison says. She turns to Groves. "Josef Silverman was a hero. He helped destroy the Leipzig reactor with Heisenberg, and because of that, he's dying of radiation poisoning."

"That is sad to hear," Szilard say. "Josef was a good man."

"Anyway," Allison says, "the two of them should be honored. They should be given a medal or something. Some kind of recognition."

Groves gently shakes his head. "I'm very sorry about your father, Nathan, and as much as we would like to honor him, and indeed honor you and Allison and Günther as well, the entire operation is confidential. We cannot publicly disclose any details about the Manhattan Project, or any of our nuclear activities, including your journey and our alliance of spies. All top secret."

Groves extends his hand to Nathan. "As far as I'm concerned, you are an American hero. I'd love to award you the Distinguished Service Cross, hell, I'd lobby Roosevelt for the Congressional Medal of Honor, but you and your mission have to remain a secret. Someday maybe, but not now. I can't give you a medal, but the best I can do today is promote you to captain. Captain Nathan Silverman."

"Thank you, sir," he says, saluting sharply. "What is to become of me now, sir? I'm anxious to return to my Ritchie unit. They're planning to accompany our expeditionary force when they land on the Continent."

Groves smiles and pats Nathan on the shoulder. "No, son, we have other plans for you."

"But sir, I have been trained for the landing and the march through France."

"You've already been there. You did the landing, you made your way through the French countryside, into Paris, and then into Berlin. And even back again. That is precious knowledge. General Eisenhower wants you on his staff. After a three-week furlough, you are to be transferred to SHAEF in England to help plan the invasion, Captain Silverman."

Allison raises her eyebrows. "My goodness. Captain!"

"Günther," Groves says, "Dr. Szilard and you are going to spend some time debriefing, after which, we'd like to send you to Chicago with Leo to finish up your research, and thereafter to Los Alamos to join Dr. Oppenheimer's team. What do you say to that?"

"I'd be honored."

"And me?" Allison says.

"Well, you are a civilian, and certainly one to whom our country owes a great debt of gratitude. We need you to hang around with Günther and Leo for the debriefing and tell them all about the 'wealth of material' you mentioned a few moments ago. Afterward, I'm sure Dr. Compton would welcome you back at the MetLab. There will always be a spot for you in the Manhattan Project, if that is what you want. Otherwise, I suppose you are free to pursue whatever dreams you have with our best wishes."

"General," Nathan says, "one more thing. Whenever you consider people for medals, sometime in the future, please consider Fred Gluck. As an OSS agent, he is an extraordinary asset. He risked his life for us more than once, and he is responsible for our being here today. He literally saved our lives."

"We know all about Fred Gluck," Groves says. "But I must tell you, there is some concern. We haven't heard from him since the Berlin bombing last Thursday."

Nathan firmly shakes his head. "He's a survivor. If anyone can pull through a tough situation, it's Fred."

Groves nods. "Yeah, you're probably right." He checks his watch. "I have a quick conference I have to join this morning. Why don't we break for lunch? I'll see you back here at two."

As they leave the office, Nathan notices a wreath taped to the front door, right below the words MANHATTAN ENGINEER DISTRICT. It has a red ribbon that reads, PEACE ON EARTH, GOODWILL TOWARD MEN.

Leo and Günther choose to dine at a French restaurant. Nathan tries to talk Allison into a corned beef sandwich at Katz's, but she says, "I could really go for pizza and a glass of wine."

Over a sausage and mushroom pizza and a carafe of Chianti, Allison says, "So, you're off to London?"

"Yeah, I guess so."

"On General Eisenhower's staff planning the invasion. What a posting! Captain Silverman."

Nathan blushes a little and shrugs his shoulders. "And you? Back to Chicago?"

"I guess so. Or wherever they want me. Maybe Oak Ridge, maybe Los Alamos? Maybe I'll go back to Dr. Lawrence at Berkeley?"

They sit quietly for a minute or two, and Allison says, "I'm really worried about Fred. He was a good friend."

"He's tough. He's a survivor. Like I told Groves, if anybody can get out of a jam, it's Fred."

"It wasn't a jam, Nathan. It was a bombing raid."

"Yeah. He'll make it. You know, I've been thinking about that guy who saved me in Salzburg. It had to be because of Fred. I was a dead duck, under arrest, waiting for the Germans, until this guy comes in, and he had to be some kind of German official because my captor addressed him deferentially. So he comes in the room, tells my Gestapo captor that he has detained the wrong man. He gets me released from custody and helps me exchange my ticket to Milan. I asked him if he was OSS and he said no. He said he did it to repay a favor, to settle a debt. So, think about it. A favor to whom? Who else could have sent this guy to look after us at the Salzburg station? Had to be Fred."

Allison's expression turns wistful. "When we left him at the train station in Dresden, he said he was going to miss us." She takes a sip of wine. "Actually, he said a lot of stuff."

"Like what?"

"Never mind. Just stuff."

"I saw him take you aside when we were leaving. What did he say?" Allison shrugs. Nathan presses the issue. "C'mon, tell me. Because I think I know. He took me aside too."

"I asked him if he was ever coming home, that's all."

"And what did he say?"

Allison ponders whether she should answer the question, and then gives a negative shake of her head. "No, it's not important."

"C'mon," Nathan says. "Tell me."

She takes a deep breath. "Okay. I asked him if he was ever coming home, and he said . . ." She pauses; her voice becomes unsteady. "And he said, 'God willing.' And then he said, 'When I do, I'll come visit you and Nathan and all your little Silvermans in Chicago, or wherever you two end up.'" Her eyes become a little watery.

Nathan smiles. "He said something like that to me too. He also made sure I knew that you were a keeper. That's what he said. A keeper." He blushes again. "And I told him that I knew." He looks into her eyes. "So . . . what do you think?"

"Excuse me?"

"What do you think, you know, about you and me, and ending up somewhere together, and . . ."

"Is this a proposal? Are you asking me to marry you!?"

"Wait, hold on. I can do better." He clears his throat. "Someday I want to fly you to Paris, take you dancing in a nightclub, ride with you in a carriage on the Champs-Élysées, take you to the Ritz Hotel and ply you with Champagne and—"

"My dream," she says.

"I want to be in that dream, Alli. I want to be in all your dreams. Forever." He kneels beside the table, takes a little black box out of his pocket. It says FEINGOLD'S JEWELERS, 47TH STREET. He holds it out. "Allison Fisher, will you marry me? Please. I can't imagine going through the rest of my life without you by my side. We're so good to-gether." He shrugs and smiles. "So . . . will you? I have a three-week furlough coming up."

With her lips tightly pressed together and quivering, she throws her arms around him. "Yes. In a heartbeat, yes I will."

The pizza waitress watches them kissing and smiles warmly. An American soldier and his girl.

NOTES, THOUGHTS, AND ACKNOWLEDGMENTS

On August 6, 1945, the U.S. B-29 Superfortress *Enola Gay* took off from Tinian Island 1,500 miles from Japan. It was carrying a 10,000-pound bomb, nearly ten feet long and thirty inches across, named Little Boy. It carried 64 kilograms (141 lbs.) of enriched uranium, U-235. It was a gun-type fission weapon, detonated by firing one mass of uranium into another, creating a chain reaction. At 8:15 in the morning the bomb was released. At the predetermined detonation height of 600 meters above the city of Hiroshima, the gun was fired, the chain reaction was instantaneous, and the bomb exploded. Eighty thousand people, approximately 30 percent of the population of Hiroshima, including twenty thousand Japanese military personnel, were killed. Seventy thousand more were injured.

Three days later, on August 9, 1945, the U.S. B-29 Superfortress *Bockscar* took off from Tinian Island. It carried a 10,300-pound bomb, 128 inches long and 60 inches across, named Fat Man. It was an implosion-type nuclear weapon carrying only 6.4 kilograms (14.1 lbs.) of plutonium, PU-239, that was placed in the center of a hollow sphere surrounded by several highly explosive trigger devices. The Fat Man was dropped at 11:02 A.M. local time. Following a forty-three-second free fall, at an altitude of 1,650 feet (500m) over Nagasaki, the outer explosives were detonated, producing powerful inward pressure on the plutonium, causing a chain reaction and a massive nuclear explosion. A total of sixty thousand to eighty thousand fatalities resulted, including those who died from long-term health effects.

An Affair of Spies is a work of historical fiction in which the central characters and the plot are fictional and woven into actual historic events as they occurred. Nathan Silverman, Allison Fisher, Günther Snyder, Lena Hartz, Fred Gluck, Kurt Renzel, Josef Silverman, Otto Weber, and Henning Wolf are all fictional. The plot to sneak one of Germany's top nuclear scientists out of the Kaiser Wilhelm Institute was a product of my imagination.

The Kaiser Wilhelm Institute for Chemistry, however, did exist and functioned as described herein. Otto Hahn, Abraham Esau, Kurt Diebner, Walther Gerlach, Paul Harteck, Klaus Clusius, and Werner Heisenberg were actual KWI scientists, described accurately, except, of course, they did not interact with the fictional characters.

General Leslie Groves and the Army Corps of Engineers, Manhattan Engineer District, had its offices at 270 Broadway, New York, and did manage the top secret Manhattan Project. J. Robert Oppenheimer, Enrico Fermi, and Leo Szilard are actual characters and they are depicted in the roles they played, with the exception of any imagined interaction with the fictional characters. Irène Joliot-Curie won the Nobel Prize for chemistry in 1935, and her accomplishments were accurately described.

The University of Chicago MetLab functioned as described under the leadership of Dr. Arthur Compton, who coordinated and consolidated America's nuclear research programs, which had heretofore been conducted in various university sites throughout the U.S. He succeeded in bringing Enrico Fermi and Leo Szilard to Chicago. The Chicago Pile-1 was constructed under the Amos Alonzo Stagg football field as described and did succeed in achieving a chain reaction. There is presently a statue on the grounds of the University of Chicago commemorating that work.

Camp Ritchie, in the hills of Maryland, was a secret facility established to train soldiers, most of whom were German expatriates. Colonel Charles Y. Banfill was its commanding officer. Ritchie boys, as they were called, did make a powerful contribution to the war effort.

Albert Speer was the reichminister of the Ministry of Armaments and War Production and a member of Hitler's inner circle. He did monitor the progress of nuclear development at KWI, as described, and concluded that the progress was too slow to make a difference in the war. As a result, Hitler became disillusioned with the efforts to build a nuclear bomb and did not support it. After the war, Speer was tried as a war criminal in the Nuremberg War Trials and sentenced to twenty years. He served his entire sentence. While incarcerated, he authored two autobiographies.

Germany did build a reactor in Leipzig under the supervision of Dr. Werner Heisenberg. It is true that on June 23, 1942, the reactor was opened to check for supposed blisters on the gaskets and it exploded, all as written in the story. It has been theorized that it was sabotaged.

The Kaiser Wilhelm Institute for Chemistry completed its move to Haigerloch and Hechingen in southwest Germany by the beginning of 1944. General Groves ordered the bombing of KWI in Berlin, and on the night of February 15, 1944, the bombing successfully destroyed the building, though most of the personnel had moved.

On April 25, 1945, an armored ALSOS task force under the command of Colonel Boris T. Pash surrounded the Kaiser Wilhelm Institute for Chemistry in the Haigerloch/Hechingen area. Otto Hahn was arrested and taken into custody along with Kurt Diebner, Walther Gerlach, Paul Harteck, and Werner Heisenberg. They were sent to and detained at Farm Hall, England.

ALSOS found that KWI did in fact build a nuclear reactor in the limestone gullies of Haigerloch. The reactor was contained in a concrete cylinder. There was an inner wall made of aluminum approximately seven feet high and seven feet across. Inside was another vessel of magnesium. The space between the two vessels, at the top and at the bottom, was filled with ten tons of graphite carbon bricks. Six hundred sixty-four uranium blocks had been lowered into the inner magnesium vessel and the lid was bolted onto the reactor.

The KWI reactor never became critical. It was disassembled by the ALSOS forces. Several years later the uranium was analyzed, revealing that the samples were not enriched with U-235. Thus, it is unlikely that the KWI reactor would have been able to sustain a nuclear chain reaction or produce fissile elements with those materials.

The captured KWI scientists were shocked to learn of the U.S. bombing of Japan. They were convinced that no country was further along than Germany. They were allowed to listen to the BBC report of the bombing of Hiroshima. Otto Hahn was recorded as saying: "Of course we were unable to work on that scale." On January 3, 1946, six months after they were placed in custody in Farm Hall, England, the captured scientists were allowed to return to Allied-occupied West Germany.

Hahn, Heisenberg, Max von Laue, and Carl von Weizsäcker were brought to Göttingen, which was controlled by the British occupation authorities. On April 13, 1957, during the Cold War, Hahn joined seventeen other scientists in signing the Göttingen Manifesto, protesting a proposal to deploy tactical nuclear weapons to West Germany. The Manifesto contained the following statements:

"Tactical nuclear weapons have the same destructive effect as normal atomic bombs."

"There is no natural limit for the development of life-threatening effects of strategic nuclear weapons. Today a tactical nuclear weapon can destroy a small city, and a hydrogen bomb can render an entire region such as the Ruhr Valley uninhabitable."

"We believe that a small country such as West Germany is best protected, and world peace most assisted when nuclear weapons of any type are banned."

"In any case, none of the undersigned are prepared to participate in the creation, testing or deployment of any type of nuclear weapon. At the same time we feel it is extremely important that we continue to work together on the peaceful development of nuclear energy."

———————

Once again, I express my heartfelt gratitude to all those who helped bring this project into being. To my supportive group at St. Martin's Press: my editor, George Witte; my publicist, Rebecca Lang; my copy editor, Bill Warhop; and Beatrice Jason, Brant Janeway, Brigitte Dale, and Kevin Reilly. Thanks to my literary agent, Mark Gottlieb of Trident Literary Group, for his efforts and his guidance. A big thanks to my group of rough-draft readers and editors, who took the raw manuscript and gave me their honest opinions and suggestions: David Pogrund, Cindy Pogrund, Carolann Schalk, Hon. Megan Goldish, Rose McGowan, and my sons Ben Balson and Nathan Balson. Finally, to my tireless wife, Monica, a woman of boundless energy and love, who read the manuscript pages, again and again, as they came out of the printer, who caught my mistakes, smoothed out the rough passages, and provided invaluable critiques. Thanks to you all.

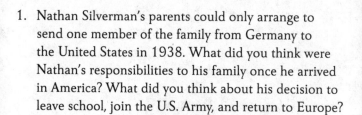

1. Nathan Silverman's parents could only arrange to send one member of the family from Germany to the United States in 1938. What did you think were Nathan's responsibilities to his family once he arrived in America? What did you think about his decision to leave school, join the U.S. Army, and return to Europe?

2. What did you think of the top-secret Ritchie Boy program? Why was Nathan a good fit for that program? Why was he an appropriate candidate for transfer to the Manhattan Project? Why did he appeal to General Groves? Why did the assignment appeal to Nathan?

3. Nathan was introduced to Dr. Allison Fisher at the University of Chicago. How was he surprised? Did you initially think that they were a good match? How were they different?

4. Nathan and Allison had discussions about the development and application of nuclear energy. How did their goals differ? Despite their differences, they agreed to go ahead in support of the Manhattan Project. Why?

5. How were Nathan's personality flaws revealed when he arrived in Berlin? Although his blunders appeared to be irresponsible, did you find them realistic?

6. Allison's initial assignment was to analyze data provided by Günther Snyder and evaluate the German progress from inside the safe house. How did those assignments broaden? In accomplishing her assignments, was it necessary to take on greater risks? In what way?

7. What were the top things you learned by reading *An Affair of Spies*? Did they surprise you?

Monica J. Balson

RONALD H. BALSON is an attorney, professor, and writer. His novel *The Girl from Berlin* won the National Jewish Book Award and was the Illinois Reading Council's adult fiction selection for the Illinois Reads program. He is also the author of *Eli's Promise,* a Target Book Club selection; *Defending Britta Stein*; *Karolina's Twins*; *The Trust*; *Saving Sophie*; and the international bestseller *Once We Were Brothers.* He lives in Chicago.